The
Sometimes
Sisters

Center Point
Large Print

Also by Carolyn Brown and available from
Center Point Large Print:

The Lilac Bouquet
The Lullaby Sky
The Strawberry Hearts Dinner
The Wedding Pearls

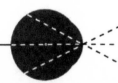

**This Large Print Book carries the
Seal of Approval of N.A.V.H.**

The Sometimes Sisters

Carolyn Brown

CENTER POINT LARGE PRINT
THORNDIKE, MAINE

This Center Point Large Print edition
is published in the year 2018 by arrangement with
Amazon Publishing, www.apub.com.

The text of this Large Print edition is unabridged.
In other aspects, this book may vary
from the original edition.
Printed in the United States of America
on permanent paper.
Set in 16-point Times New Roman type.

ISBN: 978-1-68324-737-1

Library of Congress Cataloging-in-Publication Data

Names: Brown, Carolyn, 1948- author.
Title: The sometimes sisters / Carolyn Brown.
Description: Center Point Large Print edition. | Thorndike, Maine :
    Center Point Large Print, 2018.
Identifiers: LCCN 2017061577 | ISBN 9781683247371
    (hardcover : alk. paper)
Subjects: LCSH: Large type books. | Domestic fiction.
Classification: LCC PS3552.R685275 S66 2018 | DDC 813/.54—dc23
LC record available at https://lccn.loc.gov/2017061577

A story is like a rough diamond and must be polished to show the potential luster and beauty. Thank you to my amazing editor, Krista Stroever, for applying the polish to my stories to bring out every emotion and make the whole story shine like a diamond.

Chapter One

"Promise me," Annie whispered.

"I promise." Zedekiah nodded with tears in his eyes.

"You'll bring them all home where they belong." She reached up and touched his cheek. "They need to heal."

"I'll get them here. You rest now." Zed cradled her frail body in his arms.

She'd been in and out of consciousness for two days, and each time she awoke she made him promise all over again that he'd bring her granddaughters home to the lake resort. Suddenly her eyes opened wide, and she cupped his cheeks in her hands.

"You . . ." Tears flowed down her face.

"I know, Annie." His salty tears mingled with hers when their cheeks touched.

"I've loved you since we were kids." She inhaled deeply and let it out slowly.

"Oh, Annie—" he started to say, but then he realized that she'd taken her last breath.

Time stopped as he hugged her closer to his chest. One heart beat steadily as it silently shattered. The other heart that had kept perfect time with his for decades had entered into eternity without him.

"Why, God!" he moaned. "I was supposed to go before her."

Stop it! Annie's voice was so real in his head that he watched her lips to see if she might start breathing again. *I told you that there would be no mourning. We'll be together again before long— remember when we were separated while you were in the military. You've got work to do now. So suck it up, Zedekiah, and call the girls.*

They'd talked about this moment for three months and gotten all the pieces in order. Even though they'd argue about things sometimes, the plan was in place for the next step, as she called it. And now it was up to him to make sure that her wishes were carried out. But dear sweet Jesus, he'd never thought about the pain when he'd have to let her go for good.

He laid her gently on the pillow, laced his darker fingers with her paler ones, and bent to kiss each knuckle. "Oh, Annie, life without you isn't life at all."

The girls will help, the voice in his head said sweetly. *Now let me go, Zed. You've got things to do.*

"I can't," he groaned.

He sat with her for half an hour before he made the call to the doctor, who was also the coroner for the county. When they came to get her, he accompanied the gurney to the van with his hand on hers.

"I understand that she made arrangements beforehand. Do you want to come to the funeral home and see her once more before . . ." The doctor hesitated.

Zed shook his head slowly. "She said that I wasn't to do that, and I'll abide by her wishes. I can't say goodbye. Never could say that word to her and still can't, but we've come to terms while I waited on you to get here. Call me when her ashes are ready." He choked on the last words.

The doctor patted him on the shoulder. "I'm so sorry. She was a great lady and a good friend to you, Zed."

"My best friend." He wiped his eyes. "We made a lot of memories."

"If you need anything, call me."

"Thank you. Right now I have to go call the girls, and I'm sure not lookin' forward to that job."

"They should've been here."

Zed raked his hand through his curly salt-and-pepper hair. "She wouldn't let me call them. No tears. No fussin'. That was Annie."

"Yep, it was." The doctor nodded. "I'm so, so sorry, Zed."

"Thank you." Zed watched the van until it was completely out of sight, waving the whole time, just like he did from the window of the bus that took him away all those years ago when he joined the army to get away from Annie and her new husband. He'd thought he'd forget her, but distance and time did nothing to ease the pain of watching her marry his friend Seamus Clancy and wishing that he'd been born with white skin and blond hair so he could marry his beautiful Annie. But the ache on that day was nothing compared to the one in his heart now as the coroner's van disappeared while the sun rose over the bridge crossing the lake that morning.

✦╬╫╫╫╫╬✦

With every single mile, Harper's head pounded harder. She'd been driving the same old burnt-orange truck two years ago when she came to the lake briefly on her way up to Oklahoma to work at one of the casinos just across the Red River. She hadn't spent a night on the property in ten years. Not since that summer that changed her whole life.

Ever since then, a rock the size of a Buick landed in her chest every time she got near the lake. The boulder in her heart wasn't as big as what had been there the day she signed her daughter away, but it was still painful.

She slowed down at the liquor store but didn't stop. Her sisters, Tawny and Dana, would judge her as it was. If she came in with a brown paper bag under her arm, they'd have a field day. First right-hand turn before the bridge and there it was—twelve cabins located behind the combination convenience store and café. Then just a short distance from the cabins was a small white two-bedroom house. That's where Granny Annie lived and where Harper and her two sisters had come to visit for a month every summer—but that all came to a screeching halt the summer before Harper's sixteenth birthday in August.

Beer, bait, and bologna—that's what Granny Annie called her store. It did offer a little more than that, with bread and other snacks and a shelf of over-the-counter medicine like sunblock or sunburn lotion, for those folks who forgot to bring those items with them. They also had milk and soft drinks in the refrigerator section, a big minnow tank, and a special fridge to hold stink bait, plus two gas pumps out front to keep the boats as well as the cars and trucks all fueled up and ready to go.

She could see each shelf in her mind's eye as she drove around the back of the store to the café entrance. Uncle Zed cooked up the best food in all of North Texas at the café, and Flora took care of the cleaning. Three old folks had kept the place going for decades, and now one of them was gone.

She parked her truck and leaned her head back, shutting her eyes. She'd made it. No spare tire and the gas tank, as well as her wallet, was empty. "On fumes and prayers," she whispered as she inhaled the pungent aroma of the lake water along with the smell of freshly mown grass and the first roses of spring, all mixed together with cigarette smoke. Lake Side Resort, as the faded sign above the door proclaimed, had not changed a bit.

Uncle Zed rounded the end of the porch and waved. His green eyes looked out of place in that ebony-black skin. His curly hair, once black as coal and cropped short, now had a heavy mixture of white sprinkled in it and was a little longer, but he would be at least seventy by now—maybe even seventy-one or seventy-two. He and Harper's grandmother and late grandfather were all the same age. He still looked like he needed rocks in his pockets to keep a spring breeze from blowing him into the lake, but he'd always been a beanpole and he'd always worn bibbed overalls. Some things didn't change with time—thank God.

A fresh wave of pain pounded through her head when she slid out of the seat and her feet hit the ground. "Mornin', Uncle Zed."

He wasn't really her uncle, but he'd been more like one, or maybe even a grandfather. He'd been far more than an employee at Annie's Place, that's for sure. Dana, the oldest of the three, had given him the uncle title, so Harper and Tawny followed suit.

She'd vowed when she drained the last drop of whiskey from the bottle the night before that she was through crying, but seeing him brought on a fresh batch of tears. She grabbed him in a tight hug. "What are we going to do without her?"

"I don't know, but I'm glad you're here. We'll all need one another to lean on." His voice was raspy as his tears mixed with hers.

Smoke filled her nose, wiping out all the other scents. She backed up a step but kept a hand on his shoulder. "Did she suffer?"

"No, darlin'. She was talkin' to me one minute and gone the next. The Lord took her quick." He pulled a handkerchief from his hip pocket and wiped her cheeks and then his own.

"The others here?" she asked.

"Dana and Brook are in the house," Zed answered. "Got here about an hour ago. That Brook is growing up in a hurry. You can sure tell that she's your niece. She reminds me of you when you were her age—maybe not in looks, but in her attitude. Want me to take your things to one of the cabins?"

"I'll do it later if I decide to stay. Is Tawny coming?" Harper asked.

Zed folded the hankie and returned it to his pocket. "She called last night and said she'd be here. Your granny has things set up to help you three Clancy sisters, and you shouldn't let her down."

She opened her mouth to tell him that she'd already let her grandmother down more than a

13

decade before, but snapped it shut. Now wasn't the time to peel back the lid on that can of worms. This wasn't the day to start baring her soul, especially when she'd never told anyone.

"I'll do my best. Maybe I'll unload my things in the number one unit," she said.

"That one is already booked. Fishermen are comin' in tomorrow mornin'. I'll put you in number twelve. It's closer to the house and the café anyway." He glanced over into the back of the truck at all the boxes. "Looks to me like you come to stay whether you want to admit it or not."

"Never could get anything past you, Uncle Zed." She smiled. "The question is whether or not this is where I will land permanently. I can pack and be gone in an hour if it's not."

"Well, we'll hope that you stick around here for more than an hour. My old bones can't run this place all by myself, and Flora is only stayin' on for a little longer. She wanted to leave at Christmas, but that's when—" He rolled his light-colored eyes toward the sky and finally got control. "She promised Annie she'd stick around long enough to get you girls in the groove of things. Now drive this truck on around to cabin number twelve, back it up as close as you can get it to the front door, and we'll get you unloaded."

The identical cabins were separated by enough space to park a vehicle. Yet years ago Annie had planted a weeping willow tree between each cabin, so folks parked out front these days. The trees now reached the cabin roofs, and new feathery leaves were pushing winter out of the picture and welcoming spring. Painted white with different-colored trim, each cabin had a tiny porch with a vintage metal lawn chair on the front. It seemed fitting that Harper would be staying in number twelve, with its red trim and door and red chair on the front porch.

It was her punishment for all those nights when she'd sneaked out of the house and met Wyatt in that very cabin, and red—well, that color did bring her sins home to haunt her. But Zed couldn't have chosen the cabin for those reasons—he had no idea what happened that summer. Maybe it was simply available for long term when the others weren't. She scolded herself for trying to analyze the whole thing.

Zed was already opening the tailgate when Harper crawled out of her truck for the second time. He pulled a real key on a big fob with the number twelve embossed on it from the pocket of his overalls and tossed it toward her.

She caught it in midair and stuck it in the lock but couldn't make herself turn it.

The tailgate squeaked as he got it completely down. "This thing needs some oil applied to it. What're you waitin' on, girl, Christmas?"

"Maybe Easter," she tried to tease, but it fell flat.

"Well, that's still two weeks away, and the nights are cold. You'll get your death of the pneumonia if you sleep on the porch. Open that door." He set two suitcases on the porch and went back for boxes.

She sucked in so much air that her chest ached and then let it out slowly as she unlocked the door. Drapes were open on the big back window overlooking tall pines, willows, and a few scrub oak trees. She crossed the floor and watched a bunny rabbit hop along the edge of the wooded area and a couple of squirrels chase each other through the tree limbs. Birds flitted around, singing songs about spring.

Zed shoved the suitcases inside. "Lake living at its best. None of that cable television crap or Wi-Fi stuff, either."

She turned around quickly. "That's enough for you to lift and carry, Uncle Zed. I was woolgathering. I'll get the rest. Thank you for all you've done. Especially being with Granny Annie in her last weeks. I'd have been here if you would have called."

"She wouldn't let me, and you know how she could be once she set her mind to something." The sigh that escaped from him sounded as if it came all the way from the depths of his soul. "It sure won't be the same without her."

Harper swallowed hard, but the lump in her throat refused to go down. "I thought she'd live forever. She was my rock." She didn't want Zed to leave her alone in the cabin—not yet. She needed just a few more minutes before the memories came flooding in like she knew they would.

"She was everyone's rock, darlin'," Zed whispered.

She sat down on the edge of the bed. "She told me more than once that you and my grandpa Seamus and she had always been great friends. I bet you could tell us all some stories."

Zed eased down into a straight-back chair on the other side of the room. "Maybe someday. Only time I was ever away from her was those years I was in the army. She wrote me a letter every day when I was in Vietnam. I still got them all."

Harper laid her sunglasses on the bed. "Never knew you was in Vietnam."

"I don't talk about it much. I didn't like bein' away from family. When I came home, Annie hired me to be the handyman, since my daddy passed away that year. It was 1966. I thought I'd stay in the army when I enlisted right out of high school, but that first six-year hitch was enough for me. I came home and Seamus and Annie put me to work. Then, less than two years later, in 1968, my mama died and I took over in the kitchen. Been cookin' for almost fifty years now."

"I don't ever remember you not bein' here," Harper said.

"Of course you don't. I remember the first time your daddy brought you here and me and Annie got to hold you. Lord, that was a wonderful day for sure." A weak smile turned up his mouth. "I always liked it when you girls called me Uncle Zed. Y'all with your blonde hair and all."

Harper crossed the room and patted him on the shoulder. "Sometimes blood ain't a bit thicker than water. You've been a wonderful friend and a great uncle."

Zed laid a wrinkled hand on hers. "Thank you, child. Now I'd best get on over to the café. I'm makin' hamburgers and fries for everyone to eat before the lawyer gets here. Tawny should be here by noon herself."

"Please tell me that you won't leave until . . ." Harper let the sentence trail off.

"I'll leave when the undertaker takes my body away or else when one of you girls fires me." Zed rose up from the chair and grabbed his handkerchief to cover a wicked cough. "This here is my home, Harper. If I live until the end of next month, it'll be seventy-two years since I was born right out there in a little frame house." He pointed toward the lake. "And I'll die here. I'll see you at noon, right?"

"I'd crawl through broken glass to get to one of your burgers." She smiled. "Uncle Zed, that cough sounds serious. Have you seen a doctor?"

"Lots of times, my child. Me and Annie always

went together, every three months until she got the tumor, then we went more often. Don't you worry your pretty head about me," he said as left the cabin.

She threw a suitcase on the bed and shut her eyes. A vision of Wyatt wearing nothing but lipstick kiss marks on his face floated behind her eyelids. The only thing she had on was a cowboy hat, and he chased her around the bed until she finally let him catch her. Then they fell back on a god-awful green plaid bedspread and made that kind of wild love reserved only for teenagers with raging hormones. When she opened her eyes, she realized that the bed was now covered with a puffy white duvet. That thing wouldn't be nearly as much fun to wrap around her body and pretend that she was a medieval princess when Wyatt declared he was a knight in shining armor.

"Flora might be gettin' up in years, but she still knows how to make a room look nice," she mumbled as she made her way to the bathroom. She noticed that the television on top of the chest of drawers had been upgraded to a flat screen, but she'd be willing to bet it still only got two channels.

Crossing the floor in a few long strides, she found the bathroom the same. She and Wyatt had taken lots of baths together in the old clawfoot tub. A picture of both of them on the floor with towels wiping up the water flashed into her mind.

"It was fun at the time," she muttered.

The vanity looked new, but if it was, it had been ordered from the same place as the old one. Little soaps along with shampoo, conditioner, and hand lotion were placed in a basket with fancy folded white washcloths. Towels were rolled and stuffed into slots on a wall-hung cabinet.

She turned away and groaned at the boxes stacked inside the door. If she unpacked and then couldn't get along with her two bitchy sisters, it would be a big waste of time. Finally, she decided to unload the suitcases and shove the boxes into the oversize closet, built originally to hold a foldout twin bed for a child.

When one side of the closet was filled, she set about hanging up her clothing. She'd packed in a hurry when Uncle Zed called to tell her that her grandmother had passed and that she should come prepared to stay a spell.

Harper had always gone into a job with the attitude that she wouldn't take bullshit from anyone. This would be no different. Just because Dana was her smart half sister and Tawny was her beautiful younger sister, it did not mean they could lord anything over her. Her attitude might have gotten her fired more than once from California to Texas and up into Oklahoma, but bartenders were always needed. If she couldn't get along with her two sisters for more than an hour, she might even drive a few miles up the road and apply for a job at that bar she'd passed. That should tilt Tawny's halo.

➤➤⊢⊣⊫⊨⊣⊢⊰⊱

"Hey, Mama, you sure you want to sleep in this room? Uncle Zed said that Granny Annie died in that bed." Brook shivered.

"I'm very sure," she answered. "I loved her so much that I hope her spirit visits me from time to time."

"You do know that she was cremated, right?" Brook's big brown eyes got wider with each word.

"That was her body. Her spirit lives on in her granddaughters." Dana organized her jeans in the closet by dress, work, and almost worn completely out. Zed, God love his soul, had already emptied out Granny Annie's things from the room.

Although she hadn't come around nearly enough, Dana had visited Granny Annie more often than the two "legitimate" granddaughters, so by damn she deserved the right to stay in the house.

They could each pick out a cabin—that would keep the two snooty little princesses out of her hair while she tried to run this conglomeration of businesses.

Dana's father, Gavin, wouldn't acknowledge

that she was his child, but her Clancy blue eyes said differently. She was the bastard sister—the product of a wild night of drinking during her mother and father's senior year at a party on the lake. They'd won a basketball game against their rival team and all the players were celebrating. Granny Annie had taken her in like the blood-kin granddaughter that she was and made her a part of the family. And it had been Granny Annie who'd insisted that her mother put Gavin Clancy's name on the birth certificate and make her an official Clancy even if her parents weren't married.

"Cinderella and the two mean stepsisters," Brook giggled.

"The sometimes sisters," Dana said. "That's what we called ourselves when we came to see Granny in the summertime. I'm sure not Cinderella, and they are my half sisters, not my stepsisters."

"Okay, then." Brook sighed. "But I'm glad you're stayin' in here and I get the room where we always slept when we came to visit. It's strange, her not being here."

Dana thought she'd cried until there were no more tears, but when she noticed that old, familiar quilt folded and lying across the foot of Granny's bed, the dam wouldn't hold. She sat down in the wooden rocker where she'd seen Granny rock both Harper and Tawny so many times and let the grief surface again.

Brook rushed over to her and cried with her, right on the floor in front of the chair. "We've got to stop this, Mama. This is going to wear us both out. Let's talk about something else, like where I'll be going to school."

"Frankston—it's a public school." Dana dried Brook's face with the sleeve of her knit shirt.

"That little bitty town that we came through?" Brook's voice squeaked on the last word.

"It's where I went until I finished eighth grade. It didn't kill me to go there, and I don't expect that you'll suffer, either." Dana managed a weak smile. "Change is good. Remember that. You've got your own room, and we have a house instead of an efficiency apartment at the back side of the stables."

"But Mama, I've never gone to public school. I bet they don't even have uniforms," Brook groaned.

"And you've made friends wherever we lived," Dana countered. "Maybe if things work out, you'll get to spend all of your high school years here."

"I hope not!" Brook exclaimed. "This is right on the edge of nowhere. Granny don't even have Wi-Fi, Mama."

"Get used to it, kiddo. We could be here for a long time," Dana said. "Go unpack all your things and settle in. We're supposed to be at the café at noon. If we are lucky, we'll get to start running this business tomorrow. And be glad you get to go to school, because you could be cleaning cabins all day."

"No!" Brook's hands went to her cheeks. "You're kiddin', right?"

"If you want a little paycheck like you got on the horse ranches, you'll work at whatever needs done around here weekends and in the summer. It'll probably be either cleaning rooms or else helping in the café, but it'll be work."

"But I hate housework," Brook groaned.

"Think of it as a paycheck."

Another groan escaped her daughter as she left the bedroom and headed across the hallway to her own new room.

"I hate dishes worse than any other housework," she called out.

Dana sniffed the air and couldn't pick up even a whiff of Granny Annie's trademark floral perfume. She drew in another long breath, but it was all gone. *How could that be? There should be a little of it left in the house a couple of days later.* She stuck her head inside the closet . . . still nothing.

"Are you about to sneeze or something?" Brook asked from the doorway. "It seems strange to have this much space, Mama."

"No, I was trying to get a little scent of Granny's perfume. I guess she stopped wearing it when she got sick," Dana answered. "You can't be unpacked this fast."

"No, but I heard you sniffling and thought maybe you were going to cry again and I can't let you do that alone. It's not what daughters do," Brook said.

"Well, thank you, darlin', but I think I might be finished with the crying for a few hours." Dana went to the window and pulled back the curtains. An older-model orange truck sat in front of the cabin closest to the café. A tiny bit of pride shot up and whispered that if that was either Harper's or Tawny's vehicle, then the bastard child had done better than either of them. At least she drove a newer-model club-cab truck that didn't have rust spots around the bottom of the passenger door.

"So what part of the business do you want to run, Mama?" Brook asked.

"The store."

"With that minnow smell? And having to touch worms?"

Dana nodded. "I'll do any of the jobs that Uncle Zed gives me, but that's the one I want."

"Well, good luck." Brook went back to her room.

Dana couldn't see the youngest sister, Tawny, dipping up minnows without gagging. Lord, she might break one of her fancy fingernails stocking shelves. That girl had always been spoiled. She might not even have time to leave her fancy college and come see Zed until summer. And

Harper would kill the tiny fish with her breath if she was still throwing back booze like she was the last time Dana saw her. Had to have been five years since she showed up at Granny's for ten minutes on Christmas Eve.

What are you going to do if your grandmother left the whole caboodle to Zed and Flora? God knows they've been loyal to her when you girls didn't have time to even call. Dana hated it when she could hear her mother's voice in her head.

"Then I'll ask them if they'll hire me," she said without hesitation.

>+‡‡‡‡‡‡‡+<

The call from Zed couldn't have come at a better time for Tawny Clancy, the youngest of the three sisters. Her mother, Retha, had cut her off financially when she was kicked out of college back in December. She'd managed to keep herself afloat with a job in a coffee shop while she did her community service for drug possession, but picking up trash on the highway and working with the senior citizens on bingo night had ended a week ago. She had enough money to buy gas from Austin to Tyler and a hundred dollars to spare. But that was before she got a flat tire outside Centerville. She hadn't cried when she had to sleep in her car and wait for a tire repair shop to open the next morning. In fact, she vowed she wouldn't cry at all, but guilt and grief combined when she parked her car at the resort and realized that Granny wasn't there anymore. She laid her head on the steering wheel of her fancy little red Camaro and sobbed uncontrollably.

She finally raised her head and checked her makeup in the rearview mirror. Before she could dig her kit out of her purse, Zed opened her door, and the tears started all over again. He opened up his bony arms and flashed a smile laced with sadness. Tawny slid out of the seat and laid her head on his chest.

"Uncle Zed, this isn't happening. Please tell me I'm dreaming," she whispered.

"Sorry, darlin', it's real."

"Why didn't she tell me?"

Zed patted her on the back. "She never was one to worry her girls."

She took a step back and sniffed the air. "You're still smokin' those unfiltered cigarettes, aren't you? Last time I was here, Granny was fussin' at you about those things."

"Man's got to have a little vice." He attempted to grin, but it didn't reach his eyes. He pulled a key with the number seven on it from the bib pocket of his overalls. "I was takin' a little smoke break before I get food on the table for y'all. It should be ready in about fifteen minutes. This is for you."

Tawny took it and frowned. "I thought I'd be stayin' in the house."

"You girls need your own space. You got all your stuff in that fancy car?"

"Back seat and trunk are full," she said. "Which one will Harper and Dana stay in?"

"Dana and Brook have the house. Harper is in number twelve. Annie left instructions about where you are all to stay. Drive on up to it, and I'll help you unload," Zed said.

"She's still tellin' us what to do, is she?"

"Yep." Zed nodded. "Nice ain't it?"

"Why number seven?" Tawny asked.

Zed shrugged. "Rest of them is going to be full come Friday night. I'd offer to help you unload, but I got to get the food ready."

"I'm glad you are still here, Uncle Zed," she said.

"Ain't no place but here for me, girl. This is my home."

"Harper drunk?" Tawny asked.

"Didn't appear to be. Maybe tired and a lot sad," Zed answered.

"Dana bossy?"

"She comes by that honest enough through Annie. But mostly she was feelin' bad that she hadn't been around in a while, just like you're feelin'. You stayin' out of trouble?"

"Tryin' to, Uncle Zed, but it seems to find me. I'm hopin' this place might reform me. There ain't nothin' to do out here except fish."

"And work. And both of them are four-letter

28

words." Zed left with a wave of his bony hand. "I'll see all y'all in the café at twelve sharp. If you ain't there when I serve them up, then you can eat your burgers and fries cold."

"I'll be there. That'll give me time to get my stuff out of the car. And thanks, Uncle Zed, for not putting me right next door to Harper."

"Y'all need to be friends, not enemies," Zed said. "Annie's biggest wish was that you'd be close family someday."

"Ain't damn likely," Tawny said as she got into her car and drove the short distance to her cabin.

An older truck was parked in front of cabin number twelve and, from where she was parked, she could see a crew-cab pickup down by the house. "So that's what Harper is driving these days. Looks like maybe Dana has been a little more prosperous, but then, she's older."

Who are you to judge anyone after the trouble you've been in? The voice in her head belonged to her granny for sure.

"It wasn't my fault," Tawny said out loud as she pulled into the spot in front of number seven.

I told you about that rotten boy. I knew he was trouble when y'all stopped by here last summer. Pompous and egotistical and downright rude, but you wouldn't listen. So it was *your fault.* Now it was her mother's voice in her head.

"Well, now that's a first. Mama and Granny agreeing on anything might bring on a tornado

29

right here on the lake." Tawny checked the skies, but there wasn't even a white fluffy cloud up there in all the clear blue.

She stepped out of the car and unlocked the cabin door.

"Twin beds," she groaned. Granted, the cabin was bigger than the one-room apartment that she'd had in Austin, and either of the beds would be better than the lumpy mattress she'd slept on the past three months, but she'd hoped that she'd get a unit with a queen- or king-size bed.

"I guess beggars can't be choosers, right, Granny? You used to tell us that all the time when we were kids." She choked up, and her lower lip and chin quivered. Why, oh, why hadn't she made time to come see her grandmother in the last three months?

Leaving the suitcases and boxes inside the door, she headed to the café. A strong wind whipped her long, honey-blonde hair around in her face, so she worked a ponytail holder up from the pocket of her skinny jeans. By the time she had her hair pulled up, she'd reached the door but couldn't force herself to go inside, so she sat down on the bench.

Lake water mixed with a stronger minnow smell floated on the wind, but it didn't overpower the aroma of grilled onions coming out of the café. Bless Zed's heart, he had to be heartbroken. He and Granny had been friends their whole lives, and instead of the sisters taking care of him, he was in there cooking for them. If he could do that, then she could damn sure face Dana and Harper. With new courage, she popped up off the bench and ducked inside, only to find the dining area completely empty. A dozen tables were arranged with four to six chairs around each one—just like they'd always been. The only difference was one covered with a white cloth that had been pushed into a corner. It was laden with desserts of all kinds.

"Have a seat anywhere." Zed stuck his head through the serving window between the dining room and the kitchen. "Dinner's almost ready. The ladies of the church brought all them desserts to you girls. Don't know why. Annie hadn't set foot in that place in more than thirty years. Maybe they're tryin' to get rid of the guilt they've been carryin' around about the way they treated her. But that's between them and their God."

"Chocolate cake sure looks good," Tawny said. "What guilt?"

"Whole bunch of them was ugly when your grandpa died," Zed answered. "Don't you be eatin' one bite until you finish your real food." He shook his finger at her and set a platter with eight big burgers on the serving ledge and followed it with another of tomatoes, lettuce, and pickles. "You take that on out to one of the tables. I'll bring the french fries. Reckon you can go on

31

and eat. I told everyone twelve sharp, and well, now, there's Harper, and I believe that would be Dana and Brook right behind her."

Harper pulled off her sunglasses, and a quick glance around the café let her know that nothing had changed in that area. The menu was above the counter where Flora usually took orders until right after the lunch rush—if there was one. Burgers, hot dogs, fries, and the daily blue-plate special. Mainly good old-fashioned home cooking that folks came from miles around to get. Harper suddenly wished it was Friday, because that was the day that Zed made his famous pot roast and hot rolls. And on Sunday he always made chicken and dressing, cranberry sauce from scratch, mashed potatoes and gravy, and corn on the cob. That day drew folks in by the droves, and there was always a long line.

Chrome tables with yellow tops could seat four to six people or be pushed together for a bigger crowd. Napkin dispensers, salt and pepper shakers, and a bowl of small packets of sugar and sweeteners were arranged in the middle of the tables. Chairs used to match the tables, but they'd been recently recovered in shiny red plastic. Black-and-white tile covered the floor and was so shiny that Harper wouldn't have a problem eating off it.

"Hamburgers smell amazing. Why'd you make all these desserts?" Harper asked.

"Done told Tawny. She can explain it to you," Zed answered as he headed back into the kitchen.

She whipped around to see Tawny on the other side of the room. The precious daughter who did no wrong—according to their mother—looked like hell. Tawny's blonde hair, usually perfectly styled, with not a long curl out of place, was pulled up in a ponytail. And her eyes looked like she hadn't slept well in weeks.

"What are you staring at?" Tawny snapped.

"Not much." Harper turned away from her younger sister at the same time that Dana and Brook pushed their way through the door and sat down at the table where the food waited. "What's going on with the dessert table?" Dana asked.

"Evidently Tawny knows." Harper sat down across from Dana.

"Did you make all that, Aunt Tawny?" Brook asked.

"Humph," Harper snorted. "If she tried to boil water, she'd burn down the whole house. The kitchen is as foreign to her as—"

"Being sober is to you," Tawny smarted off as she crossed the room and settled into the fourth chair.

"Put the claws away." Zed brought a basket of sweet potato fries to the table. "Or I walk right out of here for good."

Dana gasped.

Tawny's eyes got wide.

Harper laid down her burger and touched his arm. "Please don't do that. We'd be lost without you, Uncle Zed."

"The church ladies brought the desserts. Evidently they did something to upset Granny Annie a long time ago, and they're feelin' guilty," Tawny explained.

"I wish they'd ride that guilt trip for a week or two," Brook laughed. "That stuff over there looks epic."

"Epic?" Harper asked and then bit into a burger.

"It's the new 'awesome' or 'fabulous,' " Dana explained.

"I thought everything was 'dope' these days. That's what I'm used to hearing the college kids sayin'." Harper raised her voice. "Uncle Zed, these are epic, dope, and fabulous. Come on out here and eat with us."

"Naw, I'll just take my meal in the kitchen where I can watch the ribs I got cookin' for supper," he yelled back. "Y'all go on and clean up that food and then you can get into them cakes and pies. The lawyer will be here at one thirty."

"Yes, sir," Brook said seriously. "So is that old truck yours, Aunt Harper?"

"Yes." She piled lettuce, tomatoes, and pickles on her burger.

"It's been a long time since I saw you, but I

34

think you were driving that truck then and I was just a little kid," Brook said.

"I've been driving it for a long time. Little kid, huh? What are you now, twenty-one?"

Brook giggled. "I'm fourteen. What kind of job have you been doing?"

"I worked as a bartender in one of the college honky-tonks up in Oklahoma this last time and lots of other bars before that," Harper told her.

"Figures," Tawny said under her breath.

"What? That I work in a bar or that it's in Oklahoma?" Harper asked.

"Both," Tawny said.

"Stop it!" Zed said. "Y'all ain't been together here in nigh on to ten years. I ain't havin' you upset Annie with your bickerin'."

"Uncle Zed, Granny Annie is gone," Brook said softly.

"Honey, her body is gone, but her spirit is still here among us, so these three best be a little more civil to each other," Zed scolded.

"I guess we can put up a front for him," Dana whispered.

"Y'all need to remember that he's lost his best friend," Brook said. "And he don't need a lot of arguing. What's it between y'all anyway that you can't get along?"

"Long story," Harper said.

"Y'all here to stay?" Tawny looked up at her two sisters and niece.

"You?" Harper asked.

Dana glanced across the table. "It will all depend on what the lawyer says. If Granny Annie left the whole place to Uncle Zed, I'm going to beg him for a job."

Zed brought out a pitcher full of sweet tea and set it in the middle of the table. "I don't imagine you'll have to beg."

Harper refilled her glass and passed the pitcher to Tawny, who had always been the prettiest of the three. Petite and curvy, she had the lightest hair and those delicate features that made men follow around behind her like a little puppy dog. Surely she wouldn't be leaving her fancy sorority her last year at the university to work at Annie's Place and live in a cabin on the lake.

A bit of an old song played through Harper's head. The lyrics talked about three friends and said that one was pretty, one was smart, and one was the borderline fool. Dana was smart. Tawny was pretty. That only left the latter for Harper to lay claim to, and with her past mistakes, it kind of fit her well. Besides, she'd always felt like a big old sunflower among the bed of cute little miniature roses that were her sisters. Standing at just under six feet, she had what her mother called dishwater-blonde hair and light-brown eyes. And she'd sure turned out to be the biggest disappointment of the three women around the table. Hopefully Brook would get Dana's smarts, her aunt Tawny's beauty, and not an ounce from the borderline fool.

Yet Tawny's rough hands and nails hadn't seen lotion nor polish in weeks. Those were not the hands of a sorority sister. They'd seen hard work. And where were her signature high-heeled shoes? When Harper saw her three years ago, she wouldn't have been caught dead in those cheap athletic things on her feet. Just what exactly had her younger sister been doing the past year?

"Like Dana says, it depends on what the will says. I'm stayin' if she left this place to us, at least until the end of summer. If she didn't, then"—Tawny shrugged—"you goin' to use this place for a rehab center to get sober, Harper?"

"Naw, I thought I'd turn it into a brothel," Harper smarted off. "We could get us ten girls to work the cabins and . . ."

Dana's finger shot across the table. "That's enough. Brook is sitting right here."

"And I know what a brothel is, and it sounds like a moneymakin' idea to me," Brook said with a gleam in her brown eyes. "Have y'all always hated each other?"

Harper grinned. "We are the poster children for real-life sisters. All that crap about blood kin loving each other is a crock of bullshit. We learned a long time ago that we don't even like each other, but we managed to tolerate one another for a few weeks each summer for Granny's sake."

"I'm glad I don't have a sister," Brook declared.

"You are one blessed little girl." Harper nodded, meaning every word.

"Amen," Dana and Tawny said in unison.

Chapter Two

"Good afternoon, ladies. I am John Thompson of the law firm Thompson, Thompson, and Clary," the lawyer said as he entered the café.

Evidently when folks came to the lake, they didn't feel the need for three-piece suits and wing tips. The lawyer was a short man with a rim of brown hair around an otherwise bald head, giving him the look of a monk. The wire-rimmed glasses framed his baby face and a brown cardigan sweater topped a light-blue shirt and khaki trousers. He hadn't bothered with a tie.

His cowboy boots had a nice high walking heel, though, giving credence to the fact that he most likely had SMS—short man's syndrome.

Harper rose up from her chair and stuck out a hand. "I'm Harper Clancy, and this is Tawny and that's Dana and her daughter, Brook. Have you had lunch? Zed makes a mean burger."

"I've eaten, thank you." He had to look up to meet Harper's eyes, and he quickly dropped her hand after a quick shake. "Maybe we can get right down to business. It's nice to meet you all. Miz Joanna—I suppose y'all called her Annie, but on the will, it's her legal name, Joanna Clancy—anyway, she spoke well of each of you."

Harper slid back into her chair. Food had

helped the headache and the pecan pie had been wonderful, but she hoped he didn't take forever reading a bunch of legal jargon, because the banana pudding over there on the dessert table was calling her name.

He opened his briefcase, but he didn't sit down. "I have a copy of the actual will for each of you, but she also asked me to read this letter. It basically explains everything. A copy of the letter is also in the packet with the will and a copy of her death certificate for each granddaughter."

He straightened up, making himself as tall as possible, shook out the folded letter with a bit of pompous attitude, and began to read.

If John is reading this to y'all, then I'm dead and my ashes are already in Zed's care. Don't worry—when he's joined me in eternity, you'll understand why he's taking care of them. I wanted to leave everything to him, but he wouldn't have it. He said that you girls should share the resort, since you are my blood kin. So here's the deal. The resort is yours, but it cannot be sold. It's to be passed down to your children and I'd like to keep it up and going as long as possible. So if you choose not to take your share, then you are free to walk away with nothing. If you stay, then every Friday you will have a paycheck for your hard work. At the end of the year, the remaining profits will be shared between the three of you and Zed.

Dana will manage the convenience store. She knows more about running the store than you other two, because she's been around it more. Tawny will take care of the books and the business end of things like payroll and insurance and taxes. I've done that for years, but she studied it in college. Zed will help her get set up with my computer. Harper, you are going to be in the kitchen with Zed, and that will free up Flora's time to clean the cabins. You are all responsible for keeping your own living quarters tidied up whether you live in a cabin or the house. Flora is not going to pick up after a single one of you and as soon as you are comfortable with the new arrangement, I feel sure she will retire.

Harper groaned. She didn't want to do café work, but Granny Annie had promised a nice paycheck, and working with Uncle Zed wouldn't be nearly as tough as some of the bosses she'd had in the past. She glanced over at Tawny, who had a smug expression on her cute little round face. Dana looked like she was relieved that she had been given the control of the store.

"Questions?" John asked.

Harper shook her head. "Sounds pretty straight-forward to me. I'll be stickin' around for a while anyway."

John went on.

> Brook will work weekends doing what-ever needs done. Since someday this place might fall into her hands, she needs to know the operation in all its stages. Don't whine, Brook. If you want a paycheck, you have to work for it. Food is free in the café. Y'all will have to pay for what you take out of the store, including beer.

Harper threw up her palms defensively when she realized everyone else was staring at her. "Don't give me those hateful looks. I don't even like beer."

"I like beer." A big smile lit up Brook's face.

"When—what—how?" Dana stammered.

"I tasted yours when you weren't lookin' back when I was about six and I liked it," Brook said.

John cleared his throat and looked over the top of his glasses at them. "Shall I go on?"

"Yes, please," Tawny said with a sideways glance at Harper.

> Zed and Flora will keep their jobs and their paychecks will continue. Tawny will

find all that in the computer program, plus what y'all will be paid. I hate all this newfangled technology, but in order to keep the cabins full, we need to have it so they can book rooms online.

"Wi-Fi after all!" Brook pumped a fist in the air.

"No, ma'am. The Internet will only be available in one cabin, and that's where the business computer is," Zed said from the serving window. "She was adamant about that."

John checked his watch. "I'll go on now." He found his place and continued.

I've set it all up fairly. Tawny will also take care of reservations, checkouts, and rents on the cabins. When Zed goes, John will give each of you another letter. I remember when one of you said the only time you saw Dana was when you came to the lake for a while in the summer—that you were sometimes sisters. Here's your chance to be more than that. Either live in harmony or get on down the road. It's your choice. I love each of you. You've been a delight to my heart and soul. No tears or mourning. I want you to be happy and live every day as if it were your last. That's what I've done for many years, and

I'm leaving with no regrets for any of the decisions I've made.

John folded the letter and laid three bright-red folders on the table. "These are your copies of the will. Your names are on the front. My work here is done until such time as Zed passes on. Good day, ladies."

He snapped his briefcase shut, picked it up, and left without another word.

"Y'all really stickin' around?" Tawny wiped the tears from her eyes.

"Brook and I are," Dana answered. "Harper?"

"Might as well. She said no tears." Harper picked up a paper napkin and dabbed her eyes.

Dana and Tawny both nodded and bent forward in sobs anyway.

Brook hugged her mother and cried with her, but not a single one of the sisters consoled the other. Zed came from the kitchen, hugged each of them, and wiped their faces with his white handkerchief that smelled like smoke. "She didn't want this, girls. She made me promise not to weep over her ashes. It's the only promise that I made to her that I can't keep."

"I should have come more often," Dana said.

"Me too," Tawny and Harper said in unison.

"Past is past. That's what she'd say if she was here right now with us. Present is what matters and future is what we look forward to. Now, if y'all are stayin', you need to get settled in and ready for work that's startin' in the mornin'."

"Why didn't you come out here with us?" Dana asked.

"Didn't need to. I helped Annie make up that will and I knew what was in it. Here's the keys to the store, Dana." He handed off a ring with two keys on it. "You go on and reacquaint yourself with the place. The bait man comes tomorrow before noon, and there's a list tacked beside the cash register about when the other deliveries are made."

Dana took it from him. "Thank you again. It's not enough for what you've done, but I mean it."

Zed nodded, but his eyes were swimming in tears. "Annie was my best friend. I already miss her and I don't expect that time is going to do a damn thing to help it, either."

Dana quickly stood up and hugged him.

Zed inhaled and let it out slowly. "Tawny, you need to go get your cabin straightened up. Your granny had it all set up for computer stuff so you can take care of the books."

"Why no Wi-Fi?" Brook asked.

"Annie said when people come here, it's to get away from all that machinery stuff," Zed said. "I'll be bringin' the computer and printer and all that out there along with the desk to your cabin, Tawny, soon as I clean up the kitchen."

Harper looked up at him. "And me?"

"You got the afternoon to unpack. Then you'll

be helpin' me right here every day startin' at five o'clock in the mornin'. We open the doors at six and serve breakfast until ten. After that it's just burgers and hot dogs and whatever the blue-plate special is for dinner. If there's any of the special left, they can have it for supper. If not, then it's burgers until seven, when we close the doors," Zed said.

"Do we get to run a bill in the store?" Harper asked.

"Yep, but Tawny will deduct every penny from your paycheck," Zed said.

"And who is going to keep her honest? What if she skims from the funds or charges us double for what we take out of the store?" Harper asked.

"Books go to a CPA each quarter so he can pay the taxes for that time period," Zed said. "If there's a penny that can't be accounted for, he'll let me know."

"And you'll be fired." Harper pointed at Tawny. "What are you doin' here, anyway? Don't you have another year of college? Or is it ten more? When do they make you leave that fancy sorority house?"

Tawny had had enough of Harper's smart mouth. She rose up out of her chair and leaned across the table. "I haven't been in college since December. I quit and I've been working in a coffee shop,

46

doing double shifts when I can to pay the rent on a run-down apartment that I was sharing with two other girls. This job will be a huge step up for me. And for your information, I hated being poor and not knowing if I was going to have enough money to buy enough food until the next payday."

"What happened?" Dana gasped.

"Holy crap! What did you do to make Mama mad enough to cut you off?" Harper talked over her.

Tawny pushed back her chair and headed to the dessert table. "That would be my business and none of either of y'all's. I'm taking these brownies to the cabin with me. Anyone got a problem with that?"

"Not if I can have the whole banana pudding," Harper answered.

"I want the chocolate cake," Brook said.

With shaking hands Tawny picked up the pan of brownies and the folder with her name on it and left the café. By the time she reached her cabin, her cheeks were wet again with tears, only this time they were borne of anger, not grief.

She had a job, a place to live that beat the hell out of the apartment she'd lived in for the past three months, and food to eat three times a day. She set the brownies on top of the microfridge in the corner and tossed the folder on one of the twin beds. Falling face forward into the other one, she buried her face in a pillow so that no one could hear her cussing so much that it would blister the paint right off the walls.

Damn that Harper for pushing her to the limits like that. Worn out from emotion, she fell asleep and didn't wake until she heard a gentle knock on the door.

"Who is it?" she yelled.

"It's me, Zed. I've got all this computer stuff ready for you to set up."

She bounced off the bed, grabbed a washcloth from the bathroom, and quickly ran it over her face before she answered the door. "Holy smoke, Uncle Zed. What is all that? I was expecting a laptop." The back of his old pickup truck was loaded with a desk, a desktop computer, a file cabinet, and boxes with dates marked on the ends.

"It's the office. These past few years she kept it all in the corner of my little place at the back of the store. I'm glad to get it out of there, because she spent most of the time cussin' the machinery when she had to deal with it. I need help bringin' the desk in. Harper helped me load it, but she's gettin' the dining room ready for tomorrow right now. And the file cabinets are full of what Annie called hard copy. I reckon you'll learn a lot when you go through it."

Tawny got a firm grip on one end of an old oak desk. "Did this thing come over here on the *Mayflower*?"

"Naw, honey, but they used the wood from the *Mayflower* to build it." Zed's weak smile was a welcome sight for Tawny's red eyes. "It actually come out of the little country school that's out there in the middle of the lake these days. Not long before they dammed up the Neches River to make it, they had a big sale at the school. Annie's mama bought it and the office chair because they knew they were going to build this place. When Annie got the computer, I fixed a slide-out drawer for the keyboard. She was about your height, so it should be a comfortable fit."

"Where are we putting it?" Tawny asked as they maneuvered it through the door.

"Here by the door. That's where she put the special phone line in for the Internet stuff for this whole operation," Zed answered.

"Dial-up is so slow," Tawny groaned.

"Don't know nothin' about that. Just know that Annie didn't want no Wi-Fi crap out here because it ruins her idea of gettin' away from it all. That phone line is for the computer. Your regular phone is over there. Folks that bring cell phones can't get no reception, so they have to use the plain old telephones in their rooms for whatever they want. Most of them bring charge cards if they want to call home," Zed said on his way out the door to get the chair. "Come on, girl. This stuff ain't goin' to unload itself. You got to run an office out of this room tomorrow mornin'.

That means the folks check in and out through here."

"That also means I have to keep it clean, I suppose?" She groaned again.

"Exactly." Zed grinned. "You've got the cushiest job in the business, so you need a little responsibility. I'll be bringin' you all the receipts from the café, and Dana will close out each day and bring you a money bag. You'll take care of it all and put any cash in the safe that's in your closet over there. Annie did it that way, too. Then on Saturday mornin' before noon, you take a deposit to the bank in Tyler."

"Y'all got things all planned out to the letter. Was she sick a long time?"

Zed shook his head. "Three months from the time the doctor said she had a brain tumor. He wanted to do some chemo and radiation, but she said three months was enough time to get her affairs in order and she wasn't dyin' with no hair on her head."

"Why didn't you call us?" Tawny whispered.

"Wanted to. She said y'all had your own lives to live. Now let's get things done so I can get back to the café. Don't want y'all's supper to burn up," he said.

<hr>

Despite what Zed implied, Dana was fairly familiar with the convenience store. She'd been to see her grandmother more than the other two sisters through the years. But not as often as she should have or she wouldn't feel so guilty when she stepped into the store and caught a whiff of the minnow tank and the slight smell of smoke coming from the back room where Zed lived.

She'd been the only grandchild for ten years. She'd been excited the first summer that Harper came to the resort. She had a sister, a baby to play with. Then a couple of years later they added Tawny and, in her young ignorance, she'd thought they were a family.

Dana had only seen her father's wife, Retha, twice. Both times it had been when Retha brought the younger sisters to the lake for their month in the summer. The woman had looked at Dana like she was less than the dirt on the bottom of her fancy shoes, and Harper had learned early on to steer clear of Retha Harper-Clancy.

Anger filled her heart when she thought of anyone ever making Brook feel that way, and then it was suddenly replaced with sadness when she envisioned her grandmother standing behind that cash register for so many years.

"What's goin' on with Harper and Tawny and you? I don't remember much about them except that they always played with me and made me laugh. But y'all act like you hate each other," Brook asked as she checked out the place.

Dana quickly wiped her eyes and pasted on a

smile. "*Hate* is a strong word. Maybe *dislike* is better, or *indifferent* is even better than that. They have a different mama than I do, and I'm quite a bit older than they are. It's always been a little crazy," Dana said. "I think we've seen enough of the store. You ready to go to the house?"

"I'd rather go back to the kitchen and snatch that chocolate cake. I was serious about wanting to take it home. That's the best icing I've ever eaten," Brook said.

Dana inhaled deeply. Granny Annie and Zed had been family. The two sisters? They were related to Dana by blood, but not much else other than snatches of memories. Some of them good—some not so much.

"Mama?" Brook jerked her back to the present.

She blinked away the past and sighed. "I was kind of eyeballing that pan of cinnamon rolls, but we'll have to leave a little bit of stuff for Uncle Zed."

Harper was busy mopping the floors when they got to the café. She looked up at them and then down at her clean floor. "The part right inside the door is dry. What do you need?"

"Thought we'd take some desserts home with us," Dana answered.

"Take all you want. Ain't no use in keepin' them." Zed raised his voice from the kitchen. "Doctor said it was best for me to watch my sweets so I don't have to take pills or shots."

"Leave the banana pudding for me, or at least part of it. And a piece of pecan pie," Harper said and went back to mopping.

"How long has it been since you three sisters were together?" Brook asked.

Harper stopped and leaned on the mop. "I was here at Easter last year, but only for the afternoon."

"Brook and I came for Mother's Day," Dana said. "I remember that year well. It was the last time that we were all here together. Let's see, you were about fifteen, right, Harper? Tawny was almost twelve and Brook was four. It was right after my divorce and just before Brook and I moved to Houston."

"And you go by Clancy now?" Tawny asked.

"The only benefit of my divorce. Brook and I got to be Clancys again."

"So have y'all changed much?" Brook asked.

"We all got older." Harper smiled.

"Well, duh," Brook smarted off.

Harper stopped and leaned on the mop. "She reminds me of Tawny at that age."

"She's got some of you in her, too," Dana said.

"I bet that makes you real happy." Harper's tone held an edge of sarcasm.

"Nope, it does not, because that means she's like our father, and God only knows I'd rather she'd be like my mother. Mama might be wild and crazy, but she didn't abandon me," Dana said.

"There's more than one way to abandon a kid," Harper whispered.

"You got that right. Come on, Brook, let's get to the house and finish putting things right," Dana said.

They were out of the café, each of them carrying a dessert, when Brook asked her mother, "What did Aunt Harper mean by that?"

"Have no idea. You'll have to ask her, but don't expect an answer. I tried to get in touch, but . . ." She shrugged.

"And Aunt Tawny?"

"I called her on the day she graduated from high school, but she was too busy to talk to me. So I figured that they knew where I was and if they wanted to get in touch, it was on them," Dana told her.

"They're both sad," Brook said. "They remind me of you when you told me that you'd been fired at the ranch. You never told me why, Mama. I thought that those folks liked you a lot."

"It's a long story for a less stressful day. We're used to getting up early, but tomorrow we start crawlin' out at five thirty."

Brook stopped in her tracks, dropped her chin to her chest dramatically, and moaned. "Why would we do something stupid like that?"

"Store opens at six so the fishermen can get supplies for their day. And I called the school before we left the ranch. The school bus runs right by the store at seven thirty every morning," Dana said.

"But why five thirty? That's two hours before the bus runs."

Dana stopped to hug Brook. "So we can eat the fantastic breakfast that Uncle Zed makes every morning before everyone else arrives. You don't want to hurt his feelings, do you?"

"No, but I have one more question." Brook sighed.

"Well, spit it out."

"Is it too late to change my mind about moving to this place?" Brook asked.

"I'm afraid so," Dana told her.

Chapter Three

Harper awoke on Friday morning with a clear head, and although her eyes hurt from crying so much the day before, they weren't nearly as bloodshot. It was still dark at five o'clock that morning as she made her way from her cabin to the café. Stars twinkled in the sky, but the promise of a pretty day was carried in the sweet spring air. In her previous job, the bar didn't even close down until two in the morning. By the time she got things cleaned up and made her way to her tiny little apartment above the place, it was usually after three and she could still smell beer and whiskey that found its way up the back stairs. Then it took at least an hour to wind down before she could sleep.

"So I should be going to sleep about now, not waking up to the smell of roses and pure lake water. I could be happy here forever. If it weren't for my sisters."

"Mornin'. Who are you talkin' to?" Zed said when Harper entered the café. "Have a cup of coffee and sit with me for a few minutes. We'll get the breakfast goin' at five thirty. Won't be nobody here this mornin' but you girls, so we won't have too much to do."

"Good mornin' to you. So our day won't be rushed?"

"Not this mornin', but it'll pick up this evening," Zed answered.

"Why are we even open? Granny's only been gone two days."

"Because that's what she made me promise. The day she passed on I was to call you girls, and the next day we were to be closed so y'all could get settled in. But on the day after that, we were to open shop for business as usual," he answered.

The coffee machine offered decaf, dark roast, and hot water. Packages of instant hot chocolate along with a few kinds of tea were in a basket on the table. She poured a cup of the dark roast and then ripped open two of the hot chocolate packets to add to it. A double shot of half-and-half and she could pretend that it was a mocha latte.

"We got a full house checkin' in sometime between three and suppertime. That's ten cabins full, so tomorrow mornin' will be a lot different than this one. Flora's comin' about midmornin' to make sure all the cabins are up and ready. We shut them down a week ago when the doctor said it was Annie's last days. Whooo-wee!" He threw up both hands. "You can't imagine the fit she threw over that. Said that she could die without us losin' money."

Harper sipped her coffee. "That's Granny Annie.

She believed that work never hurt anyone."

"Yep." Zed's head bobbed up and down. "We worked seven days a week around here, but we got to do it together so we sure enough didn't mind. Come seven o'clock at night, we'd close up the café and watch some television." He rolled his eyes toward the ceiling to hold back the tears. "I'm glad you girls are here. Don't know if I could handle it without y'all. I could hire help, but"—he hesitated—"family needs to be with family in these times."

"Even if it's a dysfunctional one?" she asked.

"Maybe more so." He eased up out of his chair and carried his mug with him to the kitchen. Harper followed right behind him. He slid a pan of biscuits into the oven and then shook some flour over sausage that he'd already cooked in a deep cast-iron skillet.

"You can whip up those eggs, and I'll get some pancake batter ready. Dana has got to go to school and enroll Brook this mornin'. I don't expect that they'll keep the child, since they'll have to get all her records from the school she was in, but if they do, she'll need a good breakfast. What they serve in lunchrooms these days is a cryin' shame. Can't have nothin' fried," Zed fussed as he slowly added milk to the skillet.

"Who's goin' to mind the store while she's gone?" Harper picked up a whisk and went to work on a bowl full of eggs.

"Ain't nobody here until after three and the locals don't get up until midmornin', so she can leave it for an hour or so. After today, it might be tough for her to get away through the daylight hours because she'll be real busy. Not only is fishin' season in full swing, but the local folks that own summer places have started to move in. Business is pretty steady most days. It closes at seven like the café, so her evenin's are free. After breakfast you can take my grocery list to the store. We usually do our shoppin' at Walmart in Tyler. I've got it ready, and I'll send the company credit card with you," he said.

"You goin' to trust me with that?" Harper asked.

"Sure I will. You buy something not on the list, it comes out of your paycheck and I will cross-check the receipt with the list," Zed answered.

It was straight up six o'clock when Tawny arrived at the café. Covering a yawn, she sniffed the air and went straight for the table where Zed and Harper had spread out the breakfast. She loaded a plate and took it to a table, returned for a cup of coffee, and headed back.

"You don't eat our food without at least a good mornin'," Zed told her.

"Good mornin'," she grumbled. "I've never been a morning person, and I don't expect to change."

"Might be surprised what changes will come

about here on the lake. You get that computer stuff all ready to start work this afternoon?" he asked.

"I sure did and went through the program to familiarize myself with it. I learned it in my freshman year of college. It's old but pretty basic. If my work goes on after the workday closes, why do I have to be up at the crack of dawn?"

"You do your work in the mornin's when you are fresh and your mind is clear. The store and café receipts and the bankin' stuff can always wait until the next mornin' after we give them to you. You won't need to go to the bank tomorrow, since we haven't been open here for a week. That will start next Saturday mornin', and if you've a mind to be nice, then you can help either here or in the store when you ain't busy with the book stuff," Zed said as he headed back into the kitchen.

"And if I'm not in the mood to be nice?" Tawny asked.

"Then you can sit on your porch and watch the grass grow. It's up to you, girl," Zed answered.

"Grass has always fascinated me. I can't remember when I had food like this," she said between bites.

"Body needs to start off the day with something that'll stick to the ribs," he said seriously.

Harper brought her plate of food to the table. "I'm surprised you didn't die from bein' poor those few months."

"Don't you start on me," Tawny growled.

"Looks like we're the last ones to the party." Dana and Brook pushed inside the room.

Brook looked from Tawny to Harper and back again. "So what are y'all fighting about now?"

"Whether or not bein' poor is a fatal disease," Harper answered. "Tawny never had to live in a world where she needed a paycheck until this last little while."

"Shhh"—Brook nodded toward the kitchen—"don't talk about death. It'll make Uncle Zed sad all over again."

"Best get to eatin' or these two won't leave nothin' for you." Zed emerged from the kitchen with another plate of crispy bacon.

Dana quickly changed the subject. "That's the story of my life. Always comin' in last."

"That's not the way I see it. Seems to me like you were always the bossy firstborn who lorded it over us," Harper said.

"And you were the wild one and Tawny whined a lot and both of y'all were the precious little princesses who had a mama and daddy both," Dana shot back.

"You don't know that. You weren't even here when I was a teenager," Tawny said.

Brook poured two glasses of orange juice and put them on the table. "I'll be bossy, wild, and whiny if y'all will homeschool me. I've attended the same private school since pre-K. I'm nervous about all this."

"Private school?" Harper cut her eyes around at Dana.

"The kids on the ranch where I worked all went to the school. It was one of the perks of the job," Dana said.

Brook fidgeted in her chair. "This is my first time to go to public school."

"Harper and I went to a private school, but we both always wanted to go to public school," Tawny said.

"Why?" Brook cut open a biscuit and slathered it with butter.

A wicked grin spread across Harper's face. "We heard you could buy weed there better than in the private schools."

<hr>

"Harper Clancy!" Tawny raised her voice.

"Hey, don't gripe at me. I was a pretty good kid, but if I remember right, Mama had to make a sizable donation to the school to get *you* out of trouble more than once. Come on, girl. Fess up. Why do your hands look like they've been diggin' ditches?" Harper shot a look her way.

Brook jerked her head around to see what Tawny would say next.

"I've been working, and I didn't get in trouble for weed. And you're setting a bad example for this child. And how did you know about that stuff? You never came home after you ran away from that boarding school where they sent you," Tawny declared.

"You and Mama weren't the only Clancys I talked to. Until Daddy passed away, he and I talked at least once a month. If I remember correctly, the school got two nice little donations toward scholarships to keep you from being suspended."

"That was for skipping school to go shopping," Tawny explained to Brook. "Mama was angry because I ran up her credit, not because I skipped school. They were going to kick me out, but she still didn't want me to go to public school."

"Why?" Brook asked.

"Because she thought only the scum of the earth went to public school," Harper answered for Tawny.

Brook turned to face Dana. "Well, I'm not the scum of the earth. Sounds to me like y'all's mama was different than my granny Lacy."

"Little bit," Dana said and then yelled toward the kitchen, "Great breakfast. I'd forgotten how good your pancakes are, Uncle Zed."

Tawny would have traded mothers with Dana in a heartbeat. When Lacy came to pick Dana up in the summers, she'd been sweet to Harper and Dana both. And Dana actually missed her mother while they were at the resort. Tawny could never remember having that kind of feeling. Mostly she wished she never had to go home.

Zed brought out another platter with six big

63

pancakes on it and then went on back to the kitchen. "It's Annie's recipe. Secret is in beating the egg whites first and then folding them into the batter. Makes good light pancakes. I've got to get the lunch special started. Word'll get out about us bein' open, and some of the folks around these parts always eat here on Friday."

Tawny hurried through the rest of her breakfast, cramming a biscuit full of scrambled eggs and bacon to take back to the cabin for a midmorning snack. Watching grass grow might work up an appetite. A gentle morning breeze brushed against her cheeks as she walked back to the cabin. She zipped her jacket and sat down on the porch in one of the vintage metal lawn chairs. This one was red, like the one on Harper's porch. Seemed fitting—she and Harper shared parents and a bloodline, so that made them like two chairs cut from the same pattern.

A cardinal lit on the railing around the tiny porch and cocked his head toward her. She sat perfectly still and listened as he and a squirrel in the willow tree between cabins number seven and eight argued with each other. Off in the distance, she heard a rooster performing his wake-up calls. A couple of frogs joined in the mix, and a pair of robins chirped as they hopped around the yard.

The sun, a bright-orange ball sitting on the horizon, sent enough light through the trees that she could make out a few new spring leaves.

There were a few tiny little whitecaps on the lake, and by cocking her head to one side she could hear the distant drone of voices—most likely fishermen already out there in the coves trying to catch their dinner. The cardinal grew bored with her and flew away, leaving one red feather fluttering from the railing to the porch.

She picked it up, went inside the cabin, and removed her jacket. When Zed had said that strangers would be coming into her personal space, it had freaked her out. So she'd arranged the desk, file cabinets, and everything to do with the business under the window looking out over the porch. Then she'd taken down one of the twin beds and carried one piece at a time to the storage room behind the laundry house. That's where she found the bookcases and had asked Zed to borrow his old truck to take them to her cabin.

She'd pushed her bed under the window looking out over the backyard and wooded area, leaving only enough room for a nightstand on either side, and then built a wall of four bookcases to divide the room. On the back side was her personal space. Just inside the door was her office. She carefully laid the red feather on a top shelf.

She circled around the makeshift wall—bed made tight enough to pass Retha Harper-Clancy's inspection, a thousand percent tougher than anything the military required. Her mother had never cleaned a house in her life, but by damn, she expected perfection in her hired help as well as her daughters.

It was no secret that Retha hadn't wanted children. She'd made that clear, often and loudly, especially when Tawny or her sister weren't perfect little angels. It had gotten worse after they'd sent Harper off to boarding school. Whatever it was must have been horrible because they hadn't sent Tawny away when she was sixteen and got caught with a flask of tequila in her locker at school.

⋆⊹⊱⊰⊹⋆

All schools, private or public, smelled the same and for the most part looked alike. The Frankston School had changed very little since the last time Dana was in it. She'd hated leaving her friends, but at the end of her eighth-grade year her mother, Lacy, had married the first stepfather and they'd moved to Austin, where Dana had finished high school. Now Lacy was married to Richard, stepfather number three, and that marriage was on shaky ground.

"Is that really Dana Clancy?" a deep voice behind her asked.

She glanced over her shoulder and stopped in her tracks. "Well, hello, Marcus. What are you doin' here?"

"Teachin' history." His smile showed perfectly straight teeth.

"You're kiddin' me," she gasped.

Brook raised an eyebrow. "Mama?"

"This is an old classmate of mine back when I went to school here. Marcus, meet my daughter, Brook, and Brook, this is Marcus Green." No way was she going to tell her daughter that her history teacher had been one of the biggest pot smokers in junior high school.

"Pleasure to meet you." Marcus nodded toward Brook. "So you're married?"

"Was," Dana answered. "Many years ago. Right now we've got to get to the office and get her enrolled."

Marcus fell in beside her as she started down the hallway. "Moving back to the lake, are you? I was sorry to hear about Annie."

"Thank you. It came as a shock to all of us, but we are all settling in."

"That mean those other two sisters are coming back, too?" Marcus asked.

"They're here, but it's not a matter of coming back. They were only summer visitors. They never did actually live here. They were big-city girls out of Dallas, remember?"

"I do remember that about them. And they had kind of strange names." Marcus stopped by a door. "Here it is. Some things never change."

"Thank goodness for that," Dana said. "Good to see you again, Marcus."

"You too." Marcus waved over his shoulder.

He wasn't much taller than Dana, and she was

considered medium height at five feet six inches. But he carried himself differently now. When they were kids, he'd reminded her of a miniature rock star with all his kinky dark-brown hair down to his shoulders. Now it was cut close. No one would ever believe that those blue eyes could have ever been glazed over from smoking too much weed during lunch.

It took all of fifteen minutes to enroll Brook, and the principal, Mrs. Johnson, wanted her to stay. "I see you brought your backpack. I'll get Flora's granddaughter to show you around. She's enrolled in most of the same classes that you are."

"Okay," Brook said slowly, dragging out the syllables.

"You don't have to stay today if you aren't comfortable with it," Dana said.

Brook shrugged. "Beats mopping floors and cleaning rooms."

Mrs. Johnson leaned into a microphone and said, "Cassidy Jones, please come to the office."

Before she even got the last word out, a slightly overweight girl with a jet-black ponytail, a round face, and pink glasses poked her head in the door. "Yes, ma'am?"

"This is Brook Clancy, a new eighth grader. Y'all have the same schedule."

Cassidy nodded. "Then we've got English first hour and about five minutes to get there, so come on."

"Hello, Cassidy. I've known your grandma all my life. I'm Brook's mother," Dana said.

"Pleased to meet you." Cassidy smiled. "We'd better get goin'. The bell is going to ring anytime now."

Brook picked up her backpack, laid a hand on Dana's shoulder, and then followed the girl out of the office and into a hallway of chattering kids. Dana hadn't planned to leave her at school, and worry gripped her heart even worse than on Brook's first day of kindergarten.

"It's okay," Mrs. Johnson said. "Cassidy is a fine student. She'll take good care of her today, and by Monday, your daughter will be part of everything."

"I hope so. Thank you. We're out at Annie's Place. I did write down the phone number there, didn't I?"

"You did. We all know it by heart anyway from making reservations for Sunday dinner. Sorry to hear about Annie. She was always a big supporter of our school. I'm sure Brook will be fine. Besides, you brought all the paperwork, so you made my job easy. Will you pick her up, or shall I make sure she's on the right bus?" Mrs. Johnson put on her glasses and glanced down at the form in front of her. "Are you going to run the place? I'd sure hate to see it close. How's Zed doin'? He and Annie have been friends for so long and worked together for, what, fifty years?"

"About that long. Uncle Zed is sad, but so are all of us. It came as a shock to us, since she didn't want him to tell us that she was sick. We sure hope he's not thinkin' of retiring anytime soon."

"*Uncle* Zed?" Mrs. Johnson asked. "But Zed is black. Is he . . . ," she stammered.

"No, that's what we've always called him at home," Dana answered. "He's been more like a grandfather than an uncle, but—" She shrugged.

Mrs. Johnson straightened all the papers and put them to one side. "Cassidy rides the bus to the cabins some of the time, so that will make things easy. I'll just tell her to be sure that Brook is on the bus with her."

"Thanks again." Dana started toward the door.

As the phone rang, Mrs. Johnson picked it up and waved Dana out with her other hand.

Her thoughts were all over the place in the quietness of the truck as she drove back up the highway. Surely there wouldn't be a drug problem in the school. Marcus and a very small group of kids were the only ones who got into that scene when she was there. But with him being a teacher? Had she talked to Brook enough about the dangers? She made a mental note to do that over the weekend. And to warn her about what could happen if she were to take drugs and drink liquor at the same time.

She didn't remember driving home or even across the bridge, but there was the turn and she had missed it. She drove all the way to the bar up on the hill, turned around in the parking lot, and drove slower on the way back. The cabins and store were both visible when she made the right-hand turn. She parked her truck in front of the house and walked back to the store. She wished that she had seriously considered homeschooling Brook so she wouldn't have to worry about all the outside influences, but then, teaching her in front of her two aunts would probably be even worse than what she'd get in public school.

Life was not going to be a bed of roses. "Or maybe it is," she said as she opened the door and flipped on the lights. "Roses have thorns, and believe me, Tawny and Harper have always been thorns in my side."

And you are one in theirs. Granny's voice popped into her head. "Probably." She nodded.

She fished her phone out of her purse and hit the "Speed Dial" button for her mother, but nothing connected. "Dammit!" she fumed as she picked up the corded phone and punched in the phone number. Lacy answered on the third ring, panting as if she was out of breath.

"Are you there? Did they really cremate Annie?" she asked. "Why are you calling from the store?"

"I am and they did. And remember, there is no service in this spot. And no Wi-Fi, either. Brook is havin' a fit."

"Poor baby," Lacy huffed.

"Did I call at a bad time?"

"No, darlin'. I'd just walked in the door from a two-mile run. I'm not gettin' any younger, and besides, runnin' helps the stress. I'm filing for divorce today. Your stepfather has cheated on me his last time," Lacy said. "Are the two princesses there?"

"Yep, they are. I'm going to manage the store. Harper is helping Uncle Zed in the kitchen, and Tawny has an office set up in her cabin to take care of the business for the place," Dana said.

"You are jokin', right? I can't picture Tawny doin' anything but sittin' on the porch with a glass of sweet tea and lookin' pretty. And Harper cookin' and cleanin' up after people? I can't even drag up a faint vision of that," Lacy giggled.

"That's not why I called. I'm worried about leaving Brook at school. It's worse than when I had to walk away from her in kindergarten."

"That's just your mother instinct. Change never hurts any of us. I'll come see y'all sometime this summer, and I expect by then you'll be settled in and lovin' it. You always did like spendin' time with Annie."

"I loved her so much." Dana's voice broke.

"And she loved you, thank God. If it hadn't been for Annie and Zed and their help, we'd have never made it. Your father sure never gave us any support. Went off to college and we never saw him again." Lacy's voice always got that bitter edge when she mentioned Gavin Clancy. It was as if she had had no part in her pregnancy.

"So you think I'm only a worryin' mama?" Dana deliberately veered away from a conversation about her father.

"Of course I do. I've got to get a quick shower and put on a decent outfit. My lawyer and I are meeting at ten. He's a widower—very well-to-do," Lacy said.

"So you've got number four already picked out? Who was cheatin' on who?" Dana asked.

"It's not who's cheatin', but who gets caught. Why shouldn't I look at the playin' field?"

"And if you'd gotten caught?" Dana asked.

"Then I'd still be lookin' at the playin' field, but with no big fat settlement," she laughed. "Got to run, darlin'. Talk to you later. If you don't like it up there, you can always move in with me. I'm going to get the house for sure."

"Thanks, Mama. Talk to you later," Dana said and hung up the phone.

Living with her two sisters might be tough, but she'd make it work—no way in hell would she ever live with her mother.

⁕⋇⊹⧏⧐⊹⋇⁕

Zed sat down in his recliner that evening and sighed. He glanced over at the other chair and smiled. "Annie, you left me a handful with them

73

girls. Every one of them is fighting a demon. I'm tryin' to be patient with 'em and learn what keeps them from opening up to each other and bein' a family, but sometimes I just want to shake some sense into them."

He sipped at a glass of wine for a few minutes and then frowned. "Okay, I hear you. It's took a long time for them to get this way, and it will take a while for them to learn to love and trust one another. But you know, Annie, that I ain't got forever. I'm lonesome without you, and I've been ready to leave this old world for a long time now. You could have waited for me, and we could've checked out together."

Another sip of wine. "I understand it wasn't none of your doin's. You wanted us to be like that couple in *The Notebook* and die together holdin' hands. I shouldn't bitch and moan, should I? At least you knew who I was right up to your last breath and weren't like that woman in the movie. I should be grateful for that."

He finished off the wine and set the glass to the side. "Okay, it's bedtime now, so good night, my sweet Annie. I miss you even more than I thought was possible." He blew a kiss toward the wooden box where her ashes were kept. "Keep a candle in the window so I can find my way to you when the good Lord sees fit to turn me loose."

Chapter Four

Tawny would never have believed that a place so far removed from civilization would bring in enough revenue to pay Flora's and Zed's salaries, much less three more and part-time wages for Brook. But when all the rest of the cabins but one were filled up by four o'clock that afternoon and she tallied up how much they'd make in only a few days, she realized what a moneymaker the place really was.

She was busy checking the schedule for Flora's room-cleaning hours when she noticed that unit number six beside her would be filled late that evening by a Mr. and Mrs. Thomas Smith, a young honeymooning couple who'd only be there Friday and Saturday nights.

"Honeymoonin' here?" She frowned. "Are they crazy?"

"I hope I'm not crazy, but the jury is still out." A guy who looked vaguely familiar stepped inside the cabin.

Something tickled the outer edges of her memories. She'd swear on a stack of Bibles that she'd heard his voice before. She frowned as she checked the books for a name. Wyatt Simpson. The name rang a bell, but she couldn't place him.

Then it clicked. He'd been at the lake resort

that last summer that the sisters were all there together. He and Harper went to the lake every evening, and Tawny had seen them kissing. The image faded and was replaced by Harper sneaking through the back door at almost daybreak one morning. Was it Wyatt she'd sneaked out of the house to see that night?

"What?" She frowned.

"Didn't you ask if I was crazy?" He smiled.

"Sorry, I was woolgathering. And I wasn't talkin' to you. I was thinkin' out loud about a couple who are plannin' to honeymoon here. I said, 'Are they crazy?' not 'Are you,' " she answered.

"Then no, they are not crazy. I can't think of a better place to honeymoon than right here on the lake. It's downright romantic. I'm Wyatt Simpson, and you've put me in number two with a set of twin beds. I should be in number three with a queen-size bed."

"I have you down for three rooms, but you didn't specify which ones you wanted on the reservations."

"Didn't have to when Annie was here. She knew what cabin I liked."

"Well, until I get to know the customers, it would be nice if you'd tell me when you make the reservations."

He nodded. "I'm a fishin' guide. I have four guys who'll be here in half an hour. They'll need the two cabins that have twin beds," he explained.

"I can pick up the keys for them now, and I'll put my things in the cabin with the bigger bed."

"Sure thing," Tawny said as she adjusted the room numbers on the computer and handed him the keys from the rack inside the door. "You been here recently?"

"Lots of times. Came for years with my grandfather, who was a fishin' guide. When he died, I took over the business. You'd be one of Annie's granddaughters, right?"

"Yes, sir. I'm the youngest, Tawny."

"I'm sorry to hear about her passing, but I'm real glad that you are keepin' the place open," he said.

"Thank you. Anything else?" What did Harper see in him, anyway? Maybe it was because he was the only boy around that summer. Light-brown hair, hazel eyes, tall and sinewy with muscular arms but nothing outstanding about him—at least not in Tawny's eyes.

"Are you the only granddaughter that came back to this place?" Wyatt asked.

"No." She shook her head. "My sisters, Harper and Dana, are here also."

Wyatt lingered at the open door. "Harper was fifteen and Dana had a little girl with her. Maybe about three or four years old. My grandpa thought she was the cutest thing he'd ever seen."

Tawny looked up into his eyes. "That's right. That little girl is fourteen now."

"Wow, time does fly, doesn't it? I was only sixteen that year, and it was my last visit here for a long time. But after college I decided that sitting behind a desk wasn't for me, so I picked up where my grandpa left off," Wyatt said. "I should be going. Nice visitin' with you."

"See you at supper?" she asked.

"Wouldn't miss one of Zed's burgers for anything. Just sorry I missed the blue-plate special at noon." Wyatt shut the door behind himself.

She left the cabin and headed for the store. If she approached it right and didn't make Dana angry, she might find out what her older sister remembered from that summer. The store was hopping busy with fishermen wanting bait and young kids whining for ice cream bars while their parents bought picnic supplies, so she grabbed a bag of pork rinds and a root beer and held them up. Dana nodded and Tawny left without getting any answers.

Her mouth was full of pork rinds when the phone rang. "Lake Side Resort," she answered. She'd always heard the resort referred to as Annie's Place, so the official name sounded strange in her ears.

"You are talking with food in your mouth. I can hear it," her mother said bluntly.

"Sorry about that. Not bad manners, just good pork rinds."

"Good God almighty!" Retha gasped. "I hated for you girls to go to that place in the summer. Pork rinds?"

"Are amazing. Especially the barbecued ones. You should try them," Tawny giggled.

"I can't believe you are actually living in that backwoods place." Retha's voice turned icy cold.

"What does it matter where I go? You disowned me, remember?" The sharp edge in Tawny's tone could have shredded steel.

"It was to teach you a lesson. I know what's best for you," Retha said.

"I suppose you're going to tell me that's why you tied up my and Harper's inheritance from Daddy—to show us what is best for us?"

"I blame it all on that damned lake. Annie didn't watch over you like she should have."

"Whoa! Wait a minute, Mother. I know how to hang up a telephone, and a corded one makes such a lovely loud bang. I won't have you talkin' trash about Granny."

"She broke up our family," Retha countered.

"I'd say you broke it up when you sent Harper to boarding school. Why'd you do that? Daddy was never the same afterward. She was only fifteen. What did she do to get exiled?" Tawny asked.

"She left on her sixteenth birthday. That's tough love. You can have your inheritance when you are forty or when I see that you are finally acting responsibly. God knows that damn resort is breeding ground for trouble," Retha snapped.

"Trouble finds me wherever I go, Mother. There's about ten cabins here with mighty fine-lookin' men in every one. And I'm not any farther than a city block from a convenience store that sells all kinds of beer. Bet if I went down to the high school I could even score some weed." Tawny knew she was baiting her mother, but she couldn't make herself stop.

"I can't believe my kin would turn out the way you and Harper have. I would have expected it of your father's bastard daughter, but you two had the best that money could buy." Retha sighed.

"Dana probably turned out to be the best one of us. She's got her head on straight and she's a really good mom to Brook, so don't bad-mouth her." Tawny couldn't believe that she was taking up for her older sister.

"You just proved that you aren't worthy to get your inheritance yet," Retha said, and the line went dead.

"Love you, too, Mama." Tawny slammed the receiver back on the base and muttered, "If you had any idea what this place is worth, you'd be beatin' a path up here to try to get your grubby little hands on part of it."

❖⊹⊱⊰⊹❖

A bunch of guys wearing caps with fishing hooks and all kinds of pins attached to the bills arrived in the café just as Harper made the rounds to refill drinks. She set two pitchers on the drink counter and headed over to the only empty table in the café. "Looks like all y'all are wearing your lucky hats today."

"Yep, every one of us is slightly superstitious. I'll have sweet tea and a double-meat, double-cheese burger basket," the one closest to her said.

"And the rest of you?" she asked without really looking at any of them.

"Same as old Donnie," another one said.

"Me too," two more chimed in.

"Well, that makes it easy enough. And you?" she asked the guy who'd pulled up a fifth chair from a two-top.

"You got any of the cobbler left over from dinner?" he asked.

A jolt of something akin to electricity shooting through her body glued her to the floor. She'd never forgotten that deep voice or the way that her hormones whined when he was within twenty feet of her.

"We've got about eight servings, last I checked," she answered.

"Save it all for us. If we don't eat it now, we'll take it to go, and hello, Harper," Wyatt said.

"Wyatt." Her voice was at least two octaves higher than normal, and her hands trembled. "What brings you back here?"

"He's our fishin' guide. We've been comin'

here the past three years during this week. So you know this old ragtag fisherman?" the oldest guy in the group asked.

"Used to, but a lot of water has run under the bridge since we were sixteen." She fought against the desire to leave the café, get into her truck, and not even look in the rearview mirror. She could be packed up and out of there in exactly thirty minutes. When she'd gone to Tyler for supplies, she'd had both her tires fixed, so she was ready to go. But that wouldn't be fair to Uncle Zed or to her granny's memory.

She took the order all the way to the kitchen instead of pinning it up over the serving window. She only needed a few seconds to still her racing pulse and calm her thumping heart. Dammit! She'd thought she'd gotten over him for good.

Zed looked up from the grill and pointed to a bar stool by his prep table. "Sit! You look like you just saw a ghost. What's happened? Did Annie appear to you?"

She hiked a hip on the stool by the work island and leaned her elbows on it. "No. Has she appeared to you?"

"Not yet." He sighed. "I keep hopin', but it hasn't happened yet. My mama said that when her grandmother died, she saw her standing at the end of her bed one night and then she was gone. She always thought that her granny was telling her that she was happy and not to worry.

So what's happened out there that you just about fainted?"

"I saw someone, but it wasn't a ghost. He was very real. Though I wasn't expectin' to see him ever again," she answered.

Zed peeked out the window and waved.

"Would that someone be Wyatt?" He rubbed his chin. "He's here a lot. He missed a few years after his granddad passed. He finished school and went to college. Got him one of them fancy degrees in some highfalutin thing, but decided that he didn't like livin' in the big city. He come back to Lindale and started his grandpa's old business. Lot like you're doin'."

"And he's here every year?" Harper asked.

"Yep. About every week during the spring and summer." He lined up several meat patties on the grill. "We make our money off return customers and word of mouth. Annie always said that was better than placin' an ad in the newspaper. Why'd you ask about Wyatt?"

"He's out there with his fishin' crew and I recognized him. His grandpa used to bring him," Harper said.

"And one summer you had yourself a crush on that boy." He grinned.

"That was a long time ago."

"Way you looked, it don't look like it was long enough for you to forget him."

"You know what they say about first loves,

especially when you are really young," she said.

"I believe that with all my heart," he said.

"I just wasn't expecting to see him. I should get back out there and make sure everyone has what they need."

He patted her on the shoulder. "You're makin' a fine waitress. I'm proud of you, girl."

As she moved around the tables of mostly fishermen, she caught snatches of conversation about catfish the size of Moby Dick and catching so many bass that they almost sank a boat hauling them to shore. She was almost to Wyatt's table when the bell rang in the kitchen, and she hurried back to get their dinner baskets.

Setting them before each of the five men, she was very careful not to brush a hand across Wyatt's arm or to even make eye contact. Being next to him gave her hot flashes that no little white pill in the world could cure.

"Zed could put in a burger shop anywhere in the world and people would flock to it. He should write a recipe book. Bet he could make a million bucks on it," Wyatt said.

"Probably so, but I don't think he'll share his secrets with anyone," Harper said. "Anything else I can get you guys?" Working at the café was more pleasant than working at bars, but anytime someone mentioned Annie, it put a lump in her throat the size of a grapefruit.

"You ever been told that you look a lot like

Deana Carter, that country singer?" the older one in the group asked.

"Nope, and flattery won't get you anywhere with me." She blushed.

"She's younger than Deana. I'd say she looks more like Carrie Underwood."

"That won't even get you an extra dessert," she halfheartedly teased as she refilled their tea glasses and then made her way to the other side of the room to clean up a table that had been vacated. She shoved several dollar bills into her pocket. With little left to spend money on now that her truck was fixed, the tips were starting to add up.

She was very aware of when Wyatt and his fishermen left, but the rest of the evening swam with random visions that kept playing through her mind. Times she'd had with her grandmother, her sisters, and even Brook as a baby, but most of all flashes of Wyatt.

When Zed locked the door at seven o'clock on the dot and handed her a broom, she was humming an old Deana Carter tune, "Strawberry Wine." She and Wyatt had never actually drunk wine in those days, but the lyrics sure did describe the summer.

"I'll get the kitchen cleaned up. You can be in charge of the dining area. I figure it'll take about half an hour and then we can go home. What's that song you are humming?" Zed asked.

She told him the title.

"That kind of country music tells a story. Some of this new stuff is just repetitive crap. Let's get this last job of the day done and we can go home," he said.

"We are home." She went back to humming.

"Glad that you see it that way. I like to see you so happy."

One shoulder raised in half a shrug. "Look, you know I could find a job. Never been without one more than a week since I was a teenager, but this was like it fell out of heaven."

"Goin' to light out of here when you make enough money?" He stopped and turned around.

She began to sweep the floor. "Never know what tomorrow might bring."

"Ain't that the truth?" he said with a smile.

After cleanup was finished, Harper went back to her cabin, but she couldn't sit still. She flipped back and forth between the two channels on the television, but neither one kept her attention. Memories. A whole summer of them kept rising up in her mind. It was that magical time when she and Wyatt discovered sex together, when in their youthful ignorance they'd been too careless and she'd gotten pregnant. The guilt she'd felt ever since giving that precious baby girl up for adoption had never left her. Like always, she felt the need to drink or to run, but she was determined to do neither that evening.

Zed needed her, and she had to finally face her past or she'd never move on to a future. She needed something, anything, to escape from the smothering pictures flashing through her head. She dug around in her box of books until she came up with one that she'd read a dozen times and still loved, but not even her favorite author, Katie Lane, could keep her attention.

Finally, she pulled on a jacket and went out to sit in the old metal lawn chair on the corner of her tiny porch. The stars shone bright, circling around a half-moon in a black velvet sky. On many hot summer nights in that same cabin, she'd had some wild and crazy good times in cabin number twelve with Wyatt Simpson, most of them after they'd shared a six-pack of beer.

Suddenly the little short hairs on her neck prickled and her pulse jacked up a few beats a minute, letting her know that Wyatt was really close by. Then he stepped out of the shadows and into the moonlight. She drew her long legs up and wrapped her arms around them.

"Hey," he said. "I was out for an evening walk down that old trail behind the cabins. So are you living in this unit? I remember—"

She held up a palm. "That was a long time ago."

"Ten years, if I remember right. We were a couple of crazy teenagers, weren't we?"

"Oh, yes." She nodded. He didn't have any idea

of just how crazy and irresponsible they had been that summer.

"Are you just here for a few weeks or for a long time?"

"I don't really don't know. I basically live a day at a time," she answered.

He nodded. "I understand that. Mind if I sit down?" he asked.

She shrugged. "Lots of porch steps. Help yourself to whichever one looks most comfortable."

He sat on the top step and stretched his legs out over the steps to the ground. "I never forgot that summer. How about you?"

"Of course not," she answered. That summer had set the course for her life the past decade and given her the means for a guilt trip that she went on every spring.

"Two crazy teenagers finding each other, beer, and sex. You married?" he asked.

"No. You?"

He shook his head. "Not yet."

"Engaged?" Harper asked.

"Was at one time. She didn't like the idea of me being a fishin' guide."

She didn't realize she was holding her breath until he answered. Not that it made a bit of difference. They were totally different people now. "What'd she want you to do?"

"I've got a degree in commercial business and worked for a mortgage company a year before I figured out I wasn't cut out to wear three-piece suits." He grinned. "How about you?"

"Been job hopping, just makin' a livin'. Last one was working in a bar and livin' in an apartment over the place," she answered.

"You're kiddin' me!"

"Nope, didn't finish high school, but I did get my GED. Haven't spent a single day at college."

He stood up. "I figured you'd own an oil well or two by now, or maybe you'd be a model for some fancy clothing place."

"Disappointed?" she asked.

"Not in the least. We all have to find our way. As my favorite aunt used to say, it doesn't matter what you do, long as you're happy."

"Sounds like a smart woman. It's getting chilly." She shivered. "I'm going inside."

"I'd go get a six-pack of beer from my cabin if you'll invite me over." He grinned.

She shook her head and stood up. "Not tonight. We aren't those crazy kids anymore."

"I wish we were. That summer was the best time of my life. Maybe another time. See you at breakfast?"

"That's my job long as I'm here," she said. Like a famous author once wrote, that summer had been the best of times and the worst of times for Harper. What should have been a sweet awakening had turned into a bitter nightmare.

She went inside and fell forward on the bed,

burying her face in the pillow. Then she rolled over and shook her fist at the window. "Why, God? Why would you put me in this cabin and send Wyatt Simpson to the lake the first week I'm here?"

Face your demons and get on with life, the voice in her head said clearly. Was God speaking to her? If he was, then he didn't know just how big her demons were.

✦✦❈✦❈✦✦

"This is finally feeling like home," Brook said between bites of her favorite supper—spaghetti, salad, hot rolls, and chocolate pie for dessert.

"Tell me about your first day at school," Dana said.

"It was okay. I like Cassidy a lot. We're already friends and there's this one boy—" Brook laid her hand on her heart and fluttered her thick lashes. "He wears cowboy boots and tight-fittin' jeans and he's so dreamy. It's different in public school. No uniforms. Everyone don't look just alike."

Dana's heart fell into her pink fuzzy slippers. She wasn't ready for Brook to like boys or want to start dating.

"But he's got a girlfriend and he's a senior, so he'd never even look at me." Brook sighed. "But when I do get a boyfriend, he's going to look like that and make my heart go all mushy inside.

Hey, you know what?" She removed her hand and changed the subject. "We should've invited Aunt Harper and Aunt Tawny. They're probably lonely."

"They've got jobs to do just like us. Tomorrow and Sunday you'll help Flora in the laundry," Dana said. No way would she invite those two to supper. Granny had been wise in dividing their jobs. If she'd had to spend thirteen hours a day in the same room with either Harper or Tawny, she'd be ready for a straitjacket. Or worse—she might land in jail.

Brook groaned. "I'd rather clean horse stalls."

"You see any horse stalls around here?"

Her daughter shook her head. "When we get done tomorrow evening and the store is closed, can we go down to the lake? Maybe even take a sandwich or get Uncle Zed to make us up some cheeseburgers?"

"Either Friday or Saturday night used to be movie and popcorn night. Why not just keep up the way we do things, Brook?" Maybe, just maybe, if she kept the traditions alive and going, she could delay Brook's inevitable interest in boys.

"Then Sunday when we get done with work?" she asked.

"Maybe if it's not rainin'," Dana agreed.

"You know what I liked best about comin' to Granny Annie's?" Brook asked and continued before Dana could answer. "I liked sitting on the porch swing with her. When we finish supper, can we just go out there and swing? That way we can talk about her and I can tell her goodbye."

"Yes, we can sure enough do that," Dana said around the lump in her throat. "We can even take our dessert out there if you want."

"Granny would like that," Brook said.

✦✦✦

A dark cloud shifted over the moon, blocking half the light as they sat in the swing and listened to the squeak of the chains as they ate chocolate pie and shared an orange soda pop straight from the bottle.

"This taste reminds me of the chocolate-orange candy we got Granny Annie at Christmas," Brook said.

Dana bought those little foil-wrapped oranges for Granny Annie every year. She'd loved the combination of the two tastes and had always looked forward to getting one in her stocking.

And I didn't even know last Christmas would be the final time I'd ever see her. If I had, I'd have brought her a dozen of those chocolate oranges, Dana thought.

Brook pointed toward the sky. "Look at those stars. Do you think there's really holes in the floor of heaven like that country song says? Can Granny peek down and see us?"

"I don't know," Dana said. "But if there is, I bet she's real happy that we are here takin' care of things."

"Especially Uncle Zed," Brook said. "She'll miss him more than anyone else. Does he look even skinnier to you than the last time we saw him?"

"He does look like he's lost weight, but then he's taken on his and Granny's jobs for several weeks now. Maybe he'll gain a little now that we're all here to help take care of things. What makes you think that she'll miss him more than any of us?"

"They were best friends their whole lives. Granny told me that the last time we saw her. She said that her and Grandpa Seamus and Uncle Zed grew up right here before the lake was made, when it was just farm country, and they'd always been friends. If I had a friend like that, I'd sure miss her." Brook finished off her pie and licked the last of the chocolate from the plate.

"Brook Clancy, that's bad manners," Dana fussed.

"It made Granny laugh when I did it and I'm tellin' her goodbye, so it's okay."

Dana couldn't contain the smile. "So you think Cassidy will ever be a friend like Granny and Uncle Zed were?"

"Maybe if we stay here forever. We'll have to

see how things go." Brook shivered. "It's getting cold. We'd better go inside."

A burst of warm air greeted them as they entered the house, along with a phone ringing in the kitchen. The old yellow wall-hung telephone was right inside the back door, and Dana made a beeline for it. Dana caught it on the fourth ring and breathlessly said, "Hello."

"I think you're supposed to say 'Lake Side Resort,' or at least 'Annie's Place,'" Tawny said.

"Maybe I'll just say, 'Beer, bait, and bologna. Drink it, catch it, or eat it—we don't give a damn, long as you pay your bill,'" Dana shot back. "What do you want?"

"Would it be all right if I came to the house and sat on the swing for a little bit? Seems strange not to have Granny here, and I'd like to say goodbye to her," Tawny answered. "I won't disturb you."

"Fine by me," Dana said.

"Thank you."

Dana stood there with the phone in her hand staring at it for a full thirty seconds before Brook took it from her and hung it up.

"You okay, Mama?"

"Tawny said, 'Thank you.' I don't think I've ever heard her say those two words—at least not to me." She thought about all the times that she'd sat on the swing or the porch with her much younger sisters. It had been a common ground for them, so maybe that's what Tawny was thinking about.

"Think y'all will ever get along?" Brook asked.

"Probably not," Dana answered.

"But—" Brook started.

"Granny used to say, 'It is what it is,' and I've come to accept that. You'd better go take your shower, young lady. It's getting late."

"Yes, ma'am, but I love Aunt Tawny and Aunt Harper so much. I wish . . ." She hesitated.

"Me too, kiddo, me too." Dana gave her a quick hug.

She was determined not to even look outside and to let Tawny find closure however she wanted. But then she heard voices and stepped out onto the porch to find Harper sitting on the top porch step and Tawny stretched out on the swing, taking up every bit of it and not even offering to share.

"I didn't know you both were coming over here," she said.

"I didn't know I had to ask if I could." Harper raised a small bottle of Jack Daniel's. "To Granny Annie. Rest in peace and in the knowledge that we'll keep this place runnin'."

Tawny held up a can of beer. "To Granny Annie. This was your favorite kind of beer. To the legacy you left for us."

Dana sat down on the step with Harper and took the whiskey bottle from her hand. She tipped it up and held a mouthful for a few seconds before she let it slide down her throat, warming her insides. "To Granny Annie, who never thought she'd see the three of us agree on anything, but we all do want you to know that we'll do our best to keep your place alive and well."

"Huh!" Harper snorted. "Never thought I'd see the day that you'd put your lips where mine have been."

"Whiskey kills germs," Dana said. "We've made our vows. Reckon we can keep them?"

"Do my damnedest." Harper nodded. "Long as it don't mean I have to get all sweet and lovey-dovey with y'all."

"Me too," Tawny said. "We need to put on a front for Uncle Zed. He's so sad and he doesn't need us bickering in front of him. If we've got a problem, we should hold our tongues until he's not around."

"I agree. He looks so frail these days. I'm worried about him, but I can't get him to let me do more in the café," Harper said.

"I'll try not to be bitchy if y'all will," Tawny said.

Dana set her mouth in a firm line and nodded in agreement.

They both stared at Harper.

"Okay, okay! I'll give it my best shot, but don't expect miracles," she said.

"Then we're in agreement," Dana said. "I think it might have been easier on him, maybe brought about closure, if we'd had a funeral for her."

"I wonder why she didn't want a funeral." Tawny frowned.

"Guess we'll find out when she's ready to tell us," Dana answered. "Y'all want to come inside? That north wind is chilly." *Now where in the devil did that come from?* She didn't want them in the house, and she dang sure wasn't ready to be all "lovey-dovey," as Harper had said.

"Not me. This is enough for tonight. I'm goin' back to my place," Harper said.

"Before you leave—" Tawny set the empty can on the porch. "Mother called me. I pissed her off, so I don't reckon we'll see our inheritance until she's dead."

"She mention me?" Harper stood up and handed the whiskey bottle to Dana. "There's one swallow left. You can have it."

"Thanks." Dana finished off the last drop in the bottle and then set the empty on the porch.

"Yes, but it was to fuss about us both being a big disappointment. Only time she ever mentions your name. Been that way since we were teenagers and you went out to California to that boarding school. You never did come back home after that. Why?"

"She pissed me off. I don't give a rat's fanny if I never get my inheritance. I've made it this long without it, so I reckon I can go on forever without Daddy's money." Harper left without saying another word.

97

Dana leaned her back against a porch post. "What happened that summer that she went to the boarding school? Nothing was ever the same around here after that."

Tawny shrugged. "I'm not real sure. Daddy did not cross Mother when she was in a good mood and *really* didn't when she was angry, and I've never seen her as mad as she was at Harper back then. You ever see that sign that says, 'If Mama Ain't Happy, Ain't Nobody Happy'?"

Dana laughed. "I had a T-shirt with that on it a few years back."

"Well, it was the gospel truth in our house. Whatever happened when we got home sent Mother into a rage. She threw dishes and said she wouldn't be able to hold her head up in her social circles, and the next day, Harper was packed off to the West Coast. I always wondered if they found drugs in her bedroom. It was hell to pay after she left," Tawny said.

"She was so young, and so were you, Tawny."

"They sent her away on her sixteenth birthday. It must've been something really bad, because Mother didn't send me off, not even when she had to come bail me out of jail. I wondered if she'd gotten herself pregnant, but if she had there would have been a baby."

"I can't believe you were in trouble!"

"I was protesting the government's policies. I didn't really care, but my boyfriend of the day was a radical, and I got picked up and thrown in jail because I decked a policewoman who tried to cuff him."

Dana slapped a hand over her mouth. She was doomed from birth to get into all kinds of trouble—that was expected of a bastard. But the two golden-haired glory children were supposed to have wings and halos.

"It happened when I was sixteen. Mother said that if I ever got in jail again that she'd send me off to a place worse than where Harper went. Harper is tough as nails—if she couldn't handle it, there was no way I could. I'd already been in trouble twice at school, and she told me it was my third and final offense. I managed to stay out of trouble until last Christmas. Been on her bad side ever since."

Dana couldn't make herself go inside the house, no matter how cold it was. "That's horrible. I can imagine being disappointed in Brook if she made bad choices, but I'd never disown her."

"That's because you are a good mother. I should be getting back. I feel better having told Granny Annie goodbye. I think she'd even like the way all three of us did it."

"Me too." Dana nodded. "Good night, Tawny."

" 'Night," she said.

Dana sat there for a long time, a smile covering her face. Tawny had said that she was a good mother. Her youngest sister would never, not

99

in a hundred years, ever know how much she'd needed to hear that.

Finally, she went inside to find Brook wrapped in a long terry-cloth robe and wearing a towel turban-style around her hair. She hugged her daughter tightly and said, "I love you, kiddo."

"Love you more," Brook giggled. "I left you some hot water. Do I smell liquor on your breath?"

"It's whiskey. Your two aunts and I said goodbye to Granny Annie out on the porch."

"She'd like that." Brook grinned.

Chapter Five

Only a few parking spots were left at the bar up the road from the lake on Saturday night when Harper arrived. She snagged one of them, checked her hair and makeup in the rearview mirror by the streetlight behind the truck, and slung open the door. She hadn't gone five yards when she heard a long, drawn-out whistle, but she ignored it. She'd heard those noises too many times in the past to let it excite her. Paying the cover fee to a big, burly bouncer at the door, she could hear boots on a wooden floor and a few "hell, yeahs," which meant there was a line dance already going on.

She missed the days when a fog of smoke rushed out to meet her when the bouncer opened the door to let her inside. Progress, they called it—cut down on cancer. It was probably a good thing, but she still missed the gray layer up by the ceiling. There was something sexy about the smell of smoke in the air when a cowboy with whiskey on his breath kissed her after two-stepping around the dance floor.

A woman wearing enough bling to blind a person slid off the last vacant bar stool and staggered toward the bathroom. Harper made a beeline for it and had just parked her fanny when a short woman in tight jeans and dangling belly button jewelry tapped her on the shoulder.

"That's my sister's seat. I was on my way over to save it for her when you stole it," she said.

Harper pointed at the guy's beer beside her, and the bartender nodded. "Sorry about that, but it's mine now."

The woman glared at her. "So when she returns you're going to let her have the seat back."

"Nope," Harper answered.

The bartender set the longneck bottle of Coors in front of Harper and then hurried off in the other direction to wait on a couple waving bills between two old cowboys deep in conversation.

"You *will* give that bar stool back. I'm not takin' no for an answer."

Harper took a long drink from the bottle and set it back down. "Is that a threat?"

The woman glared at her. "It's a fact."

Harper ignored her and took another drink.

The woman who'd vacated the stool staggered out of the bathroom and stopped ten feet from the end of the bar. "I told you to save that for me, Daisy. Some sister you are."

Harper couldn't fathom either of her sisters ever going to a bar with her or saving her a seat if they did. Maybe they'd throw her off a stool, too.

"What are you smilin' about?" Daisy asked.

"Didn't realize I was, but if I was then it's my business," Harper told her.

"I'm makin' it mine." Daisy grabbed the half-empty beer bottle and smashed it against the bar. The jagged edge was nothing more than a flash as it came up and sliced open Harper's chin.

Tawny appeared out of nowhere, ground the heel of her cowboy boot into Daisy's foot, and then popped her right between the eyes with a fist. Daisy fell like a big oak tree, and her sister dropped down on her knees beside her. "You bitch! You've killed my precious sister," she screamed.

"Why in the hell did you do that? And why are you even here?" Harper demanded as blood ran through her fingers and dripped onto her shirt.

"She wasn't going to stop cutting you, and I'm over twenty-one and I can go where I want," Tawny said.

Daisy sat up and shoved her sister out of the way. "I'm not dead, but your damned bar stool is empty, so grab it and don't bitch at me. You'll have a good seat to watch while I whip this woman's ass."

"Honey, if you think you're big enough or mean enough to whip two Clancy girls, then you better pack a supper, because it's going to take you all damn night," Tawny told her.

Evidently Tawny had gotten there before Harper and into a couple of drinks, because she had fire in her eyes and her fists were knotted. Her little sister might be tiny and delicate-looking, but put two margaritas in her and she thought she could whip a grizzly bear with one hand tied behind her back.

One big, burly bouncer wrapped fists the size of hams around Daisy's and Tawny's arms and escorted them across the floor. Another bouncer got a firm grip on Harper and the other sister and followed right behind them. When the two men got them outside, they gave them all a push with enough force that Daisy hit the ground and Harper had to do some fancy footwork to keep from biting the gravel.

"You've ruined my night." Daisy popped up and screeched at Harper. "We were celebrating my divorce."

"Too bad." Harper continued to catch the blood dripping from her chin as she headed toward her truck.

"No husband, no kids. My first time to party in twenty years. You are a bitch for ruinin' it for me," the woman moaned.

"You shouldn't call a woman who just crippled you and bloodied your nose a bitch unless you want more of the same. You gave your kids away?" Tawny looked over her shoulder.

"Every damn one of them. I'm sick of whinin' teenagers blamin' me for the divorce." She slurred every word.

"You are batshit crazy," Harper whispered.

"What did you say?" Daisy screamed.

Harper turned around to face her and repeated the sentence.

"Don't judge me until you've had to walk in my shoes," Daisy growled.

Tawny took a step toward her, and Harper used her free hand to pull her back.

"It's not worth jail time. Just walk away," Harper said.

"Jail would be worth it," Tawny muttered.

"Then think about Uncle Zed and Granny," Harper said. "You need me to drive you home?"

"Hell, no! I'm not drunk, barely even buzzed," Tawny protested.

Daisy rushed across the parking lot and pushed Tawny backward.

Harper got between them and glared down at the woman. "Touch her again and I'll mop up this parking lot with you, woman."

Daisy backed off, and Tawny got into her little sports car, fired it up, and squealed the tires on the way out of the parking lot.

Harper crawled into her truck, locked the doors, removed her shirt, and held it against the cut on her chin while she drove south toward the lake with one hand on the steering wheel. The wound was still seeping and had begun to sting like hell by the time she parked in front of her cabin.

She got out to find Tawny waiting on her porch and Dana and Brook just coming up from the lake's edge. She started to walk right past all of them, but Tawny popped her hands on her hips and glared at Harper.

"You are welcome, by the way," she said.

"For what? I can take care of myself. I don't need you to fight my battles," Harper said. The feeling was coming back in her chin, and it stung like a son of a gun.

"Good Lord! What happened?" Dana asked.

They both started talking at once, each blaming the other one for ruining the whole evening. Finally, Dana clapped her hands, and they both turned to look at her.

"Do you need some help getting that cleaned up, Harper? Is it deep enough that we should take you to the emergency room or the urgent care for stitches?"

"I'm fine. All of you just go away and leave me alone," Harper answered.

"Fine! Next time I'll let a crazy bitch carve her initials in your face." Tawny stormed off toward her cabin.

"I'd love to have a sister, and here y'all are acting like this." Brook took off at a jog toward the house.

"Sure you don't want me to help with that?" Dana asked again.

"I told you to leave." Harper went inside and slammed the door. She didn't even make it to the bathroom before someone knocked on her door. Expecting it to be Tawny arguing some more, she slung it open and said, "Get off my porch."

"Good God, Harper," Wyatt gasped. "What happened? Car wreck?"

"I thought you were Tawny." She blushed. "It was a sister wreck. I'm fine."

"So Tawny did this?" Wyatt brushed past her into the cabin and beat her to the bathroom, where he got out peroxide and butterfly strips. "You've ruined a pretty nice shirt, and you've got blood all over your jeans."

"Cold water will take it out. Move over so I can get this cleaned up." She shoved at him, the action only serving to remind her that even a tall woman like her couldn't budge him an inch.

He put the lid down on the toilet. "Sit down and I'll do it for you. And again, which of your sisters did this?"

She sat down, suddenly aware that she was only wearing a bra on top. "Not Tawny. This girl Daisy at the bar. She tried to make me give up my stool—she wanted to save it for her sister. I protested. So she broke a beer bottle and tried to convince me otherwise. And then Tawny stepped in to rescue me. Hell's bells, Wyatt! I've been takin' care of myself for ten years. I don't need her help."

"So what does the other woman look like now? Hold your head up." He tucked a washcloth under her chin and gently poured peroxide into the wound. When it stopped bubbling, he wiped it dry and applied antibiotic ointment and three strips to hold it together.

"She'll be limpin' for a week, and all the makeup in the world won't cover up those two black eyes. Tawny packs a mean right hook when she's mad. I bet Daisy don't think she's nearly as mean right now as she was this mornin'," Harper said.

"So this all happened in a bar? Are you drunk?"

"On half a beer? God, no! I went there to dance, drink a beer or two, and blow off some steam, not get drunk and brawl. She caused it. I didn't. And I didn't even know Tawny was there, didn't know that she even went to cheap little bars. Figured she'd only be interested in swanky clubs," Harper answered.

Wyatt stepped back and tipped her chin up. "Don't get that wet for a few days and it should heal up pretty good."

"Thank you, Dr. Simpson, but I know how to take care of barroom wounds," she said, her voice only slightly elevated from the effect that he created when he touched her face.

"I should go now." Wyatt's warm breath caressed that soft spot right under her ear, and the temperature in the room jacked up several degrees.

"Thanks again," she whispered.

"Anytime. I'm just glad it wasn't one of your sisters that sliced you open." He moved out of the bathroom.

"Why does it matter who did it?" she asked.

"Sisters shouldn't act like that. Get some rest."

She raised her voice as he crossed the room. "Two aspirin and call you in the mornin' if I'm not better."

He gave her a thumbs-up and gently closed the door behind him. She removed her bra, kicked off her boots, and slid her skinny jeans down over her well-rounded hips. Once she was completely naked, she turned on the water in the old claw-foot tub and crawled into it. Her long legs reached all the way to the end, and when the water was deep enough, she turned the faucets off with her toes.

She only meant to rest her eyes for a few seconds, but when she awoke, the water was cold, her arms were asleep, and the cut on her chin was throbbing. She quickly stood up and grabbed a terry robe, wrapped it around her body, and checked her reflection in the mirror. The strips were holding and there was no blood.

"That's good," she muttered as she padded barefoot across the floor to her bed. She didn't bother taking off the robe, but curled up on top of the bedspread and pulled the edge up over her feet. In seconds she was asleep, dreaming of playing chase with a little blonde-haired girl in a field of bright Texas bluebonnets. The child wore a pure-white sundress. Her blue eyes were the same color as the flowers.

The alarm clock jerked Harper out of the dream and back into reality. No matter how tightly she shut her eyes, she couldn't bring back the peace that she felt when she was out there in the middle of that bluebonnet field.

With a sigh, she threw her legs over the edge of the bed, turned off the noisy alarm, and went back to the bathroom to check her wound. It looked fine even if it did throb with every heartbeat. She quickly dressed in jeans and a T-shirt and hurried out across the gravel lot toward the café.

Zed must've seen her coming, because he already had a mug of coffee sitting on the table for her. She picked it up and warmed her hands before taking the first sip.

"I should've put on a jacket. Morning breeze is a little nippy," she said.

"Will be until Easter is over with in a couple of weeks. After that we'll be prayin' for some of this cool wind," he said. "What happened to your chin?"

Between sips of coffee, she told him the story. "Guess some sisters are almighty protective of each other's rights to a bar stool. And others get into their sister's business uninvited."

"What demons are you chasin', child?" he asked, his tone deepening.

"What makes you think I've got any demons?" Harper pushed the chair back and brought the coffeepot to refill both their cups.

"Plain as the nose on a pig's face. What happened that last summer you came here to stay for a month? You ain't been the same since. Your granny was plenty worried about you when you ran away from that boarding school. You didn't get in touch with nobody, either. Why she didn't hear from you until you was past eighteen?" he said.

"Life happened, and believe me, Granny was the only one worried about me," she said in a flat tone.

"I was worried right along with her. So tell me about it."

"Granny used to say that the person who stirs the shit pile has to lick the spoon. I'm not in the mood for that this mornin'." She laid a hand on his bony arm.

"I'm here if you ever want to get it off your chest." Zed pushed up out of the chair and began to clear the table. "What is said in my kitchen stays in my kitchen, and that's the God's honest truth."

❈

As she and Brook entered the café before daylight, Dana held the door for the young honeymooners, who were coming out of their cabin for the first time since they arrived. They were all smiles, holding hands and looking deeply into each other's eyes. Hopefully five years down the road, the young lady wouldn't be throwing him out for cheating on her. Like what happened to some people.

"Thank you," the groom said. "It's going to be a beautiful Sunday. Kayla and I are going to have breakfast and then take a blanket to the edge of the lake and watch the sunrise."

"This place is fabulous," Kayla said. "We've agreed that we'll come back here every year on our anniversary."

Harper looked up from the cash register and smiled. "We'll look forward to havin' you. We're serving buffet-style this morning, so y'all go on and help yourselves. What can I get you to drink?"

"Orange juice and hot chocolate," Kayla said.

"Same for me." The new groom ushered her to the buffet with his hand on her back.

"Oh, to be in love," Dana whispered to Harper as she went for coffee. "How's your chin? What happened, anyway?"

"I had an argument with a busted beer bottle," she answered.

"You got so drunk that you fell on a beer bottle? From the way you and Tawny squared off, I got the impression that she helped you somehow."

"No, I was not drunk and I did not fall."

Brook headed to the kitchen. "I'm making myself some green tea with a slice of lemon. Y'all want some?"

"Not me," Dana answered.

112

"No, but I'll make it for you, princess," Harper said.

"A princess does not spend her weekends in a sweatshop," Brook grumbled.

Tawny caught the last sentence as she made her way from the door to the coffee machine. "You won't fuss next Friday when you get your paycheck for all that hard work. I'll take you to the mall Friday night if your mama don't care, and you can blow it all at Victoria's Secret."

Brook shook her head. "Not me. I might blow it all at a shoe store or a makeup place, but not for underbritches. No one can see what's under my clothing. Can I bring Cassidy with me?"

"I got no problem with that if Flora doesn't care. Where is that child? According to the payroll, she's been helping out on weekends."

Brook motioned for Tawny to follow her to the buffet. "I took her place—she's got a job babysitting every Saturday and Sunday."

Tawny stopped at the cash register and looked up at Harper's chin. "You didn't bleed to death after all."

"Disappointed?" Harper shot back.

"Maybe a little," Tawny said curtly. Trouble followed the Clancy girls like a homeless hound dog, but it found their middle sister a lot more often than it did Tawny.

In a few minutes, the whole place was filled with fishermen, and the banter started to fly again, only that morning it was about which bait was best for catfish—spinners, worms, minnows, or stink bait.

"If they're bitin', bologna or bubble gum works as good as anything," Wyatt added his opinion. "If they ain't bitin', then it don't matter what you use for bait."

"You could try singin' to them." Harper filled his cup for the third time.

"That'd scare them right up onto the bank for sure," he chuckled.

Dana could almost see the electricity between Harper and Wyatt. Whatever it was about, his singing was an inside joke from long ago.

Flora came in about that time, filled a plate, and sat down at Brook and Dana's table. "I love Sunday buffet. This is the one thing I'm going to miss when I retire at the end of summer. So you ready to go to work?" She glanced over at Brook.

Not much taller than Brook, Flora had short gray hair, bright-blue eyes, and at least three chins. She was as wide as she was tall and bustled around with the energy of a sixteen-year-old.

"Yes, ma'am. I live to fold towels and wash bedding," Brook quipped.

"Regular little smarty-pants you got there, Dana." A fourth chin popped out as she smiled, and her eyes twinkled.

"What can I say? She's Annie Clancy's great-granddaughter." Dana shrugged.

"That about covers it." Flora set to eating a tall stack of pancakes covered in warm maple syrup. "I hear that you and my granddaughter are in the same classes at school."

"She showed me around, and we are going to be friends," Brook said.

"Glad to hear it. Kids need good friends," Flora said.

Dana left Brook in Flora's care and opened the store. She made coffee, swept up a couple of dozen dead crickets, and then picked up a dusting rag and gave the shelves a quick going-over. She wasn't expecting many customers that day, because the folks in the cabins would all check out by eleven o'clock. But just as the sun rose up over the horizon, people started to come in to buy bait, soft drinks, and beer and even wiped out her stock of bologna and bread.

Evidently, not all folks were worried about their eternal souls—by midmorning she'd rung up more sales than she had since she'd been there. Maybe their church was on the lake instead of a building with poor air-conditioning and a preacher sending them to hell if they didn't get right with the Lord.

She'd finished checking out a teenage boy and his grandfather, and was about to get herself a cold root beer, when Wyatt popped into the store. "I owe forty dollars for gas, and I'm going to get an orange soda pop."

He put the can of soda on the counter. Dana made change for the fifty-dollar bill he'd handed her.

"Thanks. You are Dana, the oldest sister, right?" he continued. "We'll be seeing lots of each other this summer. I'm booked for every weekend between now and August."

"Good to know. I barely remember you from back when Harper was sixteen—you were about the same age, right?"

"Yes, ma'am, we were." He gathered up his things. "Have a nice day," he said as he shut the door behind him.

✦❈❈❈✦

Tawny had spent the entire morning checking people out of their rooms and tallying up all the receipts. She'd called Flora out in the laundry building to tell her that the honeymoon couple had checked out with two minutes to spare, so she and Brook could clean the last room of the day. She was about to head over to the café when Wyatt Simpson pulled his truck and boat up in front of her cabin.

He leaned out the window of his truck and raised his voice. "Hey, I just realized that I left my electric razor in the bathroom of my cabin. You reckon you could let me run back inside and get it? If the maids already cleaned the room, I'll be very careful."

"No problem. I'll get the key and meet you there," she said.

He was on the porch when she arrived. She unlocked the door with the old-fashioned key hanging on a big plastic fob with the number of the cabin printed on it. He followed her inside, got his razor, and was back out in seconds.

"Thanks, Tawny. I just got this one a week ago and I'd hate to buy another one." He tipped his straw hat toward her. "Now, I'd better get on out of here and not take up any more room. There'll be a big rush at noon. Everyone in these parts knows about Zed's Sunday blue-plate special."

"Which is?" Tawny asked as she locked the door.

"Chicken and dressin' and all the fixin's. I'd like to stay, but I've got to get home." He grinned.

"I remember that you and your grandpa stayed in the number one cabin and he played the harmonica in the evenings," she said.

"That's right. He loved music. See you next Thursday. I've got a crew of four comin' to stay over until Sunday. We're already on the books," he said.

As he drove away, Tawny realized she was late for the lunch crowd, so she rushed over to the café. She'd barely made it inside the door when Harper handed her two pitchers full of tea and said, "Where have you been? You're supposed to help out with the cash register during lunch hour."

"Talkin' to your crush from ten years ago."

Harper shot a dirty look her way. "You can help pour tea until someone needs to be rung up."

Tawny shook her head. "This is not my job."

Harper backed up. "You can either help me out, or I'll call Flora or Brook to do it and you can go to the laundry room. We're all in this together, whether we like it or not."

"I'm doin' this for Uncle Zed, not you. These are sticky and need washing. I'll use a couple of new ones for refills." Tawny set the pitchers down, pasted on a beautiful smile, and started making her way from table to table. Everyone had something kind to say about her grandmother, so it turned out not so bad. The line waiting outside stretched around the café and halfway to the front door of the store.

Harper picked up the pitchers, carried them to the kitchen, and sank them in a sink full of hot soapy water.

Zed's face appeared in the window. "I've got an extra pumpkin pie put aside for y'all girls and Flora to share when the rush is over."

"You are a sweetheart, Uncle Zed," she said and then stuck her tongue out at Harper.

Harper reached out and slid a fistful of soap down her younger sister's tongue.

Tawny spit and sputtered, grabbed a paper towel to get the soap out of her mouth, and then slapped Harper on the upper arm. "That was downright mean. Be careful. Last person who thought they could fight with me has a package of frozen peas on her eyes."

"Don't mess with me. I'm not in the mood for it," Harper said.

"You haven't been any fun since we were here last. Loosen up, sister. We've come home." Tawny filled two clean pitchers with tea from the huge container and went back to her second job.

Home.

Do you really believe that? the voice in her head asked.

It's the one place that I've always felt like I could be myself. Granny never told me that she was ashamed of me or that she wished she'd never had me, Tawny thought.

Chapter Six

Harper propped her feet, encased only in socks, on the porch railing and leaned back in her chair that Thursday evening. March 22—that's what the calendar said, which meant they'd been there a whole week. The evenings had gotten a little warmer as they all settled into their routines more firmly. Until summer, according to Zed, the main part of their business would be on the weekends. In some ways it seemed like the three of them had always lived at the tiny little resort; in others, she wondered why she was wasting her life in a place like this.

As usual, she knew that Wyatt wasn't far away long before he spoke. There was that little lilt in her heart like it floated. He handed her an icy-cold beer in a can, and she held it against her forehead a couple of seconds.

"So how's your week been?"

"Hours drag some through the days, but the week went by pretty fast."

He sat down on the porch step. "How's the chin healin'?"

"I took the strips off this mornin'. Don't look like it's goin' to scar." She popped the tab on the can and quickly sucked the foam off before it could run down the sides. "I'm usually a whiskey girl, but this tastes really good." Maybe she only liked beer when she drank it with Wyatt.

"I always bring a case of cold ones for the crew. Room, food, beer on the first night they arrive, and three days of fishin' for four customers at one low, low price." He grinned.

"Sounds like you should be in advertising." She set the beer on the porch rail and clapped her hands dramatically. "But wait! If you book your trip now, Wyatt will throw in a special made-in-a-third-world-country cooler to keep your catch in until you get home."

He chuckled and put up a palm, "But wait! If you book two trips, Wyatt will provide an honest-to-God old-time fish fry at the edge of the lake. Fish, hush puppies, beer, and fried potatoes."

"That sounds pretty good. Where do I sign up?" The last time she'd laughed with any sincerity had been when they were together all those years ago.

"Oh. My. God!" Tawny said loudly as she passed by the porch on the way to her cabin. "I'm hearing things. Harper just laughed. I didn't know she could do that anymore."

"Smart-ass!" Harper grinned.

"And a smile to boot! Run, Wyatt, run! The world is coming to an end. I think I see a meteorite." Tawny threw a hand up in a theatrical gesture as if shading her eyes against the imaginary ball of fire coming toward them.

"Y'all are crazier than you were when we were all kids," he laughed. "Want a beer, Tawny?" He held up a plastic ring with three still attached.

"Don't mind if I do. Thank you, Wyatt."

A stab of jealousy pricked Harper in the heart when Tawny sat down beside Wyatt on the top step. But it disappeared when he hopped up and said, "Wait, I see my first truckload of guys arriving. So I'd better get on down there. We've got a poker game in my cabin planned. See y'all around."

Unaffected, Tawny opened her beer and took a long gulp. "I called Mother after work tonight."

"And?"

"She says that if we come home and do something important with our lives, she'll forgive us," Tawny said.

"You goin' home?"

"Nope. I told her that it's not a matter of her forgiving us but of us forgiving her. You ready to tell me what it was that got you disowned? What in the devil did you do to survive? There's no way anyone would let you bartend at that age. How did you live from the time you were sixteen until now?" Tawny asked.

"Nope, I am not ready to tell you that story. I will tell you this, though. For about six months, I worked at an animal shelter. Got a free room at the back of it for taking the night shift. Anyway, one night this man left a whole litter of

122

Doberman pups on the doorstep. I had to get up every two hours all night to feed those critters. Didn't lose a single one of them." Harper smiled at the memory.

"And that has to do with what?" Tawny asked.

"Patience." Harper took the final sip of her beer. "I'm gettin' to that part. When I asked the manager lady about it, she said that Dobermans sometimes just don't have the right mother instinct. The pups start to bother the mom with their incessant whining and wanting to eat all the time, so she retaliates by biting them or pushing them away to starve."

"I think I'm gettin' your point," Tawny said.

"Yep, our mother is a Doberman. She had us because Daddy wanted kids to ease his guilt over not claiming Dana. She doesn't have any mother instinct. She left us with nannies and babysitters and only brought us out when we were all pretty and clean for family pictures. She is what she is," Harper said.

Tawny finished her beer and set the empty can on the porch. "Have you forgiven her for what she said and did to you? It was awful at the house after you left. I begged them to let me move here and live with Granny."

Harper inhaled so deep that her lungs hurt and then let it out slowly. "I forgave her a long time ago. She's not worth the pain and suffering. I just hope that I got Granny Annie's big heart when it comes to children and not hers," Harper answered.

Tawny scooted over and braced her back against the porch post. "You think you'll ever have kids? You willin' to take that kind of chance?"

Harper shrugged. "Are you?"

"I like kids, so maybe if the right man came along," Tawny answered. "What happened to all of those puppies?"

"I didn't leave that job until I'd found a good home for each of them." Harper nodded.

"That's good," Tawny said. "Maybe we should send Mama a picture of the two of us huggin' a Doberman."

"Wouldn't do a bit of good. She's never had to admit that she was wrong. Daddy adored her and let her run the place and us. She'd just wonder why in the hell we were sending her a picture of us with a dog," Harper chuckled.

"Probably so. Good night." Tawny groaned when she got to her feet. "Too many hours sitting in front of a computer, but I think I'm getting this business figured out."

"Try standing on your feet all day," Harper said.

"No, thanks. I'll take kinks over aching arches."

✦❈❈❈✦

When Brook was a little girl, she and Dana had watched animated cartoons, and then slowly they'd graduated to more mature movies and even television series on either Friday or Saturday nights. Brook's newest love was *MacGyver*, a remake of an older show that now had two seasons on DVDs, so they usually ended the week by watching it over and over. But that night she'd gone off to the mall with Tawny, and Dana felt the emptiness as she sat on the grass at the edge of the lake.

Down around Houston, when someone mentioned a beach, visions of sand, seagulls, and water all the way to the horizon came to mind. But in north central Texas, the image changed to green grass, ducks, and lights in the summer homes on the other side of the lake.

Get used to it. That's why you have sisters. The kid grows up and leaves home, and you'd have no one if it weren't for your sisters. The voice sounded a lot like her grandmother's.

"You didn't have sisters or brothers, Granny," Dana argued.

Harper sat down a few feet from her. "Who are you talkin' to?"

"You startled me," Dana said. "What're you doin' here? I figured you'd be gettin' into trouble in that bar up the road."

"Didn't feel like it tonight. Do you always talk to yourself, or do you have a feller hidin' up in the trees?" Harper asked. "We should've brought marshmallows."

"I remember when we used to do that when

125

you girls were with us in the summertime." Zed appeared out of the darkness from the other direction. "We'd start us up a fire down here on the edge of the water and have hot dogs and them things with graham crackers for dessert."

"They were s'mores. Roasted marshmallow crammed between two graham crackers along with a piece of chocolate candy bar. Pull up a chair or a piece of the grass and join us, Uncle Zed." Harper pointed to the area between them.

He eased down a couple of feet from Harper. "That's right. Me and Annie built us up a bonfire and made them things a few times, but it wasn't the same when you girls weren't here with us. I'm missin' her real bad tonight. The walls in my room got to closin' in on me, so I came out for a walk. She loved it when the trees started gettin' leaves and folks started fillin' up the summer places."

"My favorite memories of her are in the store," Dana said. "She kept me while Mama went to school to get her cosmetology license and then afterward while Mama worked."

"Did you ever know Grandpa?" Harper glanced over at Dana.

"No, he was already gone when I was born," Dana answered.

They sat in silence for ten minutes, and then Zed slowly rose to his feet and started back up the trail toward Annie's Place.

126

"You okay?" Harper called out before he disappeared.

"I'm better. It helped just to sit with y'all a spell. I can feel her presence in among us when you girls are all together. Especially when you ain't bickerin'."

"See," Harper whispered, "he's not as sad when we try to get along."

Dana rose to her feet. "I've got a movie and some popcorn if you want to join me in the house. Tawny said she'd bring Brook home by eleven."

"Think we could stand each other for two hours without arguin'? Uncle Zed isn't going to be there, you know."

"I'm willin' to give it a try if you are," Dana answered.

"What movie you got?" Harper gracefully went from sitting cross-legged to a standing position.

"Lots of them. You can even choose." She never thought she'd feel that way, but time with Harper beat being totally alone for the next three hours.

The path from the lake to the house wasn't far, but neither of them said anything. Dana stepped inside the house with Harper right behind her and stopped in the middle of the living room. "It seems like she should be coming out of the kitchen with a pan of brownies in her hand for us to eat while we play some board game," Harper said.

Dana laid a hand on Harper's shoulder. "I feel the same way, and I've been livin' in this house more than a week. If I was into hocus-pocus stuff, I'd say her spirit isn't happy and it's tryin' to tell us something."

"Is the Ouija board still somewhere in the house?" Harper flopped down on the sofa. "That thing scared the bejesus right out of me. If it's under the bed or in the hall closet, we should take it down to the lake and toss it into the water."

"Haven't seen it, thank goodness. It scared me, too. Want a beer or a glass of sweet tea?"

"Tea, please. Why wouldn't she be happy? We're all here and, with the help of Uncle Zed, keepin' the place going. We've done pretty good this past week, in my opinion," Harper said.

Dana brought in two tall glasses of tea and set them on the coffee table. "Considerin' that it's us, we've probably broken the record for doing good. Popcorn or trail mix?"

Harper picked up a glass and took a sip. "Trail mix, if it's what you made when we were here last time. The kind with M&M's in it?"

"Brook's favorite. I make it at least once a month," Dana yelled from the kitchen.

She took a bowlful to the living room and opened the hall closet where she'd stored the collection of movies that she'd brought with her. When she turned around, Harper was right behind her.

"Sweet Lord!" she gasped.

"What?" Dana asked.

"That's a lot of movies. You should put them in the store and rent them out to the folks who stay in the cabins." Harper ran her finger down the rows and rows, arranged alphabetically by the first letter in the title.

"Oh, no! This is my and Brook's private collection. We couldn't get cable out in the barn, so I bought movies." She shook her head the whole time she was talking.

"Barn? You lived in a barn? I thought you lived on a big fancy horse ranch." Harper spun around to face her.

"I lived on a horse ranch in a small apartment attached to the stables. It had a living room and bedroom combination, a small galley kitchen, and a bathroom. It was free so I didn't complain, but we couldn't get cable. Brook hasn't suffered from it." Dana ran her finger across the DVDs.

"*Hot Pursuit*," Brook yelled as she and Tawny came through the back door.

"I thought y'all were out until eleven o'clock," Dana said.

"We got bored and thought about going to a movie, but I wasn't spending my hard-earned money for that when we got better food and more comfortable chairs at home." Brook removed her jacket and set two bags on the floor. "I found a pair of jeans on a half-price rack and two shirts seventy-five percent off."

"She's a shrewd shopper." Tawny glanced over at Harper. "What are you doin' here? Is that Dana's trail mix?"

"Yes, it is, and I'm here to watch a movie," Harper answered.

"So is Aunt Tawny. Yay!" Brook clapped her hands. "We can all watch it together. Y'all seen *Hot Pursuit*?"

Harper and Tawny both shook their heads.

"Well, you're goin' to love it." Brook grabbed a pillow and a throw from the sofa and tossed them on the floor. "This is my spot. Y'all can have the sofa and the recliner."

There were two good things about watching a comedy—no one had to talk, and they felt good when it ended. As soon as the credits began to roll, Harper carried the glasses and Tawny's beer bottle to the kitchen, thanked Dana for the evening, and left by way of the back door.

Dana watched her leave and wondered again what had changed Harper from that fun-loving teenager into a person with so many demons.

"That was fun," Tawny said.

"We'll have to make it a Friday night date." Brook yawned. "Movies and popcorn at our house."

"We'll see. Thanks for loaning me your daughter and for the movie and trail mix," Tawny said.

"And the beer? Hey, Mama, when can I have a beer on movie night?" Brook asked.

"When you are forty and not a day earlier," Dana chuckled.

"She's not ever goin' to let me grow up," Brook groaned.

Tawny gave Brook a quick hug on her way out the door. "Don't get in a rush to do that, kiddo. It's not all it's cracked up to be. Good night."

Surprisingly, almost shockingly, they'd managed to spend a couple of hours in one another's presence without insults bouncing off the walls—and Uncle Zed wasn't even there. Later, Harper was sitting on her porch when Tawny passed by, so she stopped and sat down on the step.

"You remind me of that cop in the movie," Harper said.

"In looks or in actions?"

"Both," Harper told her. "Mother was right. You are the pretty one."

"She said that?" Tawny wasn't sure she'd heard right.

"Said that God made you pretty to make up for the fact that you were a girl. Daddy wanted a son so bad, but she said she wouldn't do that to her body a third time for any man on the face of the earth. And that he was cursed for having a bastard to begin with."

Tawny let it soak in for a little while. "Guess it's not much of a compliment after all, is it."

"Better than being the tall, gangly daughter that

131

looked like Granny Annie. Too big to ever be pretty," Harper said.

"Looking like Granny is not a bad thing, is it?" Tawny asked.

"It seemed like it was at the time. If she said it now, I'd thank her." Harper smiled.

"For a couple of privileged kids, we sure got a lot of baggage, don't we?" Tawny said. "Seems like Dana has less than we do, and our father wouldn't even claim her. 'Course, he wouldn't stand up to Mother for us, either."

"Crazy, ain't it?"

Tawny yawned. "Tomorrow comes around pretty early. I'm going to bed."

"Me too." Harper stood up and stretched with her hands over her head.

Tawny had always envied Harper for her height and her brown eyes. She was anything but an ugly duckling. Tawny was suddenly sorry that their mother had made her feel like that. But then Retha had never considered anyone else's feelings—except maybe her husband's, and then only if it suited her mood and her need for his paycheck. She'd always been his trophy wife with her gorgeous blonde hair and big blue eyes.

"I wonder if he ever had a mistress," Tawny mused as she passed cabin after cabin.

"If he did, he better hope his wife don't find out about it," a voice said from the porch of cabin number six.

The masculine voice startled her. She stopped in her tracks and tried to remember who was renting that particular unit. Finally the face that went with that deep drawl materialized.

"Evenin', Mr. Richman," she said.

"That makes me sound like an old man. I'm just Tony, not Mr. Richman," he chuckled. "But it is a right nice evenin', ain't it?" He leaned forward and rested his hands on the porch railing.

Tawny remembered him checking in, but it was a blur with all she had to do that day. Now she could see that his clear blue eyes were rimmed with heavy black lashes and his smile lit up the whole porch.

"Yes, it is. Supposed to be in the eighties tomorrow. Good fishin' weather," Tawny said.

"I don't fish. I'm here because my wife threw me out."

Tawny was not a sounding board for domestic fights, but he reminded her so much of her last boyfriend that she sat down on his porch. "Did you deserve it?"

"Oh, yeah. I didn't want to marry her at all, but she was pregnant and my daddy is the preacher in a little church up in Lindale."

"Why are you tellin' me this?" Tawny asked.

"Just need to bare my soul to a stranger who don't give a damn what I did," he said. "I was sittin' here prayin' to God to give me a sign about what I'm supposed to do come Sunday mornin', and you walked by. I figured you might be my sign."

"God wouldn't send me to be anyone's sign," Tawny laughed.

"My girlfriend, also a preacher's daughter, and I had this big fight and I got drunk," he said. "So I wound up in bed with another preacher's daughter for a whole weekend. My girlfriend and I made up the next week, but . . ." He let the sentence trail off.

"But then the other preacher's daughter turned out pregnant, right?"

"We shouldn't have been drinking or having sex, but things happen." He shrugged. "It was a shotgun wedding, and then she had a miscarriage at two months."

"Life ain't fair, is it?" Tawny said.

"My girlfriend and I were still in love . . .you can guess the rest. My wife's religion does not believe in divorce. My parents don't believe in it, either, even though our church doesn't send folks to hell for it."

"Twisted-up mess, if you ask me. How old are you?" Tawny asked.

"Twenty-two. Been married six months."

"Sounds like you've got a lot of soul searching to do in the next couple of days."

He rubbed a hand across his chin. "If you were my wife, what would you do?"

"I'd never have married you to begin with,

but since she did, I imagine I'd shoot you for cheating on me," she answered.

"And if you were the woman I've loved since I was in the third grade?"

"I hope I would have had enough sense to back off until you were a free man."

"Hope?" he asked.

"I can't judge. I haven't walked a mile in either of those women's shoes. Maybe your wife loved someone else, too, but she doesn't know how to get out of this horrible marriage and she's puttin' the job on you. You should talk to her—and listen to what she has to say. Just the two of you."

Maybe you should practice what you are preachin'. There was Granny Annie's voice in her head again. *You should try paying attention to Zed and your sisters like you do to strangers.*

"Thanks for listenin' to me. You might have been my sign after all. I'll probably check out early tomorrow mornin' and go back across the river. See if I can get this straightened out," he said.

"Sure thing." As she covered the distance to her own little cabin, Tawny could hear all kinds of night insects and animals who'd come out to play under the light of the moon. When she was inside, she slid down the back of the door and wrapped her hands around her knees. "Granny, I've done some really stupid things that I don't want to tell Dana and Harper about. They've

135

never been on probation or made the bad choices that I have. I just can't tell them. Don't leave me. I need to hear your voice sometimes."

She cocked her head to the side, but all she heard was wind rattling through the trees.

Chapter Seven

For the second night in a row, Harper was restless. When not even an evening of mindless drinking and dancing or picking up a sexy cowboy for a one-night motel fling sounded good, she considered taking her temperature to see if she was sick. She paced around the cabin a few times and finally pulled an old gray sweatshirt over her head and went outside. She didn't even slow down at the porch but kept walking, following the trail by moonlight to a little cove in the bend of the lake where she couldn't even see the cabins.

She went right to a big flat rock jutting out at the shore. It was one of Granny Annie's favorite places to take the girls fishing in the summer. Sometimes they'd talk, but most of the time they just enjoyed the quiet. If they were lucky, they'd take home a whole string of fish to fry. The memories calmed her—right up until the tiny hairs on the back of her neck started to prickle and Wyatt walked out of the shadows. He sat down beside her and covered her hand with his. Peace surrounded her like a warm blanket on a cold Texas night.

"The guys are having a *Die Hard* marathon tonight in one of the cabins. I couldn't sit still and watch the third one, so I told them I was going for a walk," he explained. "I figured you'd be out dancin' the leather off your boots."

"I might have learned my lesson with that business last week," she answered. Suddenly, the sweatshirt was too warm despite the chilly night breeze coming off the water. Not one of the men that she'd used to get Wyatt Simpson off her mind had ever caused the kind of heat waves he did simply by touching her hand. "What do you do when you're not fishin'?"

"Get my stuff ready for another fishin' trip. What about you? What did you do before you came here?" He gently squeezed her hand. "They say you never forget your first love. I think they might be right."

"Is that a pickup line?"

"Nope." He lowered his voice to a whisper. "I have not been a saint, believe me. But no one ever quite measured up to the feelings that I had with you. I don't know where you are in your life right now, but I just wanted you to know that."

"Thank you," she muttered.

She'd been flattered by the best of smooth-talking men, but none of their lines had ever made her heart skip a couple of beats. "I guess I could say, 'Back atcha,' but a lot of water has run under that bridge since we were kids. I'm not even sure there's a bridge anymore."

"Ever hear that old song called 'One Wing in the Fire'?" He smiled again. "It comes to mind

138

when I think of us. Maybe we are angels with no halos and one wing in the fire."

"Honey, nobody ever called me an angel," she laughed. "I think maybe 'Strawberry Wine' applies to us more. Heard it?"

"Oh, yeah." He nodded. "And I agree with you. We did find love growing wild on the banks of the lake, didn't we?"

Her heart twisted up like a pretzel the way it always did when she let herself go back to that place. She pulled her hand free. One bittersweet young love had brought such pain into her life— the kind that nothing, not alcohol, wanton sex, or even friendship could erase, and she'd tried all three.

"We did." She finally nodded. "It was a sweet summer, Wyatt."

"Would you go to dinner with me sometime?" he blurted out.

"You think it's wise for us to go down that path?"

"Won't know unless we give it a try." He slipped an arm around her shoulders and brushed a sweet kiss across her cheek. "I'm still every bit as attracted to you as I was then. I'd like to see what happens if we give things a go as adults."

She couldn't go there. Not after giving away their child. Not after the guilt trips and certainly not at this time of year—around her daughter's birthday.

"Friday night. Dinner and maybe a walk on the edge of the lake?" he pressed.

"I can't, Wyatt. I just can't."

"Okay, then. How about just sitting on your porch and watching the lightning bugs? We don't even have to talk if you don't want to," he asked.

"The lightning bugs are pretty." She should run from him, not cave in, but she wanted to be near him and hear his voice. Her chest tightened like it had a decade ago when she'd thought she'd never see him again. Talk about life being complicated.

"Then it's a date. I'll be here with a bag of barbecue chips and a six-pack of root beer. Those are still your favorites, right?"

"Yes, they are," she answered. He remembered—after all these years he remembered her favorite snacks.

"I should be going. Can I walk you back to your cabin?" he asked.

"I think I'll just sit here a little longer," she said.

"See you tomorrow at breakfast, then." He hugged her to his side but didn't kiss her again.

❈─═╫╫╫═─❈

Tawny pulled a chair up to the table in the café where Harper and Zed were already seated on Sunday afternoon. "Either of y'all ever hear Granny Annie's voice in your head?"

"All the time." Zed nodded. "And I talk to her, too. Tell her everything that I can remember

140

before I go to bed at night. Makes me feel good. Like she's still here. Why are you askin'?"

"What's happenin' in here?" Brook asked as she popped inside the door. "Flora sent me for takeout cups of iced tea."

"We were talkin' about whether any of us hear Granny Annie's voice in our heads," Harper answered.

Dana came in through the kitchen. "Back door was open, so I didn't walk all the way around to the front. I heard Granny's voice all the time before she died. If I was going to mess up, she'd be there telling me what to do. I love it when it happens," Dana answered.

"Harper, did you ever hear Dad's voice after he died?" Tawny asked.

She shook her head. "I did at the funeral, though."

"Really?" Tawny asked.

"I came in late, sat on the back pew of the church, and left. I didn't walk past the casket," Harper said softly. "I was also at your high school graduation."

"Got any regrets about not letting anyone know about that?" Zed asked.

"Not a single one," Harper answered. "I visit his grave when I'm in the area. Sometimes if I have the money, I bring flowers."

Zed laid a hand on her arm. "That's a good thing that you do, child."

141

"You ever wish Granny Annie had a grave?" Tawny's eyes filled with tears at the thought of Harper being that close and no one had even acknowledged her presence. She would have felt so alone—much like Tawny did when her mother turned her back on her.

"I'd like to visit her, but then again, if I go to the lake and sit on that big rock—well, that's as good as a grave," Zed said with a nod. "I take her ashes with me some nights just so she'll be close to me."

"What are they in, Uncle Zed?" Harper asked.

"A little wooden box that looks a lot like a cigar box. I keep them on my dresser and that way she's not far from me," he answered.

Brook carried two big cups of tea across the floor. "I hear her voice in my head, too. I was wishin' I was old enough to date that sexy boy at school the other day, and Granny Annie popped into my head and said, 'That boy ain't nothin' but trouble.' And I wanted to argue with her, but the bell rang." She backed out of the café, and the door slammed behind her.

"I wish Granny would've given me that warnin'," Tawny said.

"Why?" Harper asked.

"Long story I'm not sure I want to tell."

"Well, then let's make Harper tell us the story about what happened down at the lake last night." Zed's old eyes glittered in amusement.

Tawny jerked her head around to stare at her

sister. "You went to the lake and didn't even invite us?"

"I damn sure didn't want you or Dana to be there with me," Harper said. "I wanted peace and quiet, not another argument with y'all."

"Maybe we should be visitin' about that boy that you talked to about his problems, Miz Tawny?" Zed grinned.

"It wasn't nothin'," Tawny protested, but the way they were all staring said that they didn't believe her. "Okay, okay, it was something, but it wasn't anything between us. He just needed a stranger to talk to, and I was there." She went on to tell them what had happened with Tony Richman and exactly what she'd told him.

"Good advice," Dana said with a nod.

Tawny could hardly believe that her oldest sister had said something nice about her. She wanted to ask her to repeat it so that she'd know for a fact she'd heard right, but before she could say a word, Zed spoke up.

"Now it's your turn." Zed turned to Harper.

"I went to the big rock that was Granny's favorite spot. While I was there, Wyatt came by. He asked me out and I turned him down," she said bluntly.

"There was something between you and Wyatt way back when y'all were teenagers. Why wouldn't you go out with him now?" Tawny asked.

"I'm not ready to rekindle that fire. I may not ever be," Harper said. "Besides, this is my life, not yours."

"It was all your fault that Mother wouldn't let me come visit anymore." Tawny sighed loudly. "She told me that Granny Annie was too old to put up with me and that Dana was grown and had a job so she couldn't come."

"Hey, don't blame me for what Mother decided." Harper's tone went cold.

Zed's expression turned from happy to sad in an instant. "It broke your granny Annie's heart when you girls couldn't come back. She looked forward to that month all year and planned for it like a little girl does for her birthday party."

Harper pushed her chair back and carried her tea glass to the kitchen. "If it's okay with you, Uncle Zed, I'm going to my cabin for a short nap." Her voice cracked.

"Sure thing. Sleep as long as you can," Zed said. "Don't set an alarm. If you aren't awake, Tawny can help out. We won't have much of a supper rush anyway, since everyone has checked out of their cabins."

"Thank you." Harper escaped, but Tawny saw her wipe her cheeks as she hurried to her cabin.

✦╍╫╫╫╫╍✦

After the café was cleaned up that evening, Zed went to his little efficiency apartment in the back of the store. He poured himself a glass of elderberry wine from the last bottle he and Annie had made the year before, and then he put a DVD of the first season of *The Golden Girls* into the player. He sat down in his recliner, picked up the remote, and laid his hand on the arm of the matching chair right beside his.

"We had us a good day, Annie. Didn't have a spoonful of dressin' left after the lunch rush and only had one piece of pumpkin pie. I brought it home and put it in the refrigerator. I'll have it for a night snack like you would. I'm watchin' Blanche tonight because she reminds me of you. Full of sass and spunk, but she won't never be as pretty as you. So don't go gettin' jealous. The girls weren't as hateful to each other tonight. It's like pullin' hen's teeth to get them to be civil. But I think we're makin' progress."

He pushed a button on the remote and chuckled at Dorothy and Sophia's argument. "Kids and their mamas. I wonder what it was that set Retha off after that summer. I bet Harper went home and told her that she'd rather live with you.

"You don't think so?" He patted the arm of the chair. "It's not all water under the bridge, to my mind. Harper and Wyatt are talkin' to each other. I think they got a little chemistry back up between them. They'd make a good pair, don't you think? I know. I know. I shouldn't put the cart before the horse, but they would and you know it. I wish

145

you was sittin' in this chair for real. God, I miss you so much."

He turned down the volume and looked up at the ceiling. "I hear you loud and clear. I promise I won't interfere—well, not too much, anyway. Sometimes folks need a little push. But I'll go at it easy like, I promise. But I got to admit that it's good to have them all home again where they belong. Poor little things. One who never had any support from her daddy, and the other two with a raw deal on their mama. But I'll fix it so you can rest easy, Annie, I promise."

At nine thirty he got up out of his chair, groaned as he straightened his back, and got the pie from the little dorm-size refrigerator, though he'd never have called it that. "A bite for me and one for you," he said as he went back to the recliner.

At exactly ten o'clock he went to the bathroom, had his shower, and then curled up in the bed on his side, hugging a pillow to his chest. "Good night, Annie. Don't get too far from them gates now, girl. I'll be on up there in a little while and I want yours to be the first face I see when I get there. It's goin' to be just downright glorious to be in a place where my skin isn't black and yours ain't white. We'll be the same."

His thoughts went to the time when he and Annie and Seamus were just little kids, taking their fishing poles to the river. Seamus's folks had a cotton farm in those days. Annie's mama and daddy ran a little grocery store. Zed's daddy was a handyman around the area and his mama was the cook at the school. Then the area got dug out and flooded for the lake, and Annie's daddy hired Zed's daddy and mama both to work for him full-time.

Looking back, he knew that he'd fallen in love with Joanna—or Annie, as everyone already called her—when they were too young to even go to school. But in those days a man of color could get himself strung up for even looking at a blonde girl like Annie. So they'd all played together, and when they graduated from high school, she'd married Seamus. And Zed had gone straight into the army.

Seamus Clancy was his friend right up until the day he died. Zed missed him like a limb.

But Zedekiah Williamson had never stopped loving Annie.

Chapter Eight

The phone rang five times, quit, and then rang five more before Zed finally grabbed it from the wall and grumpily said, "Hello?"

"Hello, Zed. This is Mrs. Johnson from the Frankston School. Could I speak to Dana, please?"

"She's busy in the store. What can I help you with? Need reservations for Sunday?" Zed asked.

"No, sir. I need to speak to Dana about Brook," she answered.

"Is she sick?"

"I just need to talk to her mother, please," Mrs. Johnson said.

"Is she alive?"

"Yes, she is."

"We'll be there in ten minutes." Zed hung up and called Flora in the laundry room. "Go to the store and tell Dana to meet me out front of it in two minutes. We've got to go to the school, so I need you to mind the store while we are gone."

"Will do," Flora said.

Dana was standing in front of the store when he arrived. The expression on her face said that she was every bit as worried as he was. He'd promised Annie that he'd take care of the sisters as long as he could. That meant every one of them.

"What's happening? Is Brook all right? Is she hurt? What kind of trouble is she in? She's never been in trouble at school before in her life," Dana said as she crawled into his twenty-year-old truck.

"Mrs. Johnson wouldn't tell me, but I didn't want you to go alone," he said.

"Thanks," Dana whispered.

He made it in eight minutes and would have arrived there sooner if he hadn't gotten behind a poky old woman who didn't have anyplace to go and a year to get there. He was grumbling and praying both as he parked his truck.

Zed beat Dana to the door and practically jogged down the hallway to the office. Didn't even knock on the principal's door but barged right in and heaved a sigh of relief when he saw Brook sitting in a chair without a mark on her. He put his hands on the desk and looked Mrs. Johnson right in the eye.

"What is this all about?"

Dana stopped and laid an arm around her daughter's shoulders. "What's going on, Brook?"

"I do not use, buy, or sell drugs," Brook said with a stiff upper lip. "But no one will believe me because I'm the new girl and they don't know me."

Zed whipped around and nodded seriously. "I believe you, child." Then just as quick, he was staring down the principal. "Now you'd best tell me what happened."

149

"Brook came to us with exemplary records, but when the drug dogs came in for a random check today, they hit on her purse and we found marijuana in it," the principal said.

"There must be a mistake," Dana gasped.

Zed backed up and sat in the chair next to Brook. "Want to tell me where you got it?"

"It's not mine," she said, reddening to her hair part. "I don't do drugs. Mama would ground me until I was fifty if she caught me with any kind of drug, even marijuana."

"Then how did it get in your purse?" Dana asked. "You've got to know that—and probably who put it there."

Brook shrugged.

Zed turned back to the principal. "How much did she have?"

"A bagful, enough to get her expelled from school and likely put in jail."

Zed laid a hand on her shoulder. "Who are you protecting?"

"I'm not a rat," she said.

"Well then, I guess you'd better expel her from school and we'll take her on home. Her mama and aunts can homeschool her. Smart as she is, I expect that she can get her work done in a couple of hours every evening and work through the daytime in the laundry with Flora. We can use the help." Zed's hand dropped into his lap.

"No!" Brook squealed.

"Brook Clancy, you had better start tellin' me right now what you know." Dana's tone didn't leave a bit of wiggle room. "This can ruin your chances for college. It will be a mark on your record for the rest of your life. Start talking."

There were several awkward moments during which Brook was no doubt weighing the pros and cons. On one hand she would be cut off from the social aspect of school. On the other she wouldn't have to be branded a drug dealer. Finally she raised her head.

"I'm barely fittin' in here, and if anyone finds out that I ratted them out, then . . ."

"Do what's right, child," Zed said.

"Okay," she sighed. "My purse was sitting beside my desk and it was open. Someone in the class saw some dogs comin' into the school with policemen and pointed out the window."

"And?" Dana asked.

"And there was a rustling behind me and the next thing I knew the dogs stopped at my purse. That bag had come from the back of the room and was passed up, probably from Ryson, but I can't prove it. I promise that's all I know," Brook said. "I'm the new kid. They'll hate me if they think I told on someone, but I truly did not see who had it first. I promise. Mama, I've never even seen marijuana. I didn't know what it was when they took it out of my purse."

151

"Is she expelled, Mrs. Johnson?" Dana asked.

"School policy says that she is, but I believe she is telling the truth because I'm pretty sure I know who's responsible for this. So I'm going to send her home for the rest of the day," she answered.

"And can she make up whatever work she misses?" Dana asked.

"No, but there's only one more class today and then we're having an assembly."

"And what are you going to do about it if the kids start bullying her because they think she's really a drug dealer?" Zed asked.

"Believe me, they all know who that bag belonged to. If they bully her, I'll take care of it."

"If you know who is responsible for this, why isn't he or she in this room?" Dana asked.

"Because I can't catch him red-handed with the drugs. When I do, I'm putting him into the in-school suspension program for a long, long time," she answered.

"Why don't you fingerprint that bag of marijuana?" Zed asked.

"The police have assured me that they will do that, but think about how many hands it had to pass through on the way to her purse. By tomorrow morning, we'll have a definite answer, or at least no sign of her fingerprints, and there will be no problem with Brook coming back to school."

Zed was proud of the girl. She'd stood up for

herself like Annie had done so many times when she was that age.

Dana met the principal's gaze. "And tomorrow when she comes back to school, I want the word in the halls to be that those drugs did not belong to her."

"It will be," Mrs. Johnson said. "And Brook, I know you don't want to be a snitch, but it might help if you'd—"

Zed rose up and gave the principal a quick nod. "She's told you what she knows and the rest is your job, not hers." Then he turned to Brook and Dana. "You ladies ready to go home?"

"Yes, I am." Brook stood and wrapped her arms around Dana. "Mama, they aren't goin' to find my prints on that bag. I promised you a long time ago that I'd never do drugs. We don't keep secrets from each other."

Dana hugged her tightly. "I know that and I trust you."

Zed marched out to his truck, laid his head on the steering wheel, and let out a long whoosh of breath. Yes, sir, Brook was going to be all right. He didn't have to worry about her, but the three sisters—they still needed a lot of work.

"Annie, I was really worried. My heart was pumping so hard I thought I might be comin' to see you sooner than we ever expected, but she's okay. She ain't hurt and I'm right proud of her."

He started the engine and pulled around to the

door where Dana and Brook would be coming out of the school. "Raisin' kids ain't for us old dogs, Annie, but I gave you my word that I'd make things right for them if you went first. I didn't know that a bag of pot was going to be the first big hurdle."

"Is something wrong with our truck, Mama?" Brook slung open the door and slid across the bench seat to the middle to sit between her mother and Zed.

"No, Uncle Zed took the call in the kitchen and . . ." Dana slammed the door shut and glanced over at him.

He pulled around the rows of vehicles and back out onto the road. "I knew you'd be nervous and worryin' about what was goin' on, so I didn't want you to drive."

"Thank you for that, Uncle Zed, but I've been takin' care of myself and Brook for years with no help," Dana said.

"Yep, you have, but you don't have to anymore. I'm here, and you got two sisters who'll come through in a pinch," he told her.

"I might trust you to be there for me and Brook, but my two sisters—not so much," she chuckled. "Now, Annie Brook Clancy, who put that bag of pot in your purse?"

Brook stiffened her spine and stared out the windshield without blinking. "I know it was Ryson Taylor. I've seen him during the noon hour giving kids something and they hand him money. He sits about six seats behind me. But Mama, I didn't want to say anything because Cassidy is right in front of him and she thinks he's cute. She's the only friend I got so far."

"That means her fingerprints will be on that bag, too. I imagine Flora is going to be really upset," Dana said. "What if that kid blames it all on her?"

"You think they won't go back and look at the seating chart and see who all was close enough to drop it in your purse?" Zed asked.

Brook threw her head back dramatically. "I work with Flora, and I really like her and Cassidy. They are going to hate me."

"No, they are not!" Dana said emphatically. "If this happened to Cassidy, we wouldn't hate Flora for it or Cassidy, either. But if she's doin' drugs, you better tell me."

"She's not, but she likes him a lot. I bet she'll protect him," Brook said.

Zed crossed the bridge and made the turn back to the resort. "Crazy what love will make a person do, whether it's the old folks or the young'uns," he muttered.

"What was that?" Dana asked.

"Just mumblin' to myself." Zed parked at the back of the café. "Y'all might as well come on in and get a glass of tea or a soda pop."

"Sounds good to me. Got any of that gingerbread you were makin' for lunch?" Brook asked.

"Little bit," Zed said. "And kiddo, I'm real glad that you ain't hurt or sick."

"Me too, Uncle Zed." She gave him a quick hug as the three of them entered the café by the kitchen door.

"Are you okay? Did someone hurt you? Do I need to go to the school and whip someone's ass?" Harper started the minute they were inside. "I've been worried out of my mind. Talk to me."

"I'm fine. Someone put a bag of marijuana in my purse, and I'm expelled until tomorrow morning," Brook said as if that happened every day.

"What little bastard did it?" Tawny peeked through the serving window. "I'll go up there and take care of him or her."

"I'm not really sure, but he'll get caught eventually. Thanks, Aunt Harper and Aunt Tawny, for worrying about me." She grinned. "Now let's have some of Uncle Zed's gingerbread with lemon sauce."

Tawny giggled.

"It's not funny," Dana said.

"No, it's not, but I smarted off to my mother the other day about going to the school to score some marijuana. Looks like I was right," Tawny said.

Harper's hand flew up to her heart. "I can't believe you said that to her."

Tawny's shoulders popped up in a dramatic shrug. "Did you think it was all rainbows and unicorn farts after you left? The only thing that changed was that I got all the bitchin' instead of sharin' it with you."

Zed stuck a bowl of lemon sauce in the microwave and set half a pan of gingerbread on the table. "Life is what you make it, girls. The past is all over and done with. What you got is the present, because tomorrow might never get here. Annie told me that a lot when I got to frettin' about things, so we worked hard at makin' today a good one."

"That's a good sermon," Dana said. "Brook and I'd better take our gingerbread to go since Flora will need to get back to her regular job."

"Fifteen minutes more ain't goin' to make a difference," Zed said when the microwave bell dinged. "Y'all sit down and have a snack and then we'll all go back to work."

"Will you sit with us?" Brook asked.

A grin spread across his face. "Naw, honey, I'm going to use my fifteen minutes to go outside and smoke a cigarette. You bring that pan of gingerbread to a table, Harper, and I'll get this sauce. Y'all will be more comfortable out there in the dinin' room."

Dana didn't realize that her heart was still pounding or that there was a knot the size of a grapefruit in her stomach until she sat down at the table. But she'd learned to handle fear by putting on a hard shell. Then, when the situation was over, she fell apart in private.

"So do you know who did this thing?" Harper asked Brook.

"Got a pretty good idea," she answered.

"What are you goin' to do about it?" Tawny asked.

"Keep my purse zipped up from now on."

Harper chuckled. "And your backpack, right?"

"Yep, and if I'm right about who that weed belonged to, he'd better stay away from me. I don't like bein' a scapegoat." She finished off her snack and carried her plate to the kitchen. "I'm going to the house and get into my work jeans. Flora will probably need some help since she'll be behind and I'm the cause of it."

When the back door slammed, Harper glanced over at Dana. "You got a really good kid there."

"Yes, I do." Dana's voice cracked. "God, I was worried, especially when Uncle Zed went with me. I thought she'd died and they just weren't tellin' me."

Tawny laid a hand on her shoulder and squeezed gently. "We all worry, too. I came out here to get a glass of tea and Harper was pacing."

"I was not. I was sweeping," Harper said. "I'd spilled coffee on my shirt, so I went to change it. When I got back, Uncle Zed was gone. When I called the store to see if he was there, Flora told me there was a problem at school. But anyway, Brook can take care of herself, and if she's not quite big enough, she's got two aunts, a mama, and an uncle Zed who'll help her out."

Dana pushed back the uneaten square of gingerbread and laid her head on the table. "Thank you. I just need a minute to unwind."

"Need a shot of whiskey?" Harper asked.

"Or a beer?" Tawny patted her on the back.

Dana raised her head. "Thank you both. I'll be fine. I can keep my cool in the middle of a crisis, but when it's over, well, that's a different story."

"Me too," Harper whispered.

"Not me." Tawny went back to eating. "I fall apart right then. My nose runs and I cry like a baby. I'm not tough like y'all are."

"Bullshit," Harper said. "I've seen your tough side."

Tawny carried her plate to the kitchen and returned with three glasses and a pitcher of tea. "I used to be tough when I had you around to back me up, but after you left, everything went to hell. Mother and Daddy started fighting more and more and everything was my fault. Then Daddy died and she never wanted kids anyway and how dare he leave her with a teenage daughter. Her words, not mine. Believe me, she could break steel down into a puddle of liquid. I was so glad to go to college that I didn't even go home that first year, not even for Christmas."

Dana whistled through her teeth. "Wow. My mother is a piece of work, but she didn't go that far. I never one time felt unloved or unwanted. She told me that she'd made a mistake, but that I was a blessing from that and not a burden. She didn't even fuss at me when I got married without telling her. 'Course, we know how that ended."

"We've all got parent baggage," Harper said.

"Yes, you do, but you don't have to carry it," Zed said as he entered the café. "It's your choice whether you have a funeral for that baggage or strap it to your shoulders."

"Good advice, but a hard thing to get done," Tawny said. "I'm going back to my cabin. If anyone needs me, just holler. And Uncle Zed, I would have taken care of the store if you'd called me."

"I know that now, but me and Flora, we been doin' it alone so long, I clean forgot. Next time I'll remember that we've got more help now," he said.

"Good," Harper said. "I see a couple of cars pulling into the lot—we've got some customers, Uncle Zed."

"Time to get to work. I like it when we're busy. Makes the day go by faster," Zed said.

"We'll get on to the store. Flora can go back to her jobs." Dana picked up the plate with the gingerbread and carried it with her. "I can't bear to see this wasted, so I'm takin' it with me."

A blast of lemony cleaner met Dana when she entered the store. Flora, who could put the fear of God into a speck of dust, looked up from the back of the store, where she was wiping down the baseboards.

"Perfect timin'. I ain't had the time to give this store a good goin'-over in a few weeks," she said as she carried a bucket of soapy water and her rag to the bathroom. "Brook came through a few minutes ago and gave me the story. That damn boy has been trouble since the day he was born. His mama grows weed out in the woods behind their house and he sells it. I hope they put her in jail with him. Any of that gingerbread left?" She eyed the plate as she crossed the floor. "I could sure use a pick-me-up now."

"There's still a third of a pan in the kitchen. It smells and looks great in here, Flora, thank you." It was on the tip of Dana's tongue to spit out that Cassidy had a crush on the drug boy, but she clamped her mouth shut.

"See you later, then." The bell above the door rang as she left.

Dana got her phone from her purse and hit "Speed Dial" for her mother before she remembered there was no service in the area. She tossed it back into her purse and hiked a hip on the bar stool behind the cash register. It took her a few minutes to remember her mother's number

161

after she'd picked up the landline phone. She waited for five long rings before Lacy picked up.

"Hey, kid, what's goin' on in the boondocks?" Lacy giggled.

"Your granddaughter got in trouble at school today," Dana said and went on to tell her the whole story.

"And how are you?" Lacy's tone had gone from happy to serious.

"Why do you ask that?" Dana could not mask her anger at anyone thinking Brook would have drugs in her purse.

"Brook is a tough kid. She'll get things straightened out. But, as a mother, you will worry about how this will affect her. You'll be second-guessing yourself about whether you did the right thing by moving there. Don't! Simply don't. You are an amazing mother. Much more so than I ever was. You got that from Annie. Brook is going to hit rough spots growing up. We all do, so just trust her like I trusted you and everything will work out in the end," Lacy said.

"Thanks, Mama. You always make me feel better," Dana said.

"You can always still come and live with me," Lacy told her.

"We'd kill each other after the first six weeks," Dana chuckled.

"Probably so, but the first few days would be

162

great. Got to go now, kiddo. I've got an appointment to get my nails done. Did those two princess sisters take up for Brook?"

"Yes, believe me, they are very protective of their niece," Dana answered.

"Well, imagine that," Lacy said before the line went dead.

Dana returned the receiver to the base. "It *is* a bit of a miracle."

"Hey." Marcus Green pushed into the store. "I thought I'd stop by and see how you are after the fiasco at school today. I also want to assure you that all of us teachers know exactly who is to blame for what happened today. It's not your daughter."

"Thanks, Marcus." Dana nodded. "Cup of coffee? It's on the house. Isn't school still in session?"

"We had an assembly, and I wasn't required to be there," he explained as he added cream and two packages of sugar to the cup of steaming-hot coffee. "I wanted to talk to you. I hated to hear what happened."

"That's sweet," Dana said. "Want a chunk of gingerbread to go with that?"

"Love it, especially if it's Zed's. I can't get up here on Wednesdays for lunch during the school year, and that's the only day he makes it."

Dana dragged an old chair from behind the deli counter so that he could sit across the counter

163

from her, and then she propped a hip on the bar stool. "Place hasn't changed and neither has Uncle Zed. The menu pretty much stays the same."

"Which is a good thing. We all know the burgers are the best in the whole state. How about you, Dana?" Marcus asked.

"I have a fourteen-year-old daughter, so I guess the answer is yes, I've changed."

"But you both still go by Clancy," Marcus said.

"Yes, we do—it' a long story, but I'm not married," Dana said. "And you? Have you changed, Marcus? Still living right around here?"

"Hell, yes! I'm not half as smart as I was in junior high school or even high school." He flashed a brilliant smile. "I hope you noticed that I'm a responsible adult now and not a pot-smokin' wannabe rock star. I still live with my mother. She doesn't like being alone and we get along really well, so it's not a problem." He took a sip of the coffee and changed the subject. "I'd sure like to ask you to dinner sometime. Think you might say yes?"

"Never know until you ask." He seemed like a good person and she didn't want to hurt his feelings, but there wasn't a single bit of a spark between them. She hoped that he didn't ask.

"Hey, Dana, I'm here for two dozen minnows. I hear the bass are bitin' today," an old guy with gray hair and a big straw hat said as he entered the store. "Good God, has Flora been in here with

164

that cleanin' crap? I like this place better when it smells like minnows. Howdy, Marcus. Didn't know you was a fisherman."

"Just dropped in for a cup of coffee," Marcus answered. "How are you, Billy Tom?"

"Arthritis is actin' up, but it won't hurt no worse if I'm fishin'. And besides, the wife ain't fussin' at me if I'm out on the lake," Billy Tom laughed.

"You got that right." Marcus nodded on his way out.

"That's a good boy there," Billy Tom said. "Now, about them minnows. Maybe you better give me three dozen."

＊━┿━╢╟╢╟━╈━＊

Zed sat in Annie's chair that evening. "I want to catch a whiff of your perfume long as it lingers here. I hope it never leaves. I got a story to tell you this evenin'." He went on to tell her all about the school incident.

"I'll tell you one thing, Annie. They might fuss and fight among themselves. Oh, they think I don't see it or know about it, but I do. They try to cover it up when I'm close by so as not to make me sad, but I can tell by their body language if they've been at it again. Makes me want to put them on time-out chairs like you did when they was little. But today, they all stood together when it came to Brook, and the other night . . ." He went on to tell the story that one of the regulars at the café shared with him two days after Harper's bar incident. "We both know that I've lived a lot of years longer than any of them, and I have my ways of findin' out things."

He moved over to his chair. "So I see some progress in them getting along, Annie. And that's my good news. Good night, darlin' Annie."

Chapter Nine

March 30—the day had arrived, according to the miniature calendar stuck to the front of the mini fridge in Harper's cabin that morning. Of all the days in the whole year, this was the one that always, always put a big black cloud over her head, a rock in her chest, and tears in her eyes.

The weeping would begin that evening at exactly eight thirty. Until then she'd just deal with the blackness of the whole day. She dressed in a blue T-shirt and jeans and was sitting on the bench when Zed arrived to open up the café.

"Looks like it's goin' to be a beautiful day. I need to get a key made so you don't have to wait on me in the mornin's," he said. "What time is Wyatt pickin' you up tonight?"

"Crap," she muttered under her breath. She hadn't even looked at a calendar when she said she'd go out with him. No way could she do it. Especially not with him. This was the day that she normally didn't go to work. This was the day when she usually drank herself into a stupor to forget.

"What was that? My hearin' is gettin' bad these days." Zed flipped on the lights and adjusted the thermostat. "I'll get the coffee goin'. Go be sure the saltshakers and napkin dispensers are filled up for the day."

The phone rang, and Harper grabbed it. "Lake Side Resort. This is Harper Clancy."

"Great. I was hoping you might answer," Wyatt said.

"I've got to—" she started.

"I've got bad news—" he said at the same time.

They both stopped for a long, silent moment and finally he said, "You go first."

"No, you," she said.

"I was coming to the lake with four clients for a weekend fishin' trip. Buddies of mine now. But one of them had a heart attack about an hour ago. I'll call later and cancel our reservations, but I'm going to have to cancel our date tonight. I'm so, so sorry." His deep drawl seemed sincere. "Now you."

"It wasn't a date. You didn't even have to call. You just stay with your friend, and I'll take a rain check," she said.

"Thank you. If I can get away later this evening, I'll call you," he said.

"Don't worry if you can't," she said, already planning to unplug the phone in her cabin as soon as she got home that evening.

" 'Bye, then."

" 'Bye, Wyatt."

Zed finished making coffee and glanced over his bony shoulder. "No date tonight?"

"It wasn't a date to begin with. He was just going to come by and visit on the porch for a while. And we lost the rent on three cabins. His

168

friend has had a heart attack," she said flatly.

"I'm sorry," Zed said.

"About the heart attack or the fact that we lost rent?"

"Both, but mostly because I think you wanted to see him this evenin'," he answered.

"I've gotten over worse in my life," she answered. "But I bet that some of your good strong coffee will help everything."

"Always does." Zed nodded.

It was ham day at the café, and every chair was filled by twelve o'clock. Harper spun, taking orders and refilling glasses. And then a man and wife arrived with three little daughters, blondes spread out from about a year old to somewhere around nine.

Harper stopped halfway across the floor and turned around so fast that the room did a couple of hard spins. She made it to the kitchen before she slid down on the linoleum, wrapped her hands around her knees, and began to sob. Zed stopped what he was doing and sat down beside her, drew her into his arms, and let her soak his shirt with her tears.

"What is it, child?"

"Little girls," she sobbed.

"Do they remind you of when you sisters were little?"

She shook her head. "No, they're . . ." And the sobbing started again. "I need a drink."

"You need to let go of this burden, child. Talk to me."

"I gave her away and those little girls remind me of how she'd look," she answered in short bursts of words.

"Gave who away?" Zed asked.

"My baby daughter. I was only sixteen and I couldn't raise her and Mother was mortified about what her friends would think. She and Daddy wouldn't help me . . ." She clung to Zed as if he were a lifeline in a category-five tornado.

"So that's what happened that summer that changed everything." Zed patted her back. "Why didn't you call your granny?"

"Mama said that Granny'd hate me and I loved her too much to have her disappointed in me. Oh, Uncle Zed, today she's nine years old . . ." She clamped a hand over her mouth. "I've never told anyone."

"Your secret is safe with me, child." Tears dripped off Zed's chin and joined hers on the front of his shirt. "I'm so sorry that your mother made you believe that about me and Annie. We would have taken you right in here to live with us."

"I was sixteen, scared, and angry, and halfway across the United States."

"Did you love the father?"

"I thought I did, but he was only sixteen, too,

and I couldn't . . ." She wiped her face. "We've got customers."

"And they'll wait or leave. You are more important than any of them people," he said.

"I love you, Uncle Zed," she whispered.

"And I've always loved all you girls. Y'all was my family as much as you were Annie's."

She stood up as gracefully as she could and held out a hand toward Zed. He put his into hers; lifting him was like pulling up a bag of air. She hadn't realized how thin he'd gotten until that moment.

"Wyatt?" he asked.

She nodded.

"You ever goin' to tell him?"

"I don't know if I can. Tellin' you was the second hardest thing I've ever done."

Zed hugged her tightly. "You're in the right place to lay down this heavy burden, child. Let me and your sisters help you with this."

"Please don't tell my sisters," she whispered.

"That's not my place, honey. You take the rest of the day off. Tawny can come help me out. You go on out the back door, so you don't have to see them little girls. I'll tell Tawny that you're sick and we don't want to spread it around," he said.

"You sure?" Harper asked.

"Of course I'm sure, and from this day on, you are going to have March 30 off." He smiled, the pain on his wrinkled face echoing hers. He reached for the wall-hung phone and called

Tawny. "She'll be here in three minutes. Won't hurt them folks to wait a little longer."

"Thank you, Uncle Zed." Harper pulled off her apron and laid it on the worktable. "For everything."

"Just wish things could've been different for you, child," he said. "There she is comin' in the front. You get on out of here before she sees them swollen eyes and all that black eye stuff on your face."

Harper hung the DO NOT DISTURB sign on her door, dragged a full bottle of Jack Daniel's from the closet, and took a long drink right from the bottle before she ran a bathtub full of hot water. Sinking down into it, she held the bottle in one hand and took another long drink before she came up for air. It burned like hell all the way to her stomach, yet like always, it did not quite take the pain or the guilt away.

Knowing that Zed didn't hate her and that he and Granny Annie would've helped her actually made it worse, so she took another drink right from the bottle. She could have had a lovely little blonde-haired daughter, just five years younger than Brook. The baby could have grown up right there on the lake, and Harper would have been there with Granny Annie all these years rather than jumping from job to job, dreading the end of March every year.

"Lord, why did I believe my mother?" she

mumbled as she turned the water off with her toes and leaned back. Exhaustion, mixed with the whiskey, made her eyes heavy, and she fell asleep.

The sun was going down by the time she awoke with a nasty taste in her mouth, a half-empty bottle of Jack floating in the cold water like a ship on the ocean, and the vision of those three little girls still on her mind. She carefully picked up the bottle and set it on the floor, pulled the plug on the tub, and shivered when the cold air hit her naked, wet body. She wrapped a towel around herself and carried the bottle of whiskey with her to the bed, where she sat down and stared blankly out the window at the wooded area.

The couple who had adopted her baby named her Emma, and they'd even let Harper choose the middle name. Somewhere out there was a nine-year-old girl named Emma Joanna. And Granny never even knew about her second great-granddaughter.

She threw off the towel and dressed in a faded nightshirt and a pair of cotton underwear. Turning up the bottle again, she took a couple of gulps and then threw it across the room, shattering it on the far wall. She fell back on the bed and heartbreaking sobs racked her body as her hands went to cradle her stomach.

"I'm so sorry, Emma," she moaned. "But I was so young and so afraid I'd be a mother like mine. You deserved more than that."

She shut her eyes and images of the older little girl who'd come into the café flashed in her mind. Would her daughter be blowing out birthday candles right now? Did she get a bike for her ninth birthday, or better yet, a puppy? The couple lived out in the country, so maybe she already had a pet and a bike. Perhaps she got a pony for her birthday and a pair of new boots.

Harper kept her eyes closed and imagined a little blonde-haired girl giggling as she opened her birthday presents. Then someone knocked on her door and ruined the whole vision. She ignored it, and they knocked again, louder.

"Harper, please open the door," Wyatt yelled. "Zed said you're in there."

"Dammit, Uncle Zed. You promised not to interfere." She stumbled toward the door.

He didn't break his promise. Granny Annie's voice was in her head. *Zed keeps his word. You can count on that, so don't go blamin' him.*

Another knock and she slung open the door, hanging on to it to keep from falling through the screen and landing at Wyatt's boots. With blurry eyes, she looked at him and could see by his expression that he was hurting.

"My friend died, Harper," he said hoarsely. "He had another heart attack and they couldn't revive him."

"I gave away our daughter," she blurted out. "Guess we're both in pain."

The floor kept getting closer and closer and everything was spinning out of control. She felt the heavy weight of blackness surrounding her, and then strong arms cradled her like a baby and carried her to the bed. He stretched out beside her and held her so close that she could hear his heartbeats and his quiet weeping for his friend.

"Sweet Jesus!" she slurred. "Did I say that out loud?"

The last thing she smelled as she passed out was a mixture of coffee on Wyatt's breath, remnants of his shaving lotion—the same that he'd used when he was sixteen—and the Jack Daniel's that was in a puddle on the floor with all the glass from the broken bottle.

When she came back to her senses again, Wyatt was propped up on an elbow and staring into her eyes. "What did you say at the door, Harper?"

"I'm sorry about your friend," she said.

"No, that wasn't it. You said we were both in pain and for me to come on in, but before that you said something about our daughter. Were you dreaming or just drunk?"

"All of the above," Harper answered.

"You had a baby?"

"I did. A little girl that I gave away."

"Why?" Wyatt asked.

"Because my mother said I couldn't come home if I didn't, and then I got to thinkin' about what a horrible mother I would be. I was only sixteen and you were just a kid, too, and it didn't seem fair to her to . . ." She stopped to catch her breath and then realized she was out of words.

"It was my baby, right?" Wyatt asked.

She nodded.

"And you didn't even tell me?"

She shook her head.

"Why?"

"We were sixteen, for God's sake, Wyatt. Were you goin' to slap on your shinin' armor and marry me? We weren't old enough to do that, probably not even with parental consent. I chose her adopted parents carefully. I'm sure she's been in a good home, but today is her birthday and the guilt trip is . . ." A fresh batch of tears rushed down her cheeks like a river, dripping onto his shirt this time. "The family offered to send pictures to me or even to let me see her, like on her birthday, or be a part of her life, but I couldn't, Wyatt. I just couldn't bear the thought of seeing her and then having to say goodbye."

"I'm so sorry." Wyatt's voice cracked. He held her so close that their tears mingled together. "I don't know what I would have done. Probably freaked out, but I had a wonderful grandpa who would have helped if he'd known."

"Mother said Granny Annie would hate me, and I didn't want to disappoint her, so I didn't even tell her." Harper bounced off the bed and barely made it to the toilet before the Jack Daniel's came back up.

Wyatt followed her and held her long blonde hair back, then washed her face with a wet cloth. "It's okay, darlin'. You've got every right to drink. Let me hold you and ease the pain."

"She was your daughter, too, Wyatt. Why in the hell aren't you mad at me?" Harper bent over the toilet and dry heaved.

"I'm numb," he said.

"When that goes away, you'll be angry and hate me." She tried to stand, but her knees were weak.

He slipped an arm under her knees and one around her shoulders and carried her back to the bed. "I'm stayin' with you tonight. We'll mourn together."

"She's not dead. She's happy and riding a pony that her parents gave her for her ninth birthday," Harper argued.

"I'm sure that they are good parents." He wrapped her up in his arms and held her tightly. "But we don't get to buy her that pony or take her fishin' or sing songs to her or read books to her before she goes to sleep, so we're goin' to mourn that."

"You don't hate me?" she asked.

"You were only thinkin' of me and of her, so how could I be mad at you, darlin'?" He brushed her hair away from her eyes, his fingertips feeling like a feather on her skin.

"Some first date, huh?" she whispered. "Your friend passed away, and I unloaded all this on you."

"I'm here and I'm with you. We'll get through this together."

"Her name is Emma Joanna. They let me pick her middle name."

"That's beautiful." Wyatt held her even closer. "Shut your eyes, darlin', and let this day pass on. I'm not going anywhere, and everything will be better when morning arrives."

For now, she thought. But she'd take that much right then. She snuggled in so close to him that light couldn't find its way between them, and in that moment some of the pain and guilt finally floated away.

✦✦✦✦✦

Zed poured two glasses of blackberry wine and carried them across the floor to the recliners. He sniffed the air as he set them on the table between the chairs. "You're fading, Annie. I don't see you in the chair as clear as I did here at first, and your perfume is getting so faint I have to imagine it. I can't have that happenin'."

He padded barefoot across to the bed behind the chairs, opened the drawer in the bedside table, and took out a small bottle of perfume that he'd intended to give her for her next birthday. Giving it a quick spray toward the chair, he inhaled deeply. "There you are. I feel like you're in the room again now. I got to have your spirit with me tonight, Annie, so I can tell you about today. I know what happened that summer with Harper."

One glass of wine later, he'd finished telling the whole story about how broken Harper was. "I just felt my heart breakin' for that child, Annie, and I could almost feel your tears dripping on my shoulder. Bless her heart, what are we goin' to do to help her get through this?"

He wrapped his veined hand around the other glass and brought it to his lips. "Oh, so you think I'm handlin' it okay, do you? Well, darlin', I'm feelin' like I need more time than I've got left to get them all straightened out."

He popped the footrest up on his recliner. "Maybe I can at least get them to open their hearts to each other, but Annie, I'm gettin' tired and weary of this old earth. I really want to go on home with you, so if you could just help me out with all this, I'd sure appreciate it. Don't fuss at me. I promised I'd see to it that they became a family, and I'll do my best."

He finished off the second glass of wine, reached across the table, laid his hand on Annie's chair, and inhaled deeply. "Oh, Annie, life ain't worth a damn without you beside me."

Chapter Ten

If it can go wrong, it will. If it can't, it might anyway. That was one of Granny Annie's sayings, and that Saturday morning started out with everything that could go wrong. Dana's alarm didn't go off, so she had to rush to the store to open up, only to find half a dozen customers waiting to buy bait and picnic supplies.

After the rush, she was out of live bait, and the minnow man didn't arrive until ten o'clock or sometimes even later. Thank goodness the last customer wanted to buy snacks for a picnic and gas for their boat instead of bait. When the store was empty of customers, she made two pots of coffee, one regular and one decaf, and ran a quick dust mop around the floor.

The bell above the door rang, and she looked over the top of the potato chip shelf to see Brook with a takeout box in her hands. "I hope that's for me."

"Uncle Zed said to bring it over on my way to the laundry this morning," Brook told her. "Aunt Harper isn't in the café yet. You think she's still sick? Maybe I ought to help out in the kitchen today."

As if summoned, Harper pushed her way into

the store. "I need a bottle of aspirin and a banana."

Dana tossed a bottle toward her. "Fruit is on the counter. Hungover?"

She caught it midair. "Little bit. How about that cleaner stuff that Flora uses?"

Brook rounded the end of the display shelving. "I can get you some of that out in the laundry. Should I bring it to the café or to your cabin?"

"To the cabin," Harper said. "Put this stuff on my bill, please."

Brook waited until she was gone to whisper, "Wyatt's truck is parked right beside hers."

Dana raised an eyebrow. "Oh, really?"

"You think she threw up and that's why she needs the cleaning stuff?"

"Could be, but it's not a bit of our business, is it?" Dana answered.

Brook drew her eyes down until her brows were almost a solid line. "That's not fair."

Dana took the box from her hands and carried it to the counter. "I tell you all the time that life is not fair, but what's the issue with it today?" She flipped the lid back to find sausage gravy covering three biscuits.

"All three—no, all four—of y'all can get up in my business and know everything that happens, but I can't know why she needs some of Flora's cleaner? It's not fair." Brook crossed her arms over her chest.

"Like I said, life's not . . ."

One of Brook's hands shot up. "I know . . . not fair."

"So we'll leave it there and get on with the day, right?" Dana scooped up a bite of the food. "It's Easter weekend. Think we should go to church tomorrow evening?"

"CEO Christians," Brook laughed.

"That's right, darlin'. Christmas and Easter only makes us CEOs."

"Would Granny Annie go if she was here?"

"Nope. Something happened when my grandpa died and she never went back."

Brook picked up a candy bar. "Then I don't want to go, either. Put this on my bill."

"I'll pay for it today." Dana reached in her purse and rang up the cost for two candy bars. "Take another one with you for Flora, and I'll see you at lunch."

"Oh, yeah, and I'll be four hours older, so maybe I'll be old enough to talk about why Aunt Harper needs cleaner." Brook waved and held the door for the bait man as she left.

"Teenagers?" a tall guy with sparkling blue eyes and blond hair pulled back into a short ponytail said with a smile. "I got a daughter that graduated a few years ago. It was amazing how much I learned while she was off to college, but some days, even though I'm forty-six years old, I still revert back to being the dumbest man on earth."

"Then there's hope that the time will come when I've got brains part of the time." Dana smiled up at him and did the math. He was ten years older than her—and probably married with two or three other kids. "Where's the regular bait man?"

"Retired—I'm out doing the deliveries until I can hire someone else." He stuck out his hand. "I'm Payton O'Riley."

"Dana Clancy." Sparks flew when she shook hands with him. "I'm completely out of minnows and low on stink bait and cut bait, too."

"I'll fix you right up." He dropped her hand and whistled as he headed outside.

She glanced down at her hand for a moment, surprised to see that it wasn't fire-engine red. She hadn't felt chemistry like that with a guy in a very long time. He was almost out of the store when she leaned over the counter to watch him swagger out. And that's when she dragged her hair through the gravy. She jumped back too fast and knocked the whole container off, splattering gravy all over the floor, the wall, and somehow even into the cash register.

Grabbing a roll of paper towels, she quickly did the best she could with her hair and then started wiping up the mess. When he returned, she was on her knees trying to get enough of it off the floor so she could get to the counter to sign the receipt for the bait.

Payton leaned over the counter. "Need some help?"

"Thanks, but I'll have it done by the time you unload." She blushed.

"This is my last stop, and I've only got half your usual order of minnows. I've got to make another run down this way tomorrow morning. All right if I bring more then?"

"That will be great." She blushed again as she swiped up the last of what was on the floor and got to her feet.

He took the roll of paper towels off the floor, ripped off one, and brushed it across her cheek, then ran it down a strand of her hair. "Some of it got on you. Shame that Zed's gravy got wasted. He makes the best biscuits and gravy I've ever eaten. Want me to go around to the café and get you another order?"

"No, thank you. I'll just grab a package of chocolate doughnuts and a cup of coffee," she stammered. What was wrong with her? She was acting like a sophomore in high school, not a mother in her midthirties.

With a brief nod, he rolled his cart back to the tank and then over to the refrigerator where the other forms of bait were kept. "I think that's the best I can do for today, but I'll be back tomorrow."

"It's Easter Sunday," Dana reminded him.

"My daughter and I go to early Mass, so there's

no problem. See you same time tomorrow." He flashed a brilliant smile and waved.

"God, you have one wicked sense of humor to send Marcus around that I have no chemistry with and then let this man walk into my life and he's got a daughter and likely a wife," she muttered as she rushed off to the bathroom. The little mirror above the sink was cracked in two places, but it showed what a mess she was. Specks of gravy dotted her hair, and sweet Lord, there was even a smudge of it, complete with sausage, behind her ear.

What's God got to do with you bein' clumsy? If you hadn't leaned over the counter to look at the way Payton filled out his jeans, you wouldn't have slung gravy halfway to the Oklahoma border. Granny Annie was back in her head, so clearly that she almost expected to see her reflection in the mirror right along beside hers.

"That's not what I was talkin' about. Marcus is probably going to ask me out and I feel nothing around him. Yet Payton is probably married and his touch makes me think unholy thoughts," she said out loud.

Like you told Brook, life ain't fair.

➤═▐▌▐▌═◄

Tawny had just finished canceling a weeklong reservation for cabin number six when a guy tapped on the door of her cabin and then eased the door open. His blue eyes met hers, and he blushed slightly.

"Can I help you?"

"I stopped at the café and Zed said to come to this cabin. It would help if you'd put an office sign on the door. I didn't know whether to knock or just walk in," he said.

"Good idea. I'll make a temporary one until I can get a permanent one ordered."

"I'm here to see if you have a vacancy. I'd like to check in now and stay until Tuesday morning," he said.

Tawny picked up the number six key and dangled it. "You are one lucky guy. I was booked solid until two minutes ago. Number six, right next door to this one, is empty, so if you want it, it's yours. But if you check in now, I'm going to have to charge you for today. Regular check-in isn't until three. Want to go fishin' or do some hiking until then?"

"I'm not a fisherman or an outdoors person. I just want three days of peace and quiet to do some reading and relaxing." He handed her his credit card and driver's license. "I'm Marcus Green. You are the youngest sister, right?"

"That's right. Do I know you?" Those blue eyes were boring right into hers, and her pulse kicked in an extra beat.

"I went to school with Dana in Frankston," he said. "I heard about y'all a lot through Zed and

Annie when I came to the café. I was so sorry to hear of her passing."

Tawny ran his credit card through the machine and handed both it and his license back to him, along with the cabin key. A copy of the transaction ran through the printer, and she laid it on the desk. "Please sign right there. Checkout is at eleven."

"I'll be gone before eight. I'm a teacher at Frankston." His hand brushed against hers when he took the pen from her. "Reckon Zed is still serving breakfast?"

Tawny glanced at the clock. "For another fifteen minutes. If you live in Frankston, why are you renting a cabin? You could come to the lake anytime and go home to your own bed at night."

"Sometimes it's good just to get away from everyday life and have some quiet time to myself." He smiled, and her heart did a couple of flips. "I don't fish, but I love the lake and the idea of unplugging for the weekend. Be seein' you around, Tawny."

She pushed back her chair and watched him get into a vintage Ford Mustang, bright red, and pull it around to park in front of the cabin right next to hers. He wasn't tall, but he was muscular, and her fingers itched to see if his curly hair was as soft as it looked.

"Marcus Green," she said out loud. "Where have I heard that name?"

"Hey, Aunt Tawny." Brook startled her when she slung the door open. "I brought you a set of clean sheets. I'll pick up the dirty ones when Flora and I get done with number one. Was that Mr. Green goin' into the unit next door?"

"That's where I heard the name. Is he one of your teachers?" Tawny asked.

"Yep, history. He also teaches some math. What's he doin' here?"

"Unplugging for the long weekend. Thanks for the sheets." She loved her niece and she didn't want to push her out, but the longer Brook stayed, the more questions she'd ask. And then she'd tell Dana. And that's when the problems could and would start, because Dana would want to boss her about Marcus being so much older.

Brook rounded the bookcase and laid the sheets on the bed. "Did you know that Wyatt probably spent the night at Aunt Harper's and that she has a hangover this mornin'?"

Whoa! Wait a minute. Maybe I don't want Brook to leave just yet. So Wyatt stayed at Harper's— did that mean she was really sick yesterday, or had she wanted time to get all pretty for a night of wild sex?

"Maybe he came to see about her. She was supposed to be sick. I filled in for her at the café. She makes some damned good tips over there. I'm beginnin' to think she might have gotten the best job of the bunch of us." Maybe since Brook was thinking about Wyatt spending the night at Harper's, she could sneak in a couple of innocent questions. "Is Mr. Green married? Got kids?"

"No to both. He's got a cat, though. There's a picture of it on his desk. A big old yellow one. Did he bring it with him? Are we a pet-friendly place?"

"No, we aren't, and he didn't mention a cat or take a carrier into the cabin, so I guess he left it at home."

"Well, I got to get back to work. Flora's knees are botherin' her today, so I been vacuuming in the cabins."

"You're a good kid," Tawny said.

"Tell that to my mama." Brook's smile reminded her of her granny Annie's.

"She already knows it."

Brook eased out the door, then broke into a jog toward the laundry room. As badly as Tawny hated to admit it, Dana was a great mother. Someday when Tawny had kids, she hoped that she was even half the parent that Dana was, but she sure wasn't going to admit to liking her older sister to anyone.

"It sure won't be someone like Matthew." She grimaced at even the thought of his name. Her old boyfriend came from a wealthy family in Austin and had been a senior at the university when they met. The rest was a downhill slide that led to her being kicked out of college and his dad's fancy-shmancy lawyer getting Matthew off with only a fine and a slap on the wrist.

"And my dear mother decided to tell me to get a public defender. She reminded me of that little bit of trouble I got into in high school, and then she turned off service to my phone and froze my credit cards," she groaned.

She remade her twin-size bed and carried the dirty sheets outside, planning to take them to the laundry. Maybe a breath of fresh, brisk air would wash away the memories of that day in court.

"Hey, got time to have a cup of coffee with me while I eat breakfast?" Marcus asked as he stepped off his porch.

"Sure, just give me time to unload this at the laundry. Be there in five." It wouldn't do any harm just to sit with him while she took a short break.

He fell in beside her. "I'll walk with you. This is a gorgeous morning. Easter weekend is always unpredictable. My mother calls it the Easter snap—she never plants her annual flowers until the weekend is over."

"That's what Granny Annie used to say. We didn't get up here very often for Easter. We always came for a month in the summer. I'll only be a minute," she said at the door.

Leaving him outside—mainly so that she didn't have to explain anything to Flora or Brook—she found the laundry room empty. She quickly tossed the sheets into a bin and hurried back outside.

"All done."

"I knew you came in the summertime." He picked up the conversation as if she'd never left his side. "My mother and Annie were great friends, and I remember seeing you when y'all came here." He opened the door to the café and stood back for her to enter first.

Most of the time the place was full and the buzz of conversations reverberated off the walls, but that Saturday morning only Harper and Zed were in the café. They were sitting at a table, and she looked like she'd been crying. The first thing that went through Tawny's mind was that their mother had died and somehow Harper had found out about it first.

"Well, hello, Marcus. You out enjoying the pretty weather?" Zed got to his feet. "I still got some breakfast stuff on the stove. Want the big platter?"

"You bet I do." He pulled out a chair for Tawny. "And this lady would like a cup of coffee."

"Comin' right up." Harper seemed eager to do something, even if it was waiting on her younger sister. "Two coffees?"

"Yes, ma'am," Marcus said. "You must be Harper. How did you get so tall when your sisters are just petite little ladies?"

"Some of us get to be delicate little pansies

and some of us have to be big sunflowers," she answered.

"And they're all beautiful." Marcus smiled.

"Flattery will get you free refills on that coffee." Harper raised an eyebrow toward Tawny.

✦⊹⊱⊰⊱⊰⊱⊰⊱⊰⊹✦

As soon as she set Marcus's plate in front of him, Harper made a beeline out the back door of the café, around the building, and into the store. Dana had just finished scooping up a net full of minnows and putting them into a plastic bag for a fisherman.

"Is Brook all right?" Dana looked worried.

"Far as I know. She brought me clean sheets this morning and got all nosy about Wyatt. Teenagers haven't changed since we were that age—they're all about drama. Don't make me love her one bit less, but it's the truth." Harper meandered around the store until the customer paid and left. She picked up half a dozen candy bars and a bag of barbecue chips, figuring she might as well stock up on snacks while she was there.

"Got the munchies, do you?" Dana asked.

"What do you know about Marcus Green?" Harper blurted out.

"He's a teacher at Frankston, where Brook goes to school. Why?"

"He's havin' breakfast with Tawny in the café

192

right now." Harper laid the stash on the counter along with a ten-dollar bill.

"Well, crap! He's probably pumping her for information about me. We were in junior high together, and he came in here on Wednesday and wanted to know if I'd go to dinner with him sometime. There's not a drop of chemistry between us, Harper. I look at him and see that long-haired pot-smokin' kid." Dana made change and handed it back to her.

Harper didn't agree—not the way he was flirting with Tawny. "Well, he's lookin' at our younger sister with stars in his blue eyes. And I don't think he's got any visions of you. Sorry to burst your little bubble." Harper crammed the change into her apron pocket with the rest of her morning tips.

"Good God, that's downright creepy!" Dana raised her voice an octave. "He's, what, fourteen years older than her? That's cradle robbin'."

Harper started for the door, but Tawny rushed inside before she made it across the floor.

"Hey, tell me about this Marcus Green. He says that he knew you in school," Tawny said. "He's got the most amazing blue eyes . . ."

"He's too old for you," Dana said flatly.

Harper leaned against a shelf and nodded. She didn't have the right to give anyone advice, but she knew men. That guy was a mama's boy. She could spot them a mile away. After the mother she and Tawny had, the girl sure didn't need a controlling mother-in-law. But what did she care? She didn't even like her sister—or did she?

"He's thirty-four—that's only twelve years," Tawny argued.

"He's my age, and I'm thirty-six," Dana shot back.

"He was the youngest kid in his class and skipped third grade, so he's thirty-four. I looked at his driver's license when he checked in." Tawny crossed her arms over her chest and glared at Dana.

"He asked Dana if she'd go out with him," Harper said. "And now that I've delivered that note, I'm going back to work."

Dana grabbed her arm. "Oh, no, you are not! You're going to stay here and back me up on this. He's too old for her even if it isn't fourteen years."

"He asked you out?" Tawny rolled her eyes toward the ceiling. "What did you say?"

"He didn't actually ask me. He wanted to know if he could ask," Dana explained.

Tawny frowned. "Well, that's different, then."

"It still don't change the fact that he's too old for you," Dana said.

"Hey," Tawny said coldly, "I'm not here to ask you to be a bridesmaid. There was just a flicker of chemistry between us and I wanted to know if he's a decent man. All I did was sit with him at breakfast and drink a cup of coffee, for God's sake."

"And then he went home?" Dana asked.

"And then he went to cabin number six. He's rented it until Tuesday morning. Said he wanted to get unplugged and have some peace and quiet over the long weekend."

Well, dammit! Harper thought. She might have to set the place on fire or jam his door shut. If he really were a mama's boy, it shouldn't be too tough to scare him. Maybe she should wrap up in a sheet and scratch on his cabin window that night and see if he'd scream like a little girl.

Dana groaned. "That means he's going to . . . crap, there he is." She nodded toward the window.

"I'm going out through Uncle Zed's quarters. He won't mind." Harper's long legs made short order of the distance and she, right along with Tawny behind her, disappeared through the curtained doorway at the same time Marcus entered the store.

Harper stopped in the middle of the spotlessly clean living area and sniffed. "I smell Granny Annie's perfume in here."

"All I smell is smoke," Tawny whispered as she stuck her ear close to the curtain in the doorway.

"What are you doing?" Harper took a couple of long strides and did the same thing. "Can you hear them?"

"Shh." Tawny put a finger over her lips and leaned against the curtain a little more.

"What's goin' on in here?" Zed whispered right behind them.

He startled Tawny so badly that if Harper hadn't grabbed her by the arm she would have burst right through the curtain.

"We're eavesdropping," Harper told him.

"On who?" Zed filled up the rest of the space when he leaned in to listen, too. "Is it Dana and Brook?"

"Nope, Dana and Marcus," Harper answered.

Marcus's deep voice came through just fine. "I need to talk to you about something, Dana. I was so tickled to see you at the school that day, and I have to admit that I had a pretty good-size crush on you in junior high school. I know I asked you to go to dinner with me, but I have to ask for that back."

"You can have it back, but you are too old for my sister," Dana spat out. "And this whole thing of you asking her out is kind of . . ."

"Kind of what? We are two consenting adults," he said.

"It's creepy," Dana blurted out.

"Because I was going to ask you out first? Are you jealous? If you'll go out with me, I won't ask her," he chuckled.

"Neither of us is going anywhere with you, Marcus," Dana said through clenched teeth.

Well, at least her older sister had enough sense to know when something wasn't right and to fix it, Harper thought. Poor Tawny must want a boyfriend pretty bad for that little short guy to appeal to her.

"Dammit!" Tawny hissed.

"Age is just numbers on paper," Marcus went on. "I'm a self-proclaimed bachelor. All I'm lookin' for is a good friend, and Tawny is old enough to make up her own mind. Don't worry, Dana. I'm not going to throw her over my shoulder and elope." Marcus laughed.

Harper clamped her mouth shut to keep from saying something obscene right there in front of Uncle Zed. Tawny had heard her swear like a drunk sailor before, but for Uncle Zed to hear her say the words that were on her mind—man, that would put a blush on her face for eternity plus four days.

There was a long, pregnant silence, and then Dana laughed with him. "She's my baby sister. I get a little overprotective."

"Bullshit!" Tawny hissed for a second time.

Harper put a finger over her sister's mouth and frowned.

"Understandable. Then we're good?" he asked.

"We are good, but I'm not changing my mind."

Harper nodded and Tawny drew back her hand to slap her arm, but Uncle Zed grabbed it in a vise grip.

"Friends, then?" Marcus asked altogether too smoothly.

"You betcha. Need some fishin' worms or minnows? I understand you're here for the weekend."

"I hate fish, and it seems a shame to spend a whole day catchin' and releasin', so no, ma'am, I do not want any worms or bait. I would like a six-pack of Coke and a big bag of potato chips. I get the munchies when I read," he said.

Harper immediately wondered if the reading caused his hunger or if this little getaway was to enjoy a few days of blissful pot smoking. She eased away from the curtain and tiptoed across the floor toward the back door with Tawny and Zed right behind her. Chalk one up for all three of them. Wyatt had driven away that morning without even coming by the café. Marcus wasn't interested in Dana and only wanted a buddy when it came to Tawny. The Clancy girls had all flunked Boyfriend 101 that weekend. They would have to take the class over at a later date.

<hr />

It had been a strange day for Dana. Stepping into Tawny's business had made her feel like a real sister, and she was still trying to analyze that emotion when she brought out a huge bowl of caramel corn as Brook chose the Saturday movie. She'd thought her sisters might come to the house tonight, since Brook had invited them the week before and reminded them at least a dozen times that day.

At eight o'clock neither of them had arrived, so she hit the button on the remote to start *Something to Talk About*. The music had barely started when Tawny knocked on the front door, and immediately Harper's heavy rap hit the back. Brook yelled for them to come on in and Dana pushed the "Pause" button so they wouldn't miss anything.

"What are we watchin'? And should we start invitin' Uncle Zed to these movie nights?" Harper flopped down on the sofa, kicked off her shoes, and propped her feet on the coffee table. "I love doing this. Mother would have passed gold bricks if we'd ever put our feet on the furniture at home, but Granny Annie was so laid-back that we could be ourselves in this house."

Brook told them the title of the movie and the two lead actors. "You're goin' to love it. Movies keep y'all from fighting, you know."

Tawny claimed the recliner after she'd loaded up a smaller bowl with caramel corn. "Anything that's got Julia in it is fantastic in my books. And we've always liked movies, so I guess this is a good place to start being really civil and not just pretend for Uncle Zed's benefit. I would've been here sooner, but the last customer had a problem with their car and didn't arrive until five minutes ago. Why were you late, Harper? Waiting on Wyatt to come keep your bed warm?"

"Hell, no, Marcus was doing that for me," Harper teased. Tawny threw a piece of popcorn at her. She caught it midair and popped it into her mouth. "Don't waste good food. You might get hungry someday and wish you had what you threw away."

"You ever been that hungry, Aunt Harper?" Brook asked.

"Couple of times. Now let's watch this movie. Is it funny?"

"Oh, yeah." Brook nodded.

Dana nudged Tawny on her way to the kitchen to get sweet tea for everyone. "You still mad at me?"

"A little bit. You aren't my mother, and you don't have the right to interfere in my life," Tawny answered. "Want some help with that tea?"

"Sure do. And I'm your older sister." Dana filled four glasses with ice and then poured tea into them. "Someone has to look out for you."

"And who's going to look out for you?" Harper called from the living room.

"I'm the oldest. I can take care of myself," Dana declared.

"Bullsh—crap!" Harper said when she realized Brook was listening. "I'll be your guardian angel when it comes to men, and you can be Tawny's."

"Then who is yours—Aunt Tawny?" Brook asked.

"Heaven help me. That *does* mean she's mine," Harper groaned.

"Backed right into that son of a bitch, didn't you?" Brook laughed.

"Brook!" Dana squealed.

"Well, Aunt Harper did." Brook giggled even harder.

"And since I'm your boyfriend keeper, what happened last night with Wyatt? Was it good?" Tawny asked. "You goin' to pick up where you left off ten years ago?"

"Probably not, and nothing happened except that he slept beside me and held me all night to get me through the hardest day of every year. And that's all I've got to say about that," she answered.

"That's a Forrest Gump answer. We'll have to watch that one next week," Brook declared. "Hit the button, Mama, and let's get this party started."

What Harper had said about it being the most difficult day of the year kept running through Dana's mind as she watched the movie for probably the tenth time. She glanced over at Harper, who wiped away a tear when she saw a little blonde-haired girl in the movie.

"Men!" Tawny said. "Can't trust them."

"Then why'd you put up such a fuss today over Marcus?" Dana asked.

"I did have a little attraction. But it was more

about you trying to run my life like my mother does than fighting for a guy I'd only met a few minutes before. I'd go out with him if he asked me whether you like it or not," Tawny answered.

"Yuck! You can do better," Brook piped up from the floor. "He's not for you, Aunt Tawny. He's got a cat and he lives with his mama."

"For real?" Tawny's face screwed up in disbelief.

"Yep, he's always talkin' about his mama's cookin' and how if he's gone for a day or two, the cat is fine, but if his mama is gone for a day, it pouts. He talks about his mama like she's got a halo," Brook said.

"So?" Dana turned to look at Tawny.

Tawny shrugged. "Not a thing to worry about. I'm just a sucker for blue eyes."

Me too, Dana thought as a picture of Payton's eyes flashed through her mind.

<hr>

"Well, Annie, we made a little progress today," Zed said as he put stuffed bunny rabbits in four Easter baskets. "They actually looked out for Tawny when Marcus Green came to stay a couple of days in a cabin. You remember his mama bringing him to the café when he was a baby? I'd never seen such a mama's boy and he didn't outgrow it, neither. I was glad when Dana and Harper took a stand together. What's it called these days? Oh, yeah, an intervention. I hope they opened up her eyes a little and she don't get involved with him, or I'll have to do something about it. Can't have one of our girls livin' with that miserable mother of his, and I sure don't see him ever moving out away from here."

He stuck a chocolate bunny in each basket. "What do you think, Annie? I wish you were here to help me get the baskets all ready. We had such fun doing this when they were little girls."

He stopped, removed a handkerchief from his pocket, and wiped his eyes. "We had good years together, didn't we? Raisin' the girls up to be teenagers, and we even kind of had the empty nest thing when they didn't come around so often anymore. Yep, we had us a good life, and if you was here, then they wouldn't be. It don't make it no easier to take."

He finished up the job and sat down in his recliner. "Just look at 'em, Annie. You think they'll be surprised?" He cocked his ear toward her empty chair. "I'm glad that you think they're pretty. I just hope the girls like them."

Chapter Eleven

Zed could hardly contain his excitement on Sunday morning. He awoke before five o'clock and lined the Easter baskets up in front of the chairs. "Just look at them, Annie. It's been years since we got to make baskets for the girls. Pink is for Brook. She was wearing a pretty pink dress the first time Dana brought her to see us. I wonder what her daddy was like. I smell a rat in Dana's story, but she'll come around with what really happened one of these days."

It took two trips to get the baskets from his quarters at the back of the store to the café. Harper always arrived first, so he put the one with a pretty little red stuffed bunny toward the front. He made coffee and fidgeted, eager for them to get there so he could see their faces. Annie would want to know every detail. At the end of her life when she couldn't remember very well, she'd beg him to tell her stories about the girls. Some days he'd kneel in front of her and repeat the same things he'd told her the day before. When she laughed, the clouds parted and he could swear that the angels in heaven were sweepin' the floors and gettin' ready for her.

He couldn't be still another minute, so he pulled on a jacket and went outside to sit on the bench.

Harper's light was on, so she would be there in a few minutes. He lit up a cigarette and shook his head slowly. "I know, darlin', but it's too late to quit now, and besides, if I had ten more years, I'd spend them miserable without you, so don't fuss at me. Aha! I believe that's Wyatt's truck." He lowered his voice to a whisper. "And he's leavin' something on the porch. Well, now, that's a step in the right direction, ain't it?"

➤❖❖❖❖❖◄

Sunday morning was just like every other day of the week. Harper got up before daylight, dressed, and twirled her hair up into a ponytail and headed over to the café. But she stopped in her tracks when she opened the door. Sitting right there on the porch was a gorgeous bouquet of red roses with a big chocolate Easter bunny propped up beside it.

"Zed." She reached for the card but was surprised when she saw the handwriting.

Sorry I left in a hurry. My friend's wife wanted me to help make arrangements, and truthfully, I didn't know what else to say or do. My heart hurts for you. I'll call this afternoon. Until then, happy Easter—Wyatt.

The first thing she did was check to see if either of her sisters was nearby. With them nowhere in sight, she grabbed up the vase and chocolate and took them into her cabin. She sank her nose into the roses and inhaled deeply and then removed the foil from around the bunny and bit off an ear.

Still savoring the taste of the chocolate, she headed toward the café. Zed stood up from the bench when she arrived and chuckled. "Guess you found your first Easter surprise. Wyatt put it out there about fifteen minutes ago and then drove away. I reckon he's havin' to come to terms with all this."

"I reckon so."

Zed dropped his cigarette into a cigarette-disposal thing that looked like a pipe stuck down in a milk bucket. He opened the door for her and switched on the lights as soon as he was inside.

She stopped and giggled, despite herself, at the sight of four big baskets filled with candy and all kinds of surprises lined up on the table.

"Uncle Zed, that is the sweetest thing." Harper hugged him. "But you shouldn't have. I didn't get you a single thing for Easter. And when on earth did you manage to get all that stuff?"

His face fairly well lit up the whole place in a big grin at her surprise. "Yeah, you did. You are here and that's what Annie wanted, so it's the best Easter present in the whole world. I go to town on Sunday night after we close up every week to get my weekly supply of cigarettes and my bottle of blackberry wine. Annie was partial to that when we ran out of elderberry wine. While I'm there, I been droppin' in to Walmart to get the stuff for the baskets. Go on and open yours up. There's a little bottle of Jack down in the bottom, because I know you like it." He winked.

"I threw my last bottle at the wall in a fit of anger and busted it all over the place," she admitted as she tore into the basket and ate a chocolate egg.

"Guess that's why you needed cleaner from Flora, right?"

Her head bobbed, and it took three swallows to get the chocolate to go down past the lump forming in her throat. "I'll never get to make a basket for her, Uncle Zed."

"Maybe someday you'll have another baby and you can make Easter baskets for that one." He walked away from the coffee machine and threw an arm around her shoulders.

"I don't deserve another baby."

"Maybe you deserve one even more. You were wise enough to realize you were too young to make a good home for the one you had." He hugged her even tighter and then went back to the business of making coffee.

Harper wanted to believe Zed, she really did, but she'd lived with the guilt so long that it was impossible.

✦❈❈❈✦

"Easter baskets!" Tawny squealed when she arrived. "Who did this? Brook?"

"Nope, Uncle Zed did." Harper wrapped the

207

long strings of an apron around her waist a couple of times and tied it in the front. She shoved an order pad and pen in one pocket and set about making sure all the napkin dispensers were filled.

Zed's head poked through the window. "The purple one is for you, Tawny. Yellow for Dana, pink for Brook."

"Mine is red and it's in the kitchen, so y'all won't steal my little bottle of Jack that Zed tucked in," Harper said.

Tawny carefully removed the cellophane and folded it, hugged the purple bunny to her chest, and then kissed it on the nose. "You can keep that. Look at all this chocolate! Man, I'm going to gain ten pounds and I don't even care." Tawny ran from the dining area to the kitchen and wrapped Zed into a bear hug that almost knocked his frail body on the ground. "I love you, Uncle Zed. I haven't had an Easter basket since I was a little girl. The last one might have been back when we got to come here one year for spring break."

"Yep, you were five, and Dana had just gotten out of high school the year before. Annie was afraid she'd be offended by an Easter basket, but I insisted that we make her one anyway." Zed grinned.

"You have a sense of fairness about you that I love."

"Just the way my mama taught me to be." His smile got even wider. "Now I got to get breakfast goin'. You get on out there and eat up some of that chocolate to keep you from starvin' before I get it cooked up."

"You ain't goin' to have to twist my arm to do that. Is that cinnamon rolls I smell in the oven?"

"It's Easter. That's the special thing for today," Zed said. "We won't have a lot of customers until dinner, and then they'll all flock in here like ducks on the lake for their blue-plate special."

Tawny was taking each item out of her basket and setting it on the table when Dana and Brook arrived. She and Harper both giggled when Brook's hand clamped over her mouth and she did a little dance right inside the café.

"Easter baskets!" Her squeals bounced off the walls. "Look how big they are. Is the pink one mine? Who made them?"

Zed came out of the kitchen and leaned on the counter. Tawny loved the expression on his face when Brook grabbed up the one with her name on it. It was the happiest she'd seen him since before Granny Annie passed on. She started to tear up but swallowed hard and kept it at bay. Zed needed a happy day, and she'd do her best to give him one.

She raised her voice to get over Brook's squeals as she found her bunny and treats. "Uncle Zed did that for us. Pretty special, huh?"

"I'm going to name my bunny Miss Jo after Granny," Brook yelled even though Dana was right beside her. "And look at all this chocolate and Peeps. I love Peeps."

"Uncle Zed, this is too much," Dana said. "But I love you for doing it. You and Granny made the last one I had, but I was already out of high school at that time. Thank you so much."

"You girls sure make an old man feel good this mornin'. Happy Easter to the bunch of you," he said and then went back to work.

<hr />

The other shoe was going to fall any minute. Dana's life was living proof that it would. The morning had started off beautifully, with the baskets designed special for each of them and then the gooey, hot cinnamon rolls straight from the oven. But good things did not last forever.

Her last job had proven that beyond the old proverbial shadow of a doubt. She'd thought that she'd stay on the ranch until Brook graduated from high school, but everything fell apart on Valentine's Day when the boss's wife came out to her apartment with the pink slip.

"You've got two weeks to get out," she'd said.

"Why?" Dana was so shocked that one word was the limit that morning.

"Two reasons. You are stealin' from us and you've been sleepin' with my husband," her boss, Linda, had said.

"I am not," she'd argued.

"I believe you are, and I will not ever give you a recommendation for another job. I just want you and that kid of yours gone." Linda had spun around and stormed back to the house.

It didn't take long to figure out that she was the scapegoat for a crooked foreman who was the real culprit, but he was Linda's cousin, so she'd never believe that he would do something like rustle a few cattle or take kickbacks from an artificial breeder. And the bit about Dana sleeping with a sixty-eight-year-old man was ridiculous. He was older than her father would have been if Gavin Clancy was alive. But she did find out that he was indeed cheating on Linda with a friend of hers, who'd probably passed the buck when Linda had gotten suspicious.

"Thank you, God, for Granny's love and for this job and house," she whispered as she raised her eyes toward the ceiling.

"Hello, Dana." A masculine voice came from the front of the store.

She had a definite new spring in her step as she rounded the end of the minnow tank, expecting to see Payton bringing in a new bait supply. But it was Marcus standing in front of the counter with a big smile on his face.

"Happy Easter. Are you going to put these chocolate bunnies on sale? If you do, save them all for me to take home to my mother. She loves them," he said with a heavy wink.

"Hadn't planned on dropping the price on them. There's only about ten left, and they'll probably go today." She'd buy them at full price and take them to the house before she sold them to him. No way would she encourage him to flirt with her or with Tawny. Good Lord! He was graduating from high school when Tawny was in first grade.

"I thought I'd enjoy my quiet time a lot more than I am. I actually miss my cat and my mother, so I'm checkin' out early and goin' on home this mornin'. I called Mama and told her that I'd take her to church and we'd go eat at her favorite little Mexican place after services. I asked Tawny if she'd like to join us, but she said she had to work," he said. "Did you have a talk with her, Dana?" His tone was far from friendly.

"I told her the same thing I told you. There's too much of an age difference." She felt like she was stepping into the role of Tawny's mother instead of a sister, and she didn't like it at all.

"I'd say that's for her to decide." Marcus tilted his chin up a notch.

"Probably, but it's my right to express my opinion. I've got work to do, if you'll excuse me," she said.

Marcus's mouth set in a firm line, and his eyes went cold. "Mama always said that you'd turn out as wild as your mother and that your grandmother got crazy after her husband died.

212

I guess she had that brain tumor for years."

Dana had visions of drowning him in the minnow tank and then burying his body back in the wooded area behind the house. Harper would help her for sure and probably Tawny, too, even if she still thought that Marcus had mesmerizing blue eyes.

"You want to say that to Uncle Zed?" Dana said through clenched teeth.

"I hear that Zed was the reason she quit going to church," Marcus said.

"Enough." Dana put up a palm so close to his face that she could feel his breath. "Granny Annie had wings and a halo and walked on water, so please just go."

Marcus took a step back. "I'm just statin' facts that you already know. I'll be seein' you around." He spun and left the store in a hurry.

His car had barely gotten out of sight when Tawny popped into the store. "Was that Marcus leaving? He checked out early with a song and dance about not wanting his mother or cat to spend the holiday alone. Was he in here asking you to go to church with them?"

Dana shook her head slowly. "He's stinging because we've both turned him down and slinging insults at Granny and me because of it."

"That son of a bitch," Tawny fumed. "Is he crazy? No one talks smack about Granny Annie and lives to see the light of day. I'll get some concrete blocks, and we'll sink his sorry ass in the middle of the lake."

"This from the sister who thought his eyes were pretty?" Dana's tone was edgy, but she needed a good solid fight to ease her anger. They'd only vowed to be nice when Zed was around, and he was in the café.

"They'll be even prettier as they bug out when we throw his body over the edge of a boat. What'd he say about you?"

Dana shrugged. "That his mama figured I'd turn out wild like my mother. Nothing I haven't heard before."

She'd never overcome the fact that she was a bastard child—not in that area of Texas where everyone knew everything about everyone and didn't mind shouting it from the rooftops. Her two sisters might have a bitchy mother, but at least they'd had both parents.

Shame on you! Granny had told her when she'd whined about the same thing when she was fourteen. *You've got beauty, brains, and a family. I won't hear you feelin' sorry for yourself.*

"That settles it. We'll drown his cat with him." The anger in Tawny's statement brought her back to reality.

It started as a weak giggle and developed into full-fledged laughter that Dana couldn't control. "What'd the cat do?" she said between hiccups.

"It had the misfortune of belonging to him,"

Tawny said. "Next time he wants to come to our cabins, I'm going to infest his sheets with bedbugs. I'll figure out where I can buy them online."

A cold chill chased down Dana's spine. "He's one of Brook's teachers. You don't think he'd be ugly to her in class because we both rejected him, do you?"

Tawny's eyes went to slits. "That had better never happen, or else the next time the drug dogs come around, they'll find a bag of pot in his desk."

"You wouldn't!" Dana gasped.

"He'd best leave my niece alone is all I got to say." Tawny picked up a bag of chips. "Put this on my bill. I need something salty to combat all that wonderful chocolate and those cinnamon rolls. And I might want to scratch your eyes out most of the time, Dana, but believe me, when it comes to Brook, I will go the distance with you."

"Thank you," Dana said sincerely. "So you still wouldn't go the distance *for* me?"

"Depends on what or who we are fighting," Tawny said as she left.

Tawny had only been gone a couple of minutes when Payton came in with a cartload of minnows and bait for the refrigerator. "Happy Easter," he called out as he backed inside the store. "Looks like it's goin' to be a lovely day to hide eggs for children. I miss doing that for my daughter. You got any little kids?"

215

"My daughter is fourteen," Dana answered. "A little too old to hunt eggs, but she still likes to get an Easter basket."

He dumped an order of minnows into the tank. "I got a lot of extra hugs this mornin' when my daughter saw her basket in the car. I don't know if she really loves me or if she loved those half a dozen gift certificates to her favorite restaurants."

Dana craned her neck around to see if he wore a wedding band, but his hands were covered by the cart. Surely a guy that sexy and with those eyes had a wife. When he brought her a ticket, she heaved a visible sigh of relief to see that there wasn't even an imprint of a ring on his left hand.

"Did the husband come with you to the lake?" he asked as he peeled the top copy of the ticket off for her to keep.

"Divorced for more than ten years," she answered.

"Widowed for more than ten years," he said.

"I'm sorry." She looked up into his eyes. "So you raised your daughter alone?"

"Yep, my parents were gone and I'm an only child, so I didn't have any support. But we managed to make it through her teenage years without too much damage to either of us," he chuckled.

"Got any secrets you want to share?" she asked.

"Lots of them. Even got the ten rules of dating my daughter written down. I'll be glad to share

216

them if you'll go to dinner with me some time," he said. "Like maybe tomorrow night after you finish up here? I could pick you up at seven thirty."

She meant to shake her head, but she nodded. "I'll be ready."

"Good. I'll see you then. And I'll bring a copy of those rules with me."

When his delivery truck pulled away, she slid down the back of the counter and put her hands over her eyes. She hadn't dated in so long that she might have to drag out a manual on how to act on a date after the age of thirty.

Chapter Twelve

The evening was pleasant enough that Harper didn't even need a jacket, so she poured a shot of her Easter whiskey and carried it to the porch. The café had been a madhouse since lunch. She and Zed had managed to squeeze out thirty minutes to eat and then folks who'd rented cabins began to filter through wanting burgers and fries.

Her feet hurt and both her body and soul were worn out from the emotional upheaval of the previous two days. The first sip of whiskey slid down her throat, warming everything it touched all the way to her stomach. The second tingled but wasn't nearly as hot.

She'd finished the last sip when Wyatt drove up in front of her cabin with the boat behind his truck. In a few seconds, he was sitting on the porch, stretching his long legs out in front of him. He nodded toward her, and she did the same. It wasn't awkward or even uncomfortable, but rather peaceful having him there and knowing that she wasn't carrying the burden alone anymore.

"I wasn't expecting you," she said.

"Got things done and thought I'd stop by," he answered. "So how was your day?"

"Busy," she said. "But I like busy days. It helps it go by faster."

"Want to go out on the boat for a little while to relax?"

She'd love to, but should she? Would it be opening up something like Pandora's box? She weighed the pros and cons. It didn't have to be anything serious like a date, and she would love to feel the night breeze off the lake.

She pushed up out of the chair. "Do I need shoes?"

"Not if I do this." He got to his feet, crossed the porch in two steps, and picked her up like a bride.

Her arms looped around his neck, and she laid her head on his chest. His heart thumped almost as fast as hers. There was so much heat surrounding them that she scarcely even felt the chilly gravel on her feet when he set her on the ground long enough to open the truck door. When she was settled and the seat belt was fastened, he quickly made his way to slide in behind the steering wheel.

He grinned. "This will be kind of like when we 'borrowed' "—he made air quotes around the last word—"that old boat and rowed to that secluded place."

The twinkle in his eyes and his dimples when he smiled had not dimmed in the past ten years. "That was the last time I saw you. After you left and I tried to call, all I got was a message that the number was no longer in service. So I wrote a dozen letters to the address you gave me," he said.

"My mother shut down my cell phone, and the unwed mothers' home where they sent me was unlisted. They didn't let us call out otherwise. If I could've, I don't know what I might have said. Lord, Wyatt, we were barely old enough to make a baby. And I never got a single letter. My mother probably shredded them. But I'm glad to know that you tried to get in touch," she said.

He expertly backed the boat down off the ramp, got it into the water, and then carried her off the end of the dock into knee-deep water. When he lifted her over the side and set her down, she noticed a cooler but no fishing equipment. In only a few minutes, he'd tied the boat firmly to a post, unhitched it, and driven his truck up to the parking area.

"You sure know your business around a ramp better than you did back then," she said when he was sitting beside her.

He fired up a trolling engine and guided them around the shoreline until they came to the same wooded area where they'd spent their last night together. The boat had rocked so hard that night as they made love that she just knew it would capsize and all her clothing would float away.

Made love, she thought. *Was that what we were doing? Maybe it was just satisfying raging hormones.*

"I hope so, since I make a living at fishin' these days. But I got to admit, every time I bring a bunch of guys to this spot, I always remember that last night we were together," he said.

"I haven't been to this spot since then," she said. "It's a wonder we didn't drown that night."

A couple of blankets and two pillows came out of nowhere. He spread out one on the floor of the boat and tossed the pillows toward one end. "Let's just lie here for a while. Imagine that you are givin' me my share of that load on your shoulders."

She stretched out on one side of the blanket. With a foot of space between them, he laced his fingers with hers.

"Look at that moon and all those stars. Makes me feel like my problems are small when I look at them," she whispered.

"It looks like the Hope Diamond lyin' on a bed of black velvet. And all the stars are small diamonds scattered around it," Wyatt said. "My fishermen would throw me in the lake if they heard me sayin' sissy stuff like that. You are the only woman I've ever felt like I could be myself with."

"Me too," she whispered.

"Okay, then, let's celebrate." He opened the cooler and brought out a bottle of Jack. "A shot to loosen us up. I want you to tell me your funniest bartending story."

"Only if you'll tell me your favorite fishin' story." She sat up, took the bottle from him, uncapped it, took a swig, and handed it back. "And you go first."

He tipped up the bottle and took two gulps, then put the cap back on before he scooted over to prop his back against the side of the cabin cruiser. "This happened just a few months ago. Your grandmother and Zed were in a really big argument. I got here on Friday night, and there was so much ice between them that not even hell's fire could melt it."

She sat up and propped her back against the cooler. "You are kiddin' me. I never saw them even have a cross word."

He did the same and pulled the extra blanket up over them. "Lookin' back, I think it might have been because they'd just found out about her sickness and he wanted her to have treatments," Wyatt said. "But to get on with the story, she booked me to take her fishin' the next Monday. I told her that I didn't go fish with fewer than four men, because it wasn't worth my time to just take one."

"Bet that went over like a roach in the punch bowl," Harper said.

"She said that she'd double my rate, but she wanted to be on the water at daybreak and she damn sure wasn't comin' back to the resort until after dark. So I got the bait and enough food ready for the whole day and picked her up at five that Monday morning. She didn't catch a single fish all mornin'."

"And that's funny why?"

"I'm gettin' to it," Wyatt said. "She reached in that big black purse that she carries and brought out a Jerry Clower CD and told me to put it in the player on the boat. I did, and he told the story about a guy who'd gone fishin' with the game warden. Claude Ledbetter was the fellow's name, and the way the story went . . . well, dammit, to get the full effect, you've got to hear it. She gave me that CD when we finished the day, and I've played it dozens of times when my fishermen aren't gettin' bites."

Harper had heard the whole CD many times and it always made her laugh, but she couldn't fathom why that would be his funniest fishing story. So Granny gave him a CD and they thought the comedian was a hoot.

"You must have had some boring trips if that's your funniest one," Harper said.

"Patience, darlin'. A good story starts out with 'Once upon a time.' That part was just the beginning. Miz Annie and I listened to the story about Claude throwin' dynamite into the river at least three times, and I laughed harder every time even though I knew what was going to happen after that first time. Now, go back to that old black purse that Annie carried. Well, she reached

223

inside it and brought out a stick of dynamite and one of Zed's cigarette lighters."

"No!" Harper gasped.

"I told her that she couldn't do that, that we'd both wind up in jail, but she lit the damn thing and handed it to me. I can still see her face when she said, 'You goin' to argue with me or are you goin' to fish?' just like Claude asked that game warden when he gave him that stick of dynamite."

"What did you do?" She could picture him holding a stick of lit dynamite and Granny sitting there with her purse by her side and a fishing pole in her hand.

"I threw it as hard as I could," he said.

"What happened then?"

He shrugged. "I gave thanks that there were no game wardens or other boats on the lake that evening. And then gathered up enough bass and catfish that they almost sank my boat."

Harper clamped her hand over her mouth. "Sweet mother of God, did y'all wind up in jail?"

"No, but we did take all that fish back behind the café and Zed had to clean them. The next day's blue-plate special was fried catfish. All you can eat."

"Did they get over their argument?"

"I asked her about that the next day, and she said that Zed made a deal with her. If she'd never use dynamite to fish again, he wouldn't fuss at

224

her about anything else. I didn't know that she was sick. Now your turn," he said.

"My brain is still reelin' from your story. I wonder where she even got that stick of dynamite."

"I didn't ask, but you might tell Dana that there could be more hidden away in the house," Wyatt said. "Did you always work in bars?"

"Since I was twenty-one. Before that I worked in an animal shelter. My funniest story was about old Barney Bailey out in Amarillo, though."

"Does it involve explosives?"

"Not really, but three guys might still think that they were hit with a bomb," she answered.

"I'm listenin'." He draped an arm around her shoulders and drew her closer.

"Barney would come into the bar and get plastered the first day of every month. I'd call a cab for him because he didn't have a car. He always sat on the end stool and told me stories if it was a slow evening."

"Did you have many slow nights?" Wyatt asked.

"Busiest times in a college bar is weekends. But if the first day of the month fell on a weeknight, things were calmer."

"Why?" Wyatt asked.

"Because that's when folks usually got paid or got their retirement checks," she said. "But this time it fell smack on a Saturday night, and the bar was full of wild college kids. So there's old Barney nursing another whiskey and Coke when it was nearly closing time. Minding his own business until three smart-ass young guys started pickin' on him. I told them to leave him alone, but he held up a hand and grinned at me."

She could still see Barney in those khaki shorts he wore year-round, white tube socks that came up to his knees, and combat boots. His T-shirts varied depending on the concert or ball game he'd attended recently. His old camouflage jacket had seen decades of wear, but his name tag above the pocket was still legible.

"Thought they were tough guys, didn't they?"

"Oh, yeah, they did." She described the little short guy to Wyatt and then went on. "One of them pushed him, and he fell off the bar stool. He dusted his shirt off and stumbled to his feet. I can still see the glimmer in his eyes when he said, 'Boys, let's take this outside. I don't want to mess up Miss Harper's floor.' They laughed at him and swaggered outside with Barney staggerin' along behind them."

"This was supposed to be a funny story," Wyatt said.

"Wait for the end." She smiled and went on. "He told me to call 911 as he left, and I was terrified. He'd lost his wife on the first day of the month years before and that was a tough day for him every single month. I was afraid that he wanted to die."

"What happened?" Wyatt asked.

"I called 911 and was on my way to the back door to see if he was all right, but he met me and went right back to his favorite bar stool. Other than bloody knuckles, there wasn't a mark on the old guy."

The look on Wyatt's face was one of total disbelief. "Are you kiddin' me?"

"Nope, that's my funny story, and before you say that it's not funny, think about it," she told him.

"Kind of like Zed says sometimes. 'That's not funny—but it is'?" Wyatt nodded. "What happened to those boys?"

"The ambulance gathered up those three guys and took them to the hospital, where they told a story about a gang of thugs attacking them as they were leaving. No way were they ever going to admit that old Barney had beat the crap out of all three of them. At once."

Wyatt chuckled. "Did they ever pick on him again?"

"Nope, they cut a wide swath around him from then on. I couldn't believe they even came back to the bar. When I asked him why he'd done it, he said that sometimes folks have to learn things the hard way. His words come back to haunt me pretty often, because I'm one of those people."

"No, darlin', you aren't. You just endured a lot of hard knocks in life, but you've eaten your toad frog." He kissed her on the forehead.

"Toad frog?"

"It's one of your granny Annie's sayin's. She said that if you get up every morning and eat a toad frog, then the rest of the day has to be better. You've had your toad frog and now it's time for you to be happy." Wyatt found her hand under the blanket and gave it a gentle squeeze.

✦⊹⊱◈⊰⊹✦

Zed quickly snuffed out the cigarette in his hand so that the red glow wouldn't attract attention. Wyatt carried a barefoot Harper to the door, set her down, and then brushed a real sweet kiss across her lips.

"Do you want to come in?" she whispered.

"No, it's late and you have to get up early."

She reached up and touched his cheek.

"I'll be back tomorrow night, if that's okay," he said.

"I'll look forward to it." She smiled. "But wait, I've promised to stay with Brook while Dana goes out with Payton," she said.

"Any reason why I can't babysit with you?" he asked.

The boy was persistent. A good sign in Zed's book.

"Not one I can think of, but it could be a boring evening," she said.

"Time spent with you could never be boring." He kissed her, this time on the forehead. "See you about seven thirty, then?"

"I'll be at the house, not here." She waved.

Zed waited until the truck and boat were completely out of sight, and then he made his way around the back of the café to his place. He removed his jacket and hung it on the coatrack inside the door and headed to the bathroom for a shower.

"It's lookin' good, Annie. She looked right happy tonight when he brought her home. It was so sweet the way he carried her from the truck to the porch because she was barefoot. Brought back some memories for sure."

He adjusted the shower water and put all his dirty clothing into the hamper as he removed each piece. Then he had a coughing fit that left him hanging onto the vanity for support. "I swear, them cigarettes is goin' to kill me just like you said they would. Sometimes I just wish they'd get on with it."

Chapter Thirteen

I'm too old for a babysitter. Cassidy is keeping kids and she's my age, so why do I have to have a sitter?" Brook was arguing with her mother when Harper poked her head in the back door that evening.

"Hey, I'm not babysitting you. Tawny might be, but not me. I want you to meet Wyatt. You can tell me what you think of him," Harper said. "He'll be here in about half an hour. I thought we might build us a bonfire in the backyard and roast some marshmallows to make s'mores with. What do you think?"

"You aren't foolin' me." Brook crossed her arms over her chest. "But I would like to meet your Wyatt. Does he have a friend we could fix up Tawny with? Then there could be three men that I'm determined not to like."

Tawny came into the house without knocking. "I heard what you said, Brook. We're paddling the same boat. No one will ever be good enough for you in my eyes, either. And I don't need Harper to fix me up with men. God Almighty, girl! Can't you just see what she'd haul in for me?"

Brook's frown ended, and a smile split her face. "But she could bring in the man who is your soul mate."

"Like Ryson is Cassidy's?" Tawny asked.

Brook shook her head. "Don't try to throw me off the subject. And Cassidy just has a crush on him. He's not her soul mate. I do feel sorry for him because he doesn't have a good life at home, and the day after that drug thing, he came to school with a black eye and a bloody lip. Cassidy said that his mama beat on him with a belt because he lost that bag of pot."

"What ever happened with that? Did the police do anything?" Harper asked.

"Don't know. He didn't get expelled. Cassidy said there were too many fingerprints on the bag to even get it processed, and since no one could prove where it came from, well . . ." She shrugged.

"Does Flora know about this crush?" Harper asked.

"Cassidy really likes him, but I'm sworn to secrecy, because Flora would have a fit. His mama is white, but his daddy is black. He kind of looks like he's Hispanic, but, well, it's a problem with Flora, I guess," Brook whispered.

"Uncle Zed's mama was half white, and Flora doesn't hate him," Tawny said.

"Yep, old people are strange," Brook said. "But I'm still not going to like Mama's new man, Aunt Tawny."

The doorbell rang, and Dana opened it wide. "Come on in and meet my sisters and daughter."

Payton's blue button-down shirt matched his

eyes perfectly, and his blond hair was slicked back into a short ponytail. His jeans hugged his body and stacked up over alligator cowboy boots. He handed her a bouquet of red roses.

"Oh, Payton, red roses are my favorite." She sank her nose into the roses and inhaled deeply. "And they even smell like roses. I love them."

"They can't come close to matching the aroma all around this house or the beauty of the first rosebushes of spring . . . or you," he said.

"Well, thank you. Now introductions." She blushed as if she'd just remembered that there were other people in the room. "This is Harper and that's Tawny, my sisters. And this is my daughter, Brook."

His hand shot out toward Brook first, and his smile lit up the whole room. "I'm pleased to meet all of you. Has anyone told you that you look a lot like your mother?"

"Of course." Brook dropped his hand. "Her curfew is eleven o'clock, and if she's not home by then, I will text her every five minutes. So I'd advise you not to be late."

"Yes, ma'am. And I will promise to walk her to the door," Payton said seriously. "Harper?" He shook hands with her and then turned around. "Tawny? Pleased to make y'all's acquaintance. Now if you're ready, Dana, our reservations are in thirty minutes. You look stunning tonight."

Brook rolled her eyes toward Harper, who had to

bite her lip to keep from giggling. Dana frowned at Brook, and Harper covered the escaping laughter with a cough.

Finally, Dana and Payton were out of the house, and Brook threw herself on the sofa with a loud moan. Harper couldn't contain it any longer and her laughter echoed off the walls.

"What's funny?" Brook asked but didn't wait for an answer. "Mama wouldn't let me leave the house with a boy if he had a ponytail like that. And did you see the way he looked at her? Like he was the Big Bad Wolf and she was Little Red Riding Hood. Like he couldn't wait to get her into a motel room. Well, I'll tell you one thing—they aren't sleepin' in this house together. Not while I'm here. Oh. My. God!" She sat up with a jerk. "What if she gets pregnant?"

"Talk about role reversal," Tawny laughed.

Harper sat down beside Brook and patted her on the shoulder. For the first time, she realized that raising a daughter wouldn't have been all sweet-smelling baby powder and cute little pink ruffles. "When was the last time your mama went out on a date?"

Brook jumped up and paced the floor. "Two years, and I didn't like him, either. I'm tryin' to remember if she's takin' the pill."

"Good grief, girl! Give your mama some credit. She's not stupid," Harper said.

"And this is a first date. He won't get lucky that fast," Tawny said.

Brook flopped back down on the sofa and put her head in Harper's lap. "Raisin' parents is so hard."

"You are doin' a good job." Harper toyed with Brook's thick hair, twisting a few strands into a tiny braid. "Me and Tawny didn't do too well with our parents."

The doorbell rang, and Brook hopped up. "Maybe she's changed her mind."

But Dana didn't come into the house when Tawny beat Brook to the door. No, sir. Dana did not fall down on her knees and tell Brook that she'd been right about Payton. It was Zed on the porch, with a pumpkin pie in his hands.

"Come right in, Uncle Zed. We were thinkin' of making a fire in the backyard and havin' s'mores. You want to join us?" Tawny asked.

"I was just bringin' over this pie that we had left over today. Thought maybe y'all might like a little snack tonight. And besides, it's startin' to rain, so you won't be buildin' no fire tonight." Zed handed the pie off to Tawny.

"Well, you can come on in and have popcorn or pie with us and we'll play Pictionary." Brook crossed the floor and got him by the hand. "And besides, I want to know where you got them green eyes." She led him to the rocking chair.

"From my mama, child. She had those light eyes from her daddy, who was white, you remember," Zed answered honestly. "And what is this Pictionary thing?"

"It's a game, and you'll be good at it. I hear someone driving up. I bet it's Wyatt. I'm not going to like him any better than Mama's date," she whispered.

"And why's that?" Zed asked.

"Because there's been enough change in my world for a while," she said.

"Change is good for us," Zed said. "And you be nice to Wyatt. He could wind up bein' your uncle someday, and you'd regret bein' ugly."

"I can stand an uncle better than a stepdad," she whispered.

"One thing at a time. One date don't make a stepdad or an uncle." Zed grinned.

"Hey, Zed." Wyatt waved at the door. "This is Brook, right? I've already met Tawny."

Brook nodded. "You any good at Pictionary?"

"I could whip you standin' on my head and cross-eyed, little girl," he answered.

"In your dreams, smart aleck. You are on!" she said. "Uncle Zed is on my team. Aunt Harper is on yours and Aunt Tawny is the scorekeeper and the referee. What's the stakes?"

"A dollar a game." Wyatt pulled a bill out of his pocket.

Zed did the same and handed it to Tawny. "I

hope you know what you are doin', child, 'cause I ain't never played this before."

"I've seen you doodle. We're goin' to whip their butts," Brook laughed.

Bad boys or blonds had never appealed to Dana. Maybe it was because of her mother's history, but whatever the reason, she'd always leaned toward dark-haired guys who were superconservative. But that night she kept sliding glances across the console of the Lincoln, and delicious little shivers chased down her spine every time. With the angles of his face and that straight nose, he could easily be a cover model for the romance books that she liked to read.

"I hope you like authentic Mexican food," he said.

"It's my favorite," she answered truthfully. "And right behind that is Italian."

"What's third?"

"Anything that Uncle Zed makes."

"I've got reservations at a Mexican place tonight, but I'll remember the other two for future dates."

A man who would remember her likes. That put an extra kick in her heartbeat, especially when she thought about the idea of a second and maybe even a third date.

He kept time with the country music on the

radio. "You can change the channel if you like."

"Don't mess with something that isn't broken. I'm a country music fan, but if you don't mind, I'll turn it up a little." She hit the button to raise the volume.

"Not a bit, but I love the sound of your voice, so please keep it low enough that I can hear you."

A slow heat started at her neck. "Is that a pickup line?"

"No, it's the truth. Your voice is like warm honey with just a few drops of good Tennessee whiskey to cut the sweet. You could read the dictionary to me and I'd be in a trance the whole time."

No one had ever said anything that romantic to her, not even her ex during the time they dated. But she wasn't going there tonight. That had been the most painful time of her life, compounded by the lies she'd told surrounding it, because she didn't want to be like her mother.

"That is definitely a line," she whispered, "and I'm changing the subject. How long have you been in this fish-and-bait business?"

Dana had learned the hard way how to read men—to know if they were interested in a one-night fling or if they were shooting her a line. She hoped that she wasn't letting those sexy blue eyes lead her into a rabbit hole when she decided that he was one of the good guys out there, one of the few sincere, decent ones left.

"Since my wife died. Alison needed a full-time parent. I had a degree in marine biology and worked for a lab, so I just turned it around and started growing minnows and making my own brand of bait. It took about a year for the business to take off, but now it's big enough that I have three full-time employees. At least I did until my delivery guy quit. I don't think I'm going to hire anyone to replace him. I kind of like doin' that part of the business," he answered. "What about you?"

"Been in the horse-training business most of my working life, but now I'm helping my sisters run the resort," she answered.

He parked in a crowded restaurant lot and turned to face her. "So do you like your job?"

"The jury is still out. I miss the horses and ranch life, but I love the idea that I'm keeping Granny's legacy alive and going," she answered.

"Plus, it's a good place to raise your daughter," he threw over his shoulder as he got out of the truck.

With his long stride, it only took a few seconds before he opened the door for her and held out his hand to help her slide out. She'd worn a flowing skirt with swirls of color and a matching knit cotton shirt. She was glad that she wasn't wearing high heels when her sandals hit the ground. For one thing, the heels would take a beating in the gravel parking lot, and the other was because the

238

electricity flowing from his hand to hers would have knocked her off balance for sure.

He kept her hand tucked into his and slowed his pace to match hers as they made their way to the restaurant. He bypassed a long line extending from the hostess podium, through the foyer, and around half the building. "This is why I made reservations. We would have been standing here for hours."

"Judging from the line, it must be a good place." She was amazed that she even had a voice, the way his touch kept sending little heat bursts through her body. It must be because she hadn't dated in so long—two or three years—that he was having that effect on her. Or maybe that little ponytail and his swagger gave him the bad-boy air.

"It's my favorite," he said.

"Do you bring all your first dates here?"

He squeezed her hand as they went through the foyer and into the restaurant. "Of course I do. Aren't we here?"

It was a vague answer, but then, she'd been fishing in waters that were none of her business. She could feel every woman in line, plus the hostess, sizing him up, so there was no way this could be him just getting back into the game now. And it was a first date for them, so she had absolutely no right to be jealous—but she was, and more than a little bit.

The hostess seated them at a corner table for

two and gave them two menus. "Carrie will be your waitress tonight. Have a lovely evening."

"Thank you." Payton picked up the menu, ran a finger down one side, and then laid it aside. "I don't know why I even look at it. I always order the same thing. The sampler platter with extra rice, because I can never make up my mind between enchiladas, tacos, or quesadillas."

She didn't even open the menu, but nodded. "Then that's what I'll have, too. Are their margaritas good?"

"Very, and they go down smooth with the Mexican food."

"Then that's what I want."

"So how long were you married?" he asked.

"How long were you?" she shot back, not wanting to lie, but not willing to tell the absolute truth.

"Fifteen years. My daughter was fourteen when her mother died. That's about Brook's age, right? Alison is twenty-four now, second year of teaching biology here in Tyler."

"I met Brook's father on the first ranch I worked at. He boarded some of his prize stock with us, and the owner of the ranch assigned me to take care of them. We lived together for a while and then I got pregnant. It's complicated."

He reached across the table and laid a hand over hers. "Life is, but we don't have to go into that tonight."

"We were never really married," she blurted out and wished she could stuff the words right back into her mouth. "He was divorced, and he'd vowed he'd never marry again. I thought he'd change his mind when the baby was born. He thought he could change mine about even wanting a real marriage. So we lived together for four years, and then he cheated on me one too many times. I don't know why I'm tellin' you this. Brook and my mother don't even know that."

"Sometimes talkin' to strangers is easier than friends and family. And when the time is right, you'll tell your family the whole story. I don't think Brook liked—" He stopped midsentence and waved at a tall lady coming toward them.

"Hi, kid, what are you doin' here tonight?" he asked.

"I might ask you the same question," she said as she bent to hug him.

"Dana, this is my daughter I've been tellin' you about. Alison, meet my date, Dana. Dana, my daughter, Alison," he said. "Is this your night out with the girls?"

"That's right." Alison stared at Dana without blinking. "You didn't mention that you were going out tonight."

"Nope, I didn't. Is this your sorority sisters or your teaching friends?"

"Sorority sisters. Remember, we always get a

table here once a month," she said and then asked, "So where are you from, Dana?"

"Presently, I live at the lake and run a little resort there. I hear you are a teacher." This must be the way Payton had felt when Brook gave him the third degree.

"Yes, I am a teacher. We'll talk later, Daddy. Pleased to meet you, ma'am." Alison's tone did not match the words coming out of her mouth.

"Well, I guess we've met each other's daughters. That step is over," Payton chuckled.

The waitress brought salsa and chips to the table and asked if they were ready to order. Payton nodded toward Dana.

"I'll have the sampler platter and sweet tea with a margarita on the side. Please leave the onions off everything."

"I'll have the same, only I want a bottle of beer instead of the margarita, and bring us some jalapeño poppers with our drinks," he said.

"Have your drinks and the appetizers right out," she said and was gone in a flash.

"That step?" Dana brought him back in.

"What step?" he asked.

"You said that step is over. Does that mean you see more steps?"

"Yes, I do. I like the way I feel with you, Dana. So if you're willin', I'd like for you to put me on your calendar for a second date," he said.

"How about a s'mores night on Friday evening?

If it's not rainin', we can make a bonfire." She might as well jump in with both feet and see if this tingle she'd felt was a passing thing or if it was truly something to build on.

"I'd love it," he said.

✦❊❊❊❊✦

Harper couldn't remember the last time that she'd had so much fun. Zed was a good artist, but so was Wyatt, and the giggles during the battles echoed off the walls. For a while she forgot about the past and concentrated on beating Brook and Zed in Pictionary. She glanced at the clock and was amazed to see that it was almost eleven when they heard Dana and Payton on the front porch.

"They're back!" Brook ran across the room and had her hand on the light switch when Tawny covered it with hers.

"You don't want to do that unless you want your mama to flash the lights when *you* come home from your first date," Tawny whispered.

"She wouldn't," Brook gasped.

"Turnabout is fair play," Zed cautioned.

Wyatt came in right behind him. "Do unto others."

Brook dropped her hand to her side. "Sounds like Sunday-mornin' sermons to me."

"Don't have to be in a church building to get a message from God," Zed chuckled.

Dana came into the house alone, but Harper

243

noticed that her cheeks were flushed and be damned if her lips weren't more than a little bit bee-stung, giving testimony to the fact that the date had gone very well. She kicked off her sandals and sat down on the sofa beside Brook.

"Before you ask, I enjoyed the evening. I like Payton. We laughed and talked and after dinner, we went by his fish place. It's massive. Never seen so many minnows. And we are definitely going out again." She pulled her knees up and wrapped her skirt tail around her legs.

"Did he kiss you?" Brook asked.

"Yes, he did, and I liked it," Dana answered.

"Well, crap!" Brook groaned.

"And I met his daughter at the restaurant. She came in with friends and didn't know that we were there. From the way she acted, I'd say that she didn't like me any better than you like him," Dana said.

Brook sat up straight, and her jawline went rigid. "She's an idiot. Everyone loves you, but maybe that's a sign that you shouldn't get involved."

"We're having a bonfire and s'mores party on Friday night right here, so you can all spend time around him."

Harper caught the sly wink that Zed sent across the room. "I've got all Annie's guns under lock and key."

Dana giggled. "Brook, you'll be good, won't

244

you? Because if you aren't, I will get even on your first date."

"Which is when?" Brook asked.

"When you are forty, but only if you take your mama with you. Fifty if you want to date alone," Zed teased.

"Thank you, Uncle Zed. I think that's a fine idea," Dana said.

"Double crap! I'm going to bed to think about all this stuff before I fight with any of y'all about it." Brook stormed down the hallway, but then turned around and came back to the living room. She crossed the room and hugged Zed. "Thanks, Uncle Zed, for helping me whip Wyatt three times."

She'd started down the hall again then stopped, turned, and sighed. "And thank you, Aunt Tawny and Aunt Harper, for babysitting me. And for helping keep my mind off my mama kissing that ponytail guy. Good night."

"Well, that settles it," Wyatt chuckled. "I'm not growing a ponytail."

Zed laughed with him. "Me neither. I'm too old to be a hippie. But it was a good evenin', Dana?"

"Yes, it was." She nodded.

"It's goin' to be a short night." Tawny yawned. "It was fun. Anytime you want to go out with your hippie, I'm glad to 'babysit' "—she made air quotes—"my niece. Good night, everyone." She picked up a couple of dirty glasses and carried them to the kitchen on her way out the back door.

"Us too." Wyatt offered his hand to Harper and pulled her up from the floor. "You are a good opponent, Zed. With your poker face, I wouldn't want to gamble with you."

Zed narrowed his eyes. "Smart man. I'd own your boat if we ever got serious about a poker game."

"Good night, and I'm glad that you had a good time, Dana. Brook will come around. Just give her some time," Harper said as she and Wyatt left the house by way of the front door.

<hr />

"Uncle Zed, can you stay just a little while longer? I did something stupid tonight and . . . you know what they say about two people keeping a secret?" Dana winced to hear those words coming from her mouth.

"It's easy if one of them is dead." Zed nodded.

"Well, one of us isn't dead but . . . dammit, this isn't easy."

"Then don't say it. When the time is right, it won't have to be hard."

"I never was married. I made up that story so you and Granny Annie wouldn't be disappointed in me. And when we broke up, I let everyone think I was getting a divorce instead. The rest of it is pretty true. I fell in love with him, got pregnant, and then found out he was cheating on me and ended it." She talked fast, as if she was afraid if she ever stopped, she wouldn't finish.

"Darlin' child, I'm so sorry you've been carryin' this load all by yourself. You should have told us. We would have understood. Does he take care of Brook?" he asked.

Dana shook her head. "There's no father listed on the birth certificate. I was eighteen when I went to work on the ranch and I was taking some online college courses toward a degree. He came into my life not long after that. He was a little older than I was, and we lived together but we never got married. He skipped out when Brook was just a toddler. He knocked me around a few times, but when he slapped my baby—well, I was so angry with him that I told him to get lost and never come back." Tears began to roll down her cheeks.

"And?" Zed asked.

"It was the third time he'd cheated on me that I knew about, so I kicked him out. He was so mad that he said she wasn't even his child—that he'd had surgery after his last child with his wife was born. She is his, but I was so mad, Uncle Zed, that I told him he was right and I was glad that she wasn't his. She'll see that birth certificate someday. What do I tell her?"

Her shoulders heaved with tears and pain. Zed reached across the distance with his long arm and wiped away the moisture. She grabbed his hand and held it to her cheek. Payton was right. Telling a stranger was so much easier than telling someone she loved like a grandfather.

"You tell her as much of the truth as she can bear to hear at that time. That's exactly what you'll do, but you don't have to worry about it tonight, child. Tonight you put all that sadness out of your mind and you go to bed and dream sweet dreams about this new person in your life."

She kept his hand in hers and held it on the sofa. "I don't deserve any of this. Not Granny's legacy, not Payton, not a daughter who means so much to me, not you for sure."

"That's only your opinion. Me and Annie see things different than you girls do," he said as he pulled his hand away and stood up. "Things look different in the daylight, darlin' girl. Get some sleep."

Zed sat down in a rusty old metal chair beside the door to his quarters. "Annie, my heart is broken. One of our girls couldn't tell us about the baby because she didn't want to disappoint us. The other one lied to us because of the same reason. It's humbling to feel so loved that someone don't want to bring you heartache, isn't it?"

Chapter Fourteen

Demons aren't little red creatures with a forked tail, and they don't carry a pitchfork around in their bony hands. Harper knew that for a fact. Her black cloud demon hovered over her head and followed her around as little bits of it oozed into her heart and soul. It came around again every April 4, the day she'd signed the papers to give her baby away. The day she'd walked out of the unwed mothers' home and didn't even look back.

She tried—God knew that she gave it her best—that Wednesday. She pasted on a smile and bantered with the regular customers in the café, but by the close of the day, her feet turned to lead as she made her way across the lawn to her cabin. She paced the floor and poured a triple shot of Jack and set it on the nightstand.

"I will not drink that." She stared at the amber liquid every time she passed it. "It only makes it worse. It's all closing in on me, Granny. I'm not as good as my sisters. They can run this place without me, and they deserve to split everything down the middle, not have to share it with me. I should pack up and leave."

Tears cannot drown a demon. They only make it angry. Still, Harper's cheeks flooded with tears as she sobbed that evening. Finally, she dragged a suitcase from the closet and threw it on her bed. Fight-or-flight mode had set in, and to fight with her sisters, she had to come clean with them. It was easier to run away and start again.

So you're going to let this misery inside you control you and make you leave?

"I can't fight it. It's stronger than me," she argued with the voice in her head.

But is it stronger than your sisters and Zed?

Harper picked up the suitcase and hurled it across the room. It hit the door with a bang and slung clothing all over the room. A pair of lacy underwear hung on the ceiling fan, and a bra floated down over the lamp beside her bed.

"You okay in here?" Tawny opened the door without knocking. "God Almighty, Harper. Why would someone trash your room?"

"Go away," Harper screamed and threw her stuffed Easter bunny at her sister.

Tawny caught it midair. "What's the matter with you? Are you drunk?"

"No, that won't fix anything now. It's time for me to leave. My heart doesn't want to go, but my mind says that I can't stay." Harper dropped to the floor, drew her long legs up, and leaned her head on them.

Tawny grabbed the phone and hit the button to call the house. "Dana, come quick to Harper's cabin. She's gone crazy, and I don't know what to do."

In seconds Zed, Brook, and Dana crowded into the room with Tawny. With so many people around her, it reminded Harper again of the day she put her name on those papers. There had been a roomful of strangers there when she'd signed the adoption papers giving that sweet couple the right to hold her baby, to comfort her when she was sick, to clap for her when she took her first steps.

"Open your eyes, child." Zed touched her shoulder.

"Go away," she sobbed.

Zed sat down on the floor and wrapped his arms around her. "We can't do that. I'm here for you. Always have been and always will be."

She opened her eyes enough to see Dana and Tawny sitting on the floor in front of her, and then Brook moved to her other side and her arms joined Zed's. She wasn't worthy of her sisters' care, of Zed's love, and she damn sure didn't deserve her precious niece's concern.

"How long until he gets here?" Tawny whispered.

"You can all go. I'll be fine." She shut her eyes again and rolled up into a tighter ball. There were too many people there already, and she damn sure didn't need another one smothering her almost to death.

"Five minutes," Zed answered.

"He's not kin. We should take care of her," Dana said.

"But he needs to be here," Zed whispered. "Until then we'll just sit with her."

"I'm not talkin' to a preacher," Harper muttered. "God don't give a damn about me."

"Annie would have my hide tacked to a big pine tree if I called a preacher," Zed chuckled. "But honey, don't you ever doubt that God loves you. Me and Annie found out years ago that we could worship our Lord without settin' foot in a church building."

Brook sat down on the other side of her and held her hand tightly. "Talk to me, Aunt Harper. Is this because I didn't like Payton?"

"Has nothing to do with him," Harper sobbed. The child didn't even need to be there, seeing her so vulnerable. She should be strong for her niece, but all her strength was gone.

"I'm here," a deep voice said from the doorway.

She looked up into Wyatt's eyes as her sisters, niece, and Zed filed out of the room.

"Why did you come?" Her voice sounded like it came from a deep well, but then, that's where her heart was, so it stood to reason the rest of her body would be there, also.

He picked her up off the floor and carried her to the bed. "Because Zed called me, and I'm glad he did. You do not have to do this alone ever again," he whispered into her hair as he laid her down and stretched out beside her, holding her tightly against his body. "Why is today so tough?"

252

"It hits me on her birthday and on April 4, the day I signed the adoption papers," she said between sobs. "But I don't want to run anymore. I hoped by being here it would be easier, but facing it is so hard, Wyatt."

"I know, sweetheart." His warm breath went from her ear straight to her heart and melted part of the cold darkness lurking there. "Tell me what to do."

She snuggled down even closer to his body. "Just hold me. Don't leave."

"I'm not going anywhere," he assured her.

The flashing numbers said that it was exactly five o'clock when she awoke, her legs tangled up with Wyatt's and both of them fully clothed. Panties remained on the ceiling fan, and her suitcase was right where it landed when she threw it. But it was a new day, and Wyatt was sleeping beside her. So why was that ugly black cloud still hanging right above her head?

She eased out of the bed and out the front door. Bare feet and cold, hard gravel did not make good partners, so she stepped gingerly until she reached the grass. Cool dew covered every blade, and it was like walking on a soft velvet carpet all the way to the edge of the lake. She sat down and stretched her feet out until they were in the chilly water.

A vision of the enormous church in Dallas came to her mind. The baptismal font was fancy, with a huge mural of trees and flowers behind it. She'd worn a white robe and the preacher said that she was leaving all her sins in the water and would be a new creature when she arose from it. At ten years old, she'd often wondered how the water felt holding the sins of so many people and where it went when the preacher pulled the plug and let it all go. Did it wash into the rivers, where the sin jumped on people as they swam?

At twenty-six she knew it was simply a symbolic gesture, but, as she looked out across the peaceful waters of the lake that morning, she wondered if wading out into it would wash away the pain once and for all. One of the old songs that Zed hummed and sang as he worked in the kitchen came to her mind.

The lyrics talking about laying her burdens down ran through her mind. She started humming, and before long she was singing the words, saying that she felt so much better since she'd laid her burdens down. She stood up and took the first step out into the lake. On the third step, the water was up to her knees and one of her favorite Jamey Johnson songs followed the old gospel tune. She thought of her grandmother as she sang the lyrics in her head, saying that she was telling the world goodbye and that her new life began with death. Had Harper's new life begun with her granny's death? She stopped singing when she was waist-deep in the water.

"Oh, Granny, did you die so that I could find peace?" she whispered.

Zed had just lit his first cigarette of the day and sat down on the bench outside the café when he caught a movement down near the lake. Some crazy fool was wading out into the cold water. Then the dark clouds across the moon shifted and lit up Harper's blonde hair, and he threw the cigarette on the ground and began removing his shoes. By the time he got the first one off, she was waist-deep and holding her hand up toward heaven.

"Sweet Jesus, don't let her do this," he prayed as he tugged on the laces of his second shoe. "Take me instead. I'm ready to go. I'm old and I've lived my life and I'm ready to go see my precious Annie. Don't take her now."

Then a blast of light streaked across the area in front of Harper's cabin as the door opened and Wyatt ran out. He leaned on the porch railing and looked toward the lake. Zed kicked off his second shoe and, of all the damned times in the world, had a coughing fit that kept him glued to the bench.

"Thank you, Jesus," he said when Wyatt cleared the porch and took off at a dead run toward the lake. Both arms were above his head when he reached the edge of the water. But before he could dive in, Harper turned around and made her way back to the shore. Wyatt opened his arms, and she walked out of that water straight into them.

Zed grabbed his chest and took several deep breaths. "Thank you, Jesus. Thank you for not taking her," he said between gasps. "I don't think I've ever been so scared, Annie, but we still got our girl."

He put his shoes on and went inside the café. Busying himself with making coffee and turning on the ovens, he mumbled to himself about how he'd like to put Harper in the time-out chair like Annie had done when she was a little girl. He was still fussing when she came into the café with a big smile on her face.

"Mornin', Uncle Zed," she said cheerfully.

"Don't you mornin' me, girl. You scared the hell out of me. I can't even swim and I was goin' to dive into that cold lake water to save you." His finger shook harder with each word. "You've got to stop this crap and get on with your life. You were sixteen damn years old and didn't have much choice in what happened."

"I know," she said softly. "I wasn't going to drown myself, honest. I was just thinking through a lot of things. I was hoping to find peace."

"Did it work?" He eyed her carefully to see if she was shooting him a line of bullshit.

"Won't know for sure until next year, but if Granny died so I can find peace, then I owe it to her to try."

"Yes, you do. I was prayin' hard that you wouldn't . . . well, you know," Zed said.

"So I had an angel in heaven and one still on the earth working for me." She crossed the floor and wrapped him up in a bear hug, then kissed him on the cheek. "Thank you for that."

"Seems to me like you're leavin' one out. Wyatt was ready to dive in there to save you, too." Zed glanced over her shoulder and smiled at Wyatt, who was coming through the door.

"I'm no angel, not by any stretch of the word, but I'm grateful for the two of you if it helped her at all," Wyatt said.

Harper walked away from Zed and wrapped her arms around Wyatt's neck. "He's a knight in shining armor, and I was so glad to see him standing on the shore waiting for me."

"I think she's okay now." Wyatt smiled.

"Maybe not totally, but I've got family and Wyatt to help me if I just ask. I promise I will, Uncle Zed, from now on." Zed held up a pinkie finger, and she crossed the room in a few long strides to lock her little finger with his. "I remember you doing this with us when we were kids."

With a firm grip, he kept her finger in his, his green eyes boring into hers. "If you don't ask for help, it'll be a long time in the time-out chair for you, young lady."

"I hate sitting on a chair," she said.

He unhooked his finger from hers and headed for

the kitchen. "Then remember that. Wyatt, come on back here with me while she gets the tables set up for the breakfast run."

"Y'all could raise your voices so that I can hear what you say about me," Harper said.

Zed slammed the door and turned on the radio that he kept on the cabinet. "I don't want her to hear what I got to say, and that can be her punishment for comin' nigh to givin' this old man a heart attack."

"You saw her go into the water?" Wyatt leaned against the door.

"I couldn't get my breath enough to get to her. I was so glad to see you," Zed said. "I was prayin' harder than I ever prayed before except the night that Annie passed. I wanted Jesus to heal her right then and there and let me keep her with me. I felt that kind of thing in my soul when Harper kept taking one step after another into the water. So thank you, but son, if you ever hurt her, it'll be your body they'll find floatin' in the lake."

Wyatt clamped a hand on Zed's shoulder. "I could never hurt her. I want to help her heal from all that I helped put her through. I was as much to blame as she was in what happened, and I don't know how I would have dealt with it at sixteen, but at twenty-six I just want to be here for her, Zed."

"Then do a good job of it so I don't have a damned heart attack. Jesus, Mary, and Joseph,

Annie will kick my black butt right down to hell if I let somethin' happen to one of her precious girls."

Wyatt chuckled. "Just think of what she'd do to me."

Zed shivered. "Don't want to think about that. It's too scary. You get on back out there and help her get things ready for the breakfast rush, and I'll give you your meal for free this mornin'."

"Thank you," Wyatt said. "And thanks for callin' me."

Zed nodded very seriously.

Wyatt opened the door to find three sisters and Brook squared off in the dining room, hands on hips, dirty looks shooting around like fire from sparklers on the Fourth of July. "I think maybe you'd better come on out here, Zed."

"What I think is that you better shut that door and stay on this side of it with me," Zed told him. "They got to work this out by themselves."

Wyatt eased the door shut. "What can I do to help you?"

"Stir this sausage. Keep it movin' real slow like. When they get done, they'll have worked up an appetite."

✦❖❖✦

"What in the hell is going on in here?" Dana hissed and nodded toward the closed kitchen door. "You know Uncle Zed is—"

"In the kitchen with Wyatt," Tawny finished for her and then pointed at Harper. "She tried to drown herself this morning."

Brook ran across the floor and put her arms around Harper. "Why would you do that?"

"I did not try to drown myself." Harper took a couple of steps back.

Tawny opened her hands, put them both on Harper's chest, and pushed her hard. "Yes, she did. She *started* to drown herself this mornin'." Tawny's voice got higher and shriller with each word. "I was havin' a nightmare about Granny Annie bein' in water that she couldn't get out of, so I went outside on the porch."

Harper grabbed the edge of a table to keep from falling. Her hands knotted into fists. "Don't push me, little sister, because I will push back. And I don't have to explain anything to you," she said. "You need to get your story straight before you go tellin' tales. I was only waist-deep in water, and I can swim like a fish. I wasn't even thinking of drowning myself. Give me some credit."

Dana took a few steps forward and got nose to nose with Harper. "Have you lost your mind? What happened, Tawny?"

"She was singing a song about facing death and then she walked right out into the water. Almost gave me a heart attack, but then Wyatt went runnin' down there and she turned around and walked into his arms," Tawny said.

Harper pulled out a chair and plopped down into it. "I was thinking about Granny. The song was about her, not me. I was wondering if she had to die to bring me peace."

"Peace for what?" Brook asked as she scooted a chair close enough to Harper that she could hold her hand.

"Just peace for all the hatred, anger, and guilt I have built up inside me," Harper said honestly.

"What's that got to do with me?" Dana asked.

"I've hated you so much." Harper pointed at Dana.

"Hey, now. I know we don't always get along, but *hate* is a strong word. Why would you feel that way?"

"Because you have a beautiful daughter and you kept her and raised her and you were old enough that you could marry her father."

"But—" Dana started.

Harper shook her head emphatically. "I didn't do the same thing you did. I gave my daughter away, and I go through this guilt trip every single year on her birthday and on the day that I gave her away and walked away from the girls' home. That's what it was, Tawny, not a boarding school. Mama sent me away because she was ashamed of me and because she couldn't face her friends if her daughter had a bastard child."

"I didn't send you away. Why would you hate *me?*" Tawny asked.

261

"Because you've always been the favorite who got all the breaks. Daddy wanted a son. Hell, they even gave me a boy's name. I always felt like I was just a replacement for his guilt over Dana and you were the wanted child."

Tawny plopped down in a chair, suddenly out of energy. "And you ran away from there because you didn't want to come back home and live with her?"

"I could've lived with Mother . . . maybe. But I couldn't face Granny Annie for a couple of years."

"You were only sixteen?" Brook gasped. "That's only two years older than I am."

"That's right." Harper nodded.

Dana's heart went out to her sister. If she'd been six years younger, if she'd not been out of college, if her mother had practically thrown her out, she might have done the same thing. A cold chill made its way slowly down her back, like an ice cube melting at her neck and sending little trickles inching down her spine. She could have easily been in Harper's shoes if any one of those statements had been her portion in life.

"Why didn't you tell us? Why did you wait . . . whoa! We've got a niece out there in the world?" Dana stammered.

"Her name is Emma Joanna, and I held her for an hour after she was born. Then I handed her to the nurse who took her to her adoptive parents."

Harper finally sat in a chair at the table with Tawny. "She was nine on March 30, and I signed the final papers on April 4. Then I walked out and I've been on my own ever since. And I still feel guilty about giving away my child."

"I'm so sorry." Brook stood up and then sat down in Harper's lap. "I love you, Aunt Harper, and Mama will share me with you to make it easier."

"Daddy fell apart when you disappeared. He was never the same after that." Tawny's voice was barely more than a whisper. "Believe me, I wasn't the favored one like you thought."

"Is Wyatt the father?" Dana asked.

Harper nodded.

"Holy smoke," Tawny sputtered. "Did you tell Mother or Daddy?"

"Nope. I didn't even tell the nuns at the home. I said I didn't know who the father was. There were lots of girls there who really didn't know, so it wasn't a big deal," Harper said. "Have all y'all been baptized? I was thinking of that this morning when I went down to the lake."

Brook shivered from her hair to her toes. "No, ma'am. In our church they sprinkle the babies. I can't imagine letting some man put my head underwater."

Harper wrapped her long arms around her petite niece and hugged her. "Well, I was baptized when I was ten. Mama believed in takin' us to church, not as much for the religious aspect as the social part. We got all dressed up and had to sit up straight."

"And not yawn or wiggle in the pew," Tawny said. "I remember when the preacher ducked you under the water. Part of me hoped that he drowned you."

"What does any of that have to do with today? And shame on you, Tawny," Dana said, her tone shrill.

"I felt guilty about that feelin' for years." Tawny whispered. "I thought maybe it was why you never came home from that girls' school, that you could read my mind."

"Had no idea how you felt. We were sisters, but we sure weren't friends. But anyway, the preacher said that I left my sins in the water, and I wondered if I walked out into the lake if the water would help me get rid of the guilt. I know it sounds crazy, but I feel more at peace right now than I have in ten years. So don't judge me."

<hr/>

Tawny hated confrontations. She'd let her sorry-ass boyfriend pin the majority of the rap for a drug deal on her because she didn't want to stand up to him and tell him that she wouldn't carry them in her purse.

"I've always hated both of you because you had a father and I didn't," Dana said bluntly.

"But you have a wonderful mother," Tawny said.

Dana finally slumped into a chair. "I can truthfully say that I never doubted that she loved me, but *wonderful* might be pushing the envelope quite a ways."

"Granny Lacy is . . . well, she's never grown up. I love her, and we get along real good, but she's a teenager at heart," Brook explained.

"Trust me, Dana," Tawny said. "The way I see it is that Daddy carried so much guilt about the way that he treated your mama that he allowed our mother to walk all over him. I guess in reality we all got the short end of the stick."

"Which brings us to this morning," Harper said. "So what do we do from this point forward?"

"Well, I'll tell the bunch of you one thing." Brook bounced up off Harper's lap. "If you don't start acting like family, I'm going to divorce the lot of you. Now, I'm hungry and I bet breakfast is ready, so I'm going in the kitchen. If y'all got some more fightin' to do, I don't want no part of it. And if anyone throws a punch, I'm sending Uncle Zed out here."

"Out of the mouths of babes. Sometimes they see things clearer than all the adults in the world put together." Tawny pushed the chair back. "I'm starving. All this drama has built up my appetite."

"I was wonderin' if maybe I should go down to the lake and baptize myself," Tawny said softly.

"For what?" Harper looked up at Tawny.

"Just makin' a statement." Tawny felt a tightening in her chest, but she couldn't make herself tell them about getting kicked out of college or about the drug charges or being so scared in court that she couldn't stop shaking.

Dana was so busy wrestling with what lay ahead in her own personal world that she didn't even see Harper get up or Wyatt come out of the kitchen. But a movement caught her eye, and she looked up in time to see Wyatt throw an arm around Harper's shoulders and kiss her on the forehead.

"I've got to go now, but I'll be back later. Want to go to dinner with me?"

"Maybe I'll just pack us a picnic supper, and we'll have a visit down at the edge of the lake," she said.

"That sounds good to me," Wyatt said. "See you at seven, then."

When he'd disappeared out the door, Zed came out of the kitchen. "Y'all through fightin' out here or do I have to line three time-out chairs up against the wall?"

"They're done with it," Brook answered for them. "Right, Aunt Tawny?"

"Okay, okay," Tawny said with a huff.

"Mama?"

Dana shrugged and headed over to the coffee

266

machine and poured three cups. "What a week. This is enough." She rolled her eyes toward the ceiling. "I'm expecting the rest of this month to be smooth sailin'."

"I don't think you get to tell God what to do," Zed said. "If you are lucky, he might tell you what he's goin' to do, but mostly he just likes surprises."

"Amen," all three sisters said at the same time.

Chapter Fifteen

Dana was more nervous on Friday night than she'd been when Payton picked her up for their first date. She made one more walk through the small house. Throw pillows were fluffed; no games or shoes littered the freshly swept hardwood living room floors. Bathroom was sparkling clean, with no bras or panties drying on the shower rod for the first time.

Brook and Tawny were busy helping Zed find enough dry wood to start a small blaze in the fire pit in the backyard. The last time they'd had a s'mores and hot dog roast they'd simply built a bonfire, but a drought years ago had put an end to that. When the authorities lifted the ban, Zed built a fire pit for Annie's birthday. That's what they were using tonight.

"Hey, I'm here," Harper called out as she entered the house through the back door. "Wow! Talk about organized."

"Seven wire hangers turned into skewers, and all the makings for hots and s'mores." Dana waved her hand over the table. "Where's Wyatt? You did invite him, right?"

"He's out there with Uncle Zed getting the fire started. What time does Payton get here?"

"Any minute. I'm so nervous that I'm having

severe second thoughts. In all her years, I've never brought a guy home for Brook to meet. She's never even met one on date night. I always made arrangements for her to stay with a friend." Dana stopped to straighten the already perfect pile of paper napkins.

"And what about second, third, or more dates?" Harper asked.

"Only one ever got past the third date, and after spending the night with him, I figured out real quick there would not be a fourth," she answered.

"So you haven't been celibate for the past ten years?" Harper picked up a sweet pickle and popped it into her mouth.

"Have you?" Dana asked.

"Hell, no! Can you count how many times you had to lay your wings and halo aside for the night?"

"Can you?" Again Dana answered a question with a question.

"I asked you first," Harper answered.

"More than once, less than five. Your turn," Dana said.

"More than five, less than fifty, but there were some nights when I didn't remember much the next day, so I can't be sure," she said honestly.

"Holy smoke, girl. You better get tested before you get into a serious relationship with Wyatt," Dana said.

"Already did a few months ago when I decided

I'd better get my life together. But who says I'm going to get into anything serious? No one wants damaged goods. Wyatt will move on in a few weeks or months."

"Hey, y'all, we got us a fire blazin'. And Payton is here." Wyatt poked his head in the back door. "I heard that last remark, Harper. I'm not going anywhere, and I'll prove it to you in the next few weeks or months."

"I thought he'd knock on the front door and I'd have a moment before I took him outside with Brook," Dana whispered just loud enough for Harper to hear.

"Well, plans changed." Harper winked. "Tell everyone to come on in here and get a hanger or stick, whatever they want to call it, and get busy roasting. Dana's got it all laid out."

"Will do," Wyatt said.

Harper laid a hand on Dana's arm and squeezed gently. "Just go with the flow."

Brook was the first one inside the house, and she hit the door talking. "Mama, I love this fire pit thing. Uncle Zed says we can sit around it anytime we want, but that pretty soon it'll be too hot to want a fire. Next winter when it's cold we can have marshmallow roasts around it every night." She stopped to catch her breath and then went on. "He built it with his own hands. He says that Granny Annie liked to sit out there even when it was snowing last winter and that he bundled her up in quilts. Can we do that next winter? You think we'll really get a lot of snow? Like enough to build a snowman?"

"Slow down, girl." Tawny came in behind her. "Granny Annie used to tell me that we only get so many words in a lifetime, and you're usin' up a lot of yours."

Harper handed Brook a wire skewer and a hot dog. "Don't listen to her. Granny just said that so she'd shut up. When Tawny told a story, she started with 'And on the first day God made dirt' and went through the whole history of mankind before she got to the part where some kid had caught more fish than she did that day down at the lake."

"So I tell a good story. There's nothing wrong with that," Tawny protested. "Maybe I'll be a writer someday."

"You'd probably be a good one, Aunt Tawny." Brook nodded.

Dana chuckled. "I used to pray that my baby girl wouldn't get that from you. I guess God said no." Dana turned to Brook. "And to answer your multitude of questions, yes, darlin', we can make a fire, and yes, it does snow sometimes in this area, but not every winter." She looked up to see Payton with Zed right behind him. "Hello. Welcome to my crazy world."

"Looks like a fun world. With no siblings, I got to admit I'm a little jealous of this kind of family gathering." Payton caught her eye and lit up the room with a brilliant smile.

"You'll be droppin' down on your knees and givin' thanks for your lot in life by the time this night is done." Dana's heart threw in a couple of extra beats and then settled into a seminormal rhythm.

"I doubt it." Payton reached for the last two hangers and threaded hot dogs on both of them. "You like yours burned or just browned up real nice?" He looked right into Dana's eyes, and his smile widened.

"Browned."

"Then with mustard, chili, and relish?" He took a step and their shoulders were touching. "And no onions, right?"

"How did you know that?" Harper stuck a hot dog on a wire and headed toward the back door, with a sideways wink at Dana.

"She asked for them to be left off everything at the Mexican place," he answered.

"Good job, Payton." She gave him a thumbs-up as she left.

"That's sweet that you remembered," Dana said softly. Her ex couldn't even pass one of those simple tests asking things like the significant other's favorite color or flower. But then, it wasn't right to compare apples to oranges or idiots to geniuses.

He brushed her hair away from her ear and

whispered, "I remember every single thing about that evening. It was the best time I've had in years."

She looked up to say something, but she barely had time to moisten her lips before his found hers in a scorching-hot kiss. When it ended, she leaned in for a second one and almost lost her balance before she realized that he'd taken a step back.

"I guess we'd better get on out there with the rest of them," he said hoarsely.

"Might be a good idea," she whispered, amazed that she could utter a single word.

Zed had circled the fire pit with old metal lawn chairs of every color and description. Two were left empty, side by side, which surprised Dana when she and Payton arrived. Holding the hot dog wires in one hand, he pulled out her chair from the circle and seated her before scooting his back far enough to get inside the circle. Then he held the hot dogs at just the right distance over the blaze to turn them the right shade of brown.

"What do you think, lovely lady? Is this about right?" he asked Dana.

"Looks good to me." She smiled.

"Then I'll bring it back all dressed up before you can blink twice. Want a beer or sweet tea?"

"Sweet tea and barbecue chips." She felt like a queen. Of course, it wouldn't last—all good things came to an end—but by golly, she intended to enjoy every single minute of the evening.

For maybe a minute she sat there with only Harper, who was busy making sure her hot dog was perfectly done, and then Tawny came out of the house with a full plate of food. "If you get tired of that guy, you can throw him into cabin number seven. He's a sweetheart."

"He's got a daughter two years older than you, girl. He's old enough to be your father," Dana said.

"Maybe I've got a daddy complex." Tawny bit into her hot dog and groaned.

Dana stole a chip from Tawny's plate. "Not while I'm in your life. So how are you today, Harper? I was so swamped at the store that I didn't have time to even take a lunch break."

"Pretty good," Harper answered. "Not over the moon ecstatic, but calmer than I've been in a very long time."

"I've been wonderin'," Dana said. "How often did y'all see each other since—well, you know?"

Tawny glanced at Harper. "Maybe half a dozen times. She came through town once, and we had lunch together. She insisted on paying for it, and I felt terrible when she dragged out change to finish out the bill. The rest of the times it was just a lunch or maybe a breakfast and I'd whip out my mother's charge card before she could dig in her purse for money. I couldn't imagine having to work for minimum wage like you did. At least not until I got booted out of Mama's good graces and

274

had to work. But when I had to work, I liked being independent."

"You paid for our meals that day with Mama's money? What happened when she found out?" Harper grinned.

"She raised hell when she checked the bill and found dinner for two at a cheap restaurant on a bad side of town. When I told her that I'd paid for your meal, she deducted that amount from my next month's allowance. It was worth it," Tawny said flatly.

Harper giggled. "It's a wonder she didn't stroke out."

"I thought she might," Tawny laughed with her.

Dana made a mental note to call her mother soon and tell her that she loved her. Maybe someday Retha would come around and realize that she was missing a relationship with her girls. But maybe she wouldn't. Sometimes folks didn't realize what they'd missed until it was too late.

And that's your lesson to yourself tonight. Don't let something fall through your fingers when you've got a good firm grip on it.

Payton squeezed between two chairs and handed her a plate of food. "Just the way you like it."

"Yes, it is, and thank you so much." She smiled up at him.

"I'm going back to get mine ready. Don't let anyone steal my chair. Can I get you anything else?"

"I think I've got everything I need." For the

first time in years, she really felt that way, and this was only their second date.

Brook sat down on the other side of her and nudged her with an elbow. "Uncle Zed's hands were shakin' when he poured his glass of iced tea. Is he all right?"

"Probably just tired. It's been a long day for him," Dana said, hoping that she was right. She'd noticed that he coughed a lot more these days and that his overalls were getting even baggier than usual. He gripped the tea glass so tightly that his knuckles turned practically white. And when he took a bite of his hot dog, he used both hands to guide it to his mouth. Surely, God wouldn't take him so soon after Granny Annie. That might be more than any of them could bear—especially Harper, who worked with him every day. She might be tall and tough-looking, but the last few days had proven just how fragile she was.

Payton returned and sat down on her right side. "How often do y'all do this?"

"First time they've used the fire pit," Zed said. "Don't expect it'll be the last. Me and Annie, we liked to sit out here with a blazin' fire goin'. We'd make up stories about where we were and what was goin' on."

"Tell us one," Brook begged.

"Well, my favorite one is that we were travelin' across country right after the Civil War and this was our fire when we unsaddled our horses that night and made camp in a place that looked like this. We could hear the coyotes howlin' in the distance and the crickets and tree frogs singin' to us," he answered.

"That's all?" Tawny asked.

"That's all." Zed nodded.

But something in the wistful look in his eyes told Dana that the rest of the story was very personal. She was about to suggest that they tell a story, but Payton beat her to it.

"Let's start our own story. Zed, would you begin?" Payton said.

Zed nodded. "There's seven of us in this covered wagon. We used to be eight, but the grandma died along the trail. Now we've circled our covered wagons with all the others. There's twenty wagons all total. We've had our supper, and each family is sittin' around their own campfire talkin' about the gold mines where we're headed. That'd be out in California. We left with a wagon train up in Missouri, so we're somewhere in the middle of Nebraska tonight. Now it's your turn, Brook."

"I hate this wagon train. I don't have air-conditioning or an indoor bathroom," Brook giggled. "I sure wish I didn't have to wear all these clothes."

"How do you know about what they wore?" Tawny asked.

"I studied it in school. We even had to dress up in period clothes from back then," she answered.

"Before I got into the time machine, I was driving a brand-new Corvette and wearing skinny jeans. Now I'm eating beans and hoping that the bushes out there give me enough cover when I have to go. Now it's your turn, Aunt Tawny."

Dana smiled at her daughter's quick wit about a time machine, but she read a lot of science fiction.

Tawny held up a finger while she ate the last bite of her hot dog. "Well, I was the one who talked you into getting into that time machine with me. I thought I dialed the number to throw us a couple of hundred years into the future, but I tend to get numbers turned around and I hit the wrong ones. Now here we are walkin' ten miles a day beside a covered wagon or else riding in the back of the thing. I think my older sister Harper has a history with the wagon master, Wyatt. She keeps flirting with him, and now it's her turn."

Well done, little sister, Dana thought and made a mental note to buy Tawny's first novel if she ever got around to writing it.

Harper took a drink of her sweet tea and smiled at Wyatt. "I'm not flirting. I'm trying to be nice to him so he'll let our wagon be first in line. You know what they say—if you ain't the lead dog, the scenery never changes. I'm tired of breathin' everyone else's dust and bein' careful not to step in mule crap all day. But tonight I'm real happy that we've got clear skies and a big old pretty moon. I'm hoping that when we get to California, the pretty dress in my trunk still fits me, because I'm losing weight. Your turn, Wyatt."

Good cover, Harper. Dana smiled.

Payton nudged Dana with his shoulder. "You've got a couple of pretty smart sisters."

"Yep. I'm finding that out." Dana nodded.

Wyatt's deep drawl picked up the story. "I'm the wagon master, and I've had my eye on Harper since we left Missouri. She's a tough woman and independent as they come—way out of my league. I'm just a common old wagon master, and she'd never look at me. Tonight I'm tickled that she's invited me to the fire where she and the folks from her wagon have made supper. I get lonely riding my horse up ahead of the wagons and I'd like her to ride with me, but I'm afraid of rejection. Now it's your turn, Payton."

"I'm the scout. So I go out a day's distance and then come back to the wagon train at night, saddle weary and tired. Y'all good people pretty often ask me to sit by your fire. It's a tough job, but I have to do it so we know if the watering holes are still where they were on the last trip. Tonight we're camped by a beautiful lake and I get to sit by the prettiest girl on the wagon train. It's full of mail-order brides going to California. I'm just hoping that this one lady hasn't signed a document to be someone else's wife, because she's kind of taken my eye with her beauty and grace. Besides, she's a fine cook. I guess it's your turn, Miz Dana."

He caught her gaze. The blaze flickered in his light-blue eyes, and she was suddenly completely tongue-tied for a full minute. She'd rather have dragged him around the house to the porch swing and made out with him like a couple of high school sophomores than continued the story.

Dana looked into the fire and started, "I had to get into the time machine with my daughter. I couldn't possibly let her make this trip alone, not even if her aunt was going with her. And now I'm enjoying the trip so much I'm not sure I want to go back to the future. But California's not my favorite choice, either. Tonight I'm about to put forth an idea to the rest of my team. How about we leave the train and settle down right here by this lake and build us a little general store? If there's going to be wagon trains on this route, we can make some money selling supplies. I really like this place."

"Hear, hear!" Zed clapped his wrinkled hands. "What an amazing end to the story. This may be my new favorite one. Now I'm going home and leavin' you kids to enjoy the rest of the evening."

"Good night, Uncle Zed. See you in the mornin'," Harper said.

Zed slowly made his way into the darkness. "Good night to everyone."

"And since I'm a good cook and we've decided to live by the lake, let's bring out the makings for the s'mores," Dana said.

It was after ten when Dana walked Payton to his vehicle. With an arm on each side of her, he pinned her against his car and kissed her eyelids and the tip of her nose and then found her lips in a series of kisses that came close to blistering the paint right off his fancy vehicle.

Her arms snaked up around his neck and her hand freed his ponytail from the rubber band so that she could tangle her fingers in his thick blond hair. It felt like strands of pure silk floating through her fingers. She'd had no idea until that moment that there were erogenous zones in her fingertips, but heat flowed from them to places in her body that begged for more.

Finally he stepped back and cupped her face in his hands. "You are such a beautiful woman, Dana. I had a wonderful time tonight. There's no way on God's great green earth that I can ever top this evening."

It was on the tip of Dana's tongue to say that she could think of a couple of ways he could make tonight pale in comparison, but that would be rushing things entirely too much. "I'm glad you enjoyed it. I sure felt like a queen tonight with all the attention you've given me."

"Oh, honey, this was just the tip of the iceberg. When can I see you again?"

"Well, definitely on Thursday, since that's the day you'll be in the store," she teased.

"I might need a cold soda pop tomorrow while

I'm out deliverin' bait." He ran a forefinger down her jawline.

"I bet I could sell you one." She closed her hand around his. "Good night, Payton."

" 'Night, Dana. Sleep tight and dream of me."

"You do the same." She started toward the house. From the porch she could see him still standing beside the car. He waved and blew her a kiss and then got inside and drove away.

Brook was sprawled out on the sofa as she entered. Dana wished for the first time that her daughter was already asleep in bed.

"I've decided that I like him," Brook said bluntly.

Dana sank down in the rocking chair. "Why?"

Brook sat up and shrugged. "Because he didn't try to impress me. He only had eyes for you. That's the kind of man you deserve. Someday I will grow up and have a house and a family of my own."

"Cabin, not house," Dana told her. "You will just move from here into a cabin."

"Okay, for today, it's a cabin, but when I'm gone, I want you to have someone who looks at you like Payton does and who'll treat you like the queen you are. Now, I'm going to bed. Tomorrow will be busy."

"I love you, little girl," Dana said.

"Just bein' honest, Mama, like we've always been with each other."

Chapter Sixteen

Tawny awoke on Sunday morning and turned on the radio to the same country music station that Zed listened to in the café. "The House That Built Me" by Miranda Lambert was midway through the song. Using the curling iron for a microphone, she sang right along. The lyrics of the song said that a person couldn't go home again. But if she could go into the house, she could find herself and start healing. Only the house that Tawny sang about wasn't the house that she'd lived in her whole life but the little two-bedroom one where Dana lived. That's the real house that built her.

When the song ended, she continued to hum it as she slipped a pair of skinny jeans up over her hips and pulled a lightweight blue cotton sweater down over her head. "Stay" by Sugarland began to play, and she sat down on the bed. Even though her rich jackass of a boyfriend hadn't been married, she'd begged him more than once to stay the night with her. Lookin' back and knowing what happened after the court hearing, she understood why he'd never stayed with her. His real girlfriend, the one he'd never ask to go with him on a drug deal, was the woman that he sat beside in church on Sunday morning—she

283

was the one who sat behind him and supported him that day in court when the judge let him off with a slap on the wrist.

"Bless her heart. She may have him now, but she ain't got much," Tawny said as she headed for the café for breakfast, humming the Miranda song as she crossed the gravel lane and the grassy lawn.

As usual, she was the last one to the café. Harper, Dana, Brook, and Zed clustered around a table with Flora. Tawny's heart dropped to her knees, because their faces all said something was terribly wrong.

"Flora is retiring as of right now," Zed said. "We've been waiting for you to get here, because she has something to say to all of us."

Tawny sat down with a thud in a chair, her mind spinning as to how they'd take care of business without Flora. "Is this a joke? Please tell me it's a joke."

"No, it's the truth. I was trying to hold out on retiring until Cassidy finished up this school year. Her mama has been settled out in Arizona for a few weeks and wanting us to join her, but Cassidy didn't want to leave her friends. But things have gotten out of control. She's been babysitting for a doctor and his wife down in Frankston on weekends. Last night they came home early, thank God. They found her and that Ryson kid tangled up on their bed. Another ten minutes and things could have been worse. They'd been drinkin' the doctor's liquor and smokin' pot. With those little kids right in the next room," Flora said.

"Oh, no!" Brook gasped.

"I'm afraid so. My daughter let me keep her while she was gettin' settled in her new job after a messy divorce. I'll be checkin' her out of school tomorrow while the moving men get started packing. We'll leave on Tuesday morning. Soon as the moving van pulls away, we will, too. I'm not lettin' this kid out of my sight until I can hand her over to her mama."

"I'm so sorry, Flora," Tawny said.

"I hate to leave y'all this quick. I wanted to stick around until summertime and give you more time to settle in."

Zed moved from his chair to hug her. "It's okay. We'll make it. Cassidy needs a change, and you're ten years past when you could have retired. I'm just grateful for every single day that you've worked with us. Annie would understand."

"I'll sure miss all y'all, but I got to do what's best for Cassidy." Flora stood up and wiped tears from her eyes. "Zed, I'll be callin' to check on y'all from time to time. You take care of yourself." She left them still reeling from the news.

"Well, now, what are we goin' to do about this turn of events?" Zed asked.

Tawny caught Dana's bewildered gaze and then shifted her eyes to Harper, who looked like she could chew up railroad ties and spit out Tinkertoys. Her oldest sister was already trying to fix the problem, just like older children did. The middle one was wishing that she could shake some sense into Cassidy.

"Okay, here's my two cents," Tawny said. "Dana, you take on the reservations and checking in and out at the store. I'll fall into Flora's place cleanin' rooms. Brook has done it often enough now that if I don't get it done right, she can show me what I'm doin' wrong. When the store closes, we'll put a sign on the door for the folks checkin' in late to come to cabin seven, and I'll take care of them. Harper can help me out in the laundry when she has downtime in the café if I'm behind. Three people used to run this place and now we've got five, so we can do this."

"Tawny, your plan sounds solid to me," Harper said. "But Brook, how do you feel about this? I don't mean the new plans. I mean your friend Cassidy leaving."

Brook sat down on her mother's lap. "To tell the truth, I been kind of steerin' clear of Cassidy, because she was gettin' more and more tangled up with Ryson."

"So this isn't goin' to hurt you too much," Zed asked.

"Nope, but Aunt Tawny, we better get some

286

breakfast, because you're goin' to be real busy all mornin'. Do I get a raise? After all, I'm the supervisor now." Brook grinned.

Zed threw back his head and guffawed until he had a coughing fit. "Y'all just proved that you are Annie's kin for sure. Dana, you didn't weigh in on takin' on that much more work."

"It's fine with me. Sounds like Tawny came up with a good plan there," Dana said.

"Yes, sir! Annie would be proud of you all. Now I'm goin' to start makin' breakfast."

"If we can have some chocolate chip pancakes, I'll help," Tawny said, and the lyrics from Miranda's song played through her head again, saying she'd heard that folks couldn't go home again.

They're wrong, Tawny thought as she followed Zed to the kitchen. *I've come home and this is where I'm staying.*

Chapter Seventeen

Heat seemed to bother Zed more than the cold lately. He was not looking forward to summer. Yet gratitude filled him Monday afternoon that the transition of jobs had gone so well and that Harper had made a run to the laundry house to help Tawny out. The rooms had been cleaned and were ready for any new guests, and Dana had taken care of checkouts without a hitch. Of course, she'd had to do it the old-fashioned way with paper and pen, but still, it looked like Tawny had come up with a good idea.

"I'm right proud of her, Annie," Zed said as he dropped a cigarette butt into the receptacle and lit up another one. "Don't fuss at me. I need two today after Flora quittin'."

"Who are you talkin' to, Zed?" Payton sat down on the bench beside him.

"Annie. I talk to her a lot since she's passed on. And if I'm lucky, she talks to me." He shifted in his seat before he went on. "Blue-plate special is wiped completely out, but I can make you a burger if you're hungry."

"I'm not in a big hurry," Payton said. "Hear you lost your longtime helper. I know how that feels, but things do tend to work themselves out in those cases."

"Yep, and better than I thought they might." Zed took a couple more long draws from the cigarette and then put it into the little hole at the top of the butt bin. Before he could stand up, Brook rounded the side of the building, her book bag slung over one shoulder and looking like she had the weight of the world sitting on her shoulders.

She plopped down on the grass in front of Zed and laid her head on his knee. "I got in big trouble at school and I have to spend this whole week in the in-school suspension place. The upside is that I got my homework done. The downside is that I have to tell Mama."

"Want to practice on us first?" Payton asked.

"The fight wasn't even my fault, but since I threw the first punch, the rules say that I started it."

"Did you finish it?" Zed asked.

Her nod was slow and her sigh audible. "Ryson came up to me in the hallway soon as I got to my locker and tried to hand me a joint. When I refused it, he tried to put it in my pocket, so I took a step back and it fell on the floor. Then he whispered that I could take Cassidy's place if I'd just pick it up. He said he didn't date good girls. So if I wanted what Cassidy got, then I had to dirty up my act. That's when I decked him."

Payton leaned forward and checked her face for bruises. "That sorry little punk. Did he hit you back?"

Zed's hands shook, and he knotted them into fists. Damn little punk, talking to his baby girl like that—he ought to be beat on like he was a piñata.

"He's a lot bigger than me, but I don't think he ever took martial arts classes like I did," she said. "He doubled up his fists and took a swing, but I blocked it and gave him a pretty good workin' over by the time the teachers pulled us apart."

"And then?" Payton asked.

"Then we went to the office right along with Mr. Green, who'd seen everything. He didn't hear what Ryson said, but he saw the business with the joint and all. Ryson was supposed to spend the rest of the year in suspension, but his mama came and checked him out of school. I heard that he'll be homeschooled."

"How would you like to be stuck at home every day like Ryson is going to be and never see kids your age?" Payton asked.

"Not very good, but I don't feel a bit sorry for him," she said. "A bunch of the kids on the bus told me that if they could they'd go to suspension a day for me, so I guess I made some new friends. But Mama is goin' to be disappointed because I didn't control my temper. It's just that I was so mad at him. Poor Cassidy thinks that he loves her and he was only using her and if I told her that, she wouldn't believe me." She stopped to catch her breath. "I'm not going to tell Mama until tonight. You think she'll ground me for the rest of my life?"

Payton chuckled. "Maybe only until you are forty."

"Or fifty," Zed laughed with him.

Brook swung her forefinger around to take both of them in. "It's not funny."

"I'd have given my right lung to have seen that fight. I bet it was kind of funny. That big boy thinkin' he could whip you or, worse yet, turn you into his little pot-smokin' girlfriend." Zed slapped his thigh and kept laughing until he had to pull a handkerchief from the pocket of his overalls.

"I bet he'll be glad to stay at home the rest of his year," Payton said. "Can you imagine how his tough friends would tease him about a little wisp of a girl whipping his butt?"

Brook stood up and slung her book bag over a shoulder. "I hope Mama thinks like y'all do. I'm off to the laundry to help Aunt Tawny. Is that where Aunt Harper is?"

"Yep, but since the boss is back, you can tell her to come on to the café." Zed continued to wipe at his eyes.

A wide grin split Brook's sweet little face, and for a second, Zed took credit for her perfectly even white teeth. He might not share actual DNA with those girls, but he figured he loved them more than blood kin, so he could have passed down his smile to her.

Harper was busy folding towels and Tawny was replenishing the maid's cart when Brook entered the small laundry building. Tawny motioned for her to come over and inspect the cart.

"I think I've got it arranged just like Flora did, but it wouldn't hurt for you to pass judgment."

"Wow, I really do feel like a supervisor," Brook laughed.

"Just remember that supervisin' brings on lots more responsibilities," Harper warned.

"Then maybe I don't want the job. I've got enough on my plate as it is." Brook sighed. "Oh, yeah. Uncle Zed says for you to come on back to the café. But can you wait just five more minutes?" She dropped her backpack on a folding table and nodded at the cart. "Looks like Flora did it herself."

"What do you need, kiddo?" Harper asked.

"I was wonderin' if maybe y'all could come to the house tonight and be there when I tell Mama about the trouble I got in today at school. She's goin' to be real disappointed in me." Brook hopped up on the folding table, her legs dangling and her shoulders sagging.

"What happened, honey?" Tawny stopped what she was doing and sat beside her.

Tawny laid a supporting hand on Brook's knee. She knew what it was like to be apprehensive about having to come home and admit to trouble at school. "Tell us what happened," she said.

Brook told them the same story, word for word, that she'd told Zed and Payton. "Mama sent me to martial arts classes for a couple of years so I could get rid of my anger, not use it on someone when I was angry, but dammit." She clamped a hand on her mouth. "I'm not supposed to cuss, either."

"But dammit"—Tawny grinned—"the way I see it is that you were protecting yourself and not taking the rap for drugs again. Flora is doing the right thing getting Cassidy away from that little thug. I'm proud of you, girl, but you are right, you've got to come clean with your mama."

"That means you'll come to the house about seven thirty, then?" Brook asked.

"Of course we will." Harper patted her shoulder. "We'll always be there to support you, but also know that we won't fight for you with your mama if we think you are wrong."

"Thanks. Now you can go on to the café. I think Uncle Zed is fixin' a burger for Payton, and it won't be long until the fishermen start comin' in for supper," she said.

"Yes, boss." Harper grinned.

"I wish I was smart enough to really be a boss." Brook let out a long whoosh of pent-up air.

"You are well on the way," Tawny said. "Let's go work over in cabins one and two. The folks in there had Do Not Disturb signs on their doors until half an hour ago."

"Yes, ma'am. I love y'all," Brook said.

"Love you more," both Harper and Tawny said at the same time.

"Y'all sounded just like Granny Annie. She used to say that all the time."

"Best compliment I've ever had." Tawny pushed the cart out the door behind Harper.

✦❈❊❉❈✦

Harper and Zed got finished in the café a little early that evening, so she had thirty minutes before she had to be at Dana's place to support Brook. The girl had spunk and she hadn't started the fight, even if she had thrown the first punch, so Dana should go easy on her when it came to her punishment for getting in trouble at school.

She'd rushed to her cabin and took a hot bath to ease some of the aches and pains out of her legs and back. Keeping an eye on the clock she'd hung beside the vanity mirror, she reluctantly crawled out after fifteen minutes and wrapped a towel around her body. She was halfway across the floor when she heard the familiar sound of a truck parking in front of her cabin. She hurriedly threw on underwear, jeans, and a clean T-shirt and slung open the door as Wyatt raised his hand to knock.

Grabbing his hand, she pulled him inside and wrapped her arms around his neck. "I'm so glad to see you, but we've only got five minutes. I've got to be at Dana's in ten."

His lips found hers in a long, passionate kiss that sent sparks bouncing off the cabin walls. Teasing her mouth open with the tip of his tongue, he deepened the next one, leaving them both panting when it ended.

"Why?" He led her to the bed and pulled her down in his lap. "Do you." Another scorching-hot kiss. "Have to go to Dana's?"

"Because Brook got in trouble and she wants me and Tawny there when she tells her mother. I'll tell you the story later, but I really have to go right now." She planted one more kiss on his lips and then hurried out the door.

Tawny was already there when she arrived, equally out of breath because she'd jogged the distance in a pair of flip-flops. Brook was curled up on the end of the sofa. Dana was in the rocking chair and, from the way she raised an eyebrow, all of what was about to go down was not a total surprise. Had Uncle Zed told her?

"Okay," Brook said. "Mama, I've got something to tell you." And she went on with the story. "I started the actual fight and I have to go to in-school suspension for a week for it. That boy's a jerk, but I shouldn't have hit him first or as many times as I did before the teacher pulled me off him."

"And what did you do when the teacher got you away from him?" Dana asked.

"I kicked him two more times and Mr. Green came runnin' out of his room and grabbed my legs and they hauled me into the office," she said. "Mr. Green was as big a jerk as Ryson when he was here at the lake, but he did stand up for me and tell the truth about what happened."

"I'm glad you told me, but I've got to admit that Marcus Green called me right after school and told me the whole story, pretty much the same way you just did. And he apologized for being such a jackass when he was here," Dana said. "You let your temper get away from you again, didn't you?"

"I sure did, but he made me so mad when he said that about Cassidy. She thinks she's in love with him, and he just used her. We might not be the friends that we were in the first week I was here, but it just isn't right for a boy to be that disrespectful. He should take lessons from Payton on how to treat a lady," Brook said.

Harper wished she'd had the wisdom that Brook had when she was that age. Suddenly, it dawned on her that they were all three sitting there together and that a child had brought them together. The morning that she'd baptized herself seemed to have been a turning point for them, and yet, something said they weren't nearly ready to take that big step from sometimes sisters to real ones.

"So if you were the mother, what would you do?" Dana asked.

Brook's brown eyebrows drew down into a solid line, and her full mouth disappeared as she gave it serious thought. "I would take away my cell phone for the week I have to go to suspension, but it doesn't work here anyway, so that wouldn't be a very good punishment for this."

"It sounds like a fantastic punishment to me," Harper said. "It's not your fault there's no service."

"But that's not right," Brook said. "Me and Mama, we got this thing about fairness and honesty."

Dana bit back tears, but one lonely little drop escaped and ran down her cheek. "I've got something to say, and I don't want any one of you to ask a question or utter a word until I'm finished. It's difficult and I'm afraid I won't be able to get it all out if you do."

She started talking, and Harper could hardly believe what she was hearing. "Brook's father cheated on me, but the real reason I left him was because of his terrible temper. He knocked me around a couple of times, but then one night he slapped Brook. She hadn't done a thing wrong, but he was furious with me because he thought I'd looked at another man. I kicked him out. She and I moved, and we've never seen him since. So, darlin' girl, I've not always been honest, and I apologize for that."

Brook rushed to her mother's side, dropped

down on her knees, and put her head in Dana's lap. "You might not have been totally honest, but it was to protect me—at least mostly. And I've known that you weren't married to my daddy for years. I found the birth certificate a long time ago. I promise I'll work harder on my temper, because I sure wouldn't ever want to get angry enough to hit one of my kids."

"Then I think two weeks without your cell phone is punishment enough for not controlling that temper." Dana swiped a hand across her cheek. "And just between us and your two aunts, thank God I paid for those martial arts lessons."

Harper's voice came out high and squeaky when she said, "Good Lord! I thought you were perfect, and now you tell us this."

"Well, I thought you two were princesses and I was the big old black sheep in the family," Dana shot back.

"Wow!" Tawny gasped. "Just plain old wow! How could you ever trust a man again after that? And why didn't you marry him?"

"He said that his first marriage taught him a lesson. I thought he'd change his mind when Brook was born. He didn't," Dana answered.

"I'd sure like to know where he lives right now, because I would just love to use *my* martial arts training on him," Tawny said.

"You can fight?" Brook asked.

"Kickboxing," Tawny answered. "Took three

classes of it in college for my phys-ed requirement. Okay, now that Dana has bared her soul, I'm going to get back to my cabin and do some book work before I go to bed. And Harper here has company waiting for her in the form of a tall, dark-haired man she's been in love with for ten years."

"I have not! That was lust and this is friendship," Harper argued.

"Uh-huh," Tawny laughed.

"I love the whole bunch of you," Brook said. "And thanks for being here for me. Mama, let's have a beer to celebrate all this being out in the open."

"You can have a beer when you are forty and not a day before," Dana declared.

Harper waved as she crossed the floor and hurried back to her cabin. She found Wyatt propped up in bed, watching one of the two television channels. She kicked the door shut with her heel, tossed her flip-flops in a corner, and curled up beside him.

"You aren't going to believe this," she said.

He hit a button on the remote to turn off the TV. "I'm all ears, darlin'."

<hr />

Zed leaned back in the recliner that Monday evening, sipped on a glass of lemonade, and told Annie all about the incident with Brook. "I so wish you could've been here, and no,

I'm not exaggeratin' one bit of it. She really did whip the snot out of that kid, and he finally got his comeuppance for what happened. I intend to tell Flora about it when she gets settled and calls me. But right now I'm rememberin' a time when Marvin Hopper made fun of me at school because I didn't have good shoes and my overalls had patches," he said with a deep chuckle. He finished off the last of the lemonade and set the glass on the table between the recliners. "She whipped on that boy just like you did Marvin. I felt bad that you fought my battle that day. I should've taken care of it, but then it didn't seem like such a big deal. My overalls did have patches and there were holes in the soles of my shoes. Only time I fought was with Seamus when he got drunk and said that you couldn't cook worth a damn. Did I ever tell you about that?"

Leaning his head back, he shut his eyes and listened intently, then smiled. "I know, darlin'. You really didn't like to cook, and you didn't have to. My mama made sure there was good food every day in the café and then I took over the job. But Seamus was disrespectin' you when he said that, and he had to pay for it. Did you know that he fired me because of that?"

He listened awhile longer. "So you did know. I'd bet my right lung, sorry as it is these days, that you're the reason that he hired me back the next day and said he'd never talk ugly about you again."

Finally, he opened his eyes. "Well, I guess you're done talkin' for tonight, so I'll go on to bed. On a final note, I think we're beginnin' to see more and more progress on our girls actin' like family should."

Chapter Eighteen

Tawny stood under the shower for several minutes, letting the cool water take away the sweat and grime of working in the laundry and cleaning rooms. If someone had tried to convince her that she would like the physical work more than sitting at a desk all day, she would have declared them insane. But it was the truth. She enjoyed the instant gratification of walking into a messy cabin and leaving it spick-and-span, smelling clean and with a bed made so tight that quarters could bounce on the chenille spread.

Besides, she got to work with Brook, who had a knack for making the simplest thing that happened at her school into a comedy act. Tawny hoped that when Brook got into high school the next year she enrolled in some drama classes and learned how to stand on a stage without fear. Not that Brook would be afraid of anything, but the classes would help her tremendously if she ever did get into comedy.

She reached out and adjusted the water to a warmer level, washed her honey-blonde hair, and used conditioner twice before she got out of the shower. With a towel around her head and one around her body, she padded out into her little office area. She waltzed around the room to

Alisan Porter singing "Deep Water" on the radio.

The song was about a girl not wanting to swim the deep waters of life alone, but one line seemed to stand out—it said that she was a child who was hungry and wild, trying to find her way home. Tawny noticed the items on her bookcase as she swayed to the music. One red feather from the first days she was there. A dried yellow dandelion flower from the evening when she was walking home from that first movie night at Dana's along with three kernels of caramel corn that were stuck firmly together. The wrapper from the candy bar that she'd brought home from the store when they'd had the conversation about Marcus Green.

"And I still don't trust that man even if he did do the right thing for Brook and apologize for being a jackass," she muttered.

She picked up the little stuffed bunny from her Easter basket and hugged it close to her face. Bless Zed's heart for remembering them all on the holiday. She'd had a whole room full of stuffed animals when she was a little girl, but none of them meant as much as the little purple bunny with a yellow bow around his neck.

Then there was the smooth rock that she'd picked up at the edge of the lake when Harper had scared the hell out of her. She set the bunny back down and ran a hand over the rock to remind herself that the inner demons were sometimes far worse than anything else. Her heart ached for her sister who'd never know what it was like to hug her daughter like Dana did Brook every single day.

And the latest thing on the bookcase was her own cell phone, dead as a doornail but there to remind her of Brook's punishment, not so much for getting in trouble, but for losing control of her temper.

"I'm so jealous I could just spit." Tawny backed up from the bookcase. "Dana has someone and Harper has someone. I know, Granny, that jealousy is a terrible thing. You don't have to get in my head and fuss at me."

She got dressed in a pair of pajama pants and a tank top and went outside to air-dry her hair. She'd barely gotten settled in her red chair when a shiny black sports car whipped into the space between her cabin and number six. Her chest tightened when the almighty Matthew Richmond IV crawled out of the vehicle. He wore a pair of designer khaki shorts, a shirt that probably cost as much as a week's salary at the coffee shop where she used to work, Italian loafers, and an air that let the whole world know exactly how important he was.

"Hello, Tawny," he said.

"Matt." She nodded. "I didn't see your name on the register to rent a cabin."

From the first time she'd met him, he'd sent

little waves of desire shooting through her entire body, but then, she'd always had a weak spot for guys with dark hair and pretty green eyes. And that night was no different. She was still attracted to him like a moth to a flame, but her wings had been singed. She'd realized just how dangerous that pretty yellow flickering fire had been.

"Honey, I wouldn't spend a night in one of these things if you gave me double what one costs for a week." He stopped at the bottom of the steps.

"What are you doing here, Matt?"

"I tried to get over you. I even let my 'girl-friend' "—he made quotes in the air as he said the last word—"plan a wedding, but I couldn't go through with it. Don't look at me like that. I didn't leave her standing at the altar. I called it off six weeks into the planning stage. My folks were not happy with me."

"I don't imagine she was, either." Tawny should have been happy that the sweet little angel didn't win in the end, but she felt sorry for the woman. She thought she knew Matthew and had loved him, probably even more than Tawny, and there she was left with embarrassment and a broken heart.

"I missed the excitement and fun I had with you, darlin'."

"How did you find me?"

"Easy. I went to the coffee shop where you worked and the owner said your grandmother had passed away. You talked a lot about her and this place, so I gave it the first try."

"And you drove all the way here from Austin to tell me that you missed me?"

"I tried to call first, but it kept going to voice mail and there's not a listing for Annie's Place or the lake. Come on, Tawny, forgive me. Come home with me."

"All the way from Austin?"

"You are worth it. Life's been so dull without you in it. I had to do a few months' work with my father in the company, and now he's sending me to Paris on a weeklong business trip. Come with me, Tawny. We can have so much fun exploring Paris together."

"You said it was a business trip. And do your parents know that you are inviting me?"

"Business only lasts a few hours a day. We'll have the evenings free, and what they don't know won't hurt them."

"What makes you think I'd trust you? I haven't seen you since court, when you threw me under the bus. I was at that coffee shop for months and you never even called." He was probably telling the truth about a business trip, but when they got home, he'd leave her high and dry in some hotel on whatever coast they flew into. She knew him well enough to know that he used people to get what he wanted. And Matthew always got what he wanted.

She looked out at the lake and then her eyes shifted back to Matthew and she held out her palms. In one she had a fantastic summer of wild, crazy fun with parties and sleeping late plus some pretty good sex. In the other she had cabins to clean, a steaming-hot laundry with a never-ending supply of sheets and towels, and all the book work for the place.

Then she added all the trinkets on her bookcase to the hand with the work and it won the contest—hands down. She smiled at the pun and shook her head.

"What's so funny?" he asked.

"That you think money could ever buy what I've got here."

"And what's that?" he asked. "A bunch of run-down cabins. You belong in five-star hotels drinking expensive champagne with me, not this, Tawny. I'm sorry I didn't get in touch earlier, but I just can't understand what you see in this place when I'm offering you a good time."

"I see family that supports me and trusts me." She stood up and, without even a glance over her shoulder, went inside the cabin, leaving him on the porch. She sat down at the desk and laid her hands on her arms. She'd made her choice, and she hadn't even had to think about it very long. This was where she belonged.

"Choices." She raised her head up.

Yep, just like what George Jones sang about.

We live and we die by the choices we make. She remembered that old vinyl record playing on the stereo system that used to sit in the living room. Nearly every time it finished, Granny would say those same words that had run through Tawny's mind.

"Granny, if you had anything to do with that jackass showing up here tonight, I want to thank you. It's put everything in the right perspective."

She eased the door open enough to see that Matthew's car was gone. He might call now that he'd figured out where she was, but it wouldn't end well for him because she'd made up her mind about her future. She opened the door farther and over there on the bench by the café, the bright-red flicker of a cigarette glowed in the dark. She didn't even slow down but marched barefoot across the grass and sat down beside Zed. He took a couple of long drags on the cigarette and then put it out.

"That was Matthew. He was my boyfriend, until he let me take the blame for a bag full of drugs that he'd bought for a party he was throwing that week. I was with him when he got caught. The drugs were in my purse."

"Kind of like the problem with Brook?"

She swallowed hard and nodded. "Only this wasn't weed and we were both of age. We could have both been sent to prison for the amount that he had."

"Were you going to that party?" Zed asked.

She thought her neck wouldn't bend, but finally she nodded a second time. "But Uncle Zed, I didn't do drugs. I drank too much and that's not much better, but I saw too many students who were addicted, even in high school, and I didn't ever want to look like that. Vanity kept me from messing with them, but I drank as much as Harper during the time I dated Matthew."

"Rich feller from the looks of it," Zed said.

"Thank goodness his family had a lot of money. They hired a fancy lawyer that got him off. I had a public defender because my mother wouldn't foot the bill for a lawyer."

"How's that lucky?" Zed asked.

"Judge couldn't give me a hard sentence when he'd just let Matt off with a warning. It was a matter of he said, she said. He said he had no idea that I was carrying drugs. I told the truth and said that I knew they were there, but they weren't mine. I'd passed the drug test and failed the alcohol one that night. He didn't pass either one but had very little drugs in his system. I got three months' community service and was told I couldn't leave Austin until I'd completed it. And I got kicked out of college," she told him.

"Why didn't you call us?" Zed asked.

"I didn't want to disappoint Granny or you, Uncle Zed. I guess you've heard that before from my sisters, right?"

He nodded. "Don't reckon the past matters much. Just the present and the future. What was that fancy dude wantin'?"

She held out her hands, palms up, and didn't have a moment's doubt about the decision she'd made. "He wanted me to go with him for a summer trip to Europe and give up what I've got here. I weighed both options in my hands like Granny told me to do when I was a little girl tryin' to make a decision."

Zed chuckled and lit up another cigarette. "I guess you won that battle, but he's used to gettin' what he wants. Will you win the war?"

"I can. I've got an army behind me."

A puff of smoke blew out into the night air. "Family." Zed summed it up in one word.

"That and choices. I thought of that old George Jones song about living with the choices we make. Granny used to play it a lot."

"George Jones was her favorite." A fancy smoke ring floated out into the air.

"That looks like a halo." She laid her head on Zed's shoulder.

"Halos for my angels," he said.

"Uncle Zed, you'd better learn to blow horns, because there isn't a single one of us deserves a halo, not even a smoke one."

He blew another perfect one. "First one for Harper. Second one for Dana. And this one is for you." The third one drifted away from them.

"Angels aren't always perfect. You've come a long way, girl." Zed patted her knee.

"Thank you, Uncle Zed, but you do know those things are bad for you."

He sent one more ring into the air. "And that one is for Brook. You remind me more of your granny every day. She might have chosen the easy way a couple of times in her life, but not many. Most of the time, she thought about the long haul and the peace and happiness it would bring into her world."

"Thank you, Uncle Zed. I need her wisdom more and more."

"Don't we all, darlin'." He disposed of the cigarette butt and stood up slowly. "These old bones are cryin' for the easy chair."

"You don't have to come outside to smoke, Uncle Zed."

"Yes, I do. I promised Annie that I'd never smoke in the house. Have a good night now. I understand we're havin' some kind of get-together at Dana's tomorrow night. Brook's planned the night, so there's no tellin' what we'll be doin'."

"It'll be fun just to spend time with everyone. 'Night, Uncle Zed."

" 'Night, Tawny."

❈❖❈

Zed took a shower, put on his pajama pants that were getting bigger every day, and then eased down into his recliner. "Well, our third baby has come clean about why she was so eager to get here, Annie. You always said that God works in mysterious ways."

He pulled a quilt that Annie had made special for him from the back of the chair and covered with it. "Seems like I get colder than I used to, but an old man's skin is thin and his body wears out. I was scared tonight, Annie. I saw that fancy feller come rollin' up in that shiny sports car and I commenced to prayin' real hard. But she made the right decision. Not that I'm any kind of angel. Lord knows, it'll take a lot of beggin' from you just to get me through them pearly gates, but I felt a lot like that angel in the show we used to watch. What was his name? Edward? No, that wasn't it."

He tugged on his ear and frowned, then slapped his thigh. "Earl. That was his name. Remember how he could be there for the girl for support, but God wouldn't let him interfere. Man, I sure felt like Earl tonight."

His eyes fluttered shut, and he sighed from deep inside his chest. "You sure put a lot of faith in me to leave me here to do this job. I just pray every mornin' that I can get the job done, darlin'."

Chapter Nineteen

It was a normal Saturday morning. The cabins were full, which meant lots of extra cleaning, but Brook was home to help all day. Tawny had unloaded her burden to Zed and made a decision that she swore she'd have no regrets about. So why did she feel like a weight was tied to her heart that morning?

She stared at her reflection in the mirror and wished she could see past the superficial and actually take a peek at her heart. Maybe then she'd know how to remove that heavy feeling. As she passed by her trinket shelf, she added a cigarette butt that she'd found beside the bench the night before and made a circle above it with her forefinger.

"Thank you, Uncle Zed."

She had a chip on her shoulder when she reached the café, and it just got bigger when she heard Harper whistling and Dana talking to Brook about the evening. They deserved their smoke rings, but she didn't, because she didn't have the nerve to tell them her big black secret. If they knew, they'd never trust her again, not with the company's books or even to fold towels in the laundry room.

"Good mornin'," Harper said.

"What's so damn good about it?" Tawny popped off.

"We're alive. We've got jobs and we're makin' good money," Dana answered.

"Sounds to me like someone has some regrets, after all." Zed's face popped up in the serving window.

"What's got your panties in a twist, Aunt Tawny?" Brook asked.

Tawny stormed off to the kitchen without answering her. She made a plate of bacon, eggs, and biscuits and pulled up a stool to eat right there in the work area.

"Young lady, you take that to the dining room or else everyone will want to eat in here and they'll get in my way. What's put you in this Jesus mood anyway? I thought you were in good shape last night." Zed's tone left no room for argument.

"They've come clean with everyone and I can't. And what is a Jesus mood?"

"Annie got in one about once a year. It's when not even Jesus himself, nor all the angels in heaven, could live with a person in such a mood. I reckon you got that from her along with the ability to make the right decision. It'll pass, but it'll take at least a day," he answered. "Now get out of my kitchen. I don't allow no Jesus moods in here. Time's too short for anything but sunshine and happiness."

She shot a dirty look toward him and carried her

314

plate back to the dining room, where she sat down at a table in the corner so that she wouldn't have to talk to her sisters. Did they get the gene for a Jesus mood, too? If they did, she sure didn't want to be around them when it hit, because it was miserable.

Zed had a radio in the kitchen, and he kept it on classic country music all day. If the folks who came into the café didn't like country, they could stay away—Granny Annie's words. She stabbed a fork full of eggs and was about to put them in her mouth when Kenny Rogers started singing "The Gambler." Even after the song ended, the lines kept running through Tawny's mind.

She'd thrown away a pretty good hand the night before. The one she was holding that morning was a dud, and she couldn't even bluff her way through it.

"You ready to tell us what's eatin' on you?" Harper asked from across the room.

"You ready to tell me if you're sleepin' with Wyatt?"

"Hey, that's personal." Harper's eyes went from warm to cold in an instant.

"What is goin' on? Y'all are actin' like you did when we first got here. Am I going to have to bring Uncle Zed out here?" Brook asked.

"Breakfast is ready. Come on in here and help yourselves," Zed yelled. "Don't mind her. She's in one of your granny Annie's Jesus moods and it'll take her a while to work things through her

315

mind and get it over. Just give her lots of space so she can figure things out."

Tawny held out her hands. The right one was empty and the left one had the story of why she had to do community service. The weight of the left one was the rock tied around her heart, but she wasn't ready to let it go. She pushed her chair back, left her breakfast on the table, and marched out of the café and to the laundry room.

Brook didn't say a word when she arrived in the laundry room but simply headed out to clean the rooms of the fishermen who'd left before daybreak. A twinge of guilt tried to hit Tawny in the heart, but it couldn't get past the hardness. She should be letting Brook talk about how happy she was that her time spent in isolation at school was over. Right then, all Tawny could think about was that empty right hand and how that it would take part of the burden from the left one if she was willing to tell her sisters and niece.

❋❖❖❖❖❋

Folks in Texas said that after Easter summer would arrive with heat and very little rain. Harper considered them prophets as she went outside after the noon rush that Saturday to catch a breath of air that didn't smell like grilled onions. She was sitting on the bench when Zed motioned her to come back inside.

"Phone's for you," he said. "We might ought to

316

look at gettin' some of that cell phone service in this area for you girls."

"We're makin' it fine without it." Harper followed him back inside the café and picked up the receiver from the wall-hung phone. "Hello."

"Hey, darlin'." Wyatt's deep voice sent tingles through her body.

"Where are you?" she asked.

"Stuck at O'Hare Airport in Chicago. I was supposed to be in Dallas right now, but there's some kind of bomb threat up here and they've grounded the planes, so I won't be there for Brook's family thing. It'll be after midnight when my plane lands and tomorrow I've got a one-day trip with some fishermen out on a lake up near Wylie, so I'll be workin' on very little sleep. See you tomorrow night."

"I'll be right here," she said.

"I wish you could have come with me. The boat show was amazing. I picked out my next one. Got to go, darlin'. My battery needs charging and I have to find a station."

If she didn't have to be in the kitchen seven days a week, she could have been there with him. He'd asked her if there was any way she could take off two days, but she wouldn't even ask her sisters, not since they'd lost Flora.

"Call me when you have time," she said.

"Will do," Wyatt said and the line went dead.

She stomped her foot and growled. "Dammit!"

"Problems?" Zed asked.

"He can't make it tonight. Brook is going to be disappointed."

Zed pursed his mouth and poured two glasses of sweet tea. "I'm goin' outside for a cigarette. Might as well join me."

She followed him outside, plopped down on the bench, and folded her arms over her chest.

"Guess Tawny ain't the only one who's in a foul mood today. Amazin' how little it takes to turn pretty blue skies to dark. Your granny Annie used to say that it wasn't the mountain that put her in a bad way, but the grain of sand in her shoe. Brook will be fine." He crushed the cigarette butt on the heel of his shoe.

She didn't need a lecture or words of advice, especially when they made her feel guilty for feeling the way she did. What she needed was Wyatt. She made it through the days just fine, but the nights were a different matter.

"Tawny hasn't got a monopoly on Granny's moods," Harper said. "But I do remember Granny saying that hard work would cure anything. I'm going to go mop the floors. That little blonde-haired girl spilled a whole glass of Coke and it's still sticky."

"I saw you lookin' at her with yearnin' in your eyes," Zed said.

"I won't ever be completely over it, but it's getting better."

Zed leaned back against the building and shut his eyes, enjoying the warmth of the sun and thinking of Annie. If she was going to have a Jesus mood day, it would usually arrive on June 1, because that's when the girls used to come for a month. He understood and prepared for it, giving her lots of space and doing all he could just to get through the big disappointment.

"You asleep?" Dana whispered.

"Naw, just restin' my eyes. Sit down and enjoy this beautiful day with me," he said without opening his eyes.

He could feel her presence and, right along with it, her anger. *Lord,* he prayed silently, *now you know it was about all I could do to handle Annie when she was havin' one of these days, but to throw three of them at me at the same time, well, that's a load that even Samson couldn't bear up under.*

"Payton called. He's got a problem with a tank and he can't come tonight," she finally huffed.

"Wyatt's stuck in Chicago at the airport and he won't be here neither and I've been feelin' a mite under the weather, so I 'spect y'all are going to have a girls' night. Why don't you go on up to Tyler and do some shoppin'? Do y'all good to get out for the evenin'. Cabins are all full and rented, so you ain't got no late folks comin' in."

He didn't say that he was all out of advice

for them or that he really wanted an evening to himself for a change. Nope, that wouldn't be something Earl from that television show would do and if Zed was going to be an angel, then he had to take care of his responsibilities.

"*Saving Grace*," he said out loud.

"What?" Dana asked. "Is that a store in the mall?"

"No, it's a television show that was on some years ago. This big guy played Grace's second-chance angel. I just now remembered the name of the series."

"I loved that series. Earl was the angel's name, and he stole my heart," Dana said. "Come to think of it, you are our Earl, Uncle Zed. You've given us all a second chance."

"Don't go gluin' no wings on me or floatin' a halo up above my gray hair. It was Annie that give y'all a second chance," he said. "You're in a mood over Payton not comin' tonight? I'd like to put all three of you in a tow sack, throw it over a clothesline, and let y'all fight it out."

Dana patted him on the knee. "I hear a vehicle pullin' up in front of the store. Go on and get that tow sack out, because none of us is fit to live with today. Brook's even in a snit. I don't think a trip to the mall would even help, especially when her two aunts—"

He cleared his throat and gave her a sidelong look.

"Okay, all three of us are in a pissy mood."

"Chocolate ice cream is in the freezer. You take a half gallon home with you and hand out four spoons. You can't stay mad at each other forever when you're eatin' out of the same ice-cream box," he said.

Chapter Twenty

Night breezes ruffled Tawny's wet hair as she walked barefoot from her cabin to the edge of the lake. After the day she'd spent, she probably should wade right out there like her sister Harper had done and leave everything in the water. But Tawny didn't like swimming in anything other than a nice clear chlorinated pool where she could see the bottom and know exactly how deep the water was.

Her flowing gauze skirt floated out around her when she sat down. She was glad she'd brought along her denim jacket, because the air was turning cool. Stretching out her legs so her toes were in the water, she was amazed to feel the water warm her skin. No monsters rose up out of the water, either, which was something.

She didn't even glance at Harper when she sat down beside her, kicked off her shoes, rolled up the legs of her jeans, and stuck her long, long legs out into the water. *There are miles and miles of shoreline along the lake, so why does Harper need that spot for a few minutes of quiet mediation?*

Then Dana copped a squat on the other side of her, pulled up the skirt tail of her sundress, and put her feet in the water.

What does a woman have to do to get a few

minutes' peace? All Tawny wanted was to sit a few minutes before she had to go to Dana's and eat ice cream. To appease Brook, she'd go, eat one bite, and then leave just to prove that it was an insane idea even if it did come from Uncle Zed.

Not a one of them said a word but just sat there in quietness for fifteen minutes, and then Dana drew her feet out of the water and started past the cabins toward the house. Harper followed her, and with a long sigh, Tawny did the same. She was the last one in the house, but no one was talking or eating. All three of the others had claimed one side of a quilt that had been spread out on the living room floor. With only one left for her, she sat down and crossed her legs, yoga-style, and stared at the container of chocolate ice cream right in the middle of the quilt. A spoon was stuck in each of the four corners. One container—one family. Four different spoons, but they all came from the same set—the sisters and niece.

Brook was the first one to dig deep into the ice cream, Tawny the last. They finished off the ice cream with only a few sighs. Brook carried the empty container to the kitchen and brought out one with pecans, pralines, and cream. She set it down and said, "I started the last one. Aunt Tawny gets the first bite of this one since she's the one that caused this pissy mood day."

"Hey." Tawny raised her voice and then lowered it. "But—"

"But be honest," Brook said.

Tawny dipped into the ice cream. "I guess I did get it started, but I had a reason. Y'all are just pissed because your fellers didn't make it to the party. And I'm pissed because I don't even have a boyfriend to get mad at—among other things," she added.

"I haven't got a boyfriend, either, so that won't float." Brook brought a big spoonful to her mouth and licked it like an ice-cream cone.

"Honey, you've got two guys who think you are a little princess—Payton and Wyatt both—and you don't have to do anything but be adored." Tawny started for another bite, but Harper shoved her spoon out of the way.

"That's mine. It's in my corner and I've had my eye on that pecan." Harper's tone was as cold as the ice cream.

Using her spoon as a battle sword, Tawny shoved Harper's away and grabbed the bite with the pecan half and shoved it into her mouth.

"You brat!" Harper sank her spoon into Tawny's corner and brought up two pecan halves. "See what you get for that stunt."

Dana leaned over and took the whole bite off Harper's spoon. "What got your panties in a twist this mornin' anyway, Tawny?" she said when she finally swallowed.

"Matt came to see me last night," she said.

"And who is Matt?" Brook asked.

"He's my Ryson, only I was Cassidy instead of you." Tawny was amazed at how easy the words came out.

"And what did your Matt want? For you to sell drugs?" Brook asked.

"He wanted me to go to Europe with him for a summer of luxury. But there would have probably been drugs and for sure a lot of alcohol." She reached over into Dana's part of the ice cream and got her hand slapped.

"Please tell me you aren't going. Is that why you've been an old bear? You don't want to tell us?" Brook stuck her spoon in the ice cream and folded her arms over her chest.

"I'm not going, darlin' girl. I'm stayin' right here, and the reason I was so cranky is because"— she took a deep breath—"y'all have been open about your problems. I haven't and . . ." She went on to tell them the whole story.

"So that's why you got so mad at Ryson. You done been there and done that and got in more trouble than I did," Brook said.

"Yes, ma'am." Tawny stuck her spoon in the center of the ice cream and leaned against the sofa. "Must be the calories and sugar, but that wasn't as hard to tell y'all as I imagined. I can't stand that Granny is gone, but—" Tears welled up in her eyes, and there was no way she could get the lump in her throat to go down.

"But if she hadn't died when she did, we'd

all be in trouble, right?" Dana said. "Y'all ever watch that television show *Saving Grace*? Uncle Zed was talking about it today."

Harper raised her hand. "It was showing when I was in the unwed mothers' home. I wished I had an Earl in my life."

"Who's Earl?" Brook asked.

"He was this big, burly angel who took care of the leading lady, Grace, in the show," Harper said.

"I've never seen it," Tawny said.

"Me neither," Brook said.

"Wild child. Second-chance angel," Dana explained. "So I feel like Granny left Uncle Zed behind to be our Earl. He's kind of stepped into her boots as best he can and helped us get to this place. We've survived a day when we've all been a hell of a lot less than our best."

"It was the chocolate ice cream," Brook said. "That will fix anything."

"Amen!" Harper said.

Dana sighed. "I was fired from my job. I didn't quit like I let y'all believe. My boss got the mistaken notion in her head that I was sleeping with her husband and stealing money, too. She said she'd give me a bad recommendation wherever I went, so I was between a rock and a hard place. Then Uncle Zed called and, Lord, I felt guilty for being grateful that Granny had left this place for us. I still do."

"Amen." Tawny raised a hand.

"Well, hot damn," Brook said loudly, raising both hands into the air.

"Brook!" Dana scolded.

"Hey, after the way y'all been today, I'm entitled to one cuss word. I had to live with the bunch of you moping around like a bunch of babies," she said.

"Girl's got a point." Harper got one more bite of ice cream, then put her spoon in the middle of what was left.

"Thank you." Brook did a mini bow from a sitting position. "I've been dyin' to tell y'all my news all day, but I didn't want to say anything until you all made up."

"Made up?" Dana asked.

Brook waved both hands in the air. "That's what I said. I have a new friend. That's my news."

Tawny was happy for Brook. But in that moment she realized that she didn't have any friends. The ones that she and Matt had partied with distanced themselves from her when she was expelled from college. The ones she had before Matt had already taken a step back because they weren't included in her new circle of rich friends.

"Good. What's her name?" Dana asked.

"Not her. His name is Johnny Eagle and he's a Native American boy."

"Oh, really." Tawny's eyebrows shot up as she remembered her best friend in high school. She crossed her fingers behind her back and hoped that

Dana didn't react to this new person the way that Retha had when she brought Andre home for a study night. The yelling when he left that evening was almost as bad as the one right before Harper left.

"Yep, he was in suspension for being late to class too many times. He gets all wrapped up in a book at noon and doesn't hear the bell."

"And he's just a friend?" Harper asked.

"Yes, Aunt Harper. He likes a girl, but he's too shy to tell her."

"If he's that shy, then how come he talks to you?" Dana asked.

"Because I talked to him first. He was reading a book I just finished and I asked him how he liked it and we got to talking and he and his uncle are coming to the lake to fish tomorrow and I invited him to come meet all y'all at the end of the day. He lives with his grandma and two uncles," Brook spit out before anyone could say another word.

"A friend that's a guy, huh?" Dana asked.

"Don't judge him until you've met him," Tawny said.

"Why would you say that?"

"Because I had a best friend in junior high school and when I brought him home, Mama threw a hissy because he was black and came from a poor side of town. He was a good kid, sang in the church choir and made excellent grades, by the way. If she'd let us be friends, who knows what path my life might have taken," Tawny said.

"Kind of like Granny and Uncle Zed?" Brook asked.

"That's right," Tawny said. "They had such a sweet friendship. It would be easy to be jealous of them. No wonder he misses her so bad."

"I wasn't going to judge him, but thanks for tellin' me that," Dana said. "It's not his race that made me flinch. It was the fact that he's a guy."

Brook frowned. "Girls are whiny and gossipy and bitchy. Boys are different. We talk about books we've read and our favorite movies and he even likes to fish. So?"

"Well, I would like to meet your new friend," Dana said.

"Thanks, Mama, and I'm real sorry about you getting fired. You should have told me, and I wouldn't have thrown such a fit about leaving the ranch."

"Water under the bridge. What does this new friend look like?" Dana moved around the quilt to drape an arm around her daughter's shoulder.

"He's a nerd. Glasses that won't stay up on his nose. Black hair that's too long. He's taller than me but only a little bit, and he's got braces. His folks are originally from somewhere in Oklahoma. Don't start, Mama." Brook gave her a knowing look.

"He can be your friend, but not on the Texas-Oklahoma football weekend. Not if he's rootin' for the Sooners," Dana said.

Brook got one more bite of ice cream and then carried the container back to the kitchen and put it in the freezer. "He's not into football, so you don't have to worry about that."

"Braces hurt when you kiss. I'm speaking from experience," Tawny giggled.

"Johnny is my friend, not my boyfriend. I don't want to kiss him," Brook yelled.

Another stab of jealousy hit Tawny in the middle of her heart. Brook had a new friend, and both her sisters had someone promising in their lives. She took a long, hard look at her niece chattering away about some book she and her new friend were both reading, then at Dana, who had to be happy that Brook hadn't let the drama with Cassidy hold her back. After that she let her eyes shift over to Harper, who was actually wearing a smile. Granny Annie would be proud of them that evening, for sure.

◆═╫║╫║╫║╫═◆

Sunday was always busy at the store, but there was usually a ten-minute break a couple of times a day. Not so that day—if a guest wasn't checking out, then the store was full of folks needing supplies. From the time Dana opened the doors that morning until noon, she hardly had time to even sip on a cup of coffee.

Pretty weather had brought folks out in droves—on the edge of the lake and out on it. Kids' laughter and the buzz of conversations filled the air. But about three o'clock in the afternoon, there was a lull that let Dana sit down on the stool behind the counter. She'd barely gotten her aching feet propped up when Brook popped into the store with a teenage boy right behind her. "Mama, this is Johnny. Johnny, this is my mama, Dana."

"Nice to meet you, Miz Clancy." The poor kid looked like he could easily either faint or run. His hand trembled when he shook hers. "I was wonderin' if it would be all right if Brook came fishin' with me."

That's when the guilt trip struck Dana. Brook went to school and worked. She and Cassidy had giggled on the telephone a few times and had talked about having a sleepover, but the child hadn't had time to play since they'd arrived.

"I can't, Johnny. Aunt Tawny needs help in the laundry," Brook answered for her mother.

"If you'd like the afternoon off, I think we can manage," Dana said. "Tawny and I can finish up after we close down the store and café this evening. You go on and have a good time. Y'all fishin' from the bank or do you have a boat?"

"From the bank today, down on that big flat rock. You know where it is?" Johnny asked.

Dana nodded. "And we're plannin' on you comin' back to the house with her this evening for pizza."

"Thank you." Johnny finally smiled, showing

off orange braces. "You ready, Brook? Me and Uncle Nick brought extra gear so you don't need to bring anything."

"You sure about this, Mama?" Brook asked.

"Yes, but I do think you should let me braid your hair. It's awfully warm out today and the wind is blowing. You'll be fighting it in your face all day. Johnny, you mind waiting about three minutes while us ladies make a trip to the bathroom?" Dana asked.

"Not a bit. Uncle Nick is gettin' us some burgers from the café and he'll be a few minutes."

Dana grabbed her purse, followed Brook into the restroom, and closed the door. "So do you want to go fishin' with him? Do I need to worry about you? And I'd like to meet his uncle before you leave," she whispered as she removed a brush from her purse and began to work on Brook's tangled hair.

"Yes, I want to go with him, Mama. And you don't have to worry. These are good people. I just know it in my heart and I'll fix it so you can meet his uncle—you'll see what I mean. Now let's braid my hair."

Dana really studied her daughter as she quickly put her hair into two Pollyanna-type braids. She was fourteen going on twenty-one, but with that hairstyle and the baggy Hard Rock Café T-shirt she wore, she didn't look a day over twelve. When they left the restroom, Johnny handed Dana a piece of paper. "This is my cell phone number."

"Thank you. That's sweet." Dana tucked the paper into her pocket.

A tall, dark-haired man poked his head into the store and looked right at Johnny. "Did you get the worms?"

Johnny groaned. "I forgot."

The guy came inside and clamped a hand on Johnny's shoulder. "I'm Nick, Johnny's uncle. We need about three dozen worms and a dozen minnows. Is this your new friend?"

"This is Brook and this is her mother, Dana. This here is my uncle Nick." Johnny continued the introductions. "Brook gets to go with us."

"Well, that settles it." Nick smiled, deepening the angles in his face and putting a twinkle in deep, dark-brown eyes. "We'll be talking about books and movies rather than baseball."

"Yes, we will."

Johnny's whole body language changed from tense to comfortable now that his uncle was beside him.

"I don't know much about baseball anyway, but I can talk football with either of you. Are you going to watch the draft on television?" Brook asked. "And who do you root for in the Texas-Oklahoma game?"

"Texas!" Nick and Johnny said at the same time.

"My kind of fellows." Dana nodded. "Y'all

got plenty of water and soda for the afternoon?"

"We sure do," Johnny answered.

"Need a couple of beers to finish your order, Nick?"

"Thanks, but no, thanks, ma'am. We ain't a drinkin' family. Our sister was killed by a drunk driver. Sweet tea and soft drinks are fine with us," Nick answered. "I'll have the kids back to your place at seven, and then come get Johnny around ten."

"I'm sorry about your sister." Dana nodded. "We're plannin' on pizza. You are welcome to stay if you'd like. Save you a trip."

"Thank you. I might just do that." Nick's smile rang sincere.

That and his comment about not drinking quieted Dana's fears. Still, at the next five-minute lull in business, she picked up the phone and called the café.

Zed answered on the first ring. "Need some help? I could send Harper. We're all caught up."

"No, but she might see if Tawny needs help. I let Brook go off with Johnny Eagle and his uncle Nick to do some fishing."

"That's a good family. Johnny's mama got killed a couple of years back in a car wreck and her brothers, Nick and Drake, took it real hard. They were a lot younger than his mama—more like older brothers than uncles to Johnny."

"What about his father?"

"His daddy is in the military and is doin' another tour over in one of them war countries. I never can remember which one. When he can, he comes and stays with Johnny, takes him places and all, but it's his grandma who is raisin' him, along with lots of help from his uncles. Don't worry about Brook. She's in good hands. You'll like that boy when you get to know him better. Brook's got a real good friend there," Zed said.

"Thanks, Uncle Zed. Here comes a truckload of guys who look like they're needin' more bait. See you later."

Dana suddenly missed her friends at the ranch. The foreman who always came in to have coffee with her in the morning, the CPA that she had lunch with once a month when they went over the ranch books, the old veterinarian she'd learned so much from in the last ten years, and even her boss, who'd been her best friend until she'd accused Dana of horrible things.

"Hey, Dana," a regular customer yelled as he led a parade of guys into the store. "We need four dozen minnows, a box of stink bait, and maybe six dozen worms. While you get that ready, we'll get our snack and beer order on the counter for you to check out."

"Plannin' on stayin' out all night?" She picked up a net and headed toward the minnow tank.

"Yep. All night or until the beer runs out. Lester's wife says she'll cook the fish up if we clean 'em, and we've all got the day off tomorrow. Catfish bite better at night," he said.

She dipped up the minnows, giving them a few extra in the container, and then filled the rest of their order. By the time she got to the counter, it was filled with chips, sandwich meat, bread, candy bars, and beer. She rang it up as all the men began to throw money on the counter.

After they left, Tawny came through the door, wiping sweat from her forehead with a bandanna.

"I need an icy-cold Pepsi and a candy bar. I never realized how much Brook helped until she wasn't there for the afternoon. That girl is a godsend. But I agree with you, she does need some time to play. We should give her every Sunday afternoon off, Dana. She needs to be a kid as long as possible. I sure didn't have to spend all my time working when I was her age."

"Neither did I," Dana said.

The phone rang, and Tawny reached across the counter to grab the receiver. She stretched it too far and the base fell on the floor with a loud clang. "Lake Side Resort," she said with a giggle.

"Dropped the phone, didn't you? Can't get used to these things with cords," Brook laughed. "Can I talk to Mama?"

"How do you know this isn't your mama talking?" Tawny asked.

"Because her voice is deeper than yours."

"It's Brook." Tawny handed the receiver to Dana

and rounded the counter to put the phone back where it belonged.

"You are kiddin' me. Did you really?" Dana covered the mouthpiece and said, "She just caught a five-pound catfish and the guys are cleaning it up for her. They're going to fillet it so we can have a fish fry sometime this week."

Tawny gave her a thumbs-up sign.

"Tell them they're all invited to supper that night," Dana said, pausing to listen again. "Okay, thirty more minutes, but then you'd better come on home because Payton is bringing the pizza about then."

She handed the receiver back to Tawny, who laid it on the base. "Where were we?"

"Talkin' about her having a guy for a best friend. You comin' to the house to meet Johnny and have pizza with us tonight?" Dana asked. "Harper called and said that she and Wyatt are going out on the boat this evening, so she won't be there."

"I've got to get cleaned up, but I'll be there. Save me a slice." Tawny picked up the bag with her snacks and disappeared just as the clock ticked to closing time.

Dana hurriedly locked the door, grabbed two large bottles of Coke, and rushed home to take a quick shower and change since Payton had agreed to join them and to pick up the pizza and pasta at his favorite place in Tyler.

Chapter Twenty-One

The cool shower water beating down on her body reminded Tawny of playing in the summer rain when she was a little girl. Her mother would have probably cut off all ties with Granny Annie if she'd known how often they were allowed to run around in the rain in their underwear.

She was padding across her bedroom with a towel around her body when the phone rang. Expecting it to be Dana fussing at her for being late, she picked it up and said, "Give me ten minutes and don't eat all the meat lover's."

"What are you talking about?" her mother asked bluntly.

"Hello, Mama," Tawny said.

"So how are things in the boondocks?"

"Great. Wonderful, actually. Why don't you come up and spend the weekend? I can get you a discount on a cabin." Tawny propped the phone on her shoulder and towel-dried her hair as she talked.

"No, thank you. I'm not interested in spending one minute there. I didn't like staying overnight when your father was alive, so I'm sure not going there again. I called to tell you that I pulled some really big strings and got you back into college for next semester."

Tawny dropped the towel. "How did you do that?"

Did this mean that her mother was finally coming around? Could they possibly have a decent adult relationship?

"Does it matter? You get to finish your degree. Of course you'll be on probation, but you'll have it all done in one semester, so that's no big deal."

Leaning back in her chair, she looked at her bookcase full of sentimental items—the latest was a beautiful monarch butterfly that had died in the laundry room that day, prompting her thought about Brook needing to spread her wings at least once a week.

"Are you there?" Retha's tone was demanding.

"Thanks, but no thanks. I'm not going back to college. I don't need a degree with this new job. But next time you are flying through Dallas on one of your trips, call me and I'll drive up to the airport and we'll have lunch or dinner."

Retha's snort said that wasn't going to happen. "I'm as disappointed in you as I am in Harper."

"Mother, you are going to end up a lonely old lady, but it's not too late to turn things around. We probably won't ever have the kind of relationship Dana has with her mother or that we all had with Granny, but we could start to build some kind of foundation." Tawny tried to reach the thermostat to turn down the air-conditioning, but the cord wouldn't go that far.

"Your granny Annie gave me a lecture one time about your father. She had the opinion that he was a king and needed to be treated like one. But anyway, she said that sometimes the door gets shut and no one can open it. You might remember that. This offer isn't for anything other than the fall semester," Retha said.

"I'll hope that you change your mind, and if you do, you know where to get in touch with us." Tawny eased the phone back onto the base. Her mother was the one shutting that door.

She jerked on a pair of denim shorts and covered a red tank top with a plaid shirt, slipped her feet into flip-flops and twisted her hair up into a wet ponytail. It didn't really matter what she looked like that evening, because she would be the fifth wheel. She thought about begging off, but she was hungry and pizza sounded really good.

The night air was muggy, so she pulled off the shirt and tied it around her waist before she got to Dana's house. Strange how for years the little two-bedroom home was Granny Annie's house, and after only a month, she was already thinking of it as Dana's. She didn't knock but yelled when she entered through the kitchen door. Everyone but Brook and Johnny was gathered around the table, paper plates in hand as they loaded them up. The two kids were in the living room sitting on one of Granny's old quilts on the floor.

Tawny glanced over at Brook and asked, "Why aren't y'all goin' outside?"

"It's too hot out there," Brook said. "And besides, we don't want to listen to old people talk, so we're having an air-conditioned pizza picnic. Get your food and come eat with us in here, Aunt Tawny. This is Johnny, and his uncle Nick is in the bathroom washing up. This is my aunt Tawny."

"Thank you for not grouping me in with the old people." Tawny smiled. "Nice to meet you, Johnny." The kid was exactly as Brook had described him. A boy with skin the color of coffee with lots and lots of cream in it, and jet-black hair that tickled his shirt collar. He blushed slightly and nodded. Poor kid was every bit as shy as Brook said, but he seemed to be perfectly comfortable with her.

"Well, I'm takin' mine outside," Payton declared. "I've been on a delivery truck all day."

"And I've been cooped up in a store with min-nows and worms, so I'm going outside, too," Dana declared.

To stay in with the kids and Johnny's old uncle or to go outside and be a fifth wheel—those were Tawny's options. She sure didn't want to hinder Dana's time with Payton, so with a sigh, she put another slice of pizza on her plate. She was on the way to the living room, hoping that Uncle Nick would be a sweet old guy like Uncle Zed, when a movement caught her eye in the hallway.

Holy almighty hell were the three words that ran through her mind when she looked up at the gorgeous hunk of man not four feet in front of her. His coal-black hair was pulled into a thick braid that hung down his back at least a foot, but the top and sides were trimmed neatly. An artist would have trouble capturing all the angles and planes in his face, and his lips—good Lord, she wanted to taste them. Speaking of, his yellow T-shirt stretched over a six-pack of abs that said he was a hardworking man.

He smiled and stuck out his hand. "I don't think we've met. I'm Nick Eagle, Johnny's uncle."

Forgetting that she had a plate in her hand, Tawny stuck it out to shake with him and the pizza started to slide to the floor. He caught it upside down before it hit the floor and put it back on her plate. Heat rose from her neck and rushed to her cheeks.

"And that clumsy lady is my aunt Tawny," Brook said from the quilt. "I'm glad you caught her pizza. I would have been tempted to eat it off the floor to keep from wasting it."

"You wouldn't!" Johnny exclaimed.

"We don't waste good pizza in this house," Brook said seriously.

"Hope you like scrambled pizza," Nick said. "I'll have to go wash my hands again before I shake yours."

"I'm so sorry. Th-thank you." She stumbled over the words like a sixth-grade girl.

"No problem. Be right back," Nick said.

She sat down at the table, grabbed a beer, opened it, and downed a fourth of it fast to cool her cheeks. He'd returned by the time she set the bottle on the table. No matter how hard she tried to keep it inside and ladylike, the burp sounded like it came from a three-hundred-pound truck driver.

"Way to go, Aunt Tawny!" Brook laughed.

"I didn't know girls could do that," Johnny whispered, but his words carried across the living room into the tiny dining area.

"Sorry." Tawny's blush deepened.

"Not bad manners, just good beer," Nick said.

"Want a beer?" Tawny asked.

"No, thanks—we all stopped after Johnny's mama was killed by a drunk driver. Made Mama happy, because me and my brother liked to party," he said. "But don't let me stop you from enjoying yours. I'll just have a root beer."

"Was it hard to . . ." She stumbled again as her mind slipped into the gutter. "Was it difficult to not drink anymore?"

"Oh, honey, you'll never know. It was worse than quittin' smokin', which I did at the same time." Nick put three slices of pizza on a plate. "We goin' to sit in here or join them kids?"

Tawny didn't trust herself to walk across the

floor. "I think maybe I'd better sit here, as clumsy as I am tonight."

"Table it is." Nick nodded. "So what do you do in this business, Miz Tawny?"

"I'm in charge of books and sheets." And there was the blush again, this time thanks to a vision of his beautiful, permanently tanned body all tangled up in white sheets. "As in the laundry," she said quickly. "Brook and I take care of maid duties, and I'm the bookkeeper, too. My sister Harper is in the café with Uncle Zed."

"I met her today when I went in there for burgers to take with us on our fishin' trip," Nick said. "And Dana takes care of the store, right?"

"Yes, and she's taken over the checkin' in and out for me so I can do the cleaning. What do you do?"

Besides modeling? Their eyes locked somewhere in the middle of the table. *Or maybe you own and run a gym?*

"I'm a carpenter. My brother and I build houses," he said. "Not big fancy ones, but small ones that people around here can afford. My mama is the one who takes care of our books. Keeps us busy, especially around the lake, where folks usually just want summer places built."

"How long have you been doing that?" She loved the sound of his soft drawl. Maybe she could take him home. He could sit beside her bed and read the phone book to her until she fell asleep.

Get ahold of yourself, girl. Someone as pretty as he is has to have a whole line of girls already on his dance card. A clumsy blonde wouldn't have a chance with this hunky guy.

"I started working with my brother before I ever graduated. Summertime and after school. Soon as I finished high school six years ago, I got brought in as a full partner." Praise the Lord! That would make him about twenty-four. Dana couldn't yell at her that he was old enough to be her father.

He leaned forward and lowered his voice. "I'm so glad that Johnny has Brook for a new friend, by the way. He's been so lost since his mama died and his daddy's tour has been long. This week he's smiled more than he has in two years."

"Brook had a bad experience with her friend last week. We're glad that she found Johnny, too," Tawny said softly.

Nick leaned back and picked up a slice of pepperoni. "How about you? What did you do before you came here?"

"I was in college until December. Got into trouble and was asked to leave, so I worked in a coffee shop until I came here."

"Freshman?" Nick reached for another slice at the same time she did, and their hands brushed.

What in the devil was wrong with her? She hadn't been this nervous about a guy since her first date. No, that was wrong. She hadn't even been this jittery back then.

"Senior. Needed a semester to have my degree, but I've decided that it's not that important. How about you? Did you go to college around here?"

"Hated school. Couldn't wait to get out so I could work full-time." He bit into the pizza. "Romano's makes the best ever."

Are you married? Do you have a girlfriend? Are all the women in this area crazy? Questions bombarded her mind, but she said, "You got that right. I even like frozen pizza. Lived on it and ramen noodles every week when my money ran out."

"Never had to eat that kind of thing. Mama makes supper for us every night so we can spend some time with Johnny."

"You live with her?" A picture flashed through her mind of Marcus Green and his cat. Lord help! Was she drawn to men who were mama's boys?

"No, me and my brother, Drake, built our own house with our first year's profit," he said proudly. "Close to her and close to the lake so we can get in some fishin' most evenings if we have the energy."

"Hey, y'all." Dana came in the back door. "I see you've met. It's starting to rain, so we're coming into the house. Anyone want to watch a movie?"

"No, let's play poker," Brook said. "Nothing smaller than a nickel or bigger than a dime."

"You serious?" Nick asked.

"Sure, the foreman at the ranch where we used to live played with me and Mama lots. He was real into gambling."

"I'm in." Tawny finished her pizza and licked her fingers.

⊹⊹⊱⊰⊹⊹

Zed leaned back under the roof as he smoked his second cigarette. There wasn't a whisper of a breeze, so the rain was coming straight down. Some of it splattered on his boots, but he didn't care. It smelled wonderful and it cleared the air, making it easier for him to breathe.

It was straight up ten o'clock when Tawny appeared out of the shadows. She carried her shoes in one hand but held both arms out as she sang and danced in the rain. Harper could sing like an angel, but Tawny, God love her little soul, couldn't carry a tune. Annie used to say that the angels used earplugs when that girl opened her mouth. But she was so happy that evening that her voice put a smile on Zed's face.

When she finished, she took a bow and ran over to where Zed was sitting. She plopped down beside him.

"Must've been some damn good pizza. You freezin'?" He chuckled.

Water made a puddle around her feet. "I'm so happy that I can't feel the cold, Uncle Zed. Do you know Nick Eagle? Is he a decent man?"

"The best. He's the baby of the family, or was until they took Johnny in to help raise. They're a good, hardworkin' family."

"Where's his daddy?"

"Died when Nick was in junior high school. He was a carpenter, like those boys are, and he fell off a house. Broke his neck," Zed said.

"Is Nick married?"

Zed could hardly sit still. He had to get into the apartment and tell Annie the good news, but he couldn't ruin Tawny's evening by leaving before she did. "Nope. Drake was for a few years, but it didn't work out. 'Bout the time that Nick got out of high school, he and his wife split the blanket. Now he and Nick got them a little house on the other side of the lake," he answered. "So you liked that little sissy braid he wears?"

"I did, and now I'm going to my cabin. Maybe I'll even dream about him," she said. "Playing in the rain reminded me of when I was a little girl and Granny let me catch raindrops on my tongue."

"There's a picture in her album of you doin' that. She'd laugh every year when we got the pictures out and looked at them," Zed said.

"Good night, Uncle Zed. I'm so glad that I'm here." She kissed him on the top of his gray head and danced all the way to her cabin as she sang the lyrics to Blake and Miranda's song, "You're the Reason God Made Oklahoma."

Tears ran down Zed's cheeks. "Annie, did you hear that? Did you see her kiss me? Oh, my darlin' Annie, this is the best night I've had since you went on ahead of me. She's happy like them other two."

Chapter Twenty-Two

It rained all day Monday and Tuesday and got serious Wednesday with lots of thunder and lightning thrown in. They'd had so many cancellations that the only two occupied cabins belonged to Harper and Tawny. No one was interested in spending time at the lake when the only thing to do was run through the rain three times a day to get something to eat at the café.

At noon a single fellow braved the weather to eat at the café, and Zed hurried back to the kitchen when he saw the man hang his raincoat on the back of a chair. Harper didn't recognize the guy, so she raised an eyebrow toward Dana.

"Zedekiah Williamson!" The man followed him across the floor and through the swinging doors. "You cannot run from me. You missed your appointment this morning and there's no excuse for it."

All three sisters slid back their chairs and crowded into the kitchen. The stranger had a rim of gray hair, beady little blue eyes set in a big, round baby face, and a paunchy gut that hung out over his belt.

"Who are you?" Harper asked.

"Dr. Glenn Tipton. Zedekiah did not make his appointment this morning. I've been his and

Annie's doctor for thirty years. Why didn't he even call to cancel? I thought maybe he'd died."

The doctor's eyes shifted from one sister to the other and then came back to settle on Harper.

"We're Annie's granddaughters," she explained. "Is it too late to get Uncle Zed in to see you today? I'll bring him myself."

"I ain't dead and I can drive myself. I didn't want to get out in this rain," Zed fussed.

The doctor handed a card to Harper. "Friday afternoon at three o'clock. You'll have him there, right?"

"I don't need a chauffeur. I'll be there. Now the bunch of you get out of my kitchen and let me make this man a cheeseburger," Zed grumbled as he pointed toward the door.

"Is Uncle Zed sick?" Tawny asked outright when she took a glass of water to the doctor's table.

Harper's chest tightened at that thought. "Is this just a routine checkup, or is it something that he'll need a driver to bring him home?"

"Are you doing tests?" Dana asked bluntly.

"Just a checkup, ladies. And I'll have the biggest glass you got back there of sweet tea to go with my lunch. So y'all are the granddaughters that Annie talked about so often?"

"Harper." She raised a hand.

"Dana." She nodded.

"Tawny. And you would tell us if Uncle Zed had something wrong with him, right?"

Zed set a basket filled with sweet potato fries and a plate with a huge double-meat, double-cheese burger in front of the doctor. "He's bound by some of them new privacy laws to keep his mouth shut, but I'm tellin' all of you that this is just my three-month checkup. Last time me and Annie went, we was together for the checkup. Besides the rain, I just didn't want to go without her. That's all there is to it."

Harper had lived on the edge long enough to smell a rat when there was one present, and Zed was not telling the whole truth and nothing but the truth. If she made him place his hand on the Bible and raise the other toward heaven and swear that he was fit as a freshly tuned fiddle, she'd bet dollars to dead fish that there was something more to be said. Doctors didn't check on patients in the pouring-down rain.

She touched each sister on the arm and nodded toward the outside. "I'm in the mood for a candy bar. Y'all want to go with me to the store?"

"There's a whole stand full of umbrellas in the kitchen. Me and Annie got them when we had to close up the door between the store and the café," Zed said.

Harper laid a hand on Zed's shoulder. "Call me if we get a big rush?"

"Ain't damn likely," he said gruffly.

The rain had slowed considerably, so the umbrellas kept them from being drenched when they reached the store. They ducked inside and Harper went straight for the candy rack, picked up three of the biggest bars, and laid them on the counter.

Harper felt like she had a stone in her chest, making it hard for her to breathe. "I'm treating today. Put these on my bill, and be honest. Do either of y'all think Uncle Zed is sick? A doctor coming to the café? It don't sound good."

Tawny peeled back the wrapper and took a big bite of the chocolate. She held up a finger, which meant she needed time to think, and when she finally spoke, her voice cracked. "He's lost weight and he's coughing more and more. Oh, Lord, what would we ever do without him?"

Dana hiked a hip on the old wooden stool behind the counter and reached for her candy. "We'll take care of him if he is, but I can't imagine runnin' this place without him. It was tough losing Flora, but Uncle Zed is the cornerstone now." She blinked several times to keep the tears at bay.

"He said it was just a checkup and he's never lied to us, so . . ." Tawny gulped twice. "I need a cup of coffee to go with this. You can put three cups on my bill and I'll get us each one."

"I'd rather have a bottle of milk," Harper said.

"Lord love a duck!" Dana laughed. "I never thought I'd hear you say that you wanted to drink milk."

"Or that Tawny wanted coffee over Pepsi or

beer." Harper tore the wrapper back from her candy.

Tawny went to the back of the store and brought back a pint of milk, then drew up two cups of coffee. "I've decided to quit drinkin' anything alcoholic. So coffee, sweet tea, and soft drinks are the future."

"Nick got something to do with that?" Dana asked.

"A lot." Tawny nodded. "He said he didn't have the courage to call until last night. He'd planned to go fishing on Monday evening and stop by my porch to see if I might be sitting outside. But it was raining. I done figured that my clumsiness and inability to say the right things scared him away."

"And?" Harper asked.

Tawny smiled. "We talked for an hour about everything and I didn't want to hang up, but he said he'd call again." The smile faded. "But that's not the issue here today. Uncle Zed is. I overheard him talking to Granny Annie last night when I had the window open in my cabin. Do you think there was anything between them other than friendship? He called her Annie *darlin'* when he was talkin' to her."

"He calls us darlin' all the time. It's just an expression," Dana said. "The cough comes from him smokin' like a chimney, but . . ." She sighed.

"But what?" Tawny asked.

"But we need to know what's wrong. Or if anything is," Dana answered.

"He'll tell us when the time is right," Harper said.

Tawny picked up her coffee and candy and said, "See y'all later. I'm going to go get completely caught up on my book work. If the sun comes out, we'll have a full house starting tomorrow and through the weekend, so I'll be busy cleaning and doing laundry."

The doctor's vehicle was gone when she passed the café, and Zed had taken up his usual place on the bench with a cigarette in his hand. "Glad to see the sun. Rain makes my old bones ache," he said.

She stopped and really looked at him. His face had always been thin and now it was wrinkled, but Tawny couldn't see that his eyes were yellowed or that his hands were shaking any more than usual.

"Me too," she said. "How often does it get this slow around here?"

"Couple or three times a year. Annie hated it. She was a real busy bee." Zed crushed the cigarette butt on his heel. "She hated for me to smoke. I started over there in Vietnam, and when I got home, I tried all that stuff to quit—the gum and patches and pills—but I just couldn't break the habit."

"Shhh . . ." She put her finger over her lips.

355

"Don't tell anyone, but I'm addicted to cherry sours."

"That a drink?" Zed asked.

"No, it's those little round sour candies that are two packs for a dollar in most convenience stores. I'd buy two on payday and make them last all week when I was working in the coffee shop. Being poor and not having anything I wanted was a real test, Uncle Zed. But the worst one was having the willpower to only eat my daily allotment and leave the rest alone," she told him.

"Better than whiskey, I guess," Zed chuckled. "I hear a couple of cars turning this way. I'd best get on inside."

She watched him closely as he got up. He didn't seem a bit slower than usual, and he wasn't shuffling like some old people who used to come into the coffee shop every morning. Maybe it was just a plain old checkup.

<hr />

On Thursday there wasn't a cloud in the sky—not even a wispy little white one up there like a big long string of cotton candy. Harper kept a close eye on Zed, though nothing seemed unusual. He had a coughing fit that morning, but it sounded dry, like those that smokers get, not rattling like someone who was sick. He wasn't as spry as he'd been when she was a little girl, but who was?

In the middle of the afternoon, she left him

alone and headed out to the laundry, where Tawny was sitting in a folding chair reading a book. She hopped up on the folding table, her legs dangling while the small oscillating fan whipped her ponytail from side to side.

Tawny laid her book to the side. "I'll be glad when tomorrow gets here. Cabins have been cleaned and my book work is caught up. I'm bored."

"Been slow in the café, too, but it picked up a lot today. We ran out of the meat loaf special at two o'clock. Brook will be here soon. Maybe she'll cheer you up," Harper said.

"Johnny is riding home with her on the bus, and they're going to study for some big test they've got tomorrow. But . . ." Tawny's eyes twinkled. "That means Nick is coming to get him this evening. And that reminds me, how are things with Wyatt?"

Harper sighed. "Haven't seen him this week at all. He's been helping his friend's widow take care of all the business involved. I wonder why we didn't have more when Granny went."

"Uncle Zed took care of it for us," Tawny said. "So is this going to get serious between y'all?"

"Might be," Harper answered. "Time will tell. I'm not rushing anything. And you and Nick?"

"Not rushing anything, either, but there's definitely a spark like I've never felt before. What if we all do get serious? What happens to this place?"

Harper raised a shoulder. "We run it like always. We just have someone to keep us warm in the evenings. I'd better get back in case some of the folks checking in want to stop in the café for burgers."

⋇⋈⋇

Friday was so busy that Zed tried his best to reschedule his appointment, but Harper wouldn't have any part of it. She said that she could make burgers and that Tawny would come in from the laundry to help her if she got into a bind. So there he was sitting in the waiting room looking at a magazine and wishing to hell he was anywhere else in the world.

"Mr. Williamson." The nurse finally called his name, and he followed her back down a hallway to a corner where they kept the scale. "First we get your weight. Put your feet on the marked places."

He held his breath and waited for the digital number to pop up. Dammit! He'd lost another eight pounds since he'd been here last, but he hadn't had much appetite since Annie had died. Besides, he'd worn his good shoes this time, not his combat boots that weighed at least five pounds.

She tapped the end of her pen against a tablet and motioned him into a room. "Sit right here, and we'll get your blood pressure and temperature." She busied herself with the blood pressure cuff and thermometer and recorded the measurements.

"Doctor will be in shortly," she said when she finished and took her fancy-shmancy tablet out the door with her.

They had always put him and Annie in a room that offered an assortment of brochures about constipation and diarrhea or about arthritis and rheumatism. He chuckled and pointed to the one about heart failure.

"That's the one I need to tuck into my pocket, Annie. I didn't mind coming here when we did our appointments together. This ain't fun," he grumbled. "Damned old doctor, anyway. Why don't he just leave me alone and let me die when the good Lord is willin' to shuffle me off this spinnin' pile of dirt? He didn't need to be comin' to the café and upsettin' our girls."

"Who are you talking to?" Dr. Tipton asked as he carried another of those abominable devices into the room.

"Myself. I'm goin' batshit crazy. Shoot me up with a double dose of tranquilizers and send me home," Zed said. "What happened to pen and paper? What're you goin' to do if all that technological crap fails?"

"Took me a long time to get used to this, but it does help keep things in order better than all that paper. How are you feelin'? Your blood pressure is elevated. You been takin' your medication?"

"When I remember it," Zed said.

"Been watchin' the salt?"

"Watchin' it go right in my mouth. I ain't goin' to stop eatin' bacon. I'd just as soon not eat if I can't salt my food. Why don't you just let me eat what I want and die when I'm supposed to?"

"Zedekiah, I'm tryin' to take care of you like Annie told me to the last time y'all came in here. But you are not makin' it easy," Dr. Tipton fussed at him. "Don't you want to spend more time with the granddaughters?"

"Much as God gives me, but I'd rather spend eternity with Annie," Zed declared.

"You are one stubborn old coot."

"That I am. Can I go home now?"

"Let me listen to your lungs and heart." The doctor pressed a stethoscope on his chest. "Promise me you won't miss your diuretics."

"I won't miss them a bit when I'm dead."

"Your heart is continuing to get weaker, and your lungs are shot. It won't be long until you are going to need oxygen." The doctor took a step back.

Zed hopped down off the table. "I'm not haulin' around one of them tanks, but the news about my heart is the best I've had in weeks. Any use in making an appointment for another three months?"

"Four weeks." Dr. Tipton wrote on his pad. "Definitely no more than six weeks or I'll come back to the café and tell those girls exactly what condition you are in."

"I hear you." Zed hopped off the table and walked out without even hesitating at the office window.

Black clouds were boiling up from the south-west, and he didn't want to be caught out in a tornado. They hadn't had a bad one in more than five years now, but the last one had picked up debris from half the state of Texas and dumped it in the lake, then sucked up enough water to baptize the beer joint up the road with it. Folks inside got sobered up real quick when the roof went flying off and the flood came down on top of them. Zed had heard that the church was packed the next day.

He was still chuckling about that when he got home. No cars in the café parking lot or in front of the store, so he wasn't a bit surprised to find all the sisters, plus Brook, waiting in the café. And just as he figured, it was Harper who asked the first question, which was no surprise, either. "So what did the doctor say?"

"He said that if I quit eatin' bacon, quit smokin', and quit havin' a shot of whiskey or a glass of wine when I want it, that I might live to be a hundred."

"And what did you tell him?" Tawny asked.

"That if I did all that I'd be in hell and I'd always intended on spending eternity in heaven," Zed joked, and then his expression went serious.

"You girls don't worry about me. You've got your own lives to live. Now let's get out a half gallon of chocolate ice cream and celebrate."

"What are we celebrating?" Brook asked.

"New friends, old times, and a sweet life," he said.

<hr />

The clouds had passed over the resort with only a few claps of thunder and raindrops but nothing major that afternoon. But now a strong wind was pushing another big bunch their way, stirring up the lake until the whitecaps looked like that frosting that Granny used to put on the tops of cupcakes. Tawny loved to watch her use the back of the spoon to make little peaks. They were so sticky that Tawny never did master eating one without getting it all over her fingers and face.

"Hey, it looks like it might brew something up out there. Those clouds look angry." Nick stepped around the end of the cabin.

Her pulse jacked up about fifty percent, and her heart threw in an extra beat. "Never know. We got a pass earlier today, so we might have to pay for it tonight."

"Mind if I sit?"

"Help yourself to all the porch that you want." Tawny smiled.

"That's pretty generous, giving me that much room."

"I'm willin' to share if I like you."

If she liked him? Now that was the understatement of the year. He almost made her believe in love at first sight.

"If not?" He caught her gaze and held it.

She recognized flirting when she saw or heard it, and they were definitely sharing sparks. Why, oh, why couldn't she have met him before now?

Because you had to go through some hard times so you'd grow up and appreciate a guy who works hard for a livin' and don't live on his daddy's credit cards. Granny Annie's voice filled her thoughts again.

"If not, then you don't get to sit on my porch while a big storm rolls in," she said.

"You ever been married?" he asked bluntly.

Wow, he got right to the point. But she kind of liked that. "I'm only twenty-two."

"My sister was married at eighteen."

"Why did you ask?"

"We talked for a long time the other night, and I didn't have the courage to ask you if you were involved with someone right now." He stopped and sucked in a lungful of air. "I'd like to ask you out, but I don't mess with another man's woman."

"Never married. Got out of a relationship right before Christmas last year, so it's been long enough. And yes, I would like to go out with you. I felt sparks, too."

"Is that why you tried to throw pizza on me?" He chuckled.

"I did not!" she exclaimed.

"That's the way I'm going to tell the story. So do you want to go for pizza on Sunday evening when you get off work?"

"I'd rather go for a big juicy steak."

He nodded seriously. "I'll cook for us, then, because there isn't a restaurant in Texas that can top my steaks. Pick you up at eight?"

"I'll be ready." Her heart threw in another extra beat.

"Okay, then. I'll call you later tonight, but right now I'd better get Johnny on home. He talks about Brook all the time." He straightened up and turned to blow her a kiss before he headed over toward Dana's place.

She caught it and wrapped it tightly in her hands. She could have sworn that it warmed her whole palm.

✦❈❈❈✦

Harper was already in bed, air conditioner lowered to where her nose was actually cold to the touch. She was curled up under an extra blanket when someone rapped gently on her cabin door.

She bailed out of bed and sent up a silent prayer that it would be Wyatt on the other side of the door. Her prayers were answered.

She grabbed one of his arms, pulled him inside,

slammed the door shut with her bare foot, and then cupped his cheeks in her hands. "I have missed you so much," she said as she brought his lips to hers.

"I love you," he said when the kiss ended.

Lightning streaked through the room, lighting it for an instant so that she could see his eyes. His eyes said that he wasn't teasing, and the passion in the kiss that followed testified that he meant what he said.

"It dawned on me as I was helping the widow settle stuff that we aren't guaranteed tomorrow or even the next minute. I don't want to die without telling you that I love you. I did when we were kids and I still do now that we are adults. I want us to have a future together. I went to bed in my house and couldn't sleep because I didn't want to waste another minute without saying the words to your face."

"I love you," she said simply and led him to the bed. "Now please hold me. I'm freezing."

"With pleasure." He kicked off his shoes and started to undress.

Chapter Twenty-Three

Harper floated into work on Saturday morning. Wyatt was gone when she awoke, but he'd left a note on his pillow saying that he'd be back after his fishing trip up near Wylie that evening. Zed had already made coffee and was sitting at their favorite table back near the kitchen. And right there in the middle of the table was a big platter stacked high with fresh doughnuts.

"Uncle Zed, how long have you been up? Those take at least two hours." She reached for one with light-brown maple frosting. "Oh. My. God! These are just like I remember you making for us when we were little girls."

"That's for you, but it stays in my kitchen." He pointed to what looked like a book of some kind lying on the table. "I never shared it with nobody, but I want you to have it, long as you promise me it'll never leave the kitchen."

She licked the frosting off her hands and scooted it across the table. "What is it?"

He handed her a wet paper towel. "Wash your hands first. Paper is old and kinda brittle."

Hand stitched and resembling a miniature patchwork quilt, the fabric cover and the hand-crocheted lace around the edges were frayed in some areas. Three strips of leather held it together. Almost afraid to even touch it, she ran a soft, feathery finger over the tiny stitches. Someone had been quite a seamstress to make all those pieces fit so well together.

"It's called a double wedding ring design. My grandma gave my mama a big quilt for her bed when she got married that had that same pattern to it."

She carefully laid the cover back to the first page where *Mama's Recipes* was written in spidery handwriting.

"Oh, Uncle Zed!" she said when she opened it.

"It belonged to my grandma, but we ain't too sure if it was her grandma's or if it's been passed down even more generations than that. It was one of my mama's prize possessions. She used it to make the blue-plate specials right here at this café, and then it was mine when she passed on. I want it to be yours, so you'll be able to keep up our traditions."

"Thank you, but I won't need it for a long, long time."

"Never know when the good Lord might knock on the door."

She turned the page to see that every single recipe was handwritten. "This is priceless. It belongs in a museum. Oh, my goodness, so that's what makes your ham so sweet. You pour blackberry wine over it before you put it in the oven."

"And cook it real slow. Don't hurry good food.

Now, burgers and hot dogs and fast food is another thing. And, honey, you got to promise me that this book will always be kept in our kitchen," he said with seriousness.

"I promise. Thank you, Uncle Zed. I'll cherish it forever and take care of it like the gem it is." Harper covered the distance and hugged him.

"Now don't go gettin' all sentimental on me. Finish your doughnut, and if you want another one of them maple ones you'd better grab it, because I see Dana and Brook comin' this way." He picked up the recipe book and carried it with him back to the kitchen. "This will be on the first shelf of the old cash safe back there. Combination is taped under the table since I have trouble rememberin' it. We don't use it for much anymore but your granny's will and letters, since everyone pays with credit cards."

"Uncle Zed." She touched her heart and bit back the tears. "Thank you so much."

"Hey, doughnuts!" Brook squealed. "That chocolate one on the top is mine."

"You better not get both of the chocolate ones," Tawny yelled from the doorway. "Guess what— I've got a date."

"If it's with Marcus Green, I'm going to use my executive power as the oldest sister and have you locked up in a convent," Dana teased.

"Nick?" Brook asked.

Tawny reached for a chocolate doughnut. "Yep."

"I knew it before you did," Brook singsonged. "He told his family that he was going to, but he was afraid you'd say no."

"Well, I didn't." Tawny bit into the doughnut.

Harper picked up a broom and swept the floor even though it didn't need it. The conversation concerning what all they were going to do that Saturday was a distant buzz as she let her mind wander back to March 15 and the mistrust between them when they'd all arrived at Annie's Place. So much had changed in such a short time, and most of it had been for the good. Little blonde-haired girls didn't send her to the liquor cabinet anymore. She would never forget the baby that she'd given away, but she was beginning to feel a little less guilty.

Granny Annie used to say that love conquered everything. That could turn out to be her most profound statement, because there was a song in Harper's heart since Wyatt had said those three words to her the night before. It wasn't something that she could hum along to or one that even had words, but it was a song of joy and peace. Then Zed had put the icing on the cake that morning when he gave her that book, giving her his trust to keep it safe but also his confidence in her to take care of the café when he was gone.

"And that's going to be a long, long time from now," she echoed her earlier words.

"What did you say?" Tawny asked.

"That it just dawned on me that Monday is Uncle Zed's birthday. I saw it on the calendar in the kitchen yesterday—in Granny's handwriting and he'd drawn lines through it like a canceled appointment," she said.

"Let's do a surprise party around the fire pit and make him start another story," Brook whispered. "And have cake and ice cream. What's his favorite food?"

Harper leaned on the broom. "I bet I can find out."

Zed's face popped up in the window. "Find out what?"

"Your meat loaf is my favorite food. What's yours, Uncle Zed? I don't think we ever talked about what you like." Harper went back to sweeping.

"Hot dogs. That was a real treat when I was a little boy, and me and Annie always got us one at that little drive-by joint when we went to the doctor. I like mine with sauerkraut and she likes hers with mustard and relish." He sighed. "I mean, *liked* hers. It's still so hard to think of her gone."

His face disappeared from the window, and in a few seconds the aroma of bacon wafted through the whole dining area. Harper winked at Brook and went back to sweeping.

✦✦❱❰❱❰❱✦✦

The breakfast rush had died down by ten o'clock, and Harper had been gone to help out for at least an hour to the laundry room until the lunch run started arriving. Zed pulled out a couple of chairs. Sitting in one and propping his feet on the other, he thought about his birthday on Monday. He and Seamus and Annie had run up and down the Neches River together as children, but he'd never been invited to their birthday parties. He'd asked them to come have his mama's carrot cake and homemade ice cream with him one time, but they didn't show up. That might have been the first time any of them realized what that big word *prejudice* meant.

Annie had been truthful when she told him that her daddy said she couldn't go to his house. He'd never forget what she said next: "But someday I'll be a big person and then I'll do whatever I want and we'll eat ice cream on your birthday."

And they had, many, many times. When he came home from the military and went to work in the café, she never forgot his birthday. Not one single time. There might not have been home-churned ice cream like his mama made when he was a child, but there was always ice cream and a store-bought cake that said "Happy Birthday, Zed" right on the top. Chocolate ice cream and white cake. Annie would laugh and say that was symbolic of their friendship.

He was so deep in his thoughts that he didn't hear Brook come into the café. When she spoke, not a foot from him, it startled him so badly that his old heart came nigh to jumping out of his chest.

"I came to get us a couple of to-go cups of sweet tea. It's hot in the laundry room this morning," she said, unaware that she'd almost given poor old Zed a heart attack.

When opportunity knocks, you invite it in for chocolate cake. You don't slam the door in its face and then have to chase it down the road for a mile.

"I've got something for you, honey. Been meanin' to give it to you for a while, but it kept slippin' my mind," he said. "Come on back here in the kitchen with me. I keep it in the safe."

"What is it, Uncle Zed?" She danced along beside him, sniffing the air. "There's nothing like hot, homemade rolls to make a place smell like home. Save a couple for when me and Tawny come over for lunch. What is this surprise? You should be the one getting the presents since your birthday is coming up."

"It is, but there's not much an old man like me needs except happiness. You girls have brought that to me this past month. Don't know how I'd have gotten through Annie's passing without y'all around me." He slung open the safe and handed her a pretty hair comb with pearls scattered over the top. "It'll look real good in your hair on your weddin' day."

"Uncle Zed," she giggled as she took it from

his hands. "That's eons away. You should keep this until that day gets here and then you can put it in my hair right before you walk me down the aisle at the church."

Tears as big as dimes rolled down his wrinkled cheeks.

She grabbed a paper towel and wiped them away. "I love the comb. It's beautiful, but I want you to play the part of my daddy when I get married and it can be my something old. Tell me where it came from."

"It was given to my grandma by her mama on the day that she got married. Then she gave it to my mama when she got married, and since I didn't have any sisters, my mama gave it to me to hold for my daughter or granddaughter." He inhaled deeply, trying to get his emotions under control, and it brought on a coughing fit. When he could catch his breath again, he said, "The pearls are real—my great-grandparents lived down in the Mississippi Delta and my grandpa did some oyster fishin' to make a few dollars."

"Uncle Zed, this is too precious for you to give away." Brook fingered the pearls, all different sizes, some even lopsided and misshapen.

He took it from her hands and deftly pulled up a strand of hair from each side of her face. Carefully putting it in her hair, he said, "There, now I've put it in your hair and you are going to take it with you. If I'm still around when you get married, I'll walk you down the aisle with honor, and I'll even tuck it back into your hair. That's a promise. Until then, you put it in a nice, safe place and take it out every now and then and remember all the good times we have here at this place."

She wrapped her arms around his waist and hugged him so tight that it almost brought on another coughing fit. "I will, Uncle Zed, I promise, and thank you so much."

"Just passin' on what was passed to me." Zed patted her on the head.

When she'd filled two cups with sweet tea and left, he closed the safe and sat down on the stool. "Well, Annie, that's two of my four possessions. I told you that if I felt like they were going to stay, I'd give each of them a little something from my side of the family. We might not be blood kin, but . . . don't fuss at me. I can already hear the lecture you're gearin' up to give me. That a feller can be a grandpa even if he's not kin to the kid. I'm right glad for that."

Harper called out from the door. "I see a whole van load of folks parkin' out in the lot, so I hurried back over. We ready for the lunch run?"

"Hot rolls comin' out of the oven in five minutes," he yelled. "Rest of it is ready to serve."

Chapter Twenty-Four

Sunday morning ushered in a quick shower, but the sun came out in the afternoon, bringing humidity and heat with it. The people at the edge of the lake didn't seem to mind the wet grass one bit if they could start on their summer tan. Folks came in and out of the store all afternoon for cold drinks, beer, and snacks.

Tawny brought over her lunch about one o'clock and grabbed a candy bar and a Pepsi before going to the laundry. Dana had just finished eating when Zed pushed his way through the curtain hanging over the door from his little apartment into the store.

"Got gravy all over my shirtsleeve, so I had to get it changed. Thought I'd get a cup of hot chocolate and visit with you since things are slowin' down and Harper can run the café without me for a little while." Zed laid a tote bag on the counter, went to the machine, and hit the right button to shoot steaming hot chocolate into a to-go cup. "Put this on my bill."

"Not happenin'. You aren't payin' for anything in this place," Dana told him with a shake of her head. "Come on back here behind the counter and sit on this stool. I remember this bag. Granny used to keep a photo album in it. I remember seeing pictures of her and Grandpa and you when y'all were kids."

"And lots of your daddy and then even more of you kids. She got a better camera when you were born and we put at least one roll of pictures in that book every summer after y'all left. She liked real pictures as she called them, never did go digital."

"Can I look at it?"

"Any time you want to. It's yours as of this day. You probably know how to go about gettin' copies made if your sisters want some of them, but I want you to have it. Annie would have wanted that, too, so I don't want no argument," he said.

"None given." She slipped the thick album from the worn black velvet bag and opened the first page. There was one picture of three little kids standing in front of a big tree.

Zed ran his forefinger down Annie's cheek. "That tree was out there in the middle of the lake. We used to lean up against it to count off the numbers when we was playin' hide-and-seek."

"Granny told me that story. Her daddy came to get her to go in for supper. He'd been takin' pictures of a dog that he'd just gotten and had his camera with him. She refused to go until he snapped a photo for her book. She said that she didn't even have a book at the time. That started when he got the pictures back."

Dana flipped through the pages and watched herself and her sisters grow up before her eyes.

Later, she'd sit down with the book and let the memories of each summer wash over her, but right then she was too glad just to know that the album was still there.

"Not much in the way of new pictures in the last ten years," Zed said. "A few of Brook and only a couple of Harper and Tawny, but you take it on." He finished the last of his chocolate and slid off the stool. "Me and Annie had us some good times with the happy memories in that book."

She rounded the end of the counter and hugged him. "Uncle Zed, this means the world to me. I will take care of it and tell Brook and my grandkids all the stories I can remember about the pictures."

"That's exactly what I want you to do," he said.

"And thank you for giving Brook that comb. It is as precious as a gold mine to her." She hugged him again. "You've been better than a grandfather to her and to me both and someday I hope you do walk her down the aisle."

"Can't you just see that? An old black man and that pretty child all decked out in white satin?"

Dana kept an arm around his shoulders. "What I see is a grandpa and a gorgeous bride. Both of them have beautiful hearts and souls."

"You got on rose-colored glasses, girl," Zed chuckled as he left by the front door.

Turning back to the first page in the book, Dana studied the picture of her grandmother, her grandfather, and Zed when they were little kids. Funny, as many times as she'd seen that picture, she'd never noticed that Annie was holding Zed's hand until that moment.

➤═╞╳╞╡╡◄

Summer was pushing spring into the history books. Proof was in the fact that there wasn't even a slight breeze that Sunday evening when Nick showed up on Tawny's porch. She'd dressed in a cute little floral sundress that left her shoulders bare, and she'd planned on taking a light sweater with her in case it got chilly.

"You look like an angel," he whispered as he handed her a bouquet of wildflowers tied with a pretty yellow ribbon.

"They're beautiful. Come on in while I put them in a glass of water." She motioned him inside.

He stepped into the room and removed his cap. Her eyes traveled from the soft dark hair showing in the V where two pearl snaps of his shirt were undone down to his slim waist and stopped there. His silver belt buckle was embossed with a Native American on a horse. When she realized that she'd been looking at it far too long, she blinked and looked up to find him smiling.

"End of the trail. That's what's on the buckle."

She whipped around and went to the bathroom to put the flowers into a carry-out cup from the café so that he couldn't see her blush. "What does it mean?"

"Something of my heritage that I like very much. What do these things on your bookcase mean?"

"Each one reminds me of something that happened since Granny Annie died. I'll keep them forever." She brought the flowers out and set them on her desk, but she laid the ribbon on the shelf beside the red bird feather.

"You sure you don't have some Native American blood in your veins?"

"Maybe," she said. "With a name like Clancy I think it's mostly Irish or Scottish, but Granny always thought there might be a little bit of Choctaw in her."

"I'd believe it. You ready for a really good steak?" He turned around and opened the door for her.

"Haven't eaten since lunch so that I could really enjoy it." She picked up her purse and stepped out into the hot night air.

She expected him to walk her to his truck, open the door for her like a gentleman, and drive to his house. But he laced his fingers in hers and started toward the lake. The touch of his calloused palm in her tender hand brought on sparks that looked like a dozen falling stars shooting from the sky and landing all around them.

They followed the bend of the lake to a

cul-de-sac that she'd never noticed before. A narrow area jutted back into the woods about fifty feet, and there at the end was a tiny little fire pit with a red plaid blanket on the ground beside it. He let go of her hand and motioned for her to sit.

"Talk to me while I fix our food. I love the sound of your voice." He brought a red cooler and a huge basket from the shadows. Opening the cooler, he took out a package wrapped in white butcher paper.

"That's a pretty good pickup line."

Deftly, he removed the paper and tossed steaks the size of dinner plates onto the grill covering the fire pit. "Never used it before, to be honest. How do you like your steak?"

"Medium rare. And do you think there's going to be a second date?"

"I hope so." He flipped the top back on the picnic basket and brought out two white dinner plates, a couple of napkins wrapped around cutlery, and a couple of packages of aluminum foil that he immediately threw on the grill with the steaks.

"What makes your steaks better than any others?"

"Good beef from a butcher, not prepackaged junk from a grocery store, and open-fire cooking, but it never works unless there's a beautiful woman to share the evening with," he said smoothly. "Tell me about your day."

"Not much to tell. I clean rooms, do laundry,

work on the books, and then start all over the next day," she answered. "How was your day?"

"I worked on a set of kitchen cabinets for a house we're building. When those are finished, probably tomorrow, I'll set them in and then go to work on putting in the baseboards and framing out the doors. The nice thing is that I love what I do, and my mama says that makes me a success." He sat down close beside her and laid a hand on hers.

"Oh, yeah?" The electricity flowed between them so hot that she'd give up the food if he'd just sit beside her all evening.

"She put it this way—it don't matter what kind of work you do in the day to make a livin'. If you are whistlin' or hummin' while you do it, then you are a big success. How about you? Do any hummin' in the day?"

She nodded slowly. "Your mama is a genius."

He chuckled and scooted over closer to her. "We all think so. Maybe you can meet her someday."

"I'd like that," Tawny whispered and then his lips closed on hers. Both passionate and sweet at the same time, it created a stirring deep inside her.

He broke off the kiss to stand and flip the steaks with a big fork that appeared out of nowhere. She crossed her legs and watched him expertly finish cooking. When the steaks were done to his liking, he pulled the cooler over in front of Tawny and set the two plates on it. Then he turned out a steak and a foil packet on each of the plates and sat down on the other side of the cooler.

"In our family we thank the father for our food. You want to do it or should I?" he asked.

You, please, she meant to say, but what came out was, "I'll do it."

Granny always said grace before supper. In her opinion, Zed had done the cooking and she should be thankful. She bowed her head and said a short grace for the first time in her life. Amazed that she could utter a word, she raised her head to find him smiling across the makeshift table at her.

"Amen," he whispered and then his dark eyes seemed to crawl through hers right into her soul. "I think there must be a touch of Choctaw in you. That sounded like one of our blessings."

"You are really proud of your heritage, aren't you?" She cut off a bite of steak and popped it into her mouth.

"Yes, I am."

"And what would your mama think of you dating outside your heritage?"

"That the heart knows no color. It only knows love," he said.

Tawny had to meet this woman, even if there was never a second or third date with Nick. She sounded so much like Granny Annie.

She cut off another bite of steak, convinced that the second one wouldn't be as tasty as the first, but she was wrong. "Oh, my goodness! You were right to tell me that your steaks beat anything that you can get in a restaurant." She undid the foil to find whole green beans, little red potatoes cut into chunks, and tiny tomatoes all covered with melted butter. "You are an amazing cook."

He reached across the cooler and tucked an errant strand of hair behind her ear. The tingling sensation started at her earlobe and went all the way to her toes. "I make this meal and a real mean bologna-and-cheese sandwich. That's the extent of my culinary skills. Oh, and I can whip up an omelet that'll take the edge off a hungry lady, but that's it. You cook?"

"Very little," she answered truthfully. "But I can make a frozen pizza in the microwave without burning it, and I bet my bologna sandwich can beat yours."

"We'll have to have a contest sometime," he said.

"And the winner gets?"

He wiggled his dark eyebrows. "Anything they want."

→⊹⊹∦⊹⊹←

Millions of stars dotted the sky around a quarter moon that Sunday night as Zed took up his regular place on the bench to smoke a final cigarette of the day. His chest felt heavy that evening, as if there was even a bigger brick sitting on it than usual. He attributed it to the weather getting warmer. Summer had not been his friend since the doctor put a name to his ailment—congestive heart failure. Of course he had congestion. He'd smoked for more than fifty years and his lungs were probably the color of Dana's fire pit after a marshmallow roast. Heart failure—he didn't doubt that one bit. Since Annie had passed on, he often wondered how it had the strength to keep beating.

He heard Tawny's tinkling laughter long before he saw two silhouettes walking so close together that they looked like one. "She's happy, Annie. Our baby girl has found her place. She had to do that before she could get into any kind of relationship."

Nick walked her to the door, lingering long enough to give her a few kisses before he brought her hand to his lips and kissed the palm. She went inside, but in only a few minutes she came back out and sank down in the chair.

Zed put his hand in his pocket to be sure the ring was still there and rose to his feet with a groan. He was almost to her porch when she noticed him. She jumped up and motioned for him to sit in her chair. "Uncle Zed, I'm so glad you're out for a smoke. I feel like I'm floating on the clouds right now. Nick cooked steaks, and we talked and talked. I'll go out with him again."

"He's a good boy," Zed said. "Comes from good, sturdy stock."

"I don't deserve all this," she sighed.

"Don't you waste a single minute feelin' like that. If we got what we deserve in life, we'd all be paupers," he told her. "I've given the other girls a little something."

"I know. Harper cried when she told me about the recipe book. She's come a long way, hasn't she, Uncle Zed?"

He nodded and fished the ring from his pocket. "You all have, and here's what I want you to have."

"You don't have to give me anything. You being here with us is a gift from the angels," she said.

He reached out his hand and opened it up to reveal a small band in his palm. "This is made from a nickel. My daddy didn't have the money to buy my mama a real wedding ring when they first got married, so he melted down a nickel and fashioned this ring to put on her finger when they went to the courthouse that day."

"I can't take that, Uncle Zed. It's too priceless."

He picked up her hand and slid it on the third finger of her right hand. "It's still got a lot of wear in it, and when you look at it, you think of an old couple that was in love their whole married life." It fit perfectly and before he withdrew his hand two big teardrops had already christened it. "Don't cry. Be happy."

"They're tears of joy, Uncle Zed. I am happy, and I think it may be for the first time in my life," she said.

"Some folks never find joy or happiness. You are a blessed child."

She knelt in front of him and put her head on his knee. "Yes, I am, Uncle Zed. I'm so blessed lately that I think I'm dreaming."

Chapter Twenty-Five

Harper awoke with the tinkling piano of the first part of Bette Midler's "The Rose" running through her head that Monday morning. Dark clouds drifted over the moon and a coyote howled in the distance, but nothing was going to spoil her day. For the first time ever, she beat Zed to the café. She turned on the lights, reset the thermostat, and started the coffee brewing before she turned on his radio in the kitchen. She smiled when Conway Twitty started singing his rendition of "The Rose."

She pulled up the old wooden stool and listened to the whole song, nodding about love being a flower. "Yes, Wyatt, our love is all of what he's saying," she whispered.

Tawny poked her head into the service window about the time the song ended. "Where's Uncle Zed? Look at what he gave me last night." She held out her hand. "It was his mother's wedding ring. I can't believe he's trusting me with it. I'm going to cherish it forever. He's given us all . . ." She stopped and clamped her hand over her mouth.

"Oh, no!" Harper felt the world drop out from under her, and she had to grab the worktable to keep from falling.

"He has to be sick. I told y'all he was losing weight and coughing more. Come on. Let's go see about him."

Dana came in through the kitchen door. Her face was absolutely gray, and tears were dripping off her cheekbones. Brook was weeping behind her, and Harper knew without even asking. She dropped to her knees and put her head in her hands.

"What? Is Uncle Zed sick? Have you called his doctor or 911?" Tawny screamed and ran toward the door.

Dana stopped her, hugging her close while they both sobbed. "He's already cold. I called 911, and they're sending the coroner. They told me not to touch anything."

Brook crossed the floor and sat down with a thud beside Harper, who leaned into her shoulder and continued to sob.

"He's sittin' in his easy chair." Brook said a word at a time. "His hand is stretched out touching the other chair. He just looks like he's sleeping. I can't believe he's not going to walk me down the aisle when I get married."

Harper gathered the child into her arms, and suddenly her other two sisters were there in a group hug, their tears mingling on their cheeks.

"What are we going to do without him?" Tawny whispered. "He was the glue that held us together."

"We'll have to rely on his and Granny's

memories. I hear sirens. That must be the ambulance," Dana said.

Harper shook her head. "I don't even know what to do next. We've got to close up shop for a couple of days."

Dana nodded in agreement. "Call the lawyer. Remember, that's what was in Granny's letter. She said there was another letter when Uncle Zed went and to call the lawyer."

"I'll do it when . . ." Harper couldn't finish the sentence.

"We are brave. We are Granny Annie's girls. Suck it up," Brook said. "Let's go to the store so we can stand by him when they put him in the vehicle. We can cry and carry on like babies later." She got up.

Harper and Tawny did the same and then followed Dana and Brook out the kitchen door. The ambulance pulled up behind the store and Dr. Tipton got out of the passenger's seat. He and the driver went inside, but he was back out in only a few seconds.

"I'm not going to do an autopsy. The congestive heart failure and bad lungs finally took their toll. Two years ago I would have bet a hundred dollars that he'd go before Annie," Dr. Tipton said. "I reckon you want him taken to the same funeral home as Annie? I can do that right now if you want, since I'm the acting coroner until we can get another one."

"Yes, please," Dana said. "Which one was it?"

"Let me write it down for you. If I don't, you'll forget ten minutes after I leave. I'm so sorry for your loss and it coming so soon after Annie." The doctor wrote on the back of one of his business cards. "His heart just played out, but from that last visit, I'd say he knew it was coming. And, girls, this is a blessing. It wouldn't have been long until he would have had to have continual oxygen—possibly a respirator in a few weeks. Y'all want to go in there and tell him goodbye before we take him?"

All four nodded. Chins quivering, backs straight, and holding hands, they entered the little apartment that had been his for more than fifty years. He could have had so much more, but he'd opted to stay and help Annie after their grandpa died.

Harper went right to him and touched his gray hair. "Goodbye, Uncle Zed. I'm going to miss you so much. I hope you know how much I love you."

Dana took a few steps forward and draped an arm around Harper's shoulder. "Is this why you gave each of us one of your prized possessions? You knew it wasn't going to be long, didn't you?"

Brook slipped an arm around her mother's waist. "I love you, Uncle Zed, and that comb you gave me will bring you right in the room with me on the day I get married. I'll feel you and Granny sittin' on the front pew, and you can wear your overalls."

Tawny stretched out her arm to embrace all three of them at once. "Peace. You helped me find it. I owe you so much. I can't say goodbye because it hurts too much, so I'm just going to say that I'll see you and Granny someday. Until then, I'll touch this ring when I need your advice, and you can pop into my memories anytime you want to."

They stood, two on each side of the gurney, as the doctor and the folks in the ambulance rolled his body out of the apartment. As it drove away, four hands went up to wave goodbye, and a fresh batch of tears started to flow.

"Let's just go in there and sit in those chairs for a little while. Maybe his spirit hasn't completely left us yet," Harper said. She led the way back inside and sat down in his recliner.

Dana eased down in the chair beside it, and Brook sat in her lap.

Harper moved over, leaving enough room for Tawny to join her.

"Smoke. I can smell his cigarettes in the fabric of this chair," Tawny whispered as she wedged in beside her sister.

"I get a whiff of Granny's perfume in this one," Dana said softly.

Harper looked around at the sparsely furnished room. Two recliners, a television on a stand with lots of movies on the shelves under it, a queen-size bed in the corner with a colorful quilt on top, and pretty lace curtains on the windows. He hadn't left much in material possessions, but what he'd left in love couldn't fit in a mansion.

✦═╣╠╣╠═✦

It was daylight when the lawyer showed up. No one had called him, but there he was, tapping on the café window while the sisters were having packaged sweet rolls from the store and coffee for breakfast. Barely able to swallow, they damn sure weren't ready to deal with him, but there didn't seem to be any other choice but to let him in.

"I'll do it." Brook headed for the locked door with a CLOSED sign hanging in the window.

"Dr. Tipton called me. I'm sorry for your loss and Zed's coming this quick." He removed his glasses and wiped his eyes. "I've known Zed my whole life. He was a good man. I am to hand this letter to Harper. You will see that it's sealed, not only with tape but with a wax seal. Annie wanted to be sure that no one read it until Zed was gone, and I am meant only to deliver it and then leave. Again, I'm so sorry, and if you have any questions, I've been retained for one year to help you get through any legalities. Good day."

He laid the letter on the table and eased the door shut behind him.

All four of them stared at the letter for a full minute before Harper finally picked it up. She turned the envelope around backward for them to see. "I bet this is either Granny's or Uncle Zed's thumbprint. I can't break it."

Tawny got up and went to the kitchen and returned with a steak knife. "Use it like a letter opener."

Harper slipped it under the flap and carefully slit the top open, leaving the seal intact. "I'm not sure I can read this out loud."

"We'll each read part of it. It looks like it's pretty long," Dana said. "I wonder why she wanted you to have it first."

"I'm sure she'll tell us," Tawny said.

"Okay, here goes." Harper pulled several hand-written pages from the envelope and unfolded them.

My girls, if you are reading this, then Zed is gone. I can't say as I'm sorry, because I want him with me. It breaks my heart to know that he is lonely without me. We've never been apart except for those years when he was away in the military, and I missed him so much then. I love you, Harper. I know life has not been an easy road for you, but I'm sending love and hopefully you will heal here at the lake. It has that effect on us.

Harper stopped reading. "Yes, Granny, it does, but I don't know if it's the lake that heals us or your spirit."

It took a while, but she finally cleared her throat and went on.

> We always thought Zed would go first with his heart troubles. But it looks more and more like I'm going to have to pave the way, and that's why I'm writing this letter to you. I expect all three of you to be strong and to keep the resort going as long as you possibly can, like I told you in my letter before. Harper, you are going to be in charge of the kitchen. If he didn't already give them to you, Zed wants you to have the recipes for the specials. Anyone can make burgers and hot dogs, so that's not a problem. Anyone but me, that is—I can burn down a house trying to boil water.

Harper tried to giggle, but it came out a sob, and she laid the paper to the side until she could get control. She pulled a napkin from the dispenser and wiped her face.

> Don't worry, my lovely granddaughter, about running the café alone. I know that your sisters are going to pitch in and help you with your job, just as you will do the

same for them. I'm hoping that Zed lived long enough to get y'all transitioned from sometimes sisters to a real family. Now give this to Dana and let me talk to her for a spell.

Without hesitating, she handed the pages across the table, and Dana began to read.

You were my first grandchild. I know my son didn't do right by you. He was my only child and I loved him, but he was too much like his father. Seamus had a stubborn streak, and once he made up his mind—enough about that. You lived the story. You don't need me to write it all down. I loved you from the first day that Lacy put you in my arms, and I appreciated her so much for letting me be a part of your life. I thought I couldn't love anyone as much as I did you, but then Harper and Tawny came along and I found out that I could give them as much love as I did you and yet not take away a bit of your portion. Then Brook came along and she was the icing on the cake for this old soul.

Brook sniffled, and Dana laid the letter down and hugged her closely. Tawny stroked Brook on the back and Harper reached across the table to pat her on the head. The moment was filled with grief and love intermingled, but Harper wondered if they'd all be able to survive this new relationship without Zed.

Keeping one arm around her daughter, Dana held the pages flat with her other hand and kept reading.

You are going to keep running the store, but I want you to call someone to turn Zed's apartment into the laundry room. That way you can help with the laundry during slow times in the café. Flora told me a year ago that she wanted to retire, but she stayed on because I was sick and we needed her, so I'm assuming that she's probably gone by now. Now give this to Tawny.

Dana slid it across the table toward her youngest sister.

As I write this, I'm seeing a picture of you girls as little children. Dana was such a good babysitter and helped me by keeping you younger sisters busy in Zed's apartment while I worked. It was pouring down rain and she stripped both you girls down to your underpants and then put on her little bikini. I looked out the store window and there you all three were, holding hands and dancing in the rain out front by the gas pumps. I hope that God lets us take memories like that into eternity with us, because it was a time when you were really sisters, and I love it so much.

Tears dripped on the page, and Tawny quickly grabbed a napkin and dabbed away the moisture before she went on.

I love you, Tawny. Your father wanted a son to carry on the Clancy name so badly, but I was elated when you were a girl. If you ever have children and are so inclined, you could name one of them Clancy. I think that would make him happy. I hope none of you ever have to endure the loss of a child.

Tawny stopped and looked across the table at Harper.

"It's okay," Harper said. "Go on. She didn't know."

We are hardwired to bear the loss of our parents and grandparents. Even though it brings grief and heartache, it's a natural thing. There is nothing natural about losing a child, and the grief is something that never leaves a mother. You have to be strong to endure it, and it helps to have three beautiful granddaughters and a great-randdaughter. Love can do miraculous things.

"Amen," Harper whispered.

Now down to business. You've been taking care of the book work, but I suspect if Flora is gone you are helping in other areas. I also know that you can't cook worth a damn. You got that from me, child. But when you have time, you might go on in the kitchen with Harper and learn a few things—without fighting about every single thing. Now pass this on over to Brook. She can read the rest of it, because I'm not sure how any of you are going to take the rest of it. Don't hate me.

Tawny handed the letter to Brook, who shook her head. "I don't think I can read it. I'm too emotional."

"Please," Harper said. "It was her wish."

"Okay, I'll try." She cleared her throat and began.

I loved your grandfather, Seamus. Never doubt that. He was a good man, a wonderful friend, and an amazing business partner. He adored our son from the day of his birth, and I don't think Gavin ever completely got over his father's death. He would have done better if I'd gone first, I'm sure, but that's not the way God planned it. Just know that I loved him.

Brook peeked over the top of the pages with a puzzled look on her face. "It's like she's trying to convince us that she loved Grandpa Seamus."

"I think she's just trying to make sure we understand before she goes on with the next part," Harper said.

Brook found her place and went on.

I'm glad that Seamus wasn't here when Gavin turned his back on Lacy and Dana. There would have been a huge family split over that. I had to put on my kid gloves when it came to loving my son enough to let him make his own decision and loving my granddaughter enough to not allow his decision to affect mine. Seamus was thirty-seven when he died. The doctor said a blood clot went through his heart and he was gone before he hit the floor. Gavin was sixteen. It was a tough time, because a boy needs his father at that age.

Brook's eyes grew wide. "That's only a year older than you are, Mama."

"Keep reading. I'm in good health. Don't worry about me," Dana said.

Brook's gaze went back to the pages.

Like I said before, I loved Seamus, but I was never in love with him. That place in my heart was given to Zed when we were just little kids. I can't remember a time when I wasn't in love with Zed. So after Seamus died and I got over the guilt of not being able to give my husband my whole heart, things fell into place for me and Zed.

You have to understand that in my young days, race was a much bigger thing than it is today. White women didn't marry black men. Two years after Seamus died, Gavin went off to college. A couple of the older women from the church came to tell me that it wasn't proper for me to have a black man living on the resort without Seamus or even Gavin here to give the appearance of rightness. They were still living in a different world, one back when they were young in the forties, when it sure wasn't right for a black man and a white woman to work together like we did. I told them what they could do with their prejudiced and self-righteous attitude, and I never went back. Besides, God does not dwell in houses made with hands, but in our hearts. It says so in the Bible. And after Gavin had been in college awhile, I decided to tell Zed exactly how I felt. And he held me like a woman, not like a friend, and told me he'd always felt the same.

"Oh, my!" Brook gasped. "Were people really prejudiced like that?"

Harper managed a weak smile. "Some people still are."

Brook went on.

Another year passed and I told Zed that we were getting married, but he wouldn't have any part of it. Gavin and Zed had a good relationship, and he was afraid it would ruin what they had, plus he was looking out for my reputation. I told him that I'd fire him if he didn't marry me. He said he couldn't live without me in his life, so we'd compromise. We'd get married, but no one could ever know about it. We went over the line into Oklahoma, got a marriage license, and were married by the judge right there in the courthouse. The license is in the safe along with birth certificates and other important papers.

"Well, I'll be damned!" Tawny gasped. "So he was our grandpa after all. I wish I would have known. I would have called him Poppa instead of Uncle Zed. Lord, I loved that man, and I'm going to miss him so much."

Brook glanced down at the last page and slid the letter across the table to Harper. "It says to give this to you now."

Harper inhaled deeply.

I have been cremated. My ashes are in a wooden box in the apartment where Zed and I spent most of our time. You are to cremate Zed and put his ashes in the same can, and shake it up good so that we are together for eternity. Then I want you to take them to the big rock and scatter them together into the lake. We were both born here and we should be buried here, but I want to be buried beside Zed, who was my soul mate, and this is the way to do it without causing some big stir. No funerals, no big memorials. Maybe a song if you want. No tears, because Zed and I are finally together in a place where it doesn't matter what color anyone's skin is. I love you all.

Harper finished, "And it's signed, Granny Annie."

"Can we do this?" Tawny asked.

"We might be down to four, but it's still better than three elderly people," Brook said.

"We are strong. Granny said so and she never lied to us," Dana said.

"Except about Uncle Zed bein' our grandpa." Harper laid the letter down on the table. "And then it wasn't actually a lie. If we'd known to ask her outright, she might have told us."

Dana's head moved from side to side. "No, she wouldn't have, because she promised Zed that she'd never tell and she was in love with him. Today is his birthday. We were going to have a surprise party for him tonight."

"Don't you wish they could have been young in this day?" Brook sighed. "But it's just titles. I couldn't have loved them any more than I did and I don't think they would have loved us any more than they did. And I bet he got his birthday wish, Mama. He's with Granny Annie today."

"What do we do now?" Dana asked.

"We'll go to the funeral home and make arrangements to cremate Uncle Zed." Harper folded the letter and gently put it back in the envelope. "I'll put this in the safe with the other papers."

Dana pushed back her chair. "I found out a couple of days ago that we can get service when we get across the bridge. So I've got a charged phone. If y'all want to use it to make any calls on the way to the funeral home, you are welcome to it."

"You'd better call the school, Mama. I need to be here today," Brook said.

"Yes, you do. And you can call Johnny. I'm sure under the circumstances the principal will let you talk to him."

Tawny popped her palm against her forehead. "All the times when I've gone to the bank, it never dawned on me that I could use my cell phone when I was away from here. I need to let Nick know what's going on, because he'd planned to come by at lunch today."

"Me neither, when I went into town for supplies," Harper groaned. "I'll take you up on that offer, so I can tell Wyatt, too."

"But let's don't change things here, okay?" Tawny said.

Harper laid her hand in the middle of the table. Tawny covered it with hers, and Brook and Dana did the same.

"By the joining of hands, we agree to keep this place as it is and run it as long as we can," Harper said.

"Amen," the other three said in unison.

Chapter Twenty-Six

The Clancy sisters, along with Brook, hit the floor running Mother's Day morning and didn't slow down until they closed up the café and store. The cabins had been full all weekend, so there was cleaning and laundry. Harper had worried for days about the chicken and dressing dinner she'd prepared from Zed's recipes, but everyone had declared that he must've left part of himself behind in her, because it was as good as it had always been.

Now it was eight o'clock. In a half an hour the sun would be sliding down past the horizon. It was time for that journey to the big rock. Tawny didn't want to go. It was the final step, and she wasn't sure she could bear to tell her grandmother and Zed goodbye for good. She gripped the handle of the chair on her porch so tightly that her knuckles ached, but she couldn't make herself rise up. Not until Nick parked his old work truck in front of her cabin and held out his hand. She put hers in his and it gave her the strength to go down the steps.

Dana appeared from the store with the wooden box in her arms. Payton's arm was around her shoulders. Brook and Johnny were right behind them, and Johnny had Brook's hand tucked into his. Before they crossed the gravel, Wyatt and Harper came out of her cabin, his arm around her waist.

"We can do this. Remember, we are strong." Tawny didn't know if she was encouraging her sisters and niece or herself—maybe it was a little of both.

It was a solemn walk all the way to the big rock where Annie loved to sit in the evenings and fish with Zed. Tawny had gone out there the day before with her cell phone and found one spot on the very edge of the rock where she could hold her phone up to the sky and get service, so she'd tucked it into her hip pocket, hoping that she could find the spot that day.

When they arrived Dana stopped at the place where Granny Annie always sat. "I don't have anything planned because she didn't leave us instructions. I guess this is for our own closure."

"She said we might sing a song," Tawny said.

"I know you have one ready," Brook said. "But I think she'd like this one." She started an old familiar gospel tune, and the others joined in. "Some glad morning when this life is over."

When the last notes of "I'll Fly Away" had drifted out over the lake, Brook said, "Happy Mother's Day, Granny. I love you and I love Uncle Zed. I'm glad that you can be together forever this way."

Dana opened the lid of the box. "From ashes to ashes."

Tawny handed her phone to Nick, who carried

it to the spot she'd marked with an old piece of concrete chalk the girls had used as children. He touched a button and Jamey Johnson's deep voice filled the air as he sang "Lead Me Home." When the lyrics said that his new life began with death, Tawny said them out loud as she brought out a fistful of gray ashes and scattered them on the still waters of the lake.

Harper's voice shook a she sang right along with the lyrics that talked about hearing the angels singing and let her handful of ashes drift slowly through her fingers. Then Brook brought out a double handful and sobbed through a line that asked for the Lord to take his hand and lead him home, only she substituted *Annie* for *Lord*.

Dana knelt and let the ashes in her hand float away on the water, but she couldn't sing or even say a word. Then Wyatt gave her the box and she gently poured the rest of Granny Annie and Zed into the lake.

When she stood up, the four Clancy ladies joined hands and sang with the music, all of them substituting *Annie* for *Lord* when he asked the Lord to lead him home. There was total silence when the song ended for several moments, and then all four of them gathered together for a group hug.

"We might be sometimes friends from now on, but you three need to be always sisters," Brook said.

"Amen," the other three agreed as their tears all mingled together.

Epilogue

One year later, Mother's Day

It was a blustery day with tornado warnings all across the northern part of Texas. Wyatt had to cut his fishing trip short because there was no way he'd take a group of men out on the water when there was lightning, so he'd gotten up early that morning and made coffee.

"I love it when we have coffee at home," Harper said as she made her way into the kitchen of their new two-bedroom house that Nick had barely finished in time for the new baby's arrival. "I've got maybe fifteen minutes before I have to get to the café. If Clancy isn't awake, you can bring him over later."

"Or I can just keep him here and not share." Wyatt grinned. "When he's over there, I seldom even get to hold him. And before you leave, Clancy said I'm supposed to give this to you." He handed her a lovely velvet box. "He picked it out all by himself."

"Yeah, right." She grinned. "He's six weeks old, Wyatt."

"And super smart. Open it."

She'd remembered to get roses to take to the big rock and toss out on the lake water for Granny Annie that day, and she'd even sent her mother a card with the newest picture of Clancy in it. Maybe someday Retha would come around, but if it never happened, Harper intended to do what was right.

She flipped open the box to find a beautiful bracelet with a tiny disk attached to it.

"It's Clancy's fingerprint from the day he was born. Each year I will add a new fingerprint to it until we can't fit another one on the bracelet," Wyatt said. "I can't love you enough. Happy Mother's Day." He gathered her into his arms and tipped up her chin for a long, sweet kiss.

"And what if we have a dozen kids? Do I get a dozen bracelets?"

"Yes, ma'am, you do," he said. "When are we having a little sister for Clancy?"

"In a couple of years," she answered with another kiss.

➤✦╫╫╢╫╫✦◄

Dana snuggled up to Payton's side and wished that she could spend the whole day in bed with him. But the store didn't run itself. They planned to have dinner with his daughter, Alison, and her new boyfriend that evening. She was slowly coming around to the idea that her father had remarried—thanks to Brook, who'd taken it all in stride with cheer.

"Good morning, my beautiful bride," Payton whispered. "Happy Mother's Day."

"Thank you," she said.

He opened the drawer of the nightstand and brought out a present, all wrapped in white paper with a red bow. "This is for you."

She tried to be gentle, but impatience got the better of her and she ripped into the package to find a necklace with entwined hearts encrusted with tiny diamonds. "Oh, Payton, it's beautiful. Put it on me. I'm going to wear it all day."

He pushed her thick blonde hair to one side and fastened it around her neck, then kissed that tender spot at the base of her skull. "I don't only love you, but I'm in love with you."

The words from Granny Annie's letter came back to her mind, and she realized just how lucky she was. "Moving here was the best thing that ever happened to me and Brook," she whispered as she touched the hearts.

"My deliveryman quitting was the best thing that ever happened to me, because if he hadn't, I would have never met you," Payton said.

"And to think we've got a whole future ahead of us." She grinned as she pushed him backward on the bed.

⊱❖❖❖⊰

Tawny was busy braiding Nick's thick black hair for him that morning. Her cabin looked different than it had a year ago. Now the bookcases were lined up against a wall, and a queen-size bed had replaced the twin one. She and Nick had figured out early on that they loved spending the nights together, but after he'd fallen off the bed twice, she'd brought in the bigger one and didn't care who knew that he spent most of his nights with her.

"Thanks, darlin'," he said. "Here's the rubber band for the end."

She reached out and gasped when he held out a rubber band and a diamond ring. "Nick, is this . . ."

He slipped off the edge of the bed and dropped down on one knee. "I've been in love with you since you threw pizza at me. Will you marry me, Tawny?"

"Yes, yes, a thousand times yes."

He put the ring on her finger, and she fell to her knees beside him. "Who says that happily ever after only happens in romance books?"

"Whoever did is downright crazy." He cupped her cheeks in his hands and kissed her long, hard, and with so much love that it made her go weak.

>+:+|*|(*|:+*

Brook was alone in the laundry when Johnny arrived from the doorway into the store. He picked up a sheet and together they folded it wrinkle-free and neatly. Then she shoved a basket of towels his way and he started on them.

"You want to go with me to the end-of-school dance?"

"You mean as a date?"

"Yep," Johnny said. "It's gettin' to be more than friends, right? At least with me."

Well, praise the Lord! You are finally getting to the place where I've been since Christmas, she thought. *I've given you all kinds of hints and clues and I thought you'd never wake up and listen.*

"Sure," she said.

"That mean you kind of like me for more than a friend, too?"

"Yep, it does, but I've felt like that for a long time. Boys are slower than girls." She smiled at him.

"That mean I might even get a good-night kiss after the dance?"

"Maybe. We'll have to wait and see."

"Fair enough. Gives me something to look forward to," Johnny said.

❋❖❋

That evening they all gathered on the rock. Harper laid a dozen red roses on the water, and they all watched them float away. Maybe next year there would be another baby to carry to the memorial.

Siblings can double the joy and halve the sorrow. Granny's voice popped into Harper's head.

She kissed Clancy on the top of his dark hair and whispered, "We've had our ups and downs this year, but we're doing our best to be more than just sometimes sisters, Granny."

Acknowledgments

Dear Readers,

When I started writing *The Sometimes Sisters*, I knew all the sisters' stories and I could see the whole book playing out in my head like a movie. But when Zed started telling me his and Annie's story, the book took on a whole new layer. The more we visited, the more I could see why Annie had loved him all those years. He was patient, loving, and he wasn't at all judgmental. I'm so happy to introduce you to all the sisters, Dana, Harper, and Tawny, but just as excited to let you meet Brook, Dana's daughter, and, of course, Zed.

It's summertime in southern Oklahoma as I finish this book, but you'll be reading it just as spring begins to bring new life to the whole world. So grab a glass of sweet tea and settle into your favorite reading chair and enjoy the story.

You've all probably heard that it takes a village to raise a child. Well, producing a book like you have in your hands takes a lot of talented people to get it from an idea to a full-fledged novel. So I'd like to thank a few people for working with me to make *The Sometimes Sisters* happen.

My deepest appreciation to my publisher, Montlake Romance, and to my editor, Anh Schluep, who continue to believe in me; to my developmental editor, Krista Stroever—you do such an amazing job; to everyone on the team at Montlake who work so hard behind the curtains, from the awesome folks who make the covers to the folks who promote my books. Please know that every one of you is appreciated!

Special gratitude to my agent, Erin Niumata, and my agency, Folio Management Inc. Thank you for every single thing and for always being there for me.

I'd also like to thank Mr. B, my husband, who doesn't complain on the days when I listen to the voices in my head more than I do to him. It takes a special person to live with an author and he does a fine job.

And once again, a big, hearty thank-you to my fans, friends, and family who buy and read my books and take time to leave reviews. Don't put away your reading glasses—there's more on the way this year!

Until next time,

Carolyn Brown

About the Author

Carolyn Brown is a *New York Times*, *USA Today*, and *Wall Street Journal* bestselling author and a RITA finalist. The author of ninety novels, she's also the three-time recipient of the National Reader's Choice Award, a Bookseller's Best Award, and a Montlake Diamond Award.

Carolyn and her husband live in the small town of Davis, Oklahoma, where everyone knows everyone else, as well as what they're doing and when—and they read the local newspaper on Wednesday to see who got caught. They have three grown children and enough grandchildren to keep them young. Carolyn's husband does *not* get to read her books before they are published.

When she's not writing, Carolyn likes to sit in her backyard with her two tomcats, Chester Fat Boy and Boots Randolph Terminator Outlaw, and watch them protect the yard from all kinds of wicked varmints like crickets, locusts, and spiders. Visit her at www.carolynbrownbooks.com.

Books are produced in the United States using U.S.-based materials

Books are printed using a revolutionary new process called THINKtech™ that lowers energy usage by 70% and increases overall quality

Books are durable and flexible because of smythe-sewing

Paper is sourced using environmentally responsible foresting methods and the paper is acid-free

Center Point Large Print
600 Brooks Road / PO Box 1
Thorndike, ME 04986-0001 USA

(207) 568-3717

US & Canada:
1 800 929-9108
www.centerpointlargeprint.com